Best Wishes

Robert Byrd

The Deadly Confluence

Robert Emmrich

EMR PUBLISHING

Cincinnati, Ohio

Publication date:
November 15, 1996 (First Printing)
EMR Publishing, Cincinnati, Ohio

In association with:
Berger McGill Inc.

Copyright number: Txu 709–069
ISBN: 0–9655460–0–4

ACKNOWLEDGMENTS

In an effort like this there is not enough room to mention each person who helped. But there are some people whose contributions were and, continue to be invaluable.

I must thank the staff of LaNormandie Taverne in Cincinnati. In many ways they inspired me to write this book. All the guests who encouraged me deserve much credit for this project. But I would be derelict if I did not mention Dan and Leslie Jones, Stella Renaker and Marv Gallisdorfer. They will never say it but they know what a contribution they made. Thanks guys, for everything.

Sometimes you have to be plain lucky. While working a lunch hour for somebody I had a fifteen minute conversation with Claude Thomas. He mentioned the Old River Structure and the idea for the novel came to me. Two months later we had lunch and he gave me about a month's worth of research material in two hours. How do you thank someone for the groundwork of an entire project?

I was able to spend an afternoon at Old River with Roosevelt Howard and Richard Ortego. Any realism in that part of the book is a direct result of their help and encouragement.

Thanks to Cheryl Cooper and Ken Williamson of "The Film House": To Cheryl for her editing and Ken for all the advice. Lori Meeker of The Brown Travel Agency arranged my research trips and the employees of Kinko's just kept binding new copies every time I brought in the latest edition. I appreciate everything.

My brothers and sisters, whether they realize it or not, encouraged me all along the way. I did my best to make them proud. Thanks Joe, Tim, Judy, Nancy and Dave.

But there is one person who, above all, shares in the creation, writing and publishing of this book. While we worked together at LaNormandie and afterward, Melissa Rodgers listened to every idea, plot twist and character development, not to mention a running commentary as the story unfolded. She acted interested, even when it was obvious she had other things on her mind, and was honest enough to tell me when something was "dumb" or just did not work. Melissa, "Thank You" seems utterly inadequate. I thought you should know that.

Finally, In 1972 I met a young woman named Cathy Saheim. We only talked a few times and, after going our separate ways, we wrote to each other for a short while. I have not seen her since but I have never forgotten her. She is, to this day, one of the most decent people I have ever encountered, and without her memory, some parts of this book could not have been written.

I will never be able to properly thank my Mother and Father, Ginny and Joe Emmrich. They showed far more confidence and support than I ever deserved. Quite simply, without their help this project would not exist. The book is a tribute to their unwavering faith in their sometimes under-achieving son, and I dedicate it to them with all my heart.

Chapter I

HUNTSVILLE, ALABAMA

The cigarette wavered between the sleeping man's fingers. As muscles of the hand relaxed ever so slightly, the lit tip fell forward, missing an ashtray that lay on the bed. A few threads of bed sheet ignited and slowly smoldered. The first wisp of smoke, merely a trace, wafted straight up. It was neither large enough to trigger the smoke detector, nor close enough to the man's face for his sense of smell to send an early warning to his sleep fogged brain.

Threads continued to silently snap as the ring of fire grew, fighting to survive. A small black circle expanded as the orange ring consumed more of the sheet's surface. Seconds later a trace of flame appeared. It wavered for a moment, as if waiting for the inevitable smothering that its discovery would bring.

The man continued his sleep as the blackened ring increased its diameter by another half inch. Growing in size and seemingly in confidence, it wavered once more in search of a direction to travel.

Suddenly the fire leapt across the five-inch expanse of sheet toward a newspaper that had draped itself over the man's waist when sleep overcame him. The paper burst into flames and he became a victim. The fire was alive and it would burn. Who or what was of no consequence. The fire did not choose its victims. It only burned.

Herbert Loman's first sensation was a feeling of enveloping warmth. His head rolled slightly and his eyes slowly blinked open. Mere slits at first, they suddenly grew to golfball size as he realized his clothing was ablaze and the bed on which he lay burned like a funeral pyre. He flailed groggily for a moment then fell back unconscious as smoke invaded his lungs and shock protected his nerve endings from the hideous pain that the flames inflicted as they engulfed his body and ended his life.

CINCINNATI, OHIO

The blinking light on the phone bank forced Daniel Harte's attention away from the conference call. "Hold on, everybody. I have to take a call." His calm delivery belied the knot forming in his stomach. Staring intently at the phone bank, he put the conference call on hold and took a deep breath. "This is Daniel Harte. What's the problem?"

He checked the clock as he scribbled some notes on his schedule; 10:09 A.M. Eastern Time. "Is your mom okay?...I can be there by about two o'clock. Find out what you can and we'll just wing it from there...No problem. Keep your chin up and I'll be right down."

Harte arranged his thoughts, and returned to the conference call. "Look, everyone, we have to cut this off. That was Andy Loman. He's in Huntsville, Alabama, and needs some help. I have to go."

"Anything we can do from our end?" a voice on the conference speaker asked.

"Yeah, Billy. Mrs. Harding is off today. Get me the most direct flight to Huntsville. Don't be picky about the airline. I want to get down there as quickly as possible. You can set it up through the Foundation."

"Anything we should know about this?" a female voice broke into the conversation.

Harte paused. "I don't know, Rita. Andy's dad died last night. There was a fire in his motel room. That's all I know at this point. I'm flying down to help with the arrangements." His voice trailed off.

"Do you want the Foundation to look into this?" William Harmon's question was tentative, but it spoke for the group.

Harte knew what the question entailed. He was already going through a mental checklist. Nothing he heard from Andrew Loman had set off any alarms. "I haven't a clue, Billy. I'm just going to see what I can do for the Lomans. We'll talk soon." A push of a button ended the conference call and Daniel Harte, 41 year old spokesman and, though only a few people knew it, President and Chief Executive Officer of the "Wilson Foundation" prepared to console a protege and his family.

NAPLES, FLORIDA

Morgan Trent shifted in his chair as he "proofed" the final copy of the document on the word processor. As head of the Southeast Endangered Species Association, he personally wrote the group's quarterly reports. Observations and counts of the various threatened species in the Everglades had been duly noted by Trent's group from its field camp near Ochopee, a dot of a town on Florida's Tamiami Trail, fifty miles east of Naples. The Naples Daily News dutifully published a synopsis of each report and copies went out regularly to all of the major environmental groups across the country.

Trent considered the news stories nothing more than a line score by which the locals and the "invaders" from the north could track the devouring of the Everglades. True, Big Cypress Swamp was saved from development, but its survival as a habitat was in doubt. Traffic arteries crisscrossed the land and construction surrounded the swamp like Grant's army extending the line at Petersburg. Humanity was slowly but surely choking the life out of South Florida's most famous and tenuous ecosystem.

Trent's attention drifted across the room to a television screen. The CNN weatherman droned on about the cold wave in the north central states... "and today in Lake Itasca, Minnesota, a forecaster for KLIM radio mentioned that a quick thaw could trigger heavier than usual floods along the Mississippi this spring. I only mention this because in recent years KLIM's weather bureau has been uncannily accurate in predicting spring flood levels.

"I have to emphasize that it is impossible to predict at this point what kind of warming trend will come along. As it is there are always four or more decent-sized floods along the Father of Waters between early March and late May.

"Heck, it's only the first week of February. That's a bit early to think about spring, though I'm sure the folks up north are about fed up with the cold by now. Anyway, we will track these and all developments as we move through this really rough winter in the northern U.S. Now here are some local conditions in cities near you."

Trent finished his document, started the printer and walked over to a geological map of the United States that spread across an entire wall of his office. He stared at the area which a pale outline defined as the state of Louisiana and for the first time that day, a smile crossed his face.

For three years he had studied the patterns and had reached the same conclusions that the KLIM forecasters had come up with. The CNN report confirmed it. "As I figured. Spring should be very interesting. I only wish Nina could be here. She would truly appreciate it," He muttered as he stared at the map.

The sound of the printer finishing its job woke him from his daydream. Quickly, Trent removed the documents from the bin, turned off the equipment and left the office.

TABRIZ, IRAN

The four Arabs shielded themselves from the wind that blew through the porous walls and doorways of the shack. Their European counterparts seemed comfortable with the conditions. Compared to the Siberian frontier, February in northern Iran was like a breath of spring. Two men from each group sat at a rickety table while the others took up sentry positions around the hut.

"I see you do not react well to the chill of winter, Hamur. In Siberia we swim on a day like this."

"I should be chasing loose women on the beaches of Bandar-Abbas, Anatoly. And do not believe the stories of the western press. There are loose women to be had on the beaches in Iran." The four men exchanged a short laugh.

"So, my Iranian comrade, how is the business in Bulgaria?"

Anatoly Kasarov noted the Iranian's look of approval at the traditional Soviet term. The General resented the fact that the new Russia had chosen to remove as many vestiges of the old-line way of life as possible.

His twenty five year military career had been reduced to a "baby-sitting job", as one of the progressive cabinet members referred to it. But Kasarov was unlike any baby-sitter these new bureaucrats had ever encountered. He presided over the pullout of Soviet forces from the former Warsaw Pact countries. He was both astounded and disgusted with what he discovered during the redeployment. What the world perceived as a seventy-division monster that could swallow western Europe was nothing more than a charade, a paper army.

He cannibalized existing units and managed to downsize the western army into eight infantry and two armored divisions, two air wings and a supply and logistics division. A perceived million-man war machine consisted of around 200,000 soldiers, their supplies and equipment. The rest were either furloughed or disappeared as the paperwork was realistically updated.

Kasarov cringed as he considered the deterioration of his beloved army. My God, he thought, if NATO had known the true condition of the Russian Western Forces they would have attacked long ago.

At least now he knew what he could call on. He determined to put the remaining units of that once proud army to work for a just and noble cause.

Across the table, Kasarov's counterpart noticed the cringe. "Comrade Anatoly, has the cold finally gotten to you?"

"I'm sorry, my friend. I was just considering things that were and things that will be."

"It is good to do so, General. I have these thoughts myself about my own country." Hamur Bantar often thought about what it would be like for his country to take its rightful place as a leader of the world. The Iranian sometimes resented resorting to terrorism in the ongoing war against his homeland's enemies. He wanted desperately to confront those foes with the pride and honor of the man who sat across the table from him, but such was not his lot in life.

His was a world of car bombs and kidnaping. For ten years his group had wreaked havoc on the daily lives of civilians in the Middle East, Africa and Western Europe. Now he stood on the brink of the ultimate quest. He had a plan in mind for the great Satan of the West. And when it came to fruition, the fat and lazy people of that nation would never be the same.

"And so we both drift off, Comrade." Kasarov's soft chide brought Bantar back to the task at hand.

"So we do, General. Where were we?"

"Somewhere in Bulgaria, I believe."

"Of course. We have removed the product. It should reach its destination in three weeks, maybe a bit more."

"Good. Here are the devices you ordered." Kasarov handed over a satchel. "What about the timing on the other end?"

"My contact has arranged for his people to be in place for quite a while without arousing any suspicion so they can wait for the optimum moment."

"Your man is resourceful, Hamur?"

"One of the best. I have used him in several other situations. I think he wants to retire after this mission. At least his fee indicates so. It would be a pity to lose such an asset," Bantar mused.

"You do realize I need some notice on my end. Things like this cannot happen overnight."

"Will ten days to two weeks' notice be acceptable?"

"That is more than sufficient. Especially when you consider how the rules of the game are about to change in Russia."

"May I ask?" Bantar respected the Russian and found him a reliable ally. But he did not like surprises in his business.

Kasarov sat a little straighter in his chair. "There is going to be another cabinet shake-up in Moscow. This one involves the Ministry of Defense."

"Your President is making more political concessions?"

"He is a drunken pig with no direction, whose time is past. He can be led around by the nose and is no longer a problem."

Bantar saw Kasarov's eyes turn an even more steely blue. The Iranian shivered, but not from the chill in the air. He realized he must not disappoint the man across the table. There would be retribution if this plan failed.

"The Saudi initiative is ready. We will implement it during Ramadan," Bantar said, trying to bring Kasarov back from whatever dark thoughts distracted him.

Kasarov jerked slightly then focused. "Do you have a time frame?"

"The plan will be initiated shortly after the holy time begins. The reaction will be swift and the results should be achieved within two weeks."

"What about the Americans?"

"They will be powerless. In the Middle East religion rules all. The politicians will be helpless."

Kasarov rose from the table. "I believe we can conclude on that note."

"Shall we meet again before the great event?" Bantar asked.

"Perhaps once more to finalize the details. I will contact you in the usual way. Good luck, Comrade."

"Allah be with you, Comrade General." Bantar said solemnly. He found himself standing nearly at attention as Kasarov left the hut.

NEW ORLEANS, LOUISIANA

South Air Flight 22 banked slightly to the left and settled into its flight path. Heading east-southeast at 16,000 feet the sleek Canadair jet streaked out over the Mississippi delta and across the Gulf of Mexico toward Tampa. In less than ninety minutes Albert Simmons would be in his car and on the way to see his associates near Ochopee, east of Naples.

Although Flight 22 continued on to Naples, Simmons preferred to let his trail end in Tampa. The options were limited for someone departing the Naples airport. From Tampa the choices were endless and surveillance became difficult. A man could disappear into the state of Florida simply by choosing any one of the countless roads out of town.

Simmons was not overly concerned with the police. Although his career had made him the target of numerous countries' law enforcement agencies, in the United States he was a nobody. For now he was simply returning from a "scouting" trip for the Southeast Endangered Species Association.

SESA had contacted the State of Louisiana concerning the possibility of doing field work. Reports indicated an increase in the population among some of the Bayou area's protected bird species. The Association wanted to do observations and write about it in the spring quarterly report. Morgan Trent told the people in Baton Rouge that the article could speak favorably of the harmony of technology and nature in the state's oil and gas fields. The positive impact of such a report on Louisiana's national image was not lost on the government. The proverbial bureaucratic red carpet had been laid out for Simmons at the state capital.

Simmons gazed out the window and considered his recent field trip. After landing in Baton Rouge, he scouted an area 70 miles northwest of the city for campsites. Returning to the capital, he borrowed a runabout and spent the next two days cruising the Mississippi from Baton Rouge up to Natchez. After a good night's sleep he flew to Huntsville, Alabama, and tied up one loose end that had nothing to do with SESA's plans. The following morning a hop to New Orleans and Flight 22 to Tampa completed a most productive five days.

"Excuse me, Mr. Russell, would you like a beverage?"

Simmons jerked slightly then cursed to himself for showing any reaction. He had been traveling as Eugene Russell for five days and the alias was as natural as his true name. Looking up, he noticed an attractive flight attendant, probably in her early thirties, and smiled. "I'll have a soft drink."

"We'll be in Tampa in about an hour," she informed him as she placed the drink on the tray next to Simmons'/Russell's papers. "Call if you need anything."

"Thanks," he replied pleasantly, and gave the attendant a quick once-over as she walked away and returned to his papers.

Samantha Schmidt wheeled the drink cart into the galley and removed a small notebook from her skirt pocket. The papers on passenger 5D's tray appeared to be the standard array of Louisiana tourist publications. The only thing that caught her eye was the handwritten word "Simmesport" in one of the margins. She noted a slight twitch when she called his name but could not be sure there was anything to it.

Other than that 5D seemed normal. But he was a cash customer, and cash customers received extra scrutiny; especially on South Air flights. Samantha scribbled a note and returned to her duties.

Simmons deplaned at Tampa International. Inside the main terminal he went to a phone bank. Entering more than enough money, he hit "O" and told the operator to let the call go through unassisted.

Samantha followed him at a discreet distance. She could not hear the conversation but noted that he had used coins to make a long distance phone call. It was impossible to tell from her position if he had dialed an area code outside Florida but there was do doubt in her mind that he had punched ten numbers. She made another entry into her notebook and hurried down the concourse to reboard Flight 22. The plane would wait for her but she did not like to be late.

HUNTSVILLE, ALABAMA

Despite the circumstances, Harte was genuinely glad to see Andrew Loman. "Are you all right?"

"I'm okay. I drove down last night." Loman kept small talk to a minimum. "My car is right outside. Shall we go?"

Harte gave the young man a sidelong glance as they walked briskly to the passenger pickup area. Something did not fit. Andrew and Herbert Loman were as close as a father and son could ever be. Yet no sense of loss pervaded the young man's actions. The words grim, determined and troubled came to mind, but none of these really described the young man's demeanor, at least not individually.

Harte stopped walking. Two steps later Loman stopped and turned. "What's the matter, Mr. Harte?"

"Am I missing something here? You called me a little more than four hours ago and told me your father died in a motel fire. Now you act like we are on the way to a sales call. Do you want to tell me what is going on?"

"Can we talk in the car?"

Harte recognized the question as the closest Loman could come to issuing an order. He straightened his back imperceptibly and walked past his young colleague. "Okay Andy, you have the ball." Once the car was moving he turned to Loman and asked point blank, "Now. What's this all about?"

Loman maneuvered onto I-565 and headed toward downtown Huntsville. "At the police station, I met with a Sergeant John Dutton. He said that dad fell asleep with a lit cigarette in his hand. Apparently when he dozed off the cigarette missed the ashtray on the bed and, well I'm sure you can finish the story yourself."

Harte thought a moment then broached the sensitive subject. "Is that why you don't seem too, how do I say it, sad or even depressed about this? Are you angry that he died this way? I don't want to sound like a bleeding heart liberal or anything but I'm not connecting with your feelings on this."

After a brief pause, both men chuckled at Harte's metaphor. The ice was broken. Loman spoke as his laugh subsided. "It's nothing like that." He looked forward in silence and with quiet understatement, set off a bomb. "Dad quit smoking, cold turkey, two months ago on his doctor's orders."

If there is such a thing as deafening silence, Harte and Loman experienced a full dose. Harte finally spoke, far less sternly than before. "What did the police say to that?"

"I didn't tell them. I wanted to talk to you first." Loman paused as if searching for justification. "Haven't you ever encountered something or someone, took a look and just pulled back until you had everything on the right page? My dad is dead and my first instinct is that it wasn't an accident. Before I turn this over to a cop I don't know, who thinks it was an unfortunate mishap, in a city I've never been to, I want to talk to the only people I really trust outside my family. That's you and the Foundation."

Harte stared ahead. Loman continued with a touch of desperation. "You probably think this is stupid but all I know is that black folks haven't always received red carpet treatment in these parts. I honestly don't know if that has changed much through the years. All I have to go on is what I've heard. I'm sorry if my thinking is not rational enough."

Harte was stunned. He had not considered the Loman family's race a factor in this situation. As far as he knew, no one had even noticed that Loman was the only black member of Harte's inner circle. The Wilson Foundation operated in the absence of the racial and ethnic hyphenations that littered the world of political correctness. Suddenly, at the precise moment when one of the its first members faced a crisis, the specter of race reared its ugly head.

Harte wondered if, through the Foundation, he had insulated himself too much from society. He scolded himself for being so naive, even as he considered a course of action. Loman's assertion had put him in a defensive mind set.

"Hello. Is anybody home in there?" Loman tried to reel Harte back from wherever his mind had wandered.

"Sorry. You tossed out quite a bit there. I think we can cover your concerns." Harte outlined his plan, finishing as they pulled into the parking lot at Baker Precinct of the Huntsville Police Department.

He got out of the car and stretched. The hair on his neck stood up for a moment as he glanced at a passing vehicle. "Did you see that car?" he asked, as Loman joined him.

"Which one?"

"The red Ford Escort that just drove by and turned down the street over there."

"They made around five million of those didn't they?" Loman said with disinterest. "I don't much notice them."

"I know," replied Harte as they walked toward the precinct entrance. "But I'd swear I saw that car and the guy driving it leave the airport when we did. He may have followed us."

"So much for the calming influence. Let's go talk to the detective." They shared a weak chuckle and entered the building.

A block away, a red Ford Escort pulled into a convenience store parking lot. The driver allowed himself a congratulatory smile. He had wagered that the sedan would go directly from the airport to Baker Precinct. There were only a couple of options but leaving the tail was a gamble nonetheless. Fortunately, the target acted by the book.

George Gansz walked to a nearby pay phone and dialed a local number. "They went to Baker just as we thought. All I got was a last name. Harte. I don't know if that's with an 'E' or what...Of course I got a picture...That's hard to say. The flight was out of Nashville on American Eagle so he could have come from almost anywhere. My guess is he took the fastest connections he could find...Check with American and see what flights in and out of Nashville during their noon complex have the shortest layover...Yeah I know that's a lot of flights...Hell, call a travel agent or something. Narrow it down to, say, fifteen or twenty minutes. That's about enough time. Then see if they had any tickets purchased for that situation. Who knows? Maybe it will be right in front of them...Of course it's never the first one. But it's a start. I'll see where they go from here and get back to you."

Gansz returned to his car. He picked up the instant photo and studied it. "Okay, Mr. Harte. Who are you and why are you running around in Huntsville, Alabama, with Andrew Loman?"

"Sorry to keep you waiting, Mr. Loman," John Dutton said as he crossed the lobby of Baker Precinct. The police sergeant seemed anxious to see them, but a little disturbed.

Baker precinct was a converted bank branch a few blocks north of the crowded Municipal Government complex. It handled misdemeanor and initial felony investigations on Huntsville's expanding north side. Important cases moved downtown once the paperwork was complete. Dutton enjoyed working out of Baker. The facility was quiet and afforded him a place to get his ideas into focus.

"Hello, Sergeant Dutton," Loman replied. "This is Daniel Harte. He is my advisor, of sorts, and he came down to help me with this matter."

Dutton shook hands with Harte. "Are you a lawyer?"

"Should I be?"

Dutton grinned slightly and shook his head. "No. Frankly I'm glad you're not. Let's go to my office. I'd rather talk there if you don't mind."

Harte and Loman followed the detective down the hall through a door with his name on it. Harte noted that Dutton was not out in the pool with the rest of the detectives. He assumed that meant HPD was looking past the obvious.

Dutton motioned them to seats in front of his slightly cluttered desk. "You can smoke if you want, and the coffee is reasonably fresh. What can I do for you, Mr. Loman?"

Loman came straight to the point. "I spoke to my mother this morning and told her how dad died. She said that he quit smoking two months ago."

Dutton stiffened a bit. "Any chance he could have decided to have one for old times' sake?"

"I don't believe so, sir. He had a doctor's order to stop. He was, by nature, pretty conscientious. I don't think he would have taken the chance."

"That makes sense. But there is a problem."

Loman leaned forward. "Like what?"

Dutton looked over the file. "We found a partial pack of cigarettes and a lighter in the motel room. It appears he was smoking again."

Harte spoke up. "What kind of lighter?"

Dutton checked the file. "Standard disposable type. The ones you get in any store for a dollar. Why?"

"Seems like a waste to me."

"Come again, Mr. Harte?" Dutton studied him.

"I don't know. If you are under doctor's orders not to smoke and you want to have one for old times' sake, as you put it, why buy a lighter when the stores hand out matches or the motel puts them in most of the rooms. Did you find any matches in the motel room?"

Dutton broke the uneasy silence. "I must be getting old or something. I never even considered that. Are you a cop?"

"No, Sergeant. I've just always looked between the lines. In the Marines years ago I worked for NSA. We learned that things are not always as they appear to be. I never quite got out of the habit."

Dutton's eyebrow rose slightly at the mention of the National Security Agency. He made no comment, choosing instead to continue with the main point. "In spite of what this conversation might show, I'm pretty much the same way, Mr. Harte." He looked back at the file then turned to Loman. "We found something else that is troubling. The fire inspector says that the fire seemed to jump from the cigarette burn over to the newspaper. They found no residue of an accelerant, like gasoline, or anything. But there is one thing that could do it and pretty much disappear in the fire."

"What's that?" Loman waited for the other shoe to fall.

"Ether. It could cause the fire to jump and then dissipate as the fire consumed everything. I need to—"

"You need to do an autopsy!" Loman leapt out of his chair. "My dad did not do drugs, dammit! I want an autopsy to show that there is no drug residue in his blood. I knew it, Dan. I told you about these things."

"Mr. Loman, relax." Dutton waited for Loman to sit down. "No one said anything about drugs."

"But you said—"

"I said ether could have caused the fire to jump. Look, I know this is not pleasant and I know what you are thinking."

"You have no—"

"Let the man talk, Andy." Harte's comment brought a little order to the scene.

"Thank you, Mr. Harte. Andy, this is not the Alabama of the fifties and sixties, okay? I kind of resent that, but I understand your fears. We found nothing in the room to indicate your father smoked anything but a cigarette. I was going to suggest an autopsy myself. We may find a residue of ether in his blood and lungs." Dutton looked at Harte before he continued. "If we do, I have to think about the possibility that your father was drugged and, in all probability, murdered."

Loman looked sheepish. "I'm sorry, Sergeant. I've had a bad feeling about this since this morning. How can I help?"

"First sign this authorization for the autopsy. Then get some rest. You look terrible, son. I'll contact you as soon as we have a finding."

Harte spoke up. "Where are Mr. Loman's personal effects? We'd like to go through them."

"No problem. I have his wallet and pocket contents here. His suitcase is still at the motel room. I can have it brought in for you."

"May we go get it?" Harte's mind raced a few thoughts ahead of the conversation. "I'd like to see the room. Maybe there is something we could learn from it and let you know."

"I can't see anything wrong with that. It's the Crown Motel over on University Avenue. I'll call and tell them to let you in. Do you have anything particular in mind?"

Harte shook his head. "No, I just thought if Andy and I saw the place we might notice something that your department missed. There may be some personal thing or whatever that we could look at. Does that make any sense to you?"

"Sure, Mr. Harte. My name is John. I understand perfectly. Do what you have to do."

"Thanks, John."

Harte and Loman walked to the car in silence. "I feel like an asshole for the way I acted," Loman said as the doors closed.

"Don't worry. You don't look like one."

"Why are we going to the motel?" Loman asked.

"It's just a feeling I have and I can't explain it. Let's go." Harte stared ahead as the car pulled away from the curb.

Ten seconds later, a red Ford Escort pulled out of a side street and followed them from a safe distance.

NAPLES, FLORIDA

Simmons breathed deeply. The aroma of the Everglades, a pleasant combination of plant life, water and earth, was overshadowed by the smell of food simmering on a grill. Right now he preferred the smell of dinner. A stomach growl reminded him that a cheeseburger had been his only meal during the busy travel day.

Stretching off the effects of a two hour flight and a three hour drive, Simmons walked into the base camp of the Southeast Endangered Species Association. He looked down at the array of food sitting in serving pans over the low heat of the gas grill. The paradox made him chuckle. Since charcoal polluted the air, SESA prepared its meals on the most advanced piece of backyard cooking technology available, a Weber®,Genesis 2000® gas grill complete with three stainless steel burners.

For all its rustic appeal and appearance of harmony with nature, the camp was a state-of-the-art facility. A gas-powered generator for electricity enabled the group to work past sundown. A huge tank held enough fresh water that they could probably install pipes and the weight would provide running tap water to all the tents. Above all else, meals did not consist of gleaned forest vegetation or trapped animals. Members of SESA ate better than many middle-class American families. Trent knew that converts don't stay around long if you did not supply certain creature comforts.

Simmons appreciated that line of thinking. Besides, at age thirty, he had spent a lot of time in far worse conditions than these people could ever dream of. He seldom took advantage of the group's two apartments in town because the base camp in Big Cyprus Preserve was far more comfortable than a lot of camps he had called home.

He poked gently at a large chicken breast. Content that it would not burn his fingers, he took it from the serving pan and ate as he walked toward the large tent set apart from the others. "Mr. Trent. Are you home?"

"Come on in, Al. I've been waiting for you."

Simmons entered to find Trent at his work table. They started to shake hands but Simmons held a satchel in one hand and the piece of chicken in the other. Both men laughed. "Sorry, Mr. Trent. It smelled so good and I hardly ate a thing all day." He put the satchel on the table and accepted the outstretched hand of his mentor.

"Good to have you back, Al. How did it go out there?"

"I got all the information we need and they don't even know I was there. I called the Office of the Environment from Tampa and the stupid bitch, sorry, the woman I spoke to, a Mrs. Reese, was so worried about the project not going forward, I thought she would cry. I told her that when we arrived we would ask that she be put in charge from their end. She is sending some literature on campgrounds in the area we want."

"Terrific. Now tell me the real good news."

Simmons tossed the unfinished piece of chicken into a waste basket. Wiping his hands on a towel, he motioned Trent to sit down at the work table. "Check folder number one."

Trent found a set of blueprints with a schematic overlay and spread them on his table. "These are impressive."

"You should see the real thing. It's a piece of work. And there's not one defensive asset in the area." Simmons silently cursed himself for uttering the military term.

Trent either missed or ignored the comment. He stared at the blueprint. "It looks big even on paper. Can we get enough product to do the job?"

Simmons breathed easier. "Check out folder number two. This may be easier than we thought." He opened the second folder and showed Trent a photograph of a dam. "Look at it. Five hundred feet long with eleven gates. A crane at each end on a railroad track lifts and lowers the gates. We pull the gates, immobilize the cranes and let nature do the rest of the work for us."

"Do you really think they will stand by and watch as someone climbs into their crane and casually opens all of those gates?'"

Simmons caught the dry humor. "Not a chance. But an official work crew would have a lot of leeway wouldn't they?"

Trent sat up a straighter. "Explain."

"There is always work taking place on site. They don't have much confidence in the thing. In fact most of the work load can be handled at the first site. They think number two could fail anyway. We can go in as a work crew, relieve the people on duty and have the place to ourselves."

Trent rubbed his hands like a man about to eat the meal of his life. He liked what he heard so far. "Is that all you could come up with?" He joked.

Simmons was emboldened. "If we do something at both sites they will have to decide where to respond. If they split the response team, it cuts their efficiency and they probably won't be able to save both structures. My guess is they will concentrate on the big one because they consider it the cornerstone of the complex. I think there is a way to render it unusable. By the time they figure that out the lower structure will be history."

"What if they go to the smaller structure first?" Trent wanted to hear contingencies.

Simmons hesitated. "The repair crews might have to suffer some casualties to reduce their efficiency." He tried to make the statement sound innocuous.

After a moment of profound silence, Trent spoke in a slow, measured voice. "There is greater good involved here. Sometimes we must defy our values to assure attainment of the higher goal. We do what we do for the betterment of all humankind." He hoped the statement sounded philosophical enough to convince the younger man.

Simmons smiled inwardly. His job would be much simpler now. Trent had accepted killing as a part of the plan. "I understand, Mr. Trent," he replied evenly, before steering the conversation back to its original subject. "My contact at the site confirmed your projections. He says that with all the snow and prolonged deep freeze in the north we may have as many as six opportunities. It's up to you but, in my opinion, the earlier the better."

"I agree, Al. Good work. Now to my original question. Will we have enough product for the job?"

"I have access to about eight hundred pounds. That's more than enough. And we have a stash for future projects." Simmons was about to continue when he realized that Trent had fixated on something. He learned long ago not to interrupt Trent during one of his dark moments. He backed away from the table and left the tent.

Trent sat staring at the blueprint. He breathed a sigh of relief when the tent flap closed. His task would be much easier now. Simmons had accepted killing as part of the plan. The others would be brought into line with little trouble. They were as radical a group as Trent had ever known. And so they should be, since he had hand-picked them.

Alone with his inner demons, Trent focused on another project, a tragically unsuccessful adventure at sea. This effort would be different. This would be for Nina.

HUNTSVILLE, ALABAMA

Harte stood in the entryway looking at the charred remains of Room 245 of the Crown Motel. He watched Loman move around the debris, still concerned about the young man's approach to his father's death. Once the situation came under question, the Huntsville Police put a stop to clean-up efforts, so the room was largely in the same condition as the fire inspectors had left it.

The bed was completely charred. The damage diminished gradually outward to the opposite walls. Harte surmised that the sprinkler system had eventually kicked in and saved part of the room from destruction. It probably prevented the fire from spreading, a blessing for other lodgers but no help at all to Herbert Loman.

Harte found it curious that the police would let civilians probe a potential crime scene. Yet he appreciated the chance for Andy to confront the loss of a parent. The younger Loman needed to relieve the emotional burden boiling inside. As a friend and sometimes mentor, Harte reluctantly welcomed the event and the chance to help in whatever way possible. "Do you see anything useful?" The question sounded so detective-like but, to an extent, that was the kind of work in which they were engaged.

"No. It all looks like standard motel stuff. There are no personal items anywhere. It's like he never even unpacked."

Harte glanced into the bathroom. It was intact except for smoke stains and heat damage to some of the fixtures. There was no sign of Herbert Loman's personal toilet items. It seemed as if he had simply walked into the motel room, put down his suitcase and lay on the bed.

That's not so odd, Harte thought. Business travelers probably do that all of the time. He himself had done it on more than one occasion. Still, something seemed wrong.

"Here it is."

Harte looked back to find Loman holding his father's suitcase. It was blackened on the outside but appeared to be intact. He also noticed Loman's expression turning slightly more sullen. Maybe now we can get somewhere, Harte thought. "Let's open it and see what we've got."

"Shouldn't Dutton be here?"

"I doubt it. He let us walk around in here unsupervised, didn't he? I'm sure he figures we'll tell him what we find."

Loman did not press the issue, so Harte did not add that he felt Dutton also knew that Andy needed to release his emotions. Maybe this was Dutton's way of giving him the dignity of doing so in private. Harte felt comfortable with the detective and quickly dismissed the stereotype of "Southern redneck cop." John Dutton was one of the good guys.

"Okay, here we go." Loman put the suitcase on the burnt Formica dresser top and wiped soot from the numbered locks. "Dad loved this thing. He bought it about a year ago. He changed the combination every three months and always told me the new one..." he hesitated, "...in case anything happened to him." Loman fumbled momentarily, then finished setting the numbers. "That's it." He pushed two buttons and the clasps jumped open.

The contents were surprisingly undamaged. Harte caught himself thinking that he needed to get one of these things some day. A normal supply of men's clothing for a four day business trip lay folded in the case. Harte noticed the toilet case that was missing from the bathroom.

Loman picked up a vinyl object. When he opened it his hands began to tremble. "I gave him this on his birthday seven years ago." It was a calculator, prehistoric by today's standards. "I tried to get him to upgrade to a better unit but he said that this worked fine. He didn't want to take the time to learn all this new technology." His voice wavered then cracked. "I knew he could use better stuff because his job was so..."

The dam broke with unexpected fury. Loman was reduced to a sobbing mass of humanity in seconds. He instinctively turned and buried his head into Harte's chest, holding on as if his own life depended on not losing his grip. "Dammit, I want him back. He was my hero and he's gone. It's not right."

Harte did the only thing he could. He held the young man as long as necessary, saying nothing. The sorrow, anger and pain poured out like a flood. Loman's moment of emotional reckoning had arrived like a runaway freight train and Harte hated every second of it. But he also knew it had to happen and was glad to be there when Andy needed someone.

Harte's eyes wandered from the ceiling to the open suitcase as Loman's sorrow played itself out. A curious feeling came over him as his view settled on a compartment on the left wall of the case. He stared at it until Andy finally regained some composure and disengaged himself.

"Thanks, Dan. I had no idea how much I needed that. I'm sorry you had to be the one that—"

Harte dismissed the comment. "Don't say it. I only wish it could have been a little easier on you. Are you okay, all things considered?"

"I'll be all right."

"That's good." Harte pointed to the compartment. "What's in there?"

Loman stared curiously as he righted himself emotionally. "What have we here?"" He removed a small pen knife from his pocket and reached toward the compartment. "Can we be so lucky?" The lock popped open and Loman unzipped a flap. It dropped down revealing a standard three-inch floppy disk, in a protective covering. Loman gingerly picked it up and handed it over to Harte. The label read "WHSO1."

"What the hell is this?" Harte spoke deliberately. "What does a man with a seven year old calculator need a floppy disk for? And why did he keep it in a protective cover in a locked compartment of a combination lock suitcase?""

"I don't know." Loman was just as puzzled.

"What was your dad doing for a living? I thought he was a salesman or something."

"He was a sales consultant. I never really knew what that meant. In the last year or so he moved into consulting with corporations that have downsized since the end of the cold war. He never said much about where he went or what he did. I figured he was computer literate, in spite of his old calculator, but this seems a little out of character."

"Who did he work for, the CIA or something?" Harte asked the question tongue-in-cheek and it brought both of them to nervous laughter, breaking the real or imagined tension in the room.

"Funny, Dan. Real funny." Loman replied. "He was doing work with space and defense technology companies, but I think it was on things like manpower redistribution and asset relocation."

"You mean layoffs and plant closings."

The light bulb went in Loman's head. "Oh no. You don't think some laid-off defense worker got pissed and took it out on my dad."

"I have no idea. But I do think your father was killed and I'd bet John Dutton thinks so too. The question is 'Where do we go from here?' I have an idea, if you are interested."

"Let's hear it," Loman quickly replied.

"All right. Take the disk home and find out what is on it. If there is anything the Huntsville P.D. needs to know we can send it to them. We'll say we didn't locate it for a few days and when we ran it through our system the information came up."

"Isn't that withholding evidence?"

"It's not officially a murder, is it. Besides, you did not know it was in the suitcase until you got home and examined it closely." Harte hesitated for a second. "For some reason I don't think this is about getting revenge. An angry aerospace engineer would just use a gun. This looks pretty sophisticated. We have some resources available that may help in this situation." The comment was vague but it would have to do.

"You don't have to get the Wilson Foundation involved," Loman said pointedly. "You've done more than enough already."

Harte put his hand on Loman's shoulder. "Hey. We're already involved and that's that. I was on a conference call with everyone when you called this morning. Don't ask me 'Why?', but everyone started asking logistical questions, as if we are going to be involved whether we want to or not. If that's the case, I want to be as far out ahead of the curve on this as I can."

"Involved in what?" Loman was genuinely confused.

"I don't know yet. For now we'll just see where things lead."

Loman shrugged. "All I know is that you and the Foundation have always made sense to me. I see no reason to change my attitude now. Just tell me what you want me to do."

"Good. Get back to Louisville. I'll head for Cincinnati and bring everyone up to speed on what we have. What you find on the disk will determine where how we proceed. Let's get out of here."

George Gansz slowly pulled into traffic. Fortunately the men in the sedan were on a narrow itinerary and he could afford the luxury of keeping his distance. They went to the police station first. After a much shorter second visit they headed, as he suspected, for the airport. He wanted to know the contents of the suitcase they removed from the motel room. From the time his targets spent at Baker Precinct, he assumed that the Hunstville Police had not asked to look through it. That surprised him.

He broke a few traffic laws to arrive at the Huntsville airport before Harte and Loman. Inside the terminal he adopted an almost movie-like pose near a newsstand and watched the two men arrange flight connections. Harte headed for the airline gates and the young black man walked out of the terminal and got into the sedan.

Gansz hesitated, then walked to the airline ticket counter. He knew the driver was Andrew Loman from Louisville. If he needed to follow him he had the license number and the only way to Louisville was I-65. Harte was the mystery and Gansz was determined to find out who he was and what he wanted in Huntsville.

GALLATIN PEAK, MONTANA

The Cessna 190 weaved its way through a series of ridges and valleys that formed the entrance to the Madison Range. One of a collection of small mountain ranges running southeast from Canada to Colorado, the range helps form the eastern gateway of the Rocky Mountains. The peaks of these ranges average from twenty nine to thirty five hundred feet. To easterners familiar with the Appalachians, the Madison Range might seem daunting. But to western Americans they are but foothills compared to the fifteen thousand foot towers of the western Continental Divide.

The plane carried four businessmen from Helena to a weekend appointment with the trout population of Henry's Lake near the Montana, Idaho and Wyoming borders. Thirty miles out of Three Forks the pilot began a sweeping left turn around the north and west face of Gallatin peak. He held the plane steady at fifteen hundred feet, keeping the face of the mountain a safe two thousand feet to the left.

Halfway through the turn the engine sputtered. Seconds later it sputtered again. The pilot calmly checked his gauges. No problems. Another series of sputtering sounds caused the Cessna to hesitate for a brief second.

The pilot nervously rechecked the fuel gauge. There was more than enough to get to Henry's Lake and back. As he tapped the gauge, a habit most pilots adopted more from some movie than from practicality, a sixty mile per hour gust of wind came off the face of the mountain. The Cessna's tail section turned in the wind like a suspended weather vane.

The passengers panicked as the pilot tried to control his craft, now flying at one hundred and twenty miles per hour straight toward the face of the mountain. Realizing that the plane would not respond in time, he shouted a universal expletive and covered his face.

The Cessna slammed into a rocky crag twelve hundred feet up the slope of Gallatin Peak. Gasoline spewed from the ruptured fuel tank and the craft burst into flames. The passengers died instantly as the fireball slowly diminished, leaving only smoldering wreckage on the mountainside.

Two thousand feet above the wreckage, sound waves from the explosion plowed into the underside of a thick overhang of ice and snow stretching along the north and west face of the mountain. A winter of record snowfall and little or no sunshine had created the massive build-up. It hung precariously, waiting for the spring thaw to melt it, or something else to remove it.

The sound waves spread out along the overhang. Directly above the crash site, a fifty ton block of ice dislodged and dropped onto an outcropping of rocks, shattering on impact. Like an archway without a keystone, the overhang began to fall, bringing with it much of the surface snow that lay on the mountain. Slowly at first, then much more quickly as sound waves continued to batter it, a three-mile-long line of snow and ice rolled down the north and west face of Gallatin Peak expanding as it went.

The avalanche literally peeled the white covering off the side of the mountain, pushing everything in its path toward the base below. The rumble of the sliding debris filled the normally peaceful valley and could be heard in Big Sky, fifteen miles to the south and Bozeman, twenty miles to the north.

It was over in minutes. Up the mountain an entire winter's snow-fall had disappeared, leaving the face an barren gray mass in contrast with the white of the mountaintop. Below, fifty million cubic feet of ice, snow and rock lay across the Gallatin river in the valley on the north side of the peak. On the western side a similar mound of debris filled the five stream beds that, in spring, would be major tributaries of the Madison river.

Chapter II

CINCINNATI, OHIO

Harte walked the short distance from the dining room to the front door. With the arrival of William Harmon, the inner circle of the Wilson Foundation would be complete.

Harte had invested his life savings, the proceeds from the sale of his small restaurant, in an idea hatched by Harmon and another former employee, Mike Prince. It was the late seventies and they wanted to enter the fledgling world of personal computer programming. They had come up with a game program and needed financing to market it.

Harmon assured him that they could protect his investment, and Prince promised that Harte would have to put in little or no actual work time. It sounded too good to be true but they had been loyal employees and Harte took the chance.

Within three months "little or no work" turned into twenty hours a week over and above his full-time job. The company was showing an income but most of it was going back into the venture as they created new programs and worked to set up a distribution system.

Harte borrowed more money to help ease the company cash flow and finally, after eighteen tenuous months they began to turn a profit and earn a small personal income. They owned a regional distribution system and the company had assets that gave it an appearance of net worth. On paper it was worth over a million dollars. The three men issued themselves penny stock and ambitiously applied for a listing on the NASDAQ exchange, hoping to raise enough capital to expand nationally.

Their lives changed forever one evening when Harmon dropped a bomb on the dinner table. "Microcom wants to buy the company for ten dollars a share."

"Is that a good offer?" Harte knew about the company that was emerging as the leader in the computer software industry and he had an idea.

Prince jumped into the discussion. "It's a great offer. They are the Cadillac of the industry. When they take a step everyone gets on the bandwagon. They will define the cutting edge of this stuff for years."

"I know all of that. So let's think this through. Do we want to be a part of that?"

"What do you mean?" Harmon asked.

"Why not take part in cash and the rest in stock? Then we can live off them for the rest of their run if we want." Silence ruled the dinner table as they all sat back and considered Harte's proposal.

Six months later Daniel Harte found himself with fifty thousand shares of the top computer software company in the world and a large chunk of cash. He was staring down a road that would become the longest period of American peacetime economic expansion since World War II.

His investments grew rapidly. After five years he rolled everything into a foundation for tax purposes. Harte named the foundation, indirectly, after the man he considered most responsible for the economic boom and started handing out some of the excess, in the form of scholarships and study grants. By the end of the eighties, The Wilson Foundation had a solid reputation in its field.

"You're late again, Billy," Harte said in mock sternness.

"Yeah, but I'm worth the wait," Harmon replied as Harte closed the door behind them.

Harte's dining room had become a conference room. At one end of the table a large television displayed a computer window. From the other end Harte surveyed the scene. The three men and two women before him represented the best of what he wanted the Wilson Foundation to stand for. They had worked hard to get to their places in life. Harte, through the Foundation, had recognized their talent and awarded them financial aid to pursue their dreams, but the attainment of these dreams was the product of their personal dedication.

The Foundation held an annual gathering so that all its members could keep in touch. But the group at the dining room table kept in closer contact with Harte and each other. No one really could say when the term "inner circle" was first used. Somewhere along the way it simply became apparent that there was an innate loyalty among them. Even though conference calls and meetings were far more frequent among them, they had never before gathered in such a somber atmosphere.

"Okay, let's get to work," Harte announced, effectively calling the meeting to order. "Show us what you have, Andy."

As Loman hunched over a computer keyboard, Harte watched him closely. "Are you comfortable with this?" The funeral had been two days ago and Harte did not know how Loman would handle this dissection of his father's business dealings.

"I'm fine, but thanks for asking." Loman looked around the table. "I appreciate the concern, but this is business now. We have reason to believe that a murder took place and I want to get to the bottom of it. Is that cool with everybody?"

Heads nodded as the tension of the moment faded. Loman continued. "It took two days to get into the thing. Dad never told me the password so I hacked around trying combinations. I finally got it on the fifth combination of my family's initials." He entered RJAH and the screen came to life.

Numerous sets of capital letters, in two and five-letter groups filled the screen. "I couldn't make anything out of this. I looked through all of Dad's belongings and could not find a code book. Whatever it is he kept it all in his head. Then I took a wild stab at something. Watch this."

He clicked on the five letter group HNTAL. Next to it he typed the words "Huntsville, Alabama." Instantly the screen displayed what looked like a daily log of activity in and around Huntsville. It contained time dated entries with corporation names that were familiar to everyone at the table.

There were also gaps in the time line. "If we accept the premise that this is a business log, there are a number of times where he was somewhere other than Huntsville. Some I can account for by his presence at home but some others I can't."

The group at the table studied the screen. Timothy Lassick, the 30 year old editor of *National Analyst*, a conservative political publication, spoke up. "I'm the investigative reporter here, so here's my insight into the obvious. Let's assume all the five-letter codes indicate cities, or at least geographic locations. Just grab an atlas and hack around until we find a place that fits."

"I know something that will work a lot faster." Rita Lowry walked around to Loman's terminal. "May I?" Loman relinquished the chair. She studied the keyboard briefly. "Are we on line?"

Loman activated the modem. Rita entered a long distance number and waited while it connected. "By the way, you guys, what comes up on this screen is not for public display. It's my classified number at JPL. We've been redoing the geodetic survey maps to reconfigure the latitudinal and longitudinal fixes of everything on planet Earth." A couple of people in the room caught their breath.

"I know. It's going to take at least a year. But the good news is that the names of everything we will be plotting are already in the computer. Rivers, mountains, cities, buildings, even dead-end streets are all ready to be pinpointed once the satellite finishes mapping everything."

She returned to the keyboard and logged on to the giant Cray mainframe at the Jet Propulsion Laboratory in Pasadena, California. Lowry, age 25, was one of the Lab's "whiz kids" and had access to the entire system for her project. She spoke as she typed and the "conversation" with the JPL computer appeared on the screen.

"Let's see. Logon RL401. That number is REALLY classified," she announced as the screen printed the greeting from Pasadena. "Correlate File One with Directory A."

She transmitted the list of five letter coded groups to the Cray. "List cities to match entries in File One and send reply." The screen indicated the Cray was working on the problem. "On completion delete all entries and record of File One requests."

Harte looked at her as the screen acknowledged her last request. "Rita, we are logged on to a major computer system of the Federal Government. Is this going to be a problem?"

Five heads turned to him in astonishment. In the excitement of the moment no one had given his suggestion a thought.

Rita laughed it off. "Are you kidding? They know it's me coming in and they know where I am. They love the Wilson Foundation out there. You've helped them out a few times when a program or two was in trouble. In fact, call Mrs. Harding at the office. She will probably tell you that a donation just arrived from the JPL. I think they want you to send them some more engineers. Or maybe they think I'll eat too much and bust your food budget while I'm here.

"This should take an hour or so. I suggest we get to work on the two-letter codes and see what we come up with." She grinned and returned to her seat at the table.

"Well that covers that, doesn't it," Harte said as Loman returned the screen to the original set of letter codes. "I'm going out to the kitchen and see about something for dinner. If you want my opinion, the two-letter codes are probably people. You might want to start from there."

Before he even stood up Harte saw that his five proteges were already absorbed in the work before them. As he walked to the kitchen, Lydia Rogers, a 33 year-old Ph.D. in Military History at Ohio State, called after him. "We may be here quite a while. Do you have room for us to sleep if we have to?"

"Of course, Lydia. It may have to be two to a room in some cases." She had returned to her work before he finished his reply. So much for his concern over imposing on their time. Opening the refrigerator, Harte congratulated himself for having the good sense to stock it with enough food for a few days.

AUGUSTA, KENTUCKY

The lockmaster brushed snow from the railing and leaned over to survey the situation. Ice around Number Ten and Eleven Gates at Meldahl Dam had firmed up in the last four days. He silently cursed the budget cuts that put him in this predicament. A problem at Markland, on the other side of Cincinnati, had tied up the repair crew longer than expected. In the old days he would have called in a civilian crew. But like almost every other agency of the federal government, the U.S. Army Corps of Engineers was forced to work within budgetary restraints. The job would have to wait for the Corps' in-house repair crew.

He descended the ladder and crossed a spillway to the Kentucky side of the river. The ice was not thick around the gates and there was enough flow to keep it from becoming a major buildup. Spring would arrive soon and that would be the end of the problem. In spite of the inconvenience, the situation seemed under control. A quick inspection of the river bank showed no break between the shoreline and the ice. The lockmaster frowned at this discovery. He jumped up and down. The normally soft sand and clay compound of the river bank did not give an inch. A fear that had nagged him since November was confirmed.

The previous fall in the Ohio Valley had been one of the wettest on record, with monthly rainfall over five inches above average. A long hot summer left the ground parched, enabling it to soak up the continuous parade of light to moderate showers. By early December the ground was completely saturated.

But now it was frozen solid, probably two to three feet down. Winter, like the fall, continued to be one of records. The temperature had remained below the freezing mark for most of the nights and days since Christmas. Even the few days when the mercury crept above thirty-two degrees did not help; cloud cover prevented the sun from doing any good.

The lockmaster considered another ramification of the peculiar weather patterns as he made his way back up the ladder and across the dam. The runoff would be bad enough with a normal thaw. But if the rain came before the ground thawed and drained, there would be hell to pay downriver. He mulled over the possibility of a three or four-hundred year flood.

Just upriver a towboat maneuvered its barges for entry into lock Number Two. He trotted the last fifty yards and climbed the stairs to the control room. He opened the upriver lock gate and made a mental note to call Charles Haisley in Vicksburg. Haisley would want to know about this. It could be a bitch of a spring on the Ohio River.

CINCINNATI, OHIO

"It's been six hours. Let's see what we have so far," Harte announced as he took his seat at the dining room table.

"So far, Rita and her Cray have given us quite a load," Harmon said. Harte was not at all surprised that Harmon had assumed the leadership role. He was Harte's oldest associate among them, in time and years.

"I should let her explain." Harmon deferred to Rita Lowry.

"We received lists of possible city and landmark names for every five-letter group in the file. All we can do is enter names under each group until we hit the right one. But it is already shaping up into an orderly series of activities."

Rita made a quick entry. The screen flashed to blue and then to white. Under the letters NAPFA, a file opened with the heading "Naples, Florida." A series of times in and out, numerous two-letter groups and the names of various businesses filled half of the screen. The file appeared to be set up to handle additional entries.

Harmon continued the briefing as hard copies of the file began to print out. "Lydia and Tim are trying to set up a chronology based on all of the times and dates. We are stuck on the two-letter groups. Maybe something will come up in the rest of the files. Right now dates and places are what's happening."

"What is this?" Harte pointed to an entry in the Naples file. "Everything else is in groups of five and two. Why is this a four-letter group?"

Everyone studied the letters. "Something just came up," said Lassick dryly. "That is probably the Southeast Endangered Species Association. We did an article on them not long ago. They are pretty radical. Hey! Wait a minute. I get a cigar for this one." He pointed to a two-letter group in the Naples file. "If the two-letter groups are in fact, initials, MT could be their leader, Morgan Trent. We did not hit it off very well. I consider him militant, at the least.

"His wife was killed a while back. She fell out of a boat while they were trying to interrupt the course of a super-tanker in the Gulf of Mexico. Those things can't stop for anything. He had a nervous breakdown over it, I guess that's understandable, and got a tidy settlement from the shipping company. Texaco threw in some money too. The next thing you know, Trent is in business in Naples and the Environmental lobby has a hero. Hold it! I think I got something else." He studied the screen for a couple of seconds. "Can I see that Huntsville file again?"

Loman put up a small window in a corner of the screen. Lassick looked over the information in the HNTAL file. "Bingo. Look here. National Electronics, Inc. does a lot of semiconductor work for NASA. We think they are a major supplier to the National Reconnaissance Office. And what do you suppose we have right here?" Lassick pointed to a two-letter group in the National Electronics entry. "If we stay on the initials theory, RW is probably Richard Willis, the CEO. He's a stand-up guy. We tried to profile him in the magazine a few issues ago but he would not talk to us."

"A corporate liberal?" Lydia asked.

"Not at all," Lassick answered. "He said we did not need to know. Now where have we heard that term before?"

"Shit!" All eyes turned toward Harte as he uttered the expletive.

He exchanged a quick glance with Loman. "I think Tim is on the right track. The two letter groups are names unless something different jumps off the screen at us. Agreed?" They were back at work before he could receive a reply. "I see a trip to Huntsville in my immediate future," Harte thought as he picked up a sheet of paper and studied it. It might as well have been blank with all the random thoughts and possibilities that invaded his normally ordered mind.

MOSCOW, RUSSIA

General Kasarov enjoyed watching the President squirm. There was no sign of a vodka bottle but he knew Cherkin could use one of his habitual stiff drinks right now. So what if it was five AM? If the President was awake he needed a drink, or so went the unofficial line in Moscow. Kasarov preferred to think that on this occasion, his proposal, not Cherkin's alcoholism, caused the need.

"It is a simple thing, Mr. President. You appoint me Defense Minister and we reconstruct the cabinet so that Agriculture and Interior work in conjunction with me."

Yuri Cherkin weighed the gravity of the proposal. He was being ordered to turn the nation's food and natural resources over to the military. That was, in effect, all his government was about. "The people will not stand for this." His protest was weak and it fell on deaf ears.

"The people need not know of this," Kasarov replied evenly. "You announce the Defense appointment. The reorganization can be done within the cabinet."

"Word will get out."

"Once oil flows and food gets to market most will not care." Kasarov wanted the meeting to go smoothly. The last thing he needed was for the unstable man across the desk to imply a coup.

"It sounds like a return to the old ways, General."

"It is the only way, Mr. President," Kasarov prodded him.

A hint of resolve found its way to Cherkin's voice. "If I do not agree will you bring the army in again? That failed the last time and it will fail again."

Kasarov smiled. "No. But if you do not agree I will be forced to furlough most of the men from the army at Zelenograd. I will put them on trains to Moscow, every fifteen minutes, with the clothes on their backs and one day's pay. They will be told that the government ordered the cutback despite my strong protest. Can Moscow accommodate another one hundred and fifty thousand unemployed angry men in the dead of winter? Not to mention that the rest of the world will know the western front is defended by fifty thousand soldiers. Shall I explain the ramifications of that situation?" Checkmate, he said to himself.

Cherkin slumped in his chair. In a perverse way he admired the genius of Kasarov's plan. He silently crossed off each of his options as they came to mind. Finally he looked up. "I will need time to put the Defense Minister into disfavor."

Kasarov flinched a little. He could not afford a long delay. "How much time do you need, Mr. President?"

"At least two weeks. We can make the announcement on the first of March."

Kasarov relaxed. "That would be acceptable. Mr. President, you must realize that this will work out for the better. Once we are in a position to deliver oil to the marketplace, our financial problems will quickly be solved. The Russia that you dream of can become a reality." He resented the boot licking but knew it was better to have Cherkin on board than to carry out the plan with the President as an adversary.

"I suppose you are right, Anatoly," Cherkin responded rubbing the effects of the early morning from his eyes.

Kasarov brightened at the use of his first name. He considered it a significant moment in the negotiations. This would be a good time to conclude, he decided. "Mr. President," he said as he rose from his chair, "we both have a long day ahead so perhaps we should end our meeting and get a little rest. That is of course, unless you have any further orders for me on this matter." He continued to play the humble servant.

"You are right, General. We have much to do today. I look forward to working together for the good of Russia."

Kasarov came to attention and saluted. "Then good day, sir. I will report to you in short order."

Cherkin returned the salute weakly and Kasarov did a precise about-face and exited the office. When the door closed Cherkin fumbled for the desk drawer. He removed a bottle of vodka and a glass and set them on the desk. He stared at the bottle and his eyes moistened as he prepared to pour a stiff shot. Suddenly he hurled the bottle against the wall opposite his desk. "That little bastard. Who the hell does he think he is?" The glass quickly followed the bottle into the wall.

The office door flew open and an aide appeared. "Is anything wrong, Mr. President?" he asked nervously. The aide noticed the broken glass. He also noticed a resolve in Cherkin's expression that had been absent for a long time.

"Nothing is wrong," Cherkin replied emphatically. "I want that mess cleaned up and I don't want anyone to know about it. Bring me a pot of coffee and a good breakfast. I have a lot of work to do today."

"Yes, Mr. President," the aide replied sharply.

While the aide was gone, Cherkin considered his situation. One option still remained open. It was worth a try. Besides, if it did not work out he could always crawl back into his vodka bottle and stay drunk until the next election.

The aide returned with the breakfast, and cleaned up the broken glass as Cherkin ate ravenously. "Will there be anything else, Mr. President?"

"What does my schedule look like today, Sergei?"

The aide was startled at the use of his first name. "It is a full schedule of meetings, Mr. President."

"As you can imagine from this, it may be difficult for me to get through everything. Do you understand what I am saying?"

Sergei smiled. "Yes sir. I can eliminate the less important appointments, if necessary."

"Good. Use the usual excuses. Everything must seem as always.

Do you understand?"

"Yes, sir. I am sure that we, uh, that you will handle this in proper fashion." He blushed at his slip of the tongue.

"I think we will too, Sergei." replied Cherkin. He trusted the young man and wanted him to feel confident. "Now, quietly bring me another pot of coffee. And do not let anyone see." The aide nodded and turned to leave.

"Sergei. Should anyone discover what happened here I will have you hanged by your testicles from the highest tower of St. Basil's. Is that clear?" Cherkin smiled ominously at the aid.

"Crystal clear, Mr. President," replied Sergei cheerfully in spite of the dire warning. "If you will excuse me I believe we both have a very busy day ahead of us."

Cherkin sipped his coffee as the door closed. His mind began to clear as he got out a notebook. He had a little over two weeks to formulate a plan. That was enough time, he thought, if he could just keep the promise he had made to himself fifteen minutes ago.

CINCINNATI, OHIO

"Let's do a final review of everything." Harte's announcement brought five heads up from their work. "I want like to get a summary of this so you can all catch evening flights home. We have worked hard and I owe you a chance to be alert on the job tomorrow morning."

"We've solved five city codes so far," Loman announced. As he worked the keyboard five separate windows came on the screen. "The common thread was that all five letters appear in some order in the name of the city and the state it is located in. You know Huntsville and Naples. We also came up with Tampa, New Orleans and Baton Rouge. The pattern is distinctly southeastern."

Each window was headed by a corresponding five letter group: HNTAL, TPAFA, NORLO, NAPFA, BARLO. The files, consisting of date/time groups and two-letter codes, all appeared active. Some contained numerous entries while others were nearly empty.

"We established a time line of sorts from all the dates and times." Lydia handed Harte a sheet of paper. "As you can see, it shows Mr. Loman in a constant travel mode over the last month or so. Naples in late December, back and forth from Huntsville. Andy filled in some gaps with time in Louisville. Here is a Naples entry from October. The picture is not complete but there are patterns developing." She moved to the screen.

"The only time he was in Baton Rouge and New Orleans was in the first five days of February. We found no other dates for those cities prior to then. It also struck me that Huntsville is the only city with major corporate listings. It seems he was doing his business in Huntsville but all the other stops were non-related. It's just a thought. Maybe when we break the other codes it will fall into place better."

"What about the two letter groups?" Harte asked.

Lassick took over the discussion. "Same as before. Naples and SESA and MT have to be Morgan Trent and his environmental group. And Richard Willis is the CEO of National Electronics in Huntsville. Unless anybody has more."

No one spoke up so Lassick continued. "Here in Naples we have MT and AS. My guess is that AS is someone in Morgan Trent's group. That is the only place that these two sets of letters appear. But look here. In Tampa, Baton Rouge, New Orleans, and again in Baton Rouge, we find the letters ER. It looks like Mr. Loman met this person in these cities on successive days in February. Find out who ER is and I bet most of this will unravel pretty easily."

"Do you think ER has ties to Trent and Willis?" Harte tossed out the leading question.

"Dan, this is all speculation. There is no way to tell from what we have here. That may take footwork and meetings."

"I assumed as much. I'll fly down to Huntsville tomorrow. What about the remaining five-letter groups?" Harte asked.

"None of them came up when we entered possible U.S. cities," answered Rita. "I'll send Andy a revised list by country and continent from California. Maybe he can hack the codes out of that. It's time-consuming but it's the only way to do it."

"You guys did a hell of a job this weekend. I'm proud of you," Harte announced. "Am I pushing it if I ask for a little more help on this?" He inquired as they began to collect their belongings.

Lydia gathered up some papers. "I'm going back to O.S.U. and try to put this time line into a more concise order."

"I'll be home working on the rest of the codes, if anyone needs to reach me," announced Loman.

"A Nexis search on Trent and his group may turn up something useful," replied Lassick. "I should have it done in time to get back here next weekend."

"I'll find us some time on the Cray this week if anybody wants to log on, and I'm free next weekend also," Rita said.

There was a short silence as they looked at Harmon. He stared back with a blank expression. "I have some friends in Baton Rouge that I haven't seen in a while. I think I'll visit them." He paused in feigned disinterest. "I'll probably ask a few questions while I'm there. Okay?"

"Asshole," Lassick said as laughter erupted in the room.

When they had assembled in the foyer to say their good-byes Loman addressed the group. "Not many people get a chance to find out what really good friends are. I miss my dad more than I can say, but his death brought us together here and I learned something that I always thought but never knew until now. As long as you guys are around I'll never have to worry about being alone out there. You are the best people I know and I am honored to be associated with you. I don't know how to thank you."

"I think you just did," said Lydia as she gave him a hug.

Rita leaned over and kissed him lightly. "You make it easy for us to want to help, Andy."

"No sweat, partner," Tim said shaking Loman's hand. "I guess we have always been here for each other. At least I've always felt that way."

Harmon tossed his car keys to Lassick. "Here, Tim. Take my car to the airport. I'll ride down to Louisville with Andy, if he doesn't mind, and fly out to Baton Rouge from there in the morning."

They stood quietly, as if not wanting the moment to end. Finally

Harte broke the silence. "You people better get going." As an after-thought he mentioned, "I will be back here by Friday if anyone wants to get started before the weekend."

Nothing could suppress the elation he felt as they drove away. They were a superior group of men and women and he loved them all. Looking up, he found Orion in the southwest sky. "It looks like we are both going to be hunters for a while, my friend," he said aloud. He loosened the zipper on his coat and turned back toward the house. Maybe it was his imagination, but the evening seemed a little warmer.

OLD RIVER AREA, LOUISIANA

Charles Haisley fidgeted as he watched the CNN forecaster go through her national report. His attention wondered during the early segments on the Southeast and Southwest. Through the office window he watched an engineer perform maintenance on one of two massive overhead cranes. The twin giants flanked the Low Sill, a six hundred foot-long gated dam, that, along with two nearby gated structures, were the heart of the Old River Flood Control Project.

This was Haisley's domain. Located sixty miles above Baton Rouge, the complex siphoned water from the Mississippi river to the west and kept the giant meandering stream in its present channel. The task was far more delicate than the huge concrete and steel structures implied. A complex flow split equation insured that the spring flood season was always a work-intensive period for the Corps of Engineers employees at Old River. As such, the late winter weather reports became more important with each passing day.

"Aaron, the jet stream report is coming on," Haisley called out as he returned his attention to the television.

"Just a second. I want to get this printout." A moment later Aaron Roosevelt, Haisley's top assistant, joined him.

A map of the United States filled the TV screen. CNN's chief meteorologist gave her report. "For much of December and all of January the jet stream maintained a stationary position. Entering the continent in Alaska it ran southeast atop the Rocky Mountains and turned sharply east around the Denver area. From there it crossed the lower plains all the way through Kentucky, before turning northeast up the Appalachian Mountains and racing into Canada.

"This pattern of air flow permitted a huge Canadian low pressure system to spread over the entire upper Midwest and Ohio River Valley and remain stationary for nearly two months. That has been the cause of the almost continuous run of sub-freezing weather that has covered this area of the country.

"But as you can see, the jet stream has flattened over the Pacific ocean and now enters the U.S. near Oregon bringing warm Pacific air across the Rockies. While it maintains its path across the lower plains states its northeast exit route is much more along the Ohio Valley than the Appalachians.

"What this means for the eastern part of the nation is still uncertain. But the folks in the northwest and the lower plains states will finally get a little relief from what has been a truly brutal winter across most of the northern half of the continental United States. Now here are some temperatures for some cities near you."

Haisley shuffled through a pile of papers. "There it is. Remember the report we received on that avalanche in Montana last week or so?"

"The one near Gallatin Peak? They said it was a monster."

Haisley walked to the chart table and studied the map of the upper Missouri River. "All the snow and ice from the top of that mountain is already in the stream beds waiting to melt and flow into the head-waters of the Missouri. If this "Jet" pattern holds, the stations on the upper Missouri are going to have their hands full real quick. And eventually so are we."

Roosevelt handed over the print out he had waited for. "This should be some consolation. Meldahl is reporting ice around some gates and floating ice in the Ohio, above Cincinnati. If that trend holds we may only have to deal with one river at a time."

"Either way there is a hell of a lot of water coming down this year. How do you want it, Aaron? All at once or three months of off-and-on torture?"

"Since when did we get a choice. If it's up to me—"

The discussion ended abruptly as the office door flew open. "Aaron, Mr. Haisley, I got dinner. Look at this."

The engineers turned to find Randall Mardi, the complex's security guard, standing in the doorway. From his right hand, a headless snake dangled to the floor. "It's a cotton mouth, a good five-footer. I got him with a head shot from over fifty feet. Did you ever eat snake?"

Haisley and Roosevelt exchanged a grimace. "There were rumors about one of my ex-girl friends, but I don't think I've ever had the pleasure."

"Hey, that was a good one, Mr. Haisley. Relax. I'll fry this baby up and you'll love it. You should have seen Henry. He nearly jumped into the out flow channel when I showed him. He probably won't want any."

Roosevelt eased passed Mardi. "That's great Randall. I'm going to run over to the Auxiliary Structure and check the silt readings in the deep water channel." He left Haisley alone with Mardi and the dead snake.

"Oh, by the way, Mr. Haisley. Do you know some guy named Bill Harmon?"

"Yeah. We went to college together."

"He called while you were out on the Low Sill. He's coming down to Louisiana this week and wanted to stop by and visit. I told him you would be here."

"Thanks, Randall. It will be good to see him again." Haisley's concerns about the river faded as he considered the renewal of an old friendship.

Chapter III

NAPLES, FLORIDA

Barbara Davaron checked the film counter. Four more shots and her afternoon observation would be finished. She was normally a SESA weekend volunteer but had recently expanded her visits to the camp to include some weekdays. This Monday was one of those extra days.

She sighted on a nest of baby alligators seventy-five yards away. Most of the young reptiles lay idly in the nest, soaking up the warm rays of the late afternoon sun. Their lack of activity made Davaron's work boring but the animals were cute at this age.

The tedium of shooting the same spot every ten minutes took a toll on her attention span, so she turned the camera lens away from the nest. Moving ten degrees to the left she was pleasantly surprised to find one of the Everglades more well known species, a white plumed egret, in her sights.

Davaron snapped a quick picture, moved the film counter forward and aimed in again. As she pushed the shutter button the bird silently exploded in a puff of red feathers and body parts. She recoiled in shock dropped the camera. Only the strap around her neck prevented the lens from hitting the ground and shattering on a rock beneath her.

Instinctively Davaron grabbed the camera and refocused in an attempt to find the source of the explosion. Moving the lens a few degrees to the left, she stared open-mouthed as a break in the line of shrubs revealed Albert Simmons. He had a trace of a smile on his face as he held up a large handgun and inspected it. Davaron recognized the weapon as a standard nine millimeter semi-automatic with a silencer attached to it

She worked her way behind a growth of bushes for cover and watched him look back toward the log and take aim. Swinging the camera slowly back she flinched as a large chip flew off the log directly below the egret's former perch. Quickly, four more notches appeared, all in an extremely tight pattern.

Davaron crouched back under her hiding spot. As a volunteer for SESA she was appalled and confused. A high-ranking member of the group had just blown a protected species off a log and reacted with a satisfied smile.

The second observation loomed far more ominously in her mind. Not only had Simmons killed the bird, but he followed up with an expert shot pattern on the same spot. And he did it with a standard issue handgun from over one hundred feet. Davaron knew of only two or three men that could shoot like that and they had over ten years on the job. This guy just walked out into the woods and put up a pattern that would qualify him for the Marine shooting team.

She snapped a picture of Simmons, then sighed with relief as he moved off, and away from the camp. Working calmly but quickly she replaced the film and shot four rapid succession pictures of the baby alligators. She made a quick surveillance check of the area with the telephoto lens before cautiously making her way back toward the main campsite.

Simmons moved deeper into the Everglades along a line of cypress trees. Though not as lush as some South American jungles nor as dense as some of the forests of Europe, it was a comfortable environment and a good place to retool his skills. There were ample targets to practice on. Numerous volunteer groups and individuals working in the swampland, unwittingly gave him an opportunity to practice cover and concealment techniques. After a year and a half he was able to make himself part of the Everglades and could pass within a few yards of most of them without their knowledge.

On one of his 'training' exercises, two of Trent's people, James Kennedy and Thomas Reilly had managed to spot him. They eagerly accepted an invitation to come along and sharpen their skills. Six months later, they were the nucleus of Simmons primary team. Not long after that, two more SESA members joined the group and Simmons was in business.

"Gotcha, Al. You are going to have to better than that."

Simmons mind had been on other things. He looked up to see Kennedy and Reilly standing a mere ten yards away. "Sorry, men. I was daydreaming."

"No problem. Besides the deck was stacked this time. There were no stationary targets. We were tracking you for a change." Reilly liked to use military terminology whenever possible.

They were coming around nicely and Simmons knew they would be ready when the time came. "Where are Amy and Mark?"

"Amy went into town on some errands and Mark wanted to stay in camp and study the operating manuals you gave him," Kennedy replied. "We came out to warn you. The eggs hatched in the alligator nest. You know how Mr. Trent is about disturbing them. We figured to divert you and save you from a half hour lecture on natural habitats or some shit."

The men shared a laugh as Simmons pulled out his gun. "I saw the little bastards this morning. Do you want some target practice before we head back in?"

"I'm always up for that," Reilly answered eagerly.

"Good. Let's try a hundred feet this time."

Reilly took the weapon and sighted on a cypress tree. He squeezed off four rounds. The pattern was not perfect but all four shots would have killed. Simmons nodded approval.

Davaron entered the camp and walked calmly to Trent's quarters. "Are you home, Mr. Trent?"

He emerged to greet her. "Hi, Barbara. How did it go today?"

"Wonderful, sir," she beamed.

"They are cute aren't they?"

"Oh yes, sir." She hoped the enthusiasm sounded authentic, but her mind was far from baby alligators. "You're going to love the pictures. I'll get them developed tonight or tomorrow. There is one that I think will be adorable. I could get a print for the next newsletter if you'd like."

"That would be fine, dear. Can you join us for dinner?"

"Oh, no thanks. I have to get back to Fort Myers this evening. I'm taking my nieces over to Lauderdale tomorrow so I'll need all the rest I can get."

"That should be a lot of fun." Trent hated patronizing the volunteers. But it was good public relations, and they were more than willing to do the menial tasks that most of the Association members found unrewarding.

"I'm sure it will," Davaron replied. "I'll bring the photos back Thursday. Go ahead and schedule me for something, because I have the whole day free."

"I appreciate it, Barbara, and we are always grateful for your help out here."

"Thanks, Mr. Trent. I'll see you on Thursday." She smiled and walked as leisurely as possible to her car.

Trent rolled his eyes and entered his tent. As he was about to return to his work Maria DeLeon's voice interrupted him.

"I don't like her. She is an uppity bitch."

"I know," Trent replied absentmindedly. "Would you rather sit out there taking pictures of alligators every ten minutes?"

"No. I'd rather be right where I am." Maria sat on his bed leaning slightly forward. Her shirt was unbuttoned to the waist and her firm right breast was nearly exposed.

"Good. Because I like you right where you are." Trent replied eyeing her for a moment.

"I'd like you where I am right now," she said, shifting a little and exposing the breast even more.

"Not now, dear. I have work to do."

Maria frowned at the rebuff.

Trent soothed her. "We have a long night ahead of us, and I do not intend to overwork myself. Okay?"

Her smile returned immediately. "All right. But when you are through over there I'm going to overwork you."

Trent smiled contentedly and returned to the building plans.

Davaron used all her self control to make an unhurried exit from the compound. After what she had witnessed there was no way of knowing who might be watching her or why. Her view of SESA had completely changed. An eccentric but relatively harmless group of people had suddenly become potentially dangerous because of a ten-second look through her camera.

She wondered if Trent knew of Simmons activities. What if he condoned them? How many others were involved? All questions and not a hint of an answer, she thought.

One question dwarfed the others. If Trent did know about Simmons, then what the hell was Trent and his organization doing out here? Davaron shivered in spite of the warm Florida sun.

As she reached the expressway all conjecture disappeared and an orderly plan began to take shape. She would go to Fort Myers for the night. It would be imprudent to have one of his associates see her in Naples, where she had planned to spend the next couple of days. Fort Lauderdale was a lie but she decided to drive up to Punta Gorda, or maybe Port Charlotte. From there she would make some calls and touch base with her people.

The situation had changed drastically in the last hour. This was no longer just a periodic surveillance job. Simmons had stirred the pot significantly and Davaron did not want it to boil over on her.

HUNTSVILLE, ALABAMA

Harte pulled into a parking garage across the street from the Huntsville Municipal building. Ignoring a spot near the exit of the five- story structure, he pulled into a stall halfway down a nearly full row of cars. Only after entering the pedestrian tunnel to the city office tower did he consider his unconscious attempt to blend in with the surroundings. Thoughts of the red Ford Escort played in his head and he was glad he had made the decision.

Sergeant John Dutton arrived at the front desk in less than thirty seconds. This struck Harte as quite a departure from his last visit when he and Loman had waited nearly twenty minutes for the detective.

"Give it a rest," Harte mumbled to himself as he considered the suspicion with which he now viewed every action.

"I'm sorry. What was that?" Dutton asked as they walked down the hallway to his office.

"Nothing, Sergeant. I was reminding myself to take a long rest when this is over with. The experience has been pretty draining."

"I hope it has not taken you away from your duties with the Wilson Foundation. They do good work there," Dutton said as he sat at his desk. "I wasn't sure if you would remember. My son got a grant to Space Camp from the Foundation four years ago. He sent in an essay about manned travel to Mars."

"John Dutton Jr., I believe," said Harte, silently thanking Mrs. Harding for the update. "Sorry I didn't make the connection on my last visit. There were other matters to attend to."

"No problem. The Loman kid didn't need to hear us reminisce about our meeting four years ago. How is he doing?"

"He's all right, considering the situation," Harte replied, grateful for the transition. "Since he is a foundation associate, I'm sure you understand our interest." He passed a sheet of paper to Dutton and gave the detective a few seconds to look it over.

"Andy found a computer disk in his father's belongings when he got back to Louisville. It contained this list of companies in the Huntsville area that Mr. Loman had been visiting. You might want to see if the CEO's have anything helpful."

Dutton looked over the sheet. He shuffled some unrelated papers and looked away, rubbing his chin.

Harte read the signs instantly. "Look, I realize this is a police matter and I probably should stay out of it. But I—"

"There is no case, Dan." Dutton said abruptly.

"What do you mean?"

"I mean I have been taken off the case."

Harte was undeterred. "I understand. Can I talk to the person who has been assigned to it?"

Dutton sighed deeply. "There is no one else assigned."

"Now I don't understand." Harte remained even tempered.

"I have a file with the investigation report and the autopsy," Dutton said holding up a folder. "When I went to my Captain to request follow up support, he said the case was out of the department's hands. Huntsville P.D. is no longer looking into the death of Herbert Loman."

"But you said it might be a homicide."

"What I said does not matter. We are off the case." He got a pained look on his face. "Excuse me, but I have to go to the bathroom. I've had a touch of the flu and well, you know how that is. I'll be back in a few minutes."

When the door had closed, Harte sat staring at the desk. He could not believe what he had heard. The Huntsville police had walked away from a possible murder case, or worse were ordered to walk away. What the hell is going on here?, he wondered.

Suddenly it dawned on him that he was alone with all of the department's paperwork right in front of him. "My God! I'm in a 'B' detective movie," he mumbled, and picked up the file.

The file contained lab reports on the motel fire. The autopsy was filled with medical terminology on the state of the body, including graphic descriptions of the effects of the fire. Much of it meant nothing to Harte.

Two things caught his eye as he skimmed down the medical examiner's report. One notation indicated trace amounts of ether in the victim's blood stream. Farther down, the space marked "cause of death" contained no entry. Harte returned the file to its original spot as he heard the sound of the door opening.

Dutton re-entered the office with a stack of files under his arm. "Sorry about the delay." He showed off the files as he sat back down. "They intercepted me in the hallway with these." He placed the files on top of the Loman folder on his desk. Harte noted the irony as the Loman file was covered up.

"I don't know what to think, John," Harte said in an effort to restart the conversation.

"There isn't much to say. We are officially off the case. You, on the other hand, are a private citizen, free to do as you please in the matter, as long as you stay within the law."

"I suppose I can still visit the companies on the list. Since they are all defense-related, Andy and I had an idea that a laid-off employee may have gone for revenge. It's probably academic at this point, but I still want to go see them." Harte looked at the wall as he sorted through his options.

Dutton pulled the corporate list from under the stack of files, folded it and offered it to Harte. "Here's your printout sheet. I don't see any reason for me to keep it." he said in resignation.

"I really don't understand this," Harte managed to say.

"I'm truly sorry, Dan. If there was anything I could do, you must know that I would." He waited until Harte put the paper back into his coat pocket. "If you stick to that sheet something may come up that will help you. Other than that I don't know what advice to give you. I really feel bad about all of this, but I appreciate the way you are handling it."

"It's probably just shock. I'm sure I'll go ballistic later today. I hope it isn't in front of some corporate bigwig."

They both knew they were lying through their teeth but, for lack of an alternative, they played the scene to completion. Harte made an attempt to inject at least one note of sincerity into the conversation. "Thanks, John. I'll look forward to reading your son's progress report in June."

"I appreciate that," Dutton replied. "I feel like saying that if there is anything I can do for you, call me. But I'm not even sure that's an appropriate response. I do hope we get to meet again."

In the parking lot Harte collected himself. A promising path had led straight into an official brick wall. The problem was that every-thing seemed totally out of sync— the ridiculous way in which Dutton had let him see the file and the complete insincerity of their final conversation, with both of them remaining in character. Dutton did not even make a copy of the computer file. It all seemed totally out of line.

He removed his appointment book from his coat pocket and the printout sheet came with it. A business card fell from the folded paper and landed in his lap. The card was Dutton's.

Harte could not recall receiving the card as he studied it. There was a handwritten phone number on the front, along with an under-lined printed number. He idly flipped the card over and a thunderbolt struck him. On the back of the card were the hand- written words, "Watch your back. If you need anything, call. JD."

Harte leaned back and stared at the roof of the car. "What in the hell have you gotten yourself into, Danny boy?" he asked aloud. A quick check showed a little over an hour until his first appointment. Maybe that would give him enough time to piece things together and come up with a rational explanation for all of this.

GALLATIN PEAK, MONTANA

The shift in the jet stream had thrown the spring runoff process into chaos. Daytime temperatures in the upper fifties bathed the valleys in warm sunshine. Cloud patterns rolling off the mountains carried rain instead of snow.

On the west side of Gallatin Peak the snowcap, which should have slowly given up its contents over the next several months, lay melting at the base of the mountain. All along the massive ice barrier the water broke through in force, instantly filling creek beds to capacity and tripling the rate of discharge into the Madison River, fifteen miles to the west. At Ennis Lake, two miles to the north, engineers quickly opened the flow gates to full capacity in an effort compensate. The lake became nothing more than an extension of the swollen river bed as the water surged through.

The Gallatin River broke through the north east ice barrier with similar force. It sent a six foot wall of water speeding north toward the confluence with the Madison and Jefferson rivers at the aptly named town of Three Forks. By mid afternoon the three rivers' total discharge was more than four times the normal rate for late February. The rivers converged in a wild clash of water and debris a mile above the town and sent their water raging on toward Helena.

At Three Forks the rivers surrender their identities to a singular name: the Missouri. It is, by far, the longest river in the United States and whatever enters it at Three Forks will eventually find its way to the Mississippi River, twenty five hundred miles later.

In Townsend, Montana, at the south end of Canyon Ferry Lake, a U.S. Army Corps of Engineers district officer looked out over the entrance to the lake. As he visually noted the increased inflow, he shuddered and reached for the phone. Along the upper Missouri River, the call went out to every water control facility from Helena to Pierre. The message was simple and ominous: "Get ready for a big one."

GHAZIR, LEBANON

Three loud bangs on the door of the one room shack froze the men at their work stations. Each counted silently, while reaching for AK-47s. As the count reached ten, two more bangs on the door brought a collective sigh of relief. One of them moved to the door, weapon at the ready. "Allah be praised."

"God is great," came the response through the door.

"Welcome, my friend," said the man as he threw the door open. "It is good to see you again."

The visitor entered the shack and greeted each occupant. When the pleasantries were completed his tone turned businesslike. "How does the work go?"

"It is nearly finished, Hamur," replied one of the men. "We brought it over stuffed in the carcasses of Rhodpe Mountain deer. The Bulgarian inspector at Burgass was quite cooperative once we supplied him with four kilos of meat."

The visitor eyed him sternly. Across the room two of the men exchanged a knowing glance. Their attitude and posture stiffened as they realized who the visitor was.

Bantar moved toward them. "Return to your work, my young friends. Time is of the essence."

The men returned to the task of cutting strips of green-gray material from the remains of what had been a substantial slab of the claylike compound. They ran a strip through an old hand-cranked clothes wringer. The result was a two by six foot pancake which they gently placed in a crate on a five by seven area carpet. They repeated the process and when both pieces were in place they covered the pancakes with another carpet and went back to the slab for more.

"We have four crates with 25 carpets in each," explained the man who had greeted Bantar. "Each weighs 230 kilograms. It was extra work since the buyer wanted the material in five pound units." He sighed. "I wish the Americans would get with the rest of the world on these matters."

"They are arrogant about such things, Hassan," Bantar replied. His friend was eager but he sometimes forgot the rules. The workmen finished their task at the clothes wringer. When the last of the material was in the crate they nailed the container shut and looked to Hassan for more orders.

"Let us load the truck. It is time to ship our wares to the market," he said with a sly grin.

When the four crates were loaded, Bantar turned to the two young packers. "Now you must clean up the work place. There can be no evidence of our presence here. Be thorough."

"Yes, sir," the men replied and moved quickly to wipe down their work station and remove any evidence of their visit to the hut. When finished they turned to see Bantar and Hassan standing just inside the doorway. "Will there be anything else?" they asked subserviently.

Bantar spoke gently to them. "Yes, my young soldiers, there is one more thing you must do for the glory of Allah." He calmly pulled a semi-automatic hand gun from under his coat. Before anyone could react he fired a round into each man's head.

Hassan stared in utter horror. "What have you done?" He nearly wailed the question. The answer was a massive jolt of pain to the side of his head as the butt of the hand gun crashed into his temple. He tumbled to the floor near the dead bodies. His head throbbed and his eyes watered profusely as he lay on the floor. When his eyes finally cleared he saw Bantar standing over him. Hassan could find no trace of emotion in the man's face.

"Why did you have to do that?" he blurted the question through his pain. "They were good men."

"I did not do that, Hassan. You did."

"But I—"

Bantar cut him off. "You said my name and mentioned the Americans. That was when you condemned them to death. If I did not find you so useful you would be with them right now." He spoke as if he were ordering lunch.

Hassan began to grasp the sheer amorality of his leader. Mortal terror tightened its grip as he lay on the floor. He was learning a valuable lesson in the most stunning manner possible and he silently vowed that from this moment, Bantar would always find him "useful".

"Get up, my impetuous young friend," said Bantar calmly, as he helped the injured man to his feet and brushed some dirt from his shoulder.

"What shall we do now? We cannot leave them here." Hassan asked sheepishly.

"Take the car and dump them near the border. Everyone will assume Mossad did this. Then go back to Teheran and wait for me."

"When will you return?"

"You will receive that information when I decide you can handle it properly. For now, obey your orders. When I return we will have more adventures." Bantar spoke dispassionately. But at the last moment he determined to give the injured man's pride a small boost.

"You did good work on this mission, Hassan. Do not let this unfortunate incident detract from a job well done. Now finish your assignment." He patted Hassan on the shoulder and left the hut.

NAPLES, FLORIDA

Davaron inspected the pictures closely. Her friend at the photo lab had done an amazing job. The last four shots of the baby alligators were perfectly tinted to produce the appearance of the proper progression of sunlight. She returned the stack of photos to its envelope, took a deep breath and pulled back onto the road.

On the last stretch of road leading to the campsite, Davaron mentally worked her way into the persona of Barbara, the dizzy volunteer from Ft. Myers. The transition was not always easy for her. A Master's degree in Political Science with an undergrad major in Accounting had given her little chance to actually be the air head everyone at SESA saw two times a week.

To the environmentalists, she was the widow of a trucker who had, for some reason, decided to over-insure himself. His untimely death in a chain reaction crash on I-95 near Savannah, left her with a lot of money, a portion of which Morgan Trent was happy to accept, and plenty of time, which SESA gladly filled with tasks of environmental awareness.

The charade began as she pulled too close to the stump of a tree and hit it with her bumper. Snickers emanated from some of the SESA members as Barbara got out of her car and inspected the damage. It was minor, but the effect was perfect. "Oh well, I guess that's just another reason to visit Joe at the body shop." She giggled and squirmed a little as she made her way past the SESA members toward Trent's tent.

"Hi, Barbara. It's always exciting to see you. I wish we could see more of you around here," Mark Rodvick, a SESA member who often acted friendly toward her, dead-panned as she passed. His companions hooted at the double barreled comment.

"Oh you boys are just so hospitable," Barbara replied. "But you know that I come as often as I can," she added innocently to another chorus of hoots and laughter. She winked at Rodvick and continued to the main tent.

Across the compound, Simmons watched the scene with a slight frown. He did not generally like the effect Davaron had on the members of the organization. But he could not argue with the fact they enjoyed having her around. At least she was good for morale. Perhaps he could put her to use when SESA moved to its new location, he thought with a snicker.

"Mr. Trent. I'm here," Barbara announced at the entrance to the command tent.

"Come on in, Barbara," Trent called out.

She found Trent at his work table studying some papers. "Just wait till you see these pictures," she announced, proudly holding out the envelope of photos. "I have them in sequence. It's like a movie or something the way they show the activity through the day. It's really neat."

Trent arranged the pictures on the table over what he had been working on. Davaron glanced at the papers, turning away before Trent noticed. "Nice place you have here," she said to distract him.

"Yes," he replied looking around. "Even a nature lover appreciates some comforts now and then. Come around and look at these with me."

She moved to his side of the table and leaned over the photos while he sat next to her. "I really like this one," she said pointing to one of the doctored shots. "As soon as the sun got on them they started lying around catching rays. I guess they were all female," she added with a giggle.

"But seriously, even at this young age they are adopting the habits of adults. Once the sun moved over the foliage line their activity picked up again. It was really fascinating."

"Barbara, you have a keen insight into this. Why do you act so dumb around here when you are obviously so aware?"

Davaron froze momentarily. She was wary of everything at the camp now, and could not tell if the question was a test or just encouragement. "You told me what to expect Mr. Trent, and I just remembered what you said. I don't understand why any of this happened. All I know is that you said would happen did. I didn't do anything special."

She decided to try a different tack for the second part of the question. "I don't act dumb. These people are all educated in this stuff. I'm just trying to fit in. If there is something about me that they like, then why not give it to them, within reason of course. I like people to be comfortable around me." Davaron felt a slight pressure on her hip as Trent leaned a little closer.

"I'm sorry I used the word dumb, Barbara. We all consider you an asset out here. Everyone is happy to have you visit us as often as you do." He smiled warmly and was about to reach out to her when the flap of the tent opened and Maria DeLeon entered.

She said nothing at first. A fire began to build in her eyes as she looked first at Davaron, and then at Trent. "Am I interrupting?"

Davaron had to keep from rolling her eyes at the comment. "Of course not, Maria. I just brought back the photos of the alligator nest and Mr. Trent was kind enough to invite me in out of the sun. Look for yourself. I think they are pretty good." She backed away from the table.

Maria's anger abated somewhat as she stood next to Trent and looked at the photos. "They are very good. You should be proud of yourself." The comment was meant to ease the tension, but even when she tried to be friendly it still came across as abrupt.

Davaron had her opening and diffused the situation once and for all. "Mr. Trent could not wait for you to see them. He thought you would like them. I'm glad you do."

Trent looked past Maria and gave Davaron a quick nod of appreciation for the lie and its effect. He considered the mental agility she had displayed and went back to the question he had posed to her. Was this bimbo thing an act?

It occurred to him that this was probably not the first time she had been forced to cope with a jealous wife or girlfriend because a man had paid her some uninvited attention. He decided her response was a survival technique. All women have them. He dismissed the thought. "What are your plans for the rest of the day, Barbara?"

"I'll go out to my observation site for a while, then come back and help with dinner. It will be late by then. If there is room I'll spend the night, if it's all right with everyone." She looked directly at Maria as if to say the decision was hers.

The show of faith embarrassed DeLeon. "Amy is spending the night in Naples. No matter. We will make room for you."

"Thank you, Maria. Now if there's nothing else, I'd like to get back out to the hatchery."

"We will talk more later." Maria attempted a pleasantry as Davaron reached for the tent flap.

"I'd like that. See you later."

Before the flap had closed, Trent encircled Maria from behind and held her close. "You have to understand there are times when I am going to be friendly with the women who live and visit here. It means nothing. It's part of my job."

"She makes me jealous," Maria said looking straight ahead. "It's not just what happened in here. She has no problems. This is all fun for her. All the men like her. She does not care about things, like the rest of us do."

"Take it easy," Trent said soothingly. "You must remember that she is not part of the mission we are on. She's had difficult times. I know what it's like to lose a mate in the prime of life. Her attitude probably hides a lot of inner pain. Give her a break. She works hard and means well." He turned Maria around and held her close. "Besides, she's not here. You are. That is what matters." He looked at the tent wall as he held Maria. A vision of Nina came to his mind, and he squeezed a tighter.

Maria felt the moisture as a tear drop touched the top of her head. She knew where Morgan Trent's mind was, even though she had his body's attention. It was something she accepted. She would always share him with his dead wife. But there would be no others as long as she was by his side.

The Davaron woman seemed harmless, but Maria would always guard her relationship with Trent vigorously. She had also seen her fair share of pain and was bound and determined not to lose the solace she found in the arms of this man who now held her. She closed her eyes and cried along with him.

"What an insecure witch," Davaron mumbled to herself as she crossed the compound toward the main trail into the Everglades.

"What was that?" asked Simmons emerging from his tent.

Davaron stopped in her tracks. A hundred thoughts raced through her mind as she tried to assess the meaning of this encounter. "Nothing, Al. I was just showing pictures to Mr. Trent. Maria came in and made things uncomfortable. I get mad when I can't talk to a man without an insecure woman thinking I'm horning in on her territory." She surprised herself with the honest answer.

"That's just Maria. Don't worry about it. Where are you heading out to today?"

"I'm going to observe the alligator nest for an hour or two and then I'll be back for dinner," she answered cautiously. By giving him her itinerary, she hoped to prevent him from repeating the performance from a few days ago. Davaron did not need that complication again.

"I was wondering if you might consider something, Barbara. You don't have to answer right now. The Association will be going on an extended field trip soon. I was thinking since you do good work and everyone likes you, even Maria in her own way, you might want to come along with us."

The sudden friendly approach startled her. "I don't know, Al. Where is the field trip?"

"Don't worry about that right now. If you are interested I can give you the details later. It's just a thought for the back of your mind while you are out in the bush today."

"Okay, I'll think about it. Thanks for asking."

"Sure. Have a good time with the 'gators." He smiled and returned to his tent.

Barbara walked unsteadily from the camp. The conversation with Simmons dumfounded her. He never gave her the time of day and now he was suggesting she accompany SESA on an extended field trip. Add to that the things she had witnessed him doing in the— Wait a minute, she thought. Didn't he just refer to the Everglades as "the Bush?" She winced at the reference. It was almost exclusively the property of the military. Who the hell is this guy?, she thought.

That question answered the one Simmons had posed moments before. She had to go on the field trip just to find out the real story of one Albert Simmons. The alligators would get minimum attention on this afternoon.

HUNTSVILLE, ALABAMA

The buzzing intercom interrupted Richard Willis' thoughts. "Yes," he said to the machine.

"Mr. Harte to see you, sir."

"Just a moment" Willis took one more look through the file then put it in a desk drawer. "Send him in." He crossed the room with deliberate calm as the door opened. "Rich Willis. Good to meet you," he said as Harte entered the office.

"Dan Harte. I appreciate your time," Harte replied.

Willis returned to his desk and Harte settled in to a chair. "Coffee or something?" the CEO asked.

"That would be great, with a little cream."

"You got it." He pushed the intercom button. "I hate to bother you, Ms. Conners, could you bring us some coffee please."

He turned back to Harte. "I always feel bad asking an executive assistant to get coffee. It can be a real thorny issue with today's working woman. Sheri is pretty good about it though. We take turns making the coffee run so I guess we've neutralized the issue."

"So many new unwritten rules," Harte replied with a grin.

"What the hell. I found that if you treat everyone right nothing is really etched in stone," Willis said.

Willis' secretary brought a serving tray in and set it on the desk. "Thanks, Ms. Conners. I'll do the serving."

"It's no problem, Mr. Willis," the secretary replied in mock servitude. She reached for the coffee pot.

"You are too kind. Give me a break." They shared a laugh.

"Whatever you say, sir. Call me if you need anything. I'll be back at my desk in ten minutes or so. Nice to meet you, Mr. Harte." She made her exit.

"I told her meeting was informal. She must have decided to drop the corporate facade," Willis said sheepishly.

"And the company probably couldn't survive without her," Harte chimed in.

"Sometimes I think the place would fall apart without her," Willis replied. "The worst part is she knows it. If she ever decides to get married I'll have to bribe her husband to share her with us."

"Maybe she is already married," Harte said.

"With a little luck maybe she is," Willis replied, instantly catching Harte's meaning. "What the hell. Let's get on to the important stuff. Have some coffee," he said with a grin.

Willis poured the coffee into gold braided china cups. He watched as Harte looked at the cup's logo before taking a sip. "Now what can I do for you, Dan?"

"I'm not sure, Rich," Harte accepted the first name basis. "I work for the Wilson Foundation. It's a small organization that deals mainly with—"

"Not so small," Willis interrupted. "I like what you did with the Space Camp project."

Jesus, Harte thought. The damn Space Camp. Is that all these people think about? "Thank you," he continued, controlling his mild exasperation. "Anyway, the father of one of my colleagues died in a motel fire recently. Right here in Huntsville."

"The fire at the Crown Motel, right?"

"You know about that?" Harte leaned forward.

"It's not far from here and I do watch the news."

Harte relaxed. "I read too much into things. Sorry."

"No problem." Willis calmly moved the conversation to the next level. "So where does NEI fit into the picture?"

"The victim was Herbert Loman. Does that ring a bell?"

"Yes, I know that name. But what does that have to do with us?" Though Harte was asking the questions, Willis wanted answers first.

"There was a business log in Mr. Loman's personal effects that revealed appointments at National Electronics and your name. I'm doing follow up work for the Foundation's records and thought you might be able to help me with some things."

Willis replied in a measured voice. "He stopped in a couple of times, now that I think about it. He was doing consulting work and wanted to see if we needed his services."

"That's the point, Rich. It appears that Mr. Loman was consulting with companies in your field on downsizing. Do you mind telling me what you two discussed? It's completely off the record, of course. I just want some background for when we publish a statement about him." Harte hoped he had lied well.

Willis assumed control. "I apologize for being evasive. I just needed to see where you were coming from on this. To be honest, we had two good meetings. He really had his finger on the pulse of this industry. The problem, at least for him, is that NEI isn't cutting back. We have actually benefited from the recent industry shake out.

"We run some pretty high-level sophisticated products out of here. Most of the defense cuts are in mass manufacturing. We just got an order for Shuttle components that makes us layoff free for a while. So Loman and I really had nothing to discuss, professionally. But he seemed like a good man. It's a shame what happened."

Harte stared at his coffee cup as Willis finished. It wasn't the NASA logo that bothered him. He'd seen it hundreds of times. The problem was the words "Langley, Va." under the logo. "What kind of facility does NASA operate out of Langley? Is that where your new contracts are going?"

"Oh, Ms. Conners," Willis said with mild frustration. "She may be the best executive assistant on earth but her timing can be somewhat inappropriate. I hope you understand that I can't say anything about our contracts. We operate on a 'need to know' basis around here. It's company policy. Sorry."

Harte shuddered at the phrase. Tim Lassick had attributed the same response to Willis four days ago. "Need to know" was the founding policy at all United States intelligence services for as long as those agencies had existed. Now here was the CEO of a medium size electronics firm tossing the phrase around as easily as "Hi how are you?." He decided to try one more probe and then quit while he was ahead. "I understand completely. Can I run something by you for an opinion?"

"Fire away," Willis answered.

"Have you ever heard of an organization called the Southeast Endangered Species Association?"

"There is not a person in this business who hasn't heard of Morgan Trent and his gang." Willis said with a note of disgust.

"I sense a lack of enthusiasm."

"Let's just say our views of the future do not find much common ground," Willis snickered slightly.

"Have you had any contact with them recently?"

"No. Why do you ask?"

"Mr. Loman's logbook has date time entries for meetings with high-tech companies. But in with all of the appointments are entries concerning SESA, in Naples. I found that a little odd. Technology corporations and a major environmental awareness group seemed a strange mix to me."

"I can't see any connection." Willis said evenly. "From what I've heard, outfits like mine are small potatoes to Morgan Trent. He thinks oil is the devil incarnate. I know people who have spoken to him. They say he hates the oil companies with a passion. Do you mind if I ask you a question or two about all of this?"

Harte was happy not to pursue the SESA line. He did not want Willis to know his suspicions. "I think I owe you an answer or two if I have them."

"Do you see a problem with the death of Herbert Loman?"

"Honestly?"

"And off the record," Willis added.

"I think he may have been murdered. The Huntsville Police have closed the case as an accident, but I'm not satisfied. I have the time and the resources available so I'm doing my own investigation."

"That explains your interest in the connection between SESA and our industry. Dan, I'm going to make a frank assumption. You think Loman may have been working with Trent and someone from the high-tech world had him removed. Am in the ballpark on this?"

Harte was overwhelmed. Seeds had taken root along those lines but he did not expect it to explode in his face like this. "I have not formed any conclusions in the matter, but I have also closed no doors." He tried to sound even-handed.

Willis decided to settle the matter. "I'll tell you this up front. No one I know in this industry would have anything to do with such an act. You can take my word for that or you can pound the streets investigating till your shoes fall off.

"Trent has no real beef with us. He hates big oil and I'm sure he feels if he could bring them down the rest of us would fall like dominoes. You don't have to be a detective to figure it out. Go visit him in Naples and you will find out what I'm saying is true." Willis paused to let Harte catch up with his line of thought.

"I've caught his act on a couple of occasions. Talk to him and you will see what I mean. He's a megalomaniac. Guys like him shoot for the top of the mountain. He isn't worried about the semi-conductor industry and we have no real quarrel with him. You do what you have to do, but I stand by my statement."

A moment of silence allowed them to assess the comment. Harte took a sip of coffee. "I appreciate your honesty, Rich," he said sincerely. "I should get going now. It looks like I may have my hands full with this."

Willis escorted him to the door. "For what it's worth, if I were Herb's son I'd be glad to have you on my side."

"Thanks. I appreciate that."

"If you need anything while you are in Huntsville give me a call. I mean it."

"I may do that," Harte replied as he walked past the secretary's desk. "Good by, Ms. Conners. Keep him on his toes."

"Good by, Mr. Harte." Sheri Conners looked back at her boss when Harte was gone.

"No phone calls until I tell you." Willis returned to his desk without waiting for her to reply. He opened a drawer and picked up a telephone. After dialing he waited impatiently for the scrambling device to log on. "How's it going. We just finished. He's probably not even to his car yet...He and the Loman kid broke Herb's code...I don't know. He got Huntsville and Naples out of it...No shit. He was looking into a possible corporate hit...I think I got him off that track, but I don't know...I threw out all the bait I could. He'd have to be pretty stubborn not to at least do a follow-up on some of it...No problem. I told him to call me if he needed anything. I'm sure I'll hear from him again...You were right. He's a pretty impressive guy... Looks like you made the right decision...Okay, I'll talk to you soon."

Harte's mind raced as he walked to his car. Two things came to the forefront. "Langley, Va." and "need to know". Willis had gone out of his way to imply CIA involvement. But that was stupid. Why would the most covert spy agency in the world even subtly announce their involvement in a situation? Willis had nearly ordered him to go to Naples and talk to Morgan Trent. It really was more than a mere suggestion.

Harte tried to sort things out. He was picking up clues in the death of Herbert—Holy shit! he thought. Willis called him Herb. That could not have been slip of the tongue. Could it? Were they friends? Or even colleagues?

From Dutton to Willis he felt stonewalled yet he had more to go on than when he started. Alarm bells should have been ringing but Harte's curiosity overcame any timidness, and he vowed to move forward. From here on caution and discretion would rule his daily routine.

Ganzs watched the car leave the NEI parking lot. The paperwork on the seat next to him indicated no urgent need to tail the vehicle. The target had a limited itinerary and there would be no problem reestablishing contact.

Some nice detective work at the Huntsville airport two weeks earlier had led him to the name Daniel Harte. When he submitted the name to the central computer, Ganzs received a standard I.D. sheet with a history of the man he was following.

According to the sheet Harte was forty one years old and single. He was employed as the spokesman for a small conservative foundation headquartered in Southwestern Ohio. Ganzs deduced that to mean someone with money was willing to give part of it away, but shielded himself with the "foundation" cover.

There was nothing noteworthy in the file. The guy was an ex-Marine who had worked for the National Security Agency while on active duty nearly twenty years ago. That might have been a red flag but Ganzs knew that a lot of people had worked in the various security agencies during the Viet Nam era. The file showed a limited combat record, probably a thirty day temporary duty assignment or two in either DaNang or Saigon. Most of Harte's time had been spent in Japan or the Caribbean.

The file was clean from a police standpoint. Basically Ganzs was dealing with a pretty straight laced individual who was just poking around on his own.

What bothered Ganzs was the second sheet of paper he had received. At age thirty-one he had been a field agent for nearly seven years. In that time he had never seen a case that cried out for FBI attention more than the death of Herbert Loman. It was obviously a murder and, from what he gleaned about Loman's job and travels, involved at least interstate and possibly international implications. Every investigative instinct told Ganzs to walk straight up to Harte and grill him about his snooping around in Huntsville.

The orders negated seven years of training in two words: "Passive Monitoring." With that phrase the Bureau had ordered Ganzs not to interfere in any way with Harte's actions. Just follow and report. The Loman case had been kicked way upstairs by someone with more clout than Ganzs knew existed.

He decided to see exactly where the line was between passive monitoring and police initiative. According to his orders he had authorization to go wherever the subject led him. Ganzs liked that. It permitted him to be where that action was, even if unofficially. That indicated the Bureau was not prepared to be left totally out in the cold on this thing.

He continued to read between the lines of his orders. To follow the subject he would need to know where and when Harte was traveling. This gave him leeway to monitor Harte and any acquaintances who might participate in his activities. It looked like the Bureau was giving him the full use of whatever resources he needed to stay at least abreast of, or better, one step ahead of Harte and whoever he worked with. Moreover, Ganzs knew that if he were on the scene when anything went down, rules of law enforcement took precedent and he could act at his discretion.

This "Passive Monitoring" deal might just work out. As Ganzs saw it he had all the investigative assets he needed and the only rule was no direct contact. He would confirm the assessment with his superior, but he had a feeling he would receive the equivalent of "no comment" in response. If that happened he would be off to the races.

The Federal Bureau of Investigation saw a far greater picture taking shape than the unfortunate death of Herbert Loman in Huntsville, Alabama. They wanted Ganzs to be there when the picture came to full focus, and they wanted him ready to take action when the moment arrived.

When he joined the Bureau, Gansz swore an oath to uphold the law and protect the United States. Like every other agent, he waded through the daily grind of paper work with a dream that one day he would be assigned a case in which his actions truly made a difference in the way Americans live their lives. He took a deep breath and wondered if that case had finally landed on his desk.

Chapter IV

ZELENOGRAD, RUSSIA

The platoon sergeant called "eyes right". One hundred heads turned sharply toward the reviewing stand. Kasarov executed a perfect salute and held it until the last row of soldiers passed. He waited at attention for the next unit to pass in review.

Kasarov loved the Friday evening parades. He got the idea during a post cold war visit to the U.S. Marine Barracks "8th and I" in Washington D.C. The company was one of the American military's prized units and the pride with which those Marines executed their maneuvers had taken Kasarov aback. Even more noteworthy was the near reverence with which the civilians stood and watched everything from the red uniformed band to the "Silent Drill Team" to the final passage in review of the troops. Even the smaller children stood at their best imitation of "attention" without need for parental correction.

Kasarov never forgot that sight. When he finally took command of the Russian Western Forces he instituted the parade along with a few other morale-building ideas he had picked up from the Americans. The Russian soldiers took to the General and his changes and quickly raised themselves from a defeated straggling mob to a top notch military force.

They had become Kasarov's own army. The men would follow him to the brink of hell if he so ordered them. Their unfailing loyalty was the leverage he needed to initiate his plan to return Russia to its rightful place in the family of nations. Perhaps the Soviet Union was truly beyond resuscitation. But Russia deserved a major seat at the world table and in eight days Yuri Cherkin would provide Kasarov with the means to that end.

Once the ministries of Agriculture and Interior were made answerable to him, Kasarov could use his men to make sure food got to the tables of the Russian people. But between now and the harvest the food would have to be imported and that took money.

It was entirely possible, Kasarov thought, that Cherkin did not even know of the Interior's newly completed pipeline from the Caspian oil fields to the Black Sea. He would most certainly find out when he informed the Interior Minister of his impending subordination to Defense. That did not matter.

Kasarov's threat of mass furloughs insured no obstacle to his plan. He knew he would never dismiss one hundred and fifty thousand of his faithful soldiers in one fell swoop. What mattered was that Cherkin did not know it and must act as if the threat was real.

All Kasarov needed was a market for the newly available Russian oil and the cash would flow into the country. With that cash he would once again surround Russia with economically dependent sycophants as the former "nations" of the Soviet Union grew more reliant on the purchasing power of their former patron. Kasarov would finish rebuilding the once-proud military and eventually return Russia to the time when she dictated policy in Europe and Asia.

The world is a large place, he thought. Russia did not need to conquer every little corner of it. She could control the continents and countries around her and her people could stand proudly and declare themselves "the other superpower." This would suit Kasarov nicely. As for his Caspian oil, the Iranian snake Bantar would soon provide an instant major market.

The evening cold nipped at him. He remained at attention, showing no reaction to the chill. Inwardly he longed for spring. More immediately he wished for the arrival of March First. On that day he would begin to bring his country back to life well ahead of nature's timetable of rejuvenation. The thought seemed to insulate him from the onset of another harsh night in the almost endless Russian winter.

CINCINNATI, OHIO

The screen on the dining room table displayed a concise chronological list of cities and dates. Next to each city was a corresponding set of two-letter groups. Lydia, Tim and Rita took turns passing information to Loman who added entries to the display. At the head of the table Harte watched the workings of what he privately called the "Wilson Foundation Brain Trust."

Rita looked up from her pile of computer sheets. "This was a real teaser," she said, pointing to the five-letter group BERLN on the screen. "All the cities on the list were in the western hemisphere. I got lazy and narrowed the search accordingly. I thought it would save time but I tortured Andy with a lot of nothing. Sorry, Andy. No more shortcuts from here on."

"No problem. The job is a pain as it is." Loman picked up the presentation. "As soon as Rita faxed me the new list, Berlin jumped right off the paper. I was so excited to see an obvious solution that I forgot all the other groups contained a state or country designation in addition to the city. Of course the file rejected Berlin. I was about to start from the top of the list when I gave it one more look over and played a hunch. Wait till you see this."

"A little theatrics?" Harte asked, noting Loman's general demeanor seemed to be returning to normal.

"A show stopper, in my opinion." replied Loman with a note of gravity. He hit the enter button on his terminal.

"What the hell are we doing here?" Lassick asked. Everyone

leaned toward the screen as if drawn by a magnet. A window had opened with the heading "Beirut, Lebanon." Beneath the name was a list of dates and times along with the letter codes ER and HB.

"I just got this last night so I haven't had time to put it together with the rest of the information," Loman said. "I was so excited that I drove up from Louisville at four o'clock this morning. There is a waitress at a truck stop ten miles south of here who must be pretty sick of my face by now. I sat there for three hours so I wouldn't roust you at seven o'clock."

Harte squeezed a piece of paper into a ball and threw it at him. "You should have called, dummy. I would have gotten up for this. Besides." He looked around sheepishly. "I was up by seven fifteen any way. Let's see how Beirut fits in."

Loman worked the keyboard and the dates in the Beirut file entered themselves neatly into the openings left in the time line on the main window. Nearly every day of the past twenty months was accounted for in Herbert Loman's computer log.

Harte studied the screen. "How long did you say your father had been involved with his consulting job?"

"A little over a year," Loman replied as his eyes widened.

"What kind of consulting?" Lydia joined in.

"Defense contractor downsizing," Harte said recalling his conversation with Loman at the motel room in Huntsville.

"It doesn't take a Ph.D. to see that this log involves a lot of places unrelated to our defense industry and a time frame that starts eight months prior to when Mr. Loman began his consulting work."

"What's your point?" Harte asked her. He wanted to see if any of his colleagues were getting a sniff of the trail.

Lydia looked at Loman and then around the table. "In my opinion the consulting job was bullshit. If I were into cloak and dagger stuff I'd say it was a cover."

"A cover for what?" Rita asked.

"I'm not sure. But just look at the time line. Prior to February of last year almost every entry is in a foreign country. Then he comes back to the States here." Lydia pointed to the "Tampa, 2/1" entry on the screen. "After that the entries are mostly in the U.S. except for

Mexico City in April and today's bombshell." She indicated the "Beirut 1/15" listing. "If this is the log of a consultant to U.S. defense contractors, why are there international entries for up to eight months prior to the time he took the job?"

Harte liked where the discussion was going. At the same time he felt uneasy about what they were uncovering. He put the fears aside and let everything play itself out.

"The two-letter codes are obviously the key to all of this," said Rita. "So far, every time we treated them as initials it proved out. Let's see what initials show up where."

Loman made the proper entries and the log on the screen realigned itself accordingly. "What do you know about that?"

"Look," Rita continued. "Three sets of initials dominate the entire sequence of entries. AF appears four times, all in Latin American cities. ER comes up in all the Louisiana entries. AS shows up in Florida. HB is the only code that does not follow a pattern. That one shows up in Beirut and Lima, Peru. All the other initials appear in one city and only one time."

Lassick sat quietly, his chin resting on his hand. He had been working a separate computer terminal. "I've been doing a Nexis search on the Latin American cities. You guys better brace yourselves for this one. It took me a while to configure my request properly but I finally got what I wanted. Do you see the initials RC and PE in Mexico City?"

All nodded. "And then there is RM in Port-Au-Prince, and RE in Lima, Peru?" He waited until everyone was following. "RC sounded vaguely familiar so I asked for similar news stories from the three cites on the dates listed. It took a while but the payoff was worth it. Pedro Estaban, Ramon Carrilo, Ricardo Enzio and Raul Mondros were all upper government officials in their respective countries. They all died on dates that correspond to the entries in Mr. Loman's business log."

The room was dead silent. Finally Harte broke the spell. "Should I even ask how they died?"

"What do you think? Three were assassinated. Enzio died in an auto accident but authorities said it seemed suspicious."

"Ladies and gentlemen, the rules of the game have just changed drastically," Harte said as calmly as possible.

"It gets better," Lassick replied. "The Mexico City police said evidence linked the assassination of Estaban to a person named Arturo Fernandez. They figured the name was an alias but it was all they had to go on."

"AF appears in all three places. What about the police in Lima and Port-Au-Prince?" Loman's mind raced ahead as he asked the question.

"No leads and no suspects." Lassick replied.

"Then why is AF in the log for those cities?" Loman was afraid to ask the obvious question.

"These files indicate that your dad knew something about four Latin American assassinations and someone with the alias of Arturo Fernandez. Those are the facts. Everything beyond that is nothing more than speculation."

Loman was becoming emotional. "You don't think my dad had anything to do with these killings do you?"

"No way," Lydia jumped in. "First, no one would keep a log of their association with killers. Second, they were our kind of guys."

"What do you mean?" Harte asked quizzically.

"The head of our Latin Studies department at OSU is an interesting person to discuss global strategies with. He is a bit to the left of Ted Kennedy. As soon as Tim said those names I remembered a discussion with Dr. Cortez. He couldn't stand them so I assumed they were people the U.S. would want to have around. It's nice to have a discussion partner whose philosophy is 180 degrees from yours. It permits a number of logical assumptions." She smiled innocently.

Lassick regained the floor. "I think Mr. Loman was working some kind of investigation. I can't say who he worked for but I think that in his mind this Fernandez guy, or whoever he is, was responsible for all four deaths."

The premise was on the table. Harte felt the time had come to add direction to the discussion. "I didn't want to bring this up until I thought at least some of you might buy into it. In Huntsville I had a weird feelings about all this. When I spoke to John Dutton of HPD and Richard Willis of National Electronics, I was sure they were stonewalling me. But then off the record, they both gave indications that I should go forward with what I was doing.

"I got so paranoid I would have sworn on my mother and father's lives that Willis was with the CIA. It was strange. I still get a shiver when I think about it."

"This is a can of worms," Rita interjected. "We haven't even gotten around to the SESA people in Naples. That's starting to look like small potatoes compared to this other stuff."

"Dammit, I wish Billy was here. I'd really like to know what he found out in Louisiana." Harte said to no one.

"Probably that the food and the women are equally hot," Rita said with a perfectly straight face.

"You are still a brat," Harte said above the collective laughter. "He should be checking in soon. I want him with me when I go to Naples to see Morgan Trent."

"I'd like to go with you," Loman volunteered.

Harte considered his reply carefully. "I know you would, Andy. But I have to nix that." He paused again. The next thing he said would be a final wake-up call to everyone in the room and he wanted to make sure he phrased it right.

"If there is a real connection between Trent's people and what we have discussed here, it could be a serious risk for you to be there. Look, I don't want to sound like James Bond or anything but, if someone in SESA had something to do with your father's death you might be in danger if they found out who you are. And to be frank, it might jeopardize any chance I have to get information out of them. The best thing is for Billy and me to go down there as if the Foundation is interested."

He looked around the table, making eye contact with each of them. "What I really would like is for all of you to get caught up with your jobs and your personal affairs. I may really impose on your time if this keeps on going like it has. If your real lives keep you from getting involved I understand. Don't answer now. Just keep the possibility in mind. Is that fair?"

"Can we get back to work?" Rita asked with an impish grin.

"Do you listen to anything I say?" he asked in frustration.

"Yeah, once in a while," she replied and turned to Loman. "Come on, Andy, let's see if we can find sub-patterns in this log." She was back to work before Harte could respond.

"It's been like this for over six years," Lydia whispered to Lassick.

"He should just adopt her. Then the whole relationship would be logical," he whispered back.

"Shut up, you two. You are no help at all," Harte called out as he left the room. He waited until he got to the kitchen and out of their sight before he relaxed and enjoyed the moment.

NAPLES, FLORIDA

Simmons handed a stop-watch and clipboard to Davaron. "Mark the time when they return to the path. I want them to finish in less than forty-five minutes. Can you handle that?"

"I think so," Barbara answered with that naively curious look Simmons had grown to find both amusing and irritating.

He could not dismiss the thought that the dizzy yet sincere woman was far more intelligent than she let on. Everything about her said she was a weak link in his plan. He was determined to take her along when they moved on to Louisiana. Leaving her behind invited exposure that would almost surely come with her idle talk to the wrong people.

"I'll give the signal when we are ready to begin the exercise." He patted her gently on the back, letting his hand linger for a second. She leaned just slightly enough into his touch that he hesitated even longer before breaking off the contact. "You'll do just fine, Barbara."

"I'll wipe that stupid look off your face when we get to Simmesport," Simmons mumbled as he approached a group of three young SESA members standing at the head of a long clearing. His frown changed to a smile as he neared his charges.

"Okay, lets put everything together on this one. This will be the final run-through for this activity. I know it's not perfect but it will have to do. Miss Goofy over there will call out the time as you complete each phase of the course."

Kennedy and Reilly nodded eagerly. The other member of the trio stood stoically at the ready. Amy Hector, a strapping twenty-three year old woman, was devoted to Trent. When his intentions became known she approached Simmons and his young charges and requested to join their training regimen. She diligently threw herself into a six month course of physical and mental conditioning. She wanted to be on the front line of any action the organization might take.

"You will catch them this time, Amy," was all the encouragement Simmons gave her. When her nostrils flared and her eyes brightened he knew he had pushed the right button.

Simmons was content he had done the best he could considering what he had to work with. Each segment of the obstacle course involved a station designed to test their precision skills under physical stress. In the absence of a proper working model of the intended site, it was all he could do. "Okay people, stand by for my signal."

He walked to a shaded area where Trent and Maria stood with the other members Of SESA. "We're as ready as we ever will be," Simmons announced.

"Let's see what they can do." Trent replied.

Simmons called across the clearing. "Ready, Barbara?"

"Yes, sir," she replied like a private to a drill instructor.

"On my mark," he announced to the team members who stood poised at the start of the course. "Now!"

Barbara clicked on the stop watch and the team disappeared down a trail off the clearing. When Kennedy emerged, followed closely by Reilly and Hector, Barbara called to Simmons, "Four minutes." She had no idea what she was watching but quickly noticed that the people assembled around Trent voiced enthusiasm and encouragement whenever she called out a time.

Trent watched the exercise with satisfaction. As the three team members went through their paces his mind shifted to another exercise some ten years earlier. He remembered the sunny day and could almost smell the sea air as the events came to life in his thoughts.

He and his wife were part of a group of six protestors who had taken a thirty-foot boat into East Cote Blanche Bay. Their goal was to interrupt the passage of a super tanker bound for the Strategic Petroleum Reserve deposit the U.S. government was stockpiling to combat another OPEC embargo.

The protests made the network news like clockwork. A pool helicopter hovered above as the protest boat darted in and out of the path of the tanker. From the sky the boat appeared more an insect trying to get the attention of an elephant. If not for the grave tone of the commentator's voice over, the footage actually had a comedic look to it.

The pilot of the protest boat was quite adept at gauging the wake of the tanker. He could get his vessel quite close to the giant ship without danger. At one point he made a sharper than expected turn and the boat nosed into a swell. Nina Trent, standing on the port side of the cabin, lost her footing on the mist-soaked deck. She went overboard just before the boat cleared the bow of the super tanker.

Trent saw his wife fall and ran to the side of the boat to help her. He watched in horror as she bobbed for a moment in her life jacket and then went under the hull of the tanker. He screamed in agony as she disappeared in the boiling forward wake of the ship. His pilot tried to contact the captain of the vessel to get it to stop but the attempt was futile. All knew that the mass of steel off their port bow would need at least three miles to come to a halt. They steered aft of the ship and watched for the result of the tragedy.

Minutes later a tattered orange life jacket surfaced behind the super tanker. The torso of Nina Trent was still in the jacket. Her head and limbs had been ripped from her body by the force of the ship's propellers as she had emerged from under the hull. Trent was too distraught to watch and went below while the crew retrieved the body.

The helicopter camera caught the entire sequence and all three networks ran the story at the top of their newscasts. In the midst of a ranting press conference Trent collapsed at the podium in a full-blown breakdown. He spent two months recuperating in a mental hospital while lawyers worked out the details of a financial settlement over the incident. When he was finally discharged, he was a wealthy but almost manically bitter widower. He was also a living martyr of the environmental awareness movement.

From the moment Trent left the hospital he began to plan his revenge. He moved to Naples, Florida, and slowly gathered a group of eighteen devoted followers around him. He made no pretense of the reason for their assembly. The goal was to avenge the death of his wife at the expense of the oil industry. All agreed to help him in his quest and to keep the ultimate aim of the Southeast Endangered Species Association in strict confidence.

The arrival of Albert Simmons gave Trent the extra help he needed in rounding the association into a disciplined unit. He never really bothered to question Simmons' lack of credentials. The man's resourcefulness and organizational abilities far outweighed any need to track down his references. Trent was confident that Simmons was not a member of a government agency and that was enough.

"Mr. Trent."

Simmons' voice brought Trent back to the present. He looked across the clearing to see Kennedy, Reilly and Hector walking exhaustedly toward him.

"They did the course in forty-two minutes," Simmons informed him. "That is good work."

"Agreed. I think a big dinner and a relaxing night are in order for everyone. Tomorrow we start preparing for the move." Trent watched Davaron cross the clearing toward them. "What should we do about Barbara?"

"She should come with us. Everyone likes her and she isn't completely useless. Besides, she's seen all this and I'd feel better if she was with us."

"Does she need coaxing?"

"It wouldn't hurt if you made a pitch to her. I hinted at it but if you asked it would pretty much lock it up."

"I'll do that." Trent turned to the assembled group. "Good work, everybody. Let's get back to camp and have some dinner. Tomorrow is a big day."

TAMPA, FLORIDA

"Sorry I missed the party," Harmon said as he met Harte at Gate 35 of Tampa International Airport. "You got luggage?"

"Just a carry-on," Harte replied. "We are only going to be in Naples a couple of days and I don't plan to socialize."

"Same here. Let's move it. The flight to Naples leaves in twenty minutes," Harmon said as they started walking.

"Why didn't we just meet in Naples, Billy? I could have gotten a non-stop right into the place."

"I figured we could use the time to get each other up to speed on where things stand. Besides, it gives us a chance to return a little on someone's investment."

"I don't understand."

Harmon pointed to the South Air ticket counter. "Didn't you tell me that the Foundation once received a donation from these guys?"

"That's right. I never could figure out why they wanted to send the Foundation money." Harte recalled the feeling of puzzlement the day he opened an envelope with the South Air logo on it and found a check to the Wilson Foundation. A pleasant note expressing appreciation of the Foundation's work accompanied the check.

He called the airline to ask about the reason for the donation. He received a somewhat canned reply that the company liked to give to various worthy causes and the board of directors liked the work of the Wilson Foundation. South Air never made any requests nor did it make inquiries as to how the Foundation operated. Harte eventually forgot about it.

As they settled into their seats for the hop to Naples, he asked what, if anything, Harmon had discovered on his trip to Louisiana.

"That the food is as hot as the women." Harmon replied.

"You're kidding me," Harte said as he burst out laughing.

"It wasn't that great a line."

"You have no idea," Harte responded as his laughter subsided. "Two days ago Rita said you'd say that."

"I always thought that girl was a genius," Harmon grinned. "How did the weekend go?"

Harte turned serious. "Not here, Billy."

"Dan, there are only about fifteen people on the plane."

"At this point that is thirteen too many."

Harmon realized that Harte was deadly serious. He crafted his statements to be meaningful to them but useless to anyone else. "A college friend, who works in the state government at Baton Rouge, says they expect a visit in the near future."

Harte wrote down "SESA" on a piece of paper and passed it to Harmon.

"Exactly, but he didn't have any specifics."

"We will want to find out about that," Harte replied.

Harmon read gravity through the nonchalance of Harte's tone. "We can do that."

"So what else managed to keep you in that area all weekend? Besides, of course, the food and women."

Harmon became animated. "I have another friend, Chuck Haisley, who works for the Corps of Engineers. We took a boat trip up to Natchez. He showed me the flood control project the Corps operates above Baton Rouge. You have to see it to believe it. They actually divert the river towards New Orleans from the path it really wants to take. It's a hell of a project."

Harmon spent the rest of the flight attempting to describe the series of levees, locks and dams that the Army Corps of Engineers employs along the lower Mississippi River. These structures and earthworks keep seventy percent of the water flowing southeast through Baton Rouge and on to New Orleans. He did his best to describe the Old River Flood Control Complex, sixty miles northwest of Baton Rouge where Haisley and three gated dams and a hydro-electric power plant keep precise tabs on the seventy/thirty flow split.

The prevailing equation, according to Harmon's friend, is that if more than thirty percent of the water diverts to the west, the Mississippi will shift its course and merge into the Atchafalaya River in western Louisiana. The result would be the elimination of the deep water port at Baton Rouge and the loss of New Orleans as the major port facility on the Gulf of Mexico.

Harmon could not truly explain the full effects of such a shift. The disruption to the oil and gas industry alone would be disastrous in the short run. The entire reshuffling of the import-export business from New Orleans and Baton Rouge to Morgan City, at the mouth of the Atchafalaya would be a nightmare. A long list of negatives made the flood control project on the lower Mississippi far more cost effective than simply permitting the river to seek its own course.

Harte was lost in thought, trying to see if this information fit anywhere into the puzzle he was trying to piece together. He was so far away mentally he did not even acknowledge the flight attendant when she stopped at their seats to offer refreshment. Harmon ordered iced tea and coffee. The attendant gave the men a once-over glance before moving on.

Harmon finished his dissertation as the plane came to a stop on the tarmac at Naples Airport. As Harte paused in the entryway enjoying the change of climate, Harmon leaned into the galley and sought out the flight attendant who had served their drinks.

"Thanks a lot. We enjoyed the flight." he said.

Samantha Schmidt looked up from her work and smiled. "You're more than welcome, Mr. Harmon."

Harmon looked startled at her response.

"Relax, sir. I study the manifest and get names down. It can come in handy in an emergency when people need a personal touch."

"Not bad," Harmon replied with a touch of admiration.

"Get your friend to lighten up," Samantha said with a smile. "This is Florida. We try not to be so stressed down here."

"I'll see what I can do about that. It's my fault. I gave him a lot to think about during the flight."

Samantha stopped herself from agreeing. They did not need to know she had overheard most of the conversation. Sometimes she wished she could just be a flight attendant. She reverted to the official friendly mode. "Enjoy Naples and thanks for flying with us."

"Canned but sincere." Harmon winked and turned away.

"You guys be careful out there," Samantha said under her breath as she watched them deplane. It only slightly occurred to her that she concentrated more on the man named Harte than on his companion to whom she had just spoken.

MOSCOW, RUSSIA

The members of Yuri Cherkin's cabinet filed out of the meeting room in stunned silence. Most stared at the floor as they exited and shuffled to their offices. It would take some time to digest the meaning of all that had just occurred.

They had listened to an astonishingly candid report from General Anatoly Kasarov on the near disintegration of the army of the Western front. His detailed account of the steps taken to restructure and preserve the army as an effective fighting unit had met with responses ranging from relief to gratitude as he finished his presentation and left the room.

The door had hardly closed before Cherkin began a long-winded criticism of the Defense Ministry. A number of the cabinet ministers found themselves staring at the always-present glass of vodka to the President's right. The rest looked blankly down at their papers as Cherkin attempted to blame the helpless Defense Minister for over fifty years of mismanagement at the department.

The ministers recognized the pattern developing before them. Cherkin, in his drunkenness, had convinced himself that one man was to blame for the ills Communism had inflicted on the country since the earliest days of the revolution. The President would bully the rest of the cabinet into agreeing the minister should either resign or, if it was politically expedient, be publicly sacked. It had happened before, at Transportation and Science. As the ministers shuffled out of the room one of them looked at the Defense Minister. "*Nostrovia*," he said in sympathy.

In their dejection no one noticed Cherkin's aide give the Ministers of Agriculture and Interior a subtle signal to return when the crowd cleared. The two men exchanged an apprehensive glance and lingered in the hallway until the rest of the members of the cabinet disappeared.

Yuri Cherkin drummed his fingers on the table, looking back and forth at the two officials sitting across from him. They returned his look with expressions of resignation. Most of their concentration centered on the half-empty vodka bottle on the table to Cherkin's right.

"Sergei, bring me two more glasses," the president called out, breaking the uneasy silence.

His aide crossed the room and set two tumblers on the table.

"Attend your duties. I will call when we have finished."

"Are you officially indisposed, Mr. President?"

"Yes. Until further notice, the president is once again unable to take visitors." Cherkin displayed a trace of a smile as he recited the official line the two ministers had become so familiar with lately. "It seems like a fine day for a drink, my friends," he said and poured a healthy shot of vodka into each of the three glasses. "As a matter of fact, I think I will have two."

He drained the vodka from his glass in one gulp and poured himself another shot. With a flick of his wrist he slid the two tumblers of across the table. They stopped almost precisely in front of the ministers. "What shall we drink to? I know. Let us drink to the superb job General Kasarov has done with the restructuring of the army."

The men exchanged a troubled look. "But Mr. President," Alexei Potemkin, the Agriculture Minister protested weakly, "It is not yet eleven o'clock in the morning."

"Then if it is too early to drink to General Kasarov, let us drink to the Defense Minister," the President chuckled.

"Mr. President, I have a very demanding day ahead, as do you," replied Dimitri Stadenko of Interior, trying desperately to dissuade Cherkin.

Cherkin brought his fist down with a force that actually caused the huge table to vibrate. He stared through them with eyes of cold steel. "Gentlemen, I am the President of Russia and I say we are going to have a drink. I am ordering you to pick up your glasses and join me."

Potemkin and Stadenko were in shock. They could not recall such a determined attitude from Cherkin. It dismayed them that it was wasted on vodka. Seeing no choice they reached for the glasses.

"That is better," said Cherkin in a much calmer voice. "Now, here's to the Russian Republic." All three raised their glasses in a toast. Cherkin gulped his drink with ease. The ministers hesitated, then threw down their drinks in one swallow.

Cherkin calmly waited for the reaction. As the ministers began to exhibit the universal expression that comes over most people on their first shot of liquor of the day or evening, they both stopped in confusion. Potemkin broke the uneasy silence.

"Mr. President, I think that, as the Americans would say, this tastes like shit."

"Yes, Alexei. And do you wonder as I do sometimes, how they are able to make the comparison." Cherkin's comment lightened things significantly.

"Mr. President," Stadenko chimed in, "This tastes more like water than vodka."

"Eighty-five percent, Dimitri, assuming Sergei has done his duty properly. He found that at that ratio there would still be enough of a vodka smell to fool anyone who might want to check on my drinking habits. I am doing my best. If you do not accept this statement, I understand, but I make it as sincerely as anything I have ever said. And if you accept what I have told you then I need your help. I had to do this to show you I am in far more control than anyone knows."

Stadenko and Potemkin stared in disbelief as their president bared his soul to them. They had joined the cabinet at his personal request two years ago. Both had inherited ministries rife with corruption and mismanagement. Cherkin's charisma and desire for a better Russia convinced them that they could make a difference. They were both reformers of the highest order and they jumped at the chance to make life better for the average citizen of Russia.

Much had happened since those days to change the men from dedicated public servants to disillusioned bureaucrats. Cherkin's drinking and the impetuous outbursts that resulted, had led to cabinet infighting and government stagnation. They found themselves discussing resignation, but stayed on in the hope it might somehow turn around. All they wanted was a chance to do some good.

Now they listened to the first honest statements from Cherkin in a long time and a spark of guarded optimism flickered. It seemed the consummate gamble to trust an alcoholic trying to kick the habit. They silently rationalized that Cherkin attempting to solve his drinking problem was far better than letting things go on as they were. The worst that could happen was he would fail and they could go back to discussing life after government. A glance confirmed that each knew what the other was thinking. They were prepared to hear more and approach the situation with an open mind.

When Cherkin felt he had their attention again he proceeded. "There is a grave threat to our country and it comes from within. General Kasarov has put us in an unacceptable position regarding the army and his ambitions. He proposes to become Defense minister and have tacit control of both your ministries. If I do not agree he will furlough three quarters of his army and leave the western front bare.

"My friends, there is absolutely no way I can turn control of Interior and Agriculture to the Army. You both know Kasarov's ties to the Soviet. He will most assuredly use his influence to return the country to the old ways. We may not have achieved all we planned, but we must not allow the republic to founder."

"Do you have a plan, Yuri?" Stadenko asked tentatively.

"Yes. But it will take time. I must announce Kasarov's appointment on the first of March. The two of you must appear to agree to his new cabinet structure. I have not initiated my plan yet because I needed to see if I am alone on this or if I have allies I can count on."

"We are listening," Potemkin said in a measured tone.

"I have no right to ask more than that, Alexei," Cherkin took a deep breath. "It is my belief that Viktor Gorki can provide a solution to our problem. He is a friend I count on and, whatever you might think of the KGB, he is a patriot who will do what is necessary."

Stadenko and Potemkin recoiled slightly at the mention of Gorki's name. The restructuring of the KGB had left the former Soviet security agency largely intact and nearly as autonomous as it had always been. "Hasn't KGB caused enough grief to last the rest of history?" Stadenko asked imploringly.

"Be calm, my friends," the President assured them. "KGB will have no direct part in what must be done." He took another deep breath. "Viktor has contacts outside Russia. There are people who can accomplish what we need without upsetting any of the forces that presently direct the affairs of the planet."

The three men silently considered the profound eloquence of the president's statement. Cherkin himself marveled at the statesmanlike quality of the comment.

"We must proceed with great caution," Stadenko warned.

"I never intended to do otherwise," Cherkin replied resolutely. "And now, my friends, this meeting should adjourn. Outside of Sergei you are the only others with knowledge of this. I suggest that you make your exits with discretion. There is much to do."

Cherkin rose and shook hands firmly with each minister. When they departed he summoned his aide. "I will be in my office and ready to see visitors. Is the coffee still fresh?"

Sergei smiled. "It can be in five minutes, sir."

"Bring some to my office and give me about twenty minutes before you start the parade." He left the cabinet room without waiting for the aide's reply.

NAPLES, FLORIDA

"Louisiana Environmental Office. Mrs. Reese speaking," the friendly voice said over the phone.

"Hello, Mrs. Reese, this is Albert Simmons of the Southeast Endangered Species Association. We spoke two weeks ago."

"Oh yes, Mr. Simmons. I've been waiting for your call. I hope the information I sent was helpful."

"It was exactly what I was looking for, thank you." Simmons hated this. He begged Trent to let someone else deal with the woman, but Trent insisted everything go as routinely as possible. They did not need a nosy civil servant asking about the polite young man she had spoken with.

"Oh, good," Mrs. Reese said eagerly. "When should I expect to meet you, Mr. Simmons?"

Over-anxious bitch, he thought. "Quite soon I'm sure, Ma'am. We have found a couple of excellent sites down in the southwest area of the state and we will be moving our operation early next week."

"Oh dear, that is the first week of March," Mrs. Reese said as she leafed through her daily calendar.

"Is that a problem?" Simmons asked tentatively

"Oh no, Mr. Simmons. I just had the impression from our last conversation it would be a little later in the month."

"I thought it would too, Ma'am. But Mr. Trent wants to get set up as early as possible so that we can do our surveys well in advance of the actual study and monitoring phase."

"That makes sense," the woman said with relief. "I can meet you at your chosen site and help with any preliminary arrangements."

"I appreciate that, ma'am, but we are a fairly autonomous operation and can handle most contingencies as they arise."

"Well all right, if you think that will work out," Mrs. Reese said with a trace of disappointment.

Simmons tossed her a carrot. "Once we get settled in, I'll come to Baton Rouge and we can get together and discuss the project. I was truly impressed by how well the material you sent us covered all of our concerns. I'm sure that a person of your resourcefulness and efficiency can be far more valuable to the association once we get settled in. Would that be an acceptable arrangement?"

"It would be more than a pleasure, Mr. Simmons."

"Then I will visit you late next week, Mrs. Reese."

"I'll look forward to it. Good luck and stay safe."

"Good bye, Ma'am."

Morgan Trent stood up from his desk and turned the computer off as Simmons finished his phone call. "Good work. I actually thought you meant most of that."

Simmons pulled a tissue from the box on the desk and wiped his face. "Is all the shit off my nose?" He chuckled, then turned serious. "If that woman gets too curious we may have to do something about her." He spoke carefully, hoping Trent would pick up on the idea.

"We have a very important mission. Whatever must be done to insure its success is acceptable. Do I make myself clear?"

"Yes, sir." Simmons was amazed at how easily Trent could be led to certain conclusions. He began to understand the extent to which revenge motivated the head of SESA. Getting Trent to put the mission into effect was becoming child's play. The difficult part would be preventing him from turning it into some "Light Brigade" event that offered no means of escape. Maybe Trent was prepared to make the ultimate sacrifice for his feelings but not Simmons. This was to be his final job and he intended to spend the rest of his life living off the fee which his sponsor would be paying him.

"It's nothing to worry about. Everything will work out fine," Simmons reassured Trent as they got into the Land Rover and headed out to the base camp.

Chapter V

NAPLES, FLORIDA

Harte pulled the sedan into a clearing and parked under the shade of a palm tree. "Okay, Billy, remember the drill." Harte went over the plan in his head once more as he entered the camp of the Southeast Endangered Species Association. As they made their way toward the main tent they received a visual once-over from a number of the camp's occupants.

Harte liked the symmetry of the setup. He noted the semicircle of ten tents on one side of the compound. Cooking equipment stood in the middle of the camp and across from the semicircle was a large tent flanked by two larger tents set back from the main canvas shelter.

One of the association's young members approached them. "Can I help you?" he inquired politely.

"I'm Daniel Harte. This is my assistant, William Harmon. We represent an organization called the Wilson Foundation. We would like to speak to Morgan Trent about a study grant. We did not make an appointment. Is he be available?" Normally Harte would never give so much information to an unknown subordinate but he wanted to appear as open and as possible.

"Thomas Reilly. Nice to meet you," the young man said. "I think Mr. Trent is working in his tent. Let me check for you." Reilly turned away and Harte and Harmon took the opportunity to inspect the area more closely.

"This is pretty posh for the great outdoors," Harmon remarked.

"An understatement if I ever heard one," said Harte, marveling at the state-of-the-art facilities.

The conversation ended with the emergence of a middle aged man from the main tent. He greeted them tentatively. "I'm Morgan Trent," he said with a lack of warmth.

"Daniel Harte. My assistant, William Harmon."

Trent motioned them to enter his tent. "I didn't expect visitors and certainly not representatives of any philanthropic organizations. What brings you to my humble camp?"

Harte ignored the chance to comment on the "humble" aspect of the camp. "To get straight to the point, Mr. Trent, the directors of the foundation I work for want to discuss the idea of a study grant for your organization. They have been concerned, for some time, about the deterioration of the Everglades and want to help. Some of our members have donated to SESA. May I use the acronym?"

"Most assuredly." Trent warmed up a bit.

"The directors feel it is time the Foundation got actively involved. SESA is, by and large the organization of record concerning the Everglades. As such, we were hoping to bypass the usual bureaucratic layers that get in the way of results, and go to the source. I apologize for arriving unannounced but my superiors think that is often the best way to view something. I hope you understand their thinking and are not offended by our visit."

Trent became more gracious. "Of course. Some of my most boring visits were to places that were prepared for me. I feel like asking what they do when no one is looking."

"I've had that experience on more than one occasion," Harte responded honestly.

"Actually, Mr. Harte, we often have unannounced visitors. Many people are far more concerned with appearing involved in the environmental movement than with partaking in it." Trent paused uncomfortably. "I was, of course, referring to the politicians and that crowd."

"No offense taken." Harte eased past the moment tactfully. "If I may return to the main topic, The Wilson Foundation prefers to function as anonymously as possible. We would make no public statement as to our involvement. That would be left to your discretion. All we want is results."

"I like that approach, Mr Harte. May I call you Dan?"

"Checkmate," Harmon said to himself as he watched Harte scrape the crust away from Trent's veneer.

"Of course, sir. I prefer informality whenever possible."

"We must maintain a certain level of discipline out here among the species, Dan. So the two of you may notice a formality and stiffness among my people. But by and large I too, prefer a relaxed approach to conversation. 'Morgan' will do nicely when we speak together."

"Excellent," Harte replied. "I'll tell you something else, Morgan. My first impression is that you and I have another thing in common."

"What is that?"

"I do not enjoy patronizing exchanges when the subject stands on its own merit."

Most of Trent's public facade lay in a heap on the ground. Sensing this, Harte held back the final bone for a more opportune moment.

"We have much to discuss." Trent replied. "Would you mind if we walked a ways into the sanctuary while we talk?"

Harte was taken slightly aback by the suggestion but saw no problem. "Why not. It's been a while since I saw the Everglades up close."

Trent eyed him curiously. As the they exited the tent a woman crossed the compound toward them. "Ah, just in time." Trent said. "Maria, I'd like you to meet Daniel Harte and his assistant, William Harmon. Gentlemen, Maria DeLeon. She brings order to a hectic way of life out here in the Big Cypress Swamp."

Harte could see the woman was both flattered and a little surprised at the compliment. He filed the reaction for possible use in the future.

"Maria," Trent announced, "Mr. Harte and I are going to take walk and discuss business. Would you be good enough to show Mr. Harmon around the camp? I'd like him to get a feel of how we do things out here."

"The Wilson Foundation will certainly be interested in how your facilities function," Harte said, in case Billy wanted to express any misgivings. "There might even be some things we can help with in regards to the living situation here. Though from what I've seen so far your operation looks fairly complete."

"We think the camp is quite adequate but things can always be improved," Trent replied graciously. "Shall we go?"

"Lead on, Mr. Trent," Harte said, reverting to the formal address in front of one of Trent's subordinates.

Trent smiled at Harte's quick pick up on that aspect of camp routine, and led Harte out of the camp into the Everglades. "You said that it had been a long time since you've been here, Dan." Trent said as they started down the trail. "When was the last time you visited this part of the world?"

"I spent the first six months after my service time down here studying ecology on a federal program. I was not the best student. It was twenty years ago and my priorities were up in the air. Mostly I used the time to unwind after three years in the Marine Corps..."

"...As I said, Dan, that is quite a project and an extremely generous offer," Trent said as they walked slowly back toward the camp. He was still trying to digest the magnitude of Harte's proposal, both in scope and funding.

"Again, SESA is the organization of record down here and the Foundation wants integrity in this project. We saw no reason to approach anyone else." Harte replied evenly. He had spent an hour discussing everything from the white plumed egret to the ongoing problem of saltwater contamination as he and Trent walked through the Everglades. He hoped his last comment put the seal of approval on the deal.

"Then it is settled. My people will contact the Wilson Foundation when we are ready to get started." As they neared the compound Trent digressed. "It isn't the construction or saltwater that causes the problems, you know. It's oil. Most of the ecological problems this planet must endure are petroleum based." His mood darkened noticeably. "As long as the oil companies continue to find new things for the consumers to spend their money on, the killing of the planet will continue unabated.

"At some point the people must say 'enough is enough' and turn to alternatives. Otherwise the world will continue to choke itself and the oil companies will simply continue to gorge themselves at the expense of the consumer." A deep frown had crossed Trent's face as they entered the camp.

Harte was glad they were back among people. Trent's change of mood alarmed him. He breathed a sigh of relief when he saw Harmon standing in the middle of the camp watching them approach.

Trent's dark mood quickly vanished and he resumed a steady demeanor. "Ah, Mr. Harmon, Maria. Daniel and I just had a remarkable conversation. It is a banner day. Have you seen Al around?"

"He left to do a little field work," Maria replied as she came to Trent's side and leaned slightly against him.

A few moments of idle social chatter ended the visit and Harmon drove down the dirt road to Highway 29. "I was never so glad to be leaving anyplace," he blurted out as they drove toward I-75.

"Billy, we got a lot to talk about this evening."

"You only know the half of it, partner."

PALERMO, SICILY

The wooden crate rose slowly from the pier. On the deck of the *Queen of Brindisi* the cargo master shouted his orders as the crane operator swung the container over the entrance to the number three hold. It hung suspended for a moment while the cargo master checked the markings with his manifest. He waved to the crane operator and the crate disappeared into the hold.

The master walked to the port side of the ship and looked down at the four men standing on the dock. "It is safe and secure, my friend. But by the time it reaches New Orleans it will smell like a big jar of olives."

The men on the dock waved back in acknowledgment. "We board within the half hour," said the one who dealt with the cargo master.

"The shipment will arrive with no problems?" Bantar asked his companions.

"Between the smell of the olives and the lining there is no possibility for detection. The priest will be there to meet the shipment. They will offer the chance to inspect the cargo. If he declines that is one less step we must take. But we should be prepared to open the crate."

"Yes," replied Bantar. "We must account for all possibilities."

A blast of the ship's whistle signaled the time to board. Bantar checked each man's papers. All carried documents marking them as Italian businessmen on a fact-finding mission.

"Everything is in order. You will make sure my cabin is ready by the time you dock in Ponta Delgada. There can be no delays or interruptions from this point forward."

"All will be as you wish," one of the "businessmen" replied.

Bantar said farewell and walked to a nearby truck, where a substantial cash payment insured the driver's silence. He checked his own papers once more. The I.D. and passport were perfect and the plane ticket was in order. When the delivery truck vanished into the maze of buildings surrounding the pier, Bantar started the engine of the car he had arrived in.

With two more blasts from her horn the *Queen of Brindisi* slowly moved away from the dock. Bantar's flight to the Azores departed in an hour. The drive to the airport could be leisurely.

NAPLES, FLORIDA

"Thank you," Harmon said, as the waitress set a glass of wine on the table.

"Can I get you some appetizers?" she asked courteously.

"This will be fine for now," Harmon replied. She smiled and departed. He turned to Harte. "Pretty suave, eh?"

"Errol Flynn incarnate," Harte replied, shaking his head. "Thanks. I've been working on my presentation. It's really depressing to discover how few women are instantly attracted to a smartass. What the hell." He returned to the topic at hand. "So how did you get Trent to buy in so easily?"

"I'm surprised that you haven't figured it out, Billy. You saw that camp. What do you think is the driving force behind that operation out there? Idealism?"

"One could hope."

"It was simple." Harte eyed his friend cynically. "I offered him a hundred and fifty thousand dollars with an option for a hundred and fifty more if the project runs two years." He sat back in his chair with a Cheshire grin on his face.

"You're kidding! What did he say?" Harmon asked, chuckling.

"I think he shit his pants, to tell you the truth." Harte managed to keep a straight face in spite of Harmon's laughter. "I'm serious, Billy. He may have soiled the old hiking outfit a bit."

"Amazing," Harmon managed to say as his laughter subsided.

"Not really," replied Harte. "The saltwater study was a no brainer. They have been bitching about it for over thirty years down here. And you know what they say about money talking. I've seen a lot of Trent types in the last few years, and talked to people who philosophically would not want to be on the same planet with me. They can be incredibly agreeable if they want money. I got burned a couple of times early on. So I said 'to hell with all that' went back to my original idea of finding people and quietly helping them."

"And look at the crew you wound up stuck with," Harmon said with a grin.

"Good point," Harte chuckled.

"You aren't going to give him the money are you?" Harmon asked tentatively.

"Get a life, you pinhead. If I really want the study done I'll give the project to Rita. I'm sure she knows some hot shot scientist out at JPL who can do a truly objective study for half the money. Enough of that. What do you think is really going on out there?"

"It's a hell of an operation. I just find it hard to believe that all they do out there is count birds, snakes and alligators."

"Same here. But everything I saw points to exactly that."

"Not everything," Harmon said thoughtfully.

"Explain."

"It was a feeling I got while the DeLeon woman was showing me around. There were places she avoided letting me see."

"Like what?" Harte asked.

"Just some of the tents. I could understand not letting me into private living areas but there was a sense of uneasiness in the way she avoided certain areas."

"What else?" Harte prodded his friend.

"Then there was Simmons and his buddies."

Harte sat bolt upright in his chair. "Who did you say?"

"Simmons was his name."

"Is that the guy Trent was asking about when he mentioned the name, 'Al' to Maria DeLeon?"

"Yeah. He went out into the Everglades with two guys. One was the Reilly kid who met us when we first arrived. I think he called the other one Jim. To be honest, Dan, the entire scene had a military feel to it when I met him."

"AS," Harte said almost inaudibly.

"What are you talking about?"

Harte looked around to confirm their privacy. "One of the letter groups in Herb Loman's Naples file was AS. And you met Al Simmons. We just found a puzzle piece, Billy boy."

Harmon broke the ensuing silence. "There's something else. A lot of their stuff looked packed for transport. I think they are moving the camp."

"They are," said a female voice from nearby.

Harte and Harmon froze in their seats and exchanged an "oh shit!" glance. A woman in her late twenties appeared from around some foliage behind Harmon. Her brown hair was colored nearly blond by the sun, and the deep tan on her shapely body confirmed the time spent outdoors. As the two men stared open mouthed, she stood in front of the table and placed a wallet sized folder in front of Harte.

"My name is Barbara Davaron. May I join you?" She waited as Harte opened the folder.

His eyes widened as he looked over the identification of Field Agent Davaron of the Federal Bureau of Investigation. Passing the I.D. to Harmon, he moved over to an empty chair and motioned the woman to his.

"I guess, 'Do you come here often?' would be completely inappropriate right now, wouldn't it." Harmon said in an effort to take the edge off the moment.

"Probably," Davaron replied. "But I can deal with it." She smiled a little and the tension eased somewhat.

"Are you on duty or can we get you a drink?" Harte asked.

"Yes to both," she replied, abandoning Bureau protocol.

The conversation went nowhere until the waitress brought a glass of wine. When they were alone again Barbara took the lead. "I was assigned to look in on SESA and make sure nobody hassles them. I don't know why but that is my job. I pose as a volunteer so I can come and go pretty much as I please. In the last week I have seen Al Simmons using an egret for target practice and I've watched some pretty intense physical training exercises." She sipped her wine and let the comments sink in.

"Why are you telling us this?" Harte asked.

"I was informed that you would be coming down, and that you would probably go see Trent. I was also told to just go with it, no matter what you did. This did not come from the same people who set my original assignment but it did come from some one I have confidence in."

Harte and Harmon were becoming quite adept at staring at each other. "So what happens from here?" Harte asked.

"SESA is moving their camp to Louisiana soon. They've invited me to go with them and I've decided that I should be there." She produced the photographs of Simmons' shooting exercise. "Hold onto these. They should be in someone else's possession for now. I'm sure we will get together again soon."

"What makes you think that?" Harte asked.

"I know you are not here to donate money to Morgan Trent. Whatever you are doing has been, at least unofficially, given a green light by the Bureau. I want these pictures in the hands of someone who can get them where they have to go. And right now you two are the best shot I have."

"Can you give us anything more to go on?" Harmon asked.

"How long are you going to be in Naples?"

"We were planning to leave tomorrow." Harte replied.

"Stay with your schedule. I'll see what I can come up with and contact you in the morning. Do you have a phone number I can reach you at?"

Harte wrote the phone and hotel room number on a napkin.

"Are you both in this room?" she asked.

"No. Billy is in 513."

"I'll contact you." she said to Harmon, then turned back to Harte. "He did not talk to Trent. It will be less conspicuous."

"This really has you spooked, doesn't it?" Harmon said.

"Yes. I have seen events I cannot explain. I don't like the way things are evolving around me. I'm not even comfortable with you two, but I see little choice but to trust that you are the good guys."

"For what it is worth, Ms. Davaron, you made a good choice," Harte said as she rose to make her exit.

"I hope so," she said and walked away from the table.

"Danny boy, what the hell is going on here?" Harmon asked as Davaron got out of earshot.

"Somebody is digging a big hole, Billy, and I think we are about to jump into it." He paused for a moment. "Look, if you want out, I have no problem with that. I feel like I've been led along for most of this trip and there is no reason for you to get dragged into something we can't even get a handle on."

"You can kiss my ass, Dan." Harmon grinned. "This is the most excitement I've had since Microcom offered us the buy out. Besides," he looked at Harte helplessly. "She is really hot. I have to stick around just to see what she's all about."

"For Chrissake, Billy! Quit thinking with your dick. This is serious stuff we are into."

"So let's get on with it."

"Okay. But we watch our backs from here on in," Harte said and then felt a shiver up his spine as he recalled those exact words from John Dutton's business card in Huntsville.

Gansz sat at the corner of the bar sipping a beer. He eyed the young woman walking toward him. Nothing about her dress or manner indicated she might want companionship but he decided to make his move anyway. As she came within reach, he enveloped her with his right arm, pulling her to his side.

"Hey, pretty lady. How about if I buy you a drink?" he said in a tipsy voice that belied his sobriety.

Davaron struggled against his grip pushing on his chest to get free. She finally extracted herself and slapped his face with a resounding crack that caused the lounge patrons to look toward them.

"If I want a man to buy me a drink, it will sure be somebody with a lot more class than you," she scolded Gansz in the diztzy voice she employed at the SESA camp.

"Jesus, lady. I'm sorry," Gansz said contritely. "I was just looking for a good time."

Gansz and Davaron looked around the room in embarrassment. Once the patrons realized the confrontation was over, they returned to matters that had occupied them before the outburst.

"Find someone else to grope, buddy," Davaron said in a slightly lower voice as she brought the charade to an end.

She walked out of the lounge and stopped in a restroom to compose herself and consider her assignment. Things were moving at a pace she could not control and it seemed, for the moment, her only option was to go with the flow.

"Check please," said the distinguished looking man at the end of the bar. On his way out of the lounge he paused in front of Gansz and looked at him through wire rimmed glasses.

Gansz looked up from his beer and returned the stare. "Can I help you with something, buddy," he said in an irritated voice.

The man rubbed the growth of beard that covered his chin and jaws. "No," he said with a hint of a British accent. "I thought you should know I considered approaching her myself. Thank you for showing me how not to."

Gansz controlled his urge to verbally lash back. "Glad to be of assistance. Now if you don't mind I'd rather be alone."

"A condition I suspect you are accustomed to," the bearded man said as he passed Gansz and left the lounge.

Gansz considered following him and finishing the discussion but he had already drawn enough attention to himself. He assumed the same look of embarrassment he had displayed after his confrontation with Davaron and stared into his lap to avoid eye contact with the rest of the lounge.

In his shirt pocket he saw the fruits of his labors. He removed the wadded up cocktail napkin, glanced quickly at the writing under the lounge's logo, refolded the napkin and slowly finished his beer.

"I don't know about you but I'm beat," Harmon said as they rode the hotel elevator.

Harte agreed. "I never thought I'd be ready for bed at ten at night in South Florida during tourist season."

"We are not your average garden variety tourists."

"Good point."

"Barbara really handled herself well with that guy at the bar," Harmon said with a touch of admiration in his voice. "I'm surprised she didn't lay him out. I was ready to jump in."

"It's a good thing you didn't," Harte said as the elevator door opened on the fifth floor.

"What are you talking about?" Harmon asked curiously.

"Billy, if you are going to get into this thing the first rule says, 'nothing is as it seems.' " Harte admonished. "After the gray-haired guy left the lounge, guess what the drunk at the end of the bar pulled out of his shirt pocket."

"Enlighten me," Harmon responded.

"The cocktail napkin with our room numbers on it," A few steps later Harte turned to see Harmon standing dead in his tracks and staring open-mouthed at him.

"They are working together?" Harmon asked the obvious.

"I hope so," Harte answered as they resumed walking.

"Keep talking. I'm all ears."

"Billy, how many people do you think Trent has at his camp?"

"Fifteen, maybe twenty I'd say."

"That's what I figured, too." Now, counting Ms. Davaron, how many people do you figure we have on our side down here?"

"That would be three of us wouldn't it," Harmon dead-panned as the numerical odds dawned on him.

"Does the math trouble you at all here or am I being just the least bit alarmist?" For all the weight of the event he could not resist the friendly taunting that had been the hallmark of his relationship with Bill Harmon.

"Do you want to save the kick in the ass for later or should we get it over with now?" Harmon said.

"I'll just file it with the rest I owe you."

"How far back are you going?" Harmon asked incredulously. He was grateful for the moment of levity and appreciated Harte's attempt to lighten things up.

"At least seven years," Harte replied in total seriousness.

"I can't believe you are counting the OSU-Michigan ticket deal. We could have gone to the game. That has to count for something."

"The game was in Ann Arbor, dummy. And it was fifteen degrees below zero!" Harte laughed as he remembered the time Harmon had called him in Cincinnati at midnight to tell him he had just bought two tickets for the Ohio State-Michigan football game the following day. They were both so excited about the prospect of attending the game it didn't dawn on them until they met at eight o'clock on Saturday morning that the game was in Michigan instead of Columbus, Ohio.

"I really meant well on that one." Harmon said sheepishly.

"I know you did. We'll decide the merits of that case another time." Harte figured the edge was sufficiently removed and they could call it an evening. "Here's the deal. We can't do athing about any of this until tomorrow. So let's sleep on it and when we get up we'll take it from there."

"Sounds like a plan to me." Harmon replied. His tone indicated to Harte that all was as calm as could be expected.

They parted company and minutes later Harte was flopped across his bed, sound asleep in his clothes.

The gray-haired man sat in his car in the motel parking lot. "Time to go," he said to himself. He had watched Davaron depart the hotel. His initial plan for dealing with her was foiled by her confrontation with the drunk at the bar. Many of the patrons had seen her face and would recognize her.

He removed his glasses and then peeled the beard from his face, rubbing away the itchy sensation of the adhesive. Finally he pulled off the wig that had been the rest of his disguise.

Most of his adult life Simmons had survived by blending with his surroundings. This job involved more recognition than he felt comfortable with but he accepted that. But it would be his last and then Albert Simmons would vanish, much to the chagrin of numerous law enforcement agencies.

As he drove to the airport to catch his late evening hop to Miami he considered the disposition of Davaron. The deed would be done, just not in Naples. Once the Association relocated to Louisiana it would be simpler and, when the plan was fully implemented, nature would remove all evidence for him. Besides, Simmons still had one or two uses in mind for the woman.

He wished he could have overheard her conversation with Harte. From all that he could see she had made a move on the men and been rebuffed. He chuckled, imagining her surprise and outrage when informed the men had no need of whatever services she was offering for the evening. It helped explain her reaction to the drunk at the end of the bar.

"Don't worry, you dizzy bitch. We'll find a use for your services when we get to Louisiana," Simmons entered the long term lot at

Naples Municipal Airport. A glance at his watch told him there would be no problem making his connection at Miami International. He sighed as he anticipated renewing a long standing relationship with his friend from the East.

OLD RIVER AREA, LOUISIANA

Haisley watched as his worst nightmare unfolded on the television screen. Across the office Roosevelt and Henry McMahon, an assistant supervisor, tracked incoming messages on the computer. Mardi delayed his rounds to watch the latest information.

A massive "Bermuda High" had waddled in and squatted over the coastal Carolinas. These high-pressure systems, named after the island four hundred miles to the east, normally began forming toward mid-March. But occasionally nature smiled early and gave the towns along the east coast a jump start for the tourist season.

Haisley traced the line on the CNN weather map. "Look at it, Randall. It hits all the good spots." The outer edge of the system extended to the Mississippi River before peeling back to the northeast along the Ohio. A clockwise flow of air brought warm Gulf moisture up the Mississippi valley. Near Nashville the jet stream grabbed the moist air and sent it careening along the southern edge of the Canadian low pressure system that dominated the winter in the Midwest.

The television screen changed to a comprehensive national radar picture. A six hour, time-lapsed image showed bright yellow blotches of heavy precipitation forming below Memphis, Tennessee and moving up the Ohio valley, along the leading edge of the front.

"It looks like a parade," Mardi said, noting the nearly uniform distance between the storm systems.

"Yeah. But the problem is that when the parade is over, it's all going to come back down on us," Haisley replied without looking up. "Hey, Aaron, anything coming in from the stations on the Missouri?"

"Henry's getting some readings right now."

McMahon tore a printout sheet from his computer terminal. "Bad news, Chuck. Big Bend and Oahe are up three feet. Garrison is up four. Fort Peck is up five feet and they expect to go up again soon."

Haisley rolled his chair to the map table and stared at the upper Midwest area of the United States. He ran his finger along the upper Missouri River from just below Pierre, South Dakota, to Helena, Montana. Four massive lakes, Sharpe, Oahe, Sakakawea and Fort Peck, formed the upper Missouri basin. They were quickly filling with water as the dams at each lake reported the opening of their flood gates. Worse yet, Fort Peck Dam, the first structure in the system, was about to open its flood control gates even farther.

Mardi had been around the engineers and the complex long enough to grasp the numbers. "Mr. Haisley, that is an awful lot of water coming in."

"About a hundred thousand cubic feet more. If this pattern holds up for any length of time it will triple the Missouri's discharge. They will be putting well over two hundred thousand cubic feet per second into the Mississippi at St Louis."

"Will they be able to handle all of it?"

"That all depends on what Aaron has to say." Haisley leaned back and looked across the room. "Talk to me, Aaron."

Roosevelt took a printout off the computer. "They report snow changing to rain in Evansville, Louisville and Cincinnati. Pittsburgh reports snow but the temperature is rising."

Haisley massaged his forehead. "Probably not, Randall."

The Ohio River was officially part of the mix. Along its 980 mile length a major runoff was beginning as the frozen, saturated ground refused to take in any more water. The oncoming flood was inevitable. Its severity and duration depended on the early season Bermuda High camped over the eastern half of the United States.

NAPLES, FLORIDA

Harte turned away from his hotel room and immediately bumped into a man walking down the hallway. "Sorry," he mumbled, as they regained their equilibrium.

"No problem," the man replied and moved on.

Harte took three steps and turned back. The hallway was empty. He tried to recall where he had seen the man. It was the drunk in the lounge who had contacted Barbara Davaron. A feeling nagged at Harte. He had seen that face before, but only for a brief glimpse. It would come to him, he decided, as he stopped at room 513.

"Are you up yet?" Harte called out as he knocked on the door. He cringed for a moment, half expecting a head or two to look out a door and tell him to keep it down.

Harmon greeted him in shorts and a t-shirt. He looked decidedly alert for a man whose appearance indicated he had been rousted from bed. Harte gave him a quick once over from bare feet to disheveled hair.

"Come on, Billy. It's almost nine thirty. I know we had a long day, but it's time to get moving," Harte scolded mildly.

"I've been up since seven o'clock, Dan. We've been waiting for you," Harmon replied as Harte passed him in the entry way.

Harte entered the living area of the hotel room to find Barbara Davaron sitting lazily in a chair. He surveyed the scene with a combination of amusement and concern, before a glance at the bed revealed evidence of one occupant. "Good morning, Ms. Davaron."

"Nice to see you again, Mr. Harte." She stood to greet him.

Harmon sat on the bed as Harte poured a cup of coffee and took a seat near the window.

Davaron remained standing and took the lead. "I realize you have a noon flight out and a schedule to keep, but I'd like to ask a favor."

"Why not? It's a regular thing lately." Harte was becoming truly annoyed at the ongoing feeling that everything he did was being choreographed.

Davaron either failed to recognize his irritation or simply ignored it. "I'd like Bill to stay in Naples for another day so we can exchange information on where everything stands with the Trent case."

"The Trent case?" Harte said emphasizing the last word.

"What else would you call it?" she asked. "I'm on official business out there, and you are here doing investigative work. My bureau contact wants me to try to correlate the information you have with what I've seen. I call that a case."

Harte agreed but he threw in one question to satisfy a nagging curiosity. "Does your contact drive a red Escort?"

"I haven't the faintest idea." Davaron replied honestly.

Harte guessed, from her expression, she was telling the truth. He knew the man in the hallway was the contact but he hoped she would confirm his suspicions about the vehicle in Huntsville. In spite of Davaron's honesty, it seemed like every answer left more questions. Cynicism nagged at him. Maybe everything she said was part of a script designed to land him dead in the middle of some intra-government play. All he knew was it sure was getting weird around there.

Harmon entered the discussion. "It's a good idea. If Trent is a bad guy, we want to know everything we can about him. Barbara has information we can use. And if she's going off with this crew, we should give her what we have on them."

"Billy, what information can you possibly have? You were in Louisiana while the Foundation was getting all of this together."

"I got in touch with everybody this morning. They brought me up to speed. I know where everything stands as of nine A.M."

"Smartass."

They shared a chuckle as Harmon recognized Harte's agreement with the proposal. "It's your fault, Dan."

"This ought to be good," Harte said, rolling his eyes.

"You always told me to pay attention. I'm just trying to make you proud." Harmon replied with mock sincerity.

"Don't give me that shit. You haven't paid attention to a word I've said in—"

"Excuse me," Davaron interrupted the exchange. "Is this for my benefit or is it always like this around you two?"

Harte shrugged. "This is pretty much the way it is with us."

"Unless I think that it can get me somewhere with you. Then it's for your benefit," Harmon chimed in hopefully.

Davaron slumped into her chair. "Terrific. I'm up to my ass in unanswered questions and I'm working with Laurel and Hardy."

"Only until it's time to ante up. Then you can count on us." Harte looked directly into her eyes, holding his stare until she understood he meant every word he said.

"That's the truth, Barbara." Harmon with similar gravity. "When the chips are on the table we don't screw around."

Davaron was nearly convinced but she tried one more test. "This isn't a card game, you guys. It's the real thing."

"We aren't gamblers," Harte replied without hesitation.

The room was quiet as they considered the exchange. Harte stood and everyone seemed to exhale at once. Harmon and Davaron exchanged a glance and a smile.

"I have a plane to catch." Harte announced. "You two be careful. I can't tell you how to proceed from here because I'm not even sure where I'm going next. Billy, I expect to see you in Cincinnati this weekend. Ms. Davaron, I honestly don't know when I will see you again, but good luck. We will do what we can to keep you a step ahead of the game."

He added an afterthought. "I know this isn't necessary, but make sure you both get a little free time in. I'm sure you can find something to do." He gave them a smile and a wink and walked out of the door.

Harte arrived back at Room 511 at the same time as the bellboy. "Good morning, Jeff."

"Hi, Mr. Harte. Should I call your car up?"

"Call me a cab and give these keys to Mr. Harmon in 513. I'm going down to check out." He handed the bellboy the keys and a ten dollar bill. "Thanks for everything."

"Thank you, Mr. Harte," the bellboy replied graciously.

Thirty minutes later Harte stood at the South Air ticket counter at Naples Municipal Airport. He looked at the chart on the wall behind the counter and noted his flight information.

"Flight 31 for Tampa is now boarding at Gate 5 and will depart on time at 11:50, Mr. Harte." the ticket agent confirmed. "Would you like to check that suitcase or would you prefer to carry it on?"

"I'll keep it with me, thank you," Harte replied. "Slow day for the airline business, isn't it?" he said, taking a final glance at the sparsely populated waiting area. He half-expected to see the man from the lounge peering over a newspaper at him.

"I guess everyone is resting up for the weekend, sir," the agent replied nonchalantly. "You can board now."

Harte nodded courteously, walked through Gate Five and quickly crossed the tarmac to the jet parked a few yards away.

The pilot, just completing his walk around inspection, met Harte at the stairs of the plane. "Good morning sir," he said politely. "The weather report says smooth sailing all the way. Enjoy the flight."

"Thanks." Harte found his seat toward the rear of the plane and settled in for the short hop to Tampa. There was much to think about and he was anxious to get together with everyone at home. He made a mental note to do something special to show his appreciation for all of the time they were volunteering.

The ticket agent worked his keyboard. On the schedule chart behind him the numbers for Flight 31 to Tampa changed slightly. The chart now listed it as departing from Gate Six at 12:05. "Ladies and gentlemen, we appreciate your patience. Flight 31 is now boarding. South Air would like to announce that drinks will be on us to compensate for the delay. Thank you again."

A dozen people stirred in the waiting area. As they milled past the counter the agent marveled at how smoothly things had gone. To a person they accepted his story about the computer malfunction which prevented him from posting the proper flight information. Daniel Harte's pre-confirmed "walk through" status made things much easier.

Chapter VI

OVER SAVANNAH GEORGIA

Harte checked his watch, looked nervously out the window and did a double-take. Land met the sea halfway to the horizon and from that point the rest of the view was ocean. A quick glance to the left revealed land as far as the eye could see. Everything was backward.

A look around the cabin revealed no clue. The flight was less than a third full and the passengers read or slept like any group of travelers. He rang for the flight attendant, trying to maintain an appearance of calm.

Samantha Schmidt looked up from her work to see the light flash over seat 7A. "It's about time." She did a uniform check and exited the galley as the light flashed again.

Harte watched the flight attendant make her way toward him. It dawned on him that she was on the Tampa to Naples hop. He wondered if this was another of what was becoming an amazing number of recent coincidences.

"How can I help you, Mr. Harte?" She smiled confidently as she spoke to him.

"I don't want to be an alarmist but," he lowered his voice, "the view out there tells me this flight is heading at least north and more likely northeast. We should have landed in Tampa forty minutes ago. Can we talk?"

"May I sit down?" Samantha asked calmly.

"Oh, please do."

"This might be a good way to start." She removed a black wallet sized object from her skirt as she settled into the seat next to him.

His eyes grow wide as he opened the small leather folder and read her CIA identification. "You're kidding, of course."

"No, sir. It's real and we are en route to Washington."

Harte maintained his composure. "Is this one of these deals that if you tell me what's going on you'll have to kill me?"

She smiled. "I'd prefer not to do that." The unexpected personal comment startled them both. She blushed and looked away in embarrasment.

"That didn't work." Harte said. "But thanks. Whether you meant it or not I needed it."

Samantha wrestled with her thoughts. The comment was intended to lighten the situation. But it came out with far more personal feeling than she wanted. She had never, in ten years at the Agency, made anything resembling that kind of comment to a male colleague or contact. From reading Harte's dossier she liked what she had learned, both professionally and personally. But she was supposed to have control of this situation. As she looked down and blushed again, her I.D. folder came into view.

"We were discussing my unscheduled trip to Washington."

"I'm sorry, Mr. Harte. I'm usually much better at this sort—"

Harte interrupted her. "I'm supposed to be the nervous one. My name is Dan." He held out his hand.

"Samantha Schmidt," she replied almost shyly as they exchanged a gentle handshake. This was not the way it was supposed to go.

"Perhaps you should be briefing me or something." Harte was confused. He should have enjoyed her discomfort, given the situation, but he did not. This was not the way it was supposed to go.

With all that was happening he had no reason to express personal feelings toward his new-found seat mate. Yet there he was, wanting to keep the conversation on the personal level. If not for the bizarre chain of events over the last few days these feelings would have worried him. At this point it seemed like part of the deal. "I assume you were going to do that at some point, weren't you, Samantha?" He noticed how comfortable he was saying her name. His first impression of Samantha was quite favorable. Somehow, he was not surprised.

"My briefing is only preliminary. Langley will have the details." Samantha resumed her official voice. "They wanted to bring you in this way rather than on a standard domestic flight. You never know who is watching."

The statement put him back in real time. "Excuse me?"

"You have been looking into the activities of SESA. They can be quite protective of their privacy. It's probably nothing to be concerned about, but the Agency has ways of doing things. We try not to leave anything to chance."

"Point taken."

"Even though I'm pretty well up to speed on this, you can see why they want to hold the briefing at agency headquarters. We do operate on a 'need to know' basis and, by definition, this is an open setting."

Harte looked around the cabin. "What about the rest of your, uh, customers?"

"I'm sorry, Dan, but it's not that open. You do not need to know about them."

He knew from the reply that everyone on the plane was an employee of the Central Intelligence Agency. For some reason he was being summoned into this shadowy realm of government service. He recalled his time with NSA nearly twenty years ago. Maybe that was the link. Or maybe there was something more. To his surprise, the idea did not anger him. It was more of a curiosity to be explored. A thought came into his head and he chuckled.

"Penny for your thoughts?" Samantha asked.

"When I was looking into Herbert Loman's death in Huntsville two weeks ago, I half jokingly asked Andy if his father worked for the CIA or something. Now I have an appointment in Langley, Virginia. I thought that was worth a chuckle. How long before we land?"

"Fifteen minutes, or so." She reluctantly rose from her seat. "I have duties to take care of. I am grateful for the way you've handled this. Most people would be a basket case by now, or maybe worse."

"Maybe I just wear it well," Harte replied.

Samantha smiled and turned away, took a few steps, and turned back to him. Since Harte had been watching her, their eyes met instantly. She hesitated, wrestling with thoughts she had no business having, and appeared utterly uncomfortable. "Look, I know this is stupid but, uh, I was thinking that, uh, maybe you might..."

"Can I ask you something, Samantha?" Harte interrupted her discomfort, hoping his question was the one she had in mind.

"Please do," she responded with a grateful sigh.

Harte crossed his fingers and took a deep breath. "I have no idea how long they want to talk to me. But I'm sure it will take until the evening. I was wondering if..." He knew what he wanted to say but needed to phrase it properly. "It may be against the rules and I'll understand if you say no, but even if I fly home tonight, I'm going to at least have dinner before I leave. If you have the time and are interested would you want to join me? I mean, if you are worried, the people you work for will act as quite a chaperon."

My God, she thought, I've met a prince! He had read her mind and still given her the option. There might really be one left out there. Her smile could not hide another sigh that escaped her lips. "I'd love to have dinner with you, Mr. Harte."

"Great. How can I get in touch with you after my briefing?"

"Don't worry. You won't lose me." She blushed slightly and stifled a giggle. "I'll be at Langley all day. Enjoy the rest of your flight, sir." She delivered the last sentence in her best official flight attendant voice, turned away and walked to the front of the cabin. Her step seemed to have a bit of a slight bounce to it.

Harte relaxed. The conversation had taken some of the edge off his situation, but there was still much to consider. The plane banked slightly to the left and the pilot came on the intercom. "Ladies and gentlemen. We are beginning our approach to Andrews Air Force base. Please observe the no smoking and seat belt signs. Samantha, make sure you get the booze back from Alan. You know how he is about taking the little Jack Daniels bottles. And make sure the guy in 7A doesn't steal a blanket."

The cabin erupted with laughter. Harte looked at a passenger a few seats away and saw him grin sheepishly and flip the bird to some imaginary person. It again occurred to Harte that he was the only civilian flying into the nation's capital on a plane full of CIA employees. Christ, they were all spies, he thought, even the one he could not wait to have dinner with and get to know better. What could he say? He joined in the laughter as he prepared for the landing.

MOSCOW, RUSSIA

Viktor Gorki watched silently as Cherkin poured two cups of coffee. He noted a steadiness in his friend's hand that had long been absent. There was even a slight tint of color in the president's face, although it had not yet completely replaced the ashen shade that government officials had grown used to.

"How long, if I may ask?"

"Nine days now," Cherkin replied as he pushed a cup toward the head of the KGB. "It is not easy and there are times, to maintain the facade, that Sergei arranges a bottle of mostly water but which still smells of vodka. It must be done in case anyone would want to check the contents."

"Is such a ruse necessary?" Gorki asked skeptically.

"I believe so, my old friend," replied Cherkin. He raised his coffee cup in a toast. "To my personal *perestroika*," he said.

Gorki arched his eyebrows and accepted the toast. "Is this the reason we have not met for over a week, Yuri?"

"It is part of the reason. I wanted to be sober when we spoke and I needed time to compose a coherent presentation. I am sorry about the delay."

Gorki was sufficiently interested. "You are obviously troubled by something," he said, signaling that he was prepared to listen.

"I will get directly to the point." Cherkin's mood turned grim. "There is a dark cloud on the horizon and it threatens all we have worked to achieve."

Gorki had heard this statement before, but not from a sober Yuri Cherkin, and not in so rational a tone. He had every right to take it with a grain of salt, but instinct told him the President was not crying wolf.

Although the KGB had been downsized and had lost some of its influence, it was still the most powerful arm of government in Russia. Gorki wanted the reforms to work and often used the KGB to insure that things were done even when Cherkin's drunken outbursts threatened to undo everything. He prodded his friend, "What is this cloud you speak of?"

"It is Anatoly Kasarov," Cherkin said in a measured voice, eying Gorki for a reaction.

"He is a hero," Gorki replied in an equally measured tone.

"He is a Soviet!" Cherkin said emphatically.

"Weren't we all at one time?" Gorki led with the question.

"Many were. Some never were. Now none of us should be." Cherkin said. "In four days I must make an announcement that may start us on the slide back into the old ways."

Gorki's attention was complete. He had seen the signs. The Defense Minister had been publicly dishonored in official announcements and the media. That assured the end of his tenure. It had always been that way, even in the Soviet Union.

Cherkin continued. "On March first, I will name Kasarov the new defense minister."

Gorki played devil's advocate. "He has earned the position. His restructuring of the western army was magnificent. No one else could have accomplished so much with so little."

"That is true." Cherkin conceded. "But this is more than just the naming of a new cabinet member."

"I was beginning to suspect so," Gorki said wryly.

"It has been decided that the Interior and Agriculture Ministries will be unofficially subordinate to Defense."

"The cabinet and parliament will not stand for this."

"They will not know." Cherkin waited for the explosion.

"How can this be?" Gorki asked as an edge came to his voice.

"Kasarov has threatened to furlough most of the Western Force and expose the front." Cherkin watched Gorki's mouth drop open. "My friend, it is not in the better interest of the Russian Republic to permit such a thing."

The KGB Director's head swam with the possibilities such consolidation of government presented. The plan would put all of the country's food and resources in the hands of one unelected military official. The people would never know, if Kasarov played his cards right and did not publicly acknowledge his actions. Gorki rubbed his sweaty palms together as he listened.

"Viktor, we have a major problem here. Kasarov has been a hero ever since Afghanistan. But we just cannot let him assume logistical control of the country. Above the threat to the structure of the government, I fear he would revert to the old ways as soon as he felt his power base secure." Cherkin gathered his thoughts.

"I may soon be thrown out of this office. But it will be by a vote of the people, not a coup led by a renegade officer. Russia has had enough of that. I will take what steps I must to stop him. You may help me, oppose me or stand aside. And when all is said and done you can decide whether the people find out if my actions were proper or just another outrageous moment in the life of a drunken bureaucrat."

Cherkin poured another cup of coffee while Gorki stared at the desk. He was proud of himself for saying what was right and for saying it without his favorite glass of courage. Gorki could simply arrest him on a conspiracy charge. No matter. If Russia was to be secretly ruled by an autocrat, like Kasarov, Cherkin wanted no part of the future of the country.

When reality had sunk in Gorki made a simple inquiry. "May I snoop around to see the extent of this situation?"

"You are my friend, Viktor, but you are also no fool. I do not expect you to blindly accept what I have told you. Find out what you can. But remember. If you are discovered Kasarov and his allies will reopen the gulag just for the two of us."

Gorki was bolstered by the warning. "I jousted with the Americans for years and did quite well considering my resources. I will handle this. If the circumstance is as grave as this conversation indicates, I will bring you a plan to remedy the situation." He stood at attention to take his leave. Forsaking a salute, he extended his hand. "You have my word on this, Mr. President." Then he added, "It is good to have you back."

"Your word has always been enough for me. Do your duty. I will see you soon." Cherkin accepted the hand of his trusted minister.

Gorki departed and Cherkin slumped back into his chair. The situation was exacting a toll on his mind and body. "Sergei, come in here a moment," he said over the intercom.

The aide appeared instantly. "Yes, Mr. President."

"I've had an exhausting meeting with General Gorki. It is time the bureaucrats heard that the president is indisposed for an hour or so. That ought to give them something to discuss at lunch. Move my appointments back accordingly."

"Yes, Mr. President," the young aid replied hesitantly.

"What is it, Sergei?" Cherkin asked paternally.

"It pains me to make these announcements. When can we stop this charade?"

"Soon, my boy. Very soon," Cherkin replied as he gently dismissed the aide with a wave of his hand. He closed his eyes hoping the world would just go away for a while.

LANGLEY, VIRGINIA

Samantha led Harte across the main lobby of the Central Intelligence Agency. He tried not appear awed by the surroundings.

"It took me a while to not be a nervous wreck every time I entered the building," Samantha said with a sheepish grin. "I don't think I will ever consider it routine. Maybe that's the way it should be."

A young man came through the security gate and greeted them.

"Good afternoon, Mr. Harte, Samantha. If you will put this on and follow me."

Harte attached the I.D. tag to his shirt. Only then did he consider that in a world full of suits he was still dressed in the casual attire of Naples. No one seemed to mind so he dismissed the thought. After leaving his luggage at the security desk, he passed through the gate into a world he had only briefly scratched the surface of, years ago.

They walked down a hallway interrupted twice by security doors. The escort shielded the wall panel each time he entered the code to allow passage to the next section. Near the end of the hall he opened an unmarked door for them.

"Mr. Harte is here," the escort announced.

"Mr. Harte to see you, sir," the secretary said unemotionally into the intercom.

Harte noticed Samantha moving away. He gave her a "what's going on?" look and she smiled. "I have a report to fill out. If they need me they will call me."

"But I need you!" Harte blushed at his Freudian response.

"You can handle this." She moved closer and whispered, "I'm not going far. We have an appointment, remember?"

"I needed that." They exchanged a warm smile as she turned to leave. Harte watched her exit.

"She's a good woman, Mr. Harte. A lot of us care about her." The secretary stared at him over her glasses. She suddenly seemed matronly, even foreboding.

"Yes, ma'am." he said, as if caught passing a note in class.

"Go on in." She motioned toward the door. "I'll let Samantha know when you are done." He nodded, took a deep breath and entered the inner office.

"Have a seat, Dan. Do you want some coffee?"

Harte stared at the back of the man at the credenza. He started to sit when his host turned and brought him to attention. "My God! This is crazy. Mike, what are you doing here and what is going on?"

Michael Prince crossed the room and shook hands with his old friend. "Good to see you again. Sorry I haven't kept in touch. As you can imagine, my outside contacts are pretty limited at this point. I still talk to Billy once in a while but that's about it." A collective burst of laughter shattered the tension. "Can you believe this shit? The Agency approached me after the Microcom deal. I started out consulting and before I knew it I was on the payroll and up to my ass in spy stuff. And you know what? I love it."

As they spent time catching up with each other's lives, Harte slowly regained his composure. The sheer volume of information he had assimilated over the past twenty-four hours was taking its toll. He gulped the coffee, hoping to jog his senses, and grabbed a refill. Even as Prince continued the small talk, tension returned to the room.

"So what do you do here?" Harte asked pointedly

"The official title is Western Hemisphere Special Operations. It's a classified title but since you are here that's kind of a moot point. Specifically, well I'm sure you've heard the old 'need to know' routine before."

"A lot lately." Harte deduced the WHSO acronym and suddenly Herbert Loman's computer disk took on a whole new focus. He needed some answers and decided to jump right into it. "Can I get right to the point?"

"By all means. What's on your mind?"

"That's my question," Harte replied in mild frustration.

"Sorry. Just trying to lighten things up a little." Prince held up a folder marked "Top Secret." "This file contains information on the Southeast Endangered Species Association. I want to know why you visited their headquarters out in the Everglades," he said pointedly.

"I was checking on a possible research grant," Harte lied poorly. The discussion quickly moved to a more serious level.

"Hey, Dan. It's your buddy Mike." His tone had a decided edge to it. "You don't have so much as piss in the wind in common with Morgan Trent. Now what the hell is going on?" All conversational frills disappeared.

Harte deferred again. "Like I said. It was simply a field trip for the Foundation."

Prince dropped the folder on the desk. His voice rose. "Don't bullshit me. I'm serious here."

Harte's frustration boiled over. His passive approach vanished and he responded in kind. "So am I, dammit! I take a flight from Naples to Tampa and the next thing I know, I'm hijacked to Washington on a plane full of spies, or something. Then I find myself sitting with someone who was once a friend and he's grilling me about where I've been and who I'm talking to. Just who the hell do you think you are?"

Prince brought his fist down on the desk top with a loud thud. "I'm the fucking Central Intelligence Agency, that's who. And we either know everything that's going on, or we find out everything that's going on. Because that's how this country survives. Is that clear enough for you?"

Harte protested. "You still have no right to—"

"Yes I do. And you gave me the right years ago." He looked straight into Harte's eyes. "All the times you talked to people about duty, honor and loyalty. I never got tired of hearing that stuff. Hell, if they hadn't recruited me here I probably would have applied. I believe in all the things you said and it's time to find out if you believe them too, or if all the talk was just a lot of bullshit."

The silence was deafening as two old friends looked away from each other. Prince restarted the discussion in a much calmer tone. "Dan, when I said I love this stuff I didn't mean all the cloak and dagger crap. I love what the Agency stands for. I love that what we do is often the difference between whether or not the nation survives as we know it. There is no greater moment of personal satisfaction than to finish a watch and leave this place knowing that what you did today made a difference. Now who the hell do you think I learned that from, you dumbass? My Little League coach? Wrong!"

He pointed at Harte. "I learned it from you. I can't count the number of times Billy and I heard that statement when we worked with you. Well, Congratulations. It sunk in. What I do makes a difference and right now I think you can help. For what it's worth I'm sorry we brought you in this way. It seemed like the best way to go."

"And the stewardess? Was she part of the official treatment too?"

"Do you mean the flight attendant?"

"Whatever." Political correctness was the last thing Harte was concerned with at the moment.

Prince showed a hint of a smile. "The answer is 'No'. Samantha had a pretty rough time a while ago so we gave her the South Air assignment as a stand down."

"What, do you own them or something?" Harte cursed his natural sense of curiosity. It was deflecting his anger at the situation.

"No. Their CEO is a former agency guy. He runs a few commuter lines that fill some of the holes in the major carriers' network. We have a few jets with the logo on them so we can ferry our people around and we fill a few positions on the civilian side. That, and a small subsidy keeps the whole operation solvent. The majors don't really mind as long as South Air doesn't try to compete with them."

Harte shook his head. "I'm having trouble keeping up with everything. So what about Samantha?"

"I told her to take her time getting herself back together. She may be coming out of her shell. If so, it's good for the Agency, good for her and to be honest, it's probably damn good for you. If she wants you to know more, I'm sure she will tell you."

Harte softened a bit. "All right, Mike, it worked. I'm back from my snit. Let's get back to the original point. Only this time I'll ask the question. What's on your mind?"

Prince breathed a bit easier. "In one sentence, I do not trust Morgan Trent or his motives as far as I can spit him."

"What does that have to do with me?" Harte probed.

"Maybe nothing. Maybe everything."

"Can I have a hint?" Harte asked.

"That depends," Prince countered and the chess game was on.

"Okay. I'll play along. Depends on what?"

"On how far into it you are willing to go." Prince drummed his fingers and shifted uncomfortably.

"Will you cut it out? I need some bearings here. What exactly do you want from me?" Harte asked directly.

"This is difficult, Dan. I can't tell you much unless you come in on this. But I have a problem with asking you to just blindly agree to help us."

"That's a start. Keep talking."

Prince got his thoughts in order. "As you know, SESA is a major speaking tool for the environmental movement. I think there is more going on with them than just saving the Florida wildlife but I can't get a handle on it."

Harte asked the obvious question. "Why don't you put an agent on it or whatever it is you people do in these cases?"

"You wouldn't believe it if I told you."

"Try me."

"Okay." Prince shook his head in exasperation. "The Director of the EPA and the First Lady have been very good friends both politically and socially for years. The Director thinks Trent is God. About a year or so ago, SESA was running a protest at the sugar cane fields in South Central Florida. A couple of the local cops hassled them. Someone talked to someone and a memo came down from the White House saying SESA is untouchable. In effect they have Presidential immunity."

"You're kidding, of course," Harte said incredulously.

"I wish. It isn't all that significant for us since SESA is a domestic outfit. But it ties the hands of the FBI and local agencies."

"Amazing," was all Harte could say.

"It's the most frustrating thing I've ever dealt with. There are twenty or so people running around in the Everglades with a license to do as they please. And I'm not convinced that their leader is a stable guy. Hell, they could go out and blow up Hoover Dam if they wanted to and I don't know if we could even arrest them. That's how crazy it is."

"You've got my attention."

"Great." Prince rubbed his hands nervously and shifted in his chair. "You accessed the computer at the Jet Propulsion Laboratory. I assume it was Rita Lowry's idea."

"How the hell did you find that out?" Harte was impressed.

"It's a Cray. We know about it when a light goes out on one of them. Those are the rules," Prince replied matter of factly. "Only this time it was no run-of-the-mill entry. When Rita uploaded the file, Herb Loman's agency code came up on my terminal. So I knew you had accessed his disk and were looking into his investigation."

"Is your life just one bombshell after another, or what?" Harte asked, trying to maintain his composure.

"We try to keep an eye on things." Prince sensed rightly that Harte's interest had overcome his anger. "Shall I go on? If we stop here you are out the door, no questions asked."

"And if we go on?" Harte asked knowingly.

"You are in and I can't guarantee you will like the rules of the game. It's that simple."

Harte turned defensive once more. "Is it? "Why should I just drop everything and get into this?"

"Because the nation needs it, that's why."

"Oh come on, Mike. Don't give me that 'Uncle Sam wants you' bullshit. Why should I help bail out some wimp in the White House who lets his wife run the country like it was her own political sewing circle?"

Prince leaned forward. "Because they aren't going to be there forever. And it's our job at the agency and your duty as a citizen to do what we can to make sure that, when they leave, the next president can run the country the way he sees fit and the one after him and the one after him or her. You know better than anyone I've met what that continuity means."

He leaned back and continued. "Presidents have been tinkering with the fringes of the nation's fabric since day one. They come and they go. But it's the people and their spirit that make us the most envied and admired nation in history. And everything we do, big or little, to keep that concept whole is worthwhile and important. It's that simple."

"How did you get so smart?" Harte gave in a little more.

Prince sighed. "I listened a lot. Or didn't you notice?"

Harte was convinced. "Fill me in."

"Here's the situation. Herb Loman was a friend of mine. He was on assignment for me, doing a deep cover investigation of terrorism in Latin America. Somehow, SESA came up in his file. We want to know why."

"What do you want me to do?"

Prince became uneasy as he prepared to give marching orders to his former mentor. "Continue to concentrate on Trent. I want to know why an investigation into international terrorism could brush up against the most famous environmental awareness group in the country."

"What help can I expect from your end?"

Prince looked away. "I guess you weren't listening, Dan. This conversation is not taking place. We have not spoken in seven years. As far as the Agency is concerned, you are a private citizen acting completely on your own. There will be no record of our contact and no electronic or paper trail. Government computers are off limits. We are not involved."

"That's really helpful. I appreciate it," Harte replied sarcastically. "What about the people working with me on this?"

"If they are in, it's all the way and the 'need to know' rules apply. I assume that Tim Lassick is on board, and probably Rita. They have dealt with this kind of stuff before, on a lower level, and should understand the situation. I don't know about Andy Loman, Lydia and Billy. Be careful how you approach them with it."

"That's it? 'Off you go. Have a nice day.' Mike, talk to me. Give me something I can use here."

"Off the record, I will help if I can. Nothing official, of course. We're assigning an agent to work with your group. This agent will be considered as on leave of absence and will contact me only in a crisis situation. I will contact you only under the same conditions."

"I have someone in mind for the job." Now that he had accepted the situation, Harte looked for a silver lining.

"I had the same idea three days ago. What a surprise."

"I knew it was a setup, you little shit." Harte feigned outrage.

"Oh Christ! Don't start that crap again." Prince did not attempt to hide his exasperation. "I thought she would be good for the job. That's all. Give yourself a break. I'm not running some sort of inter-national counter-intelligence escort service, okay? Jesus, if I didn't think so much of you I'd consider you a royal pain in the ass."

"That's a fair comment," Harte replied straight-faced and they both had a good therapeutic laugh.

"Just remember she works for us. Keep your personal and business affairs separate." Prince looked away again. "I'm sorry, Dan. You didn't need to hear that from me."

"I should let you squirm but the truth is I probably did need to hear it. Anything else?"

"No, that's all. I don't want to pile anything important on you," Prince said with a wry smile.

Harte looked at his watch. It was almost 5:30. "Good Lord! I have a dinner date tonight. Of course, you probably know that. I have to find some decent clothes to wear."

Prince rubbed his brow. "I suspect that has been taken care of. Come with me."

As they entered the anteroom Prince's secretary was hanging up the phone. On a coat rack near the door hung a suit, shirt and tie in a dry cleaner bag. Other necessities were in a bag on the shelf above.

"This looks familiar," Harte said inspecting the clothes.

"It should," the secretary said with disinterest.

"It's mine!" he exclaimed.

" Since we had to search you luggage anyway, someone thought you might need them. She dropped them off with this." The secretary held out a note without looking up from her work.

Harte took the note. "Are you always this excitable?" he asked as he read: 'I'll meet you in the lobby forty-five minutes after you are done with Mr. Prince, Sam.'

The secretary glanced up. "I keep a low profile to balance things out around here." She smiled, sort of.

Harte took the comment to mean that she approved of his dinner plans. Prince showed him to the washroom. Thirty minutes later he presented himself to the secretary for inspection. "Can I go out now, Ms. Arnold?" he asked like a teenager. It occurred to Harte that she was not nearly as old as their first meting had led him to believe.

Janice Arnold looked up from her paper work and gave him a seemingly disinterested once-over. Sighing fretfully, she walked around her desk, adjusted the knot of his tie and brushed a speck of lint from his shoulder. "It figures you would clean up nicely," She said nonchalantly as she pressed the intercom.

"Does that mean you approve?"

She relented, "I approve, Mr. Harte. Have a good time."

An escort appeared. Harte retrieved his visitor's badge. "Good evening, Ms. Arnold. Thanks for everything."

"Good evening, Mr. Harte. Enjoy dinner."

Harte had a million things on his mind as he paced the lobby. All that he had discussed with Prince rolled around in his head trying to find a place to land. Suddenly, the plate glass security doors opened and Samantha walked through. Harte stared open-mouthed at her. "Thank you," he murmured, glancing briefly toward the ceiling.

"What did you say?" asked Samantha as she approached him.

"Nothing important," he replied. "Shall we go?"

"Where should we eat?"

"Find us a restaurant that is not in a hurry," he replied as he held the door for her. The official thoughts fell into a pile in the back of his mind. They would wait until later. They could even wait until tomorrow. Right now all that mattered was getting to know Samantha Schmidt better.

PONTA DELGADO, AZORES

The last traces of light disappeared on the far horizon, yet Simmons continued to stare out over the dark ocean. The chill in the air was noticeable but not enough to drive him indoors. Alone on the veranda he contemplated his upcoming mission and his life afterward.

A noise from behind interrupted his thoughts and caused him to reach into his jacket pocket. The gun which was always with him sat in his car at Naples Airport. Metal detectors rendered any thought of carrying the weapon moot.

The new arrival put a cocktail on the table and sat down facing the sea. "Your wine will get a chill in this air, my friend," the visitor said offhandedly.

Simmons exhaled. "It is good to see you again. I was concerned. You are nearly an hour late."

"Some airlines are less efficient than others. I would have flown

Lufthansa, but they would not be pleased to have my business, I think." They chuckled at Bantar's reference. The Germans were only one of a long list of nations that had put a bounty on his head in the last ten years. A combination of skill and occasional luck had kept him free to roam the world and inflict his evil on numerous civilian populations.

"I told the waiter we would call him if we needed anything. We should not be interrupted." Bantar's comment was the green light to get down to business.

"Is the cargo on schedule?" Simmons got right to the point.

"The ship arrives here late tomorrow night. And will be on its way by morning. It is the *Queen of Brindisi* and it docks on the fifth of March."

Simmons considered the timetable. "Perfect. My people will be in place by the second. Meeting the ship will be no problem."

Bantar produced a piece of paper. "Here is the person to contact in New Orleans. He will handle everything on that end. Make what arrangements you must with him."

Simmons produced a cigarette lighter and set the paper on fire. In seconds it was a small black pile in the ashtray. Moments later it floated in pieces in a breath of wind that gently swept the veranda.

"What is your situation?" Bantar asked.

"Trent has much influence over his people. They do anything he tells them. He is completely dedicated the mission, but for different reasons. He has sought revenge for his wife's death for so long. I hardly had to persuade him. There are four in his group who are special. I have trained them and they will perform admirably for us."

"What about security?"

"One woman who volunteers at the camp may be a problem. She is an ass, but she also has a nice one." They smiled at Simmons' characterization of Barbara Davaron. "She knows far more than she should but has no idea what it all means."

"What will you do about this?" Bantar asked pointedly.

"I am taking her to Louisiana. She will be entertainment for the men and will talk to no one."

Bantar understood completely. Simmons intended to do the job for which Bantar was paying him a substantial fee and cover his tracks as he escaped.

"It is a shame that you will not be there to see the event."

"I would love to attend but there will be other business to see to that is a greater part of this thing we do." Bantar had learned a long time ago that the key to success in his line of work was to tell the lies as sincerely as the truth.

"May I ask?" Simmons inquired tentatively.

"We have quite a surprise planned for the Americans in the Persian Gulf. And their Russian friends will come to their assistance in their hour of need."

"Will it be soon?" Simmons probed.

"Have fun reading your newspapers over the next week or two. And look beyond the headlines to see my smiling face."

"I am anxious for this to be done," Simmons said wishfully. "I intend to find a quiet place and live the rest of my life in peace."

"I am more than happy to arrange it for you, my good friend," Bantar replied evenly. "You will be well taken care of when this thing is finished."

Simmons checked his watch. "I must go. My return flight leaves in forty-five minutes. I arrive in Miami fifteen minutes before departing from Ponta Delgado. I always find that odd," He said referring to the time zones he had to cross on his way west.

"It is confusing," Bantar replied. "You look tired. Some rest would do you well," he said in a brotherly tone.

"I will rest in Florida. It is more familiar there."

"Of course. In our business it is not healthy to rest in unfamiliar places. You are a master of the trade." Bantar meant the compliment, though his plans remained in place.

Simmons shook Bantar's hand. "Until we meet again, my friend."

"May it be soon." In the darkness Simmons could not see the emptiness in the smile that accompanied Bantar's words.

WASHINGTON, D.C.

Harte and Samantha walked leisurely along Madison Drive, on the west side of the Mall, toward Capitol Hill. The growing chill reminded them that, despite the pleasant day, it was still late February.

"I can't believe that of all the restaurants in this city, I picked the one where you knew everybody," Samantha said for what had to be the third time in the last hour.

"It's no big deal, Sam," Harte replied for the third time. "Besides, wasn't it nice to be Queen and King of Washington, D.C. for one evening?"

The situation at the small Italian restaurant near 18th and L street actually turned into a blessing. Harte spent much of the dinner introducing Samantha to Martin the bartender and Sue the manager, and explaining how he had come to know them. The story filled the inevitable conversation gap that occurs when a man and a woman are attempting to get to know each other and establish common ground.

The owner, Charles Naylor, operated the original Casa Roma in Cincinnati. He was a frequent guest at the restaurant where Harte worked before the Wilson Foundation came into existence.

Once when Harte took a two day trip to D.C., Naylor arranged a room at the Hotel Andrew near the restaurant. The employees adopted him from the first time he stepped into Casa Roma. Harte visited Washington periodically, often just to touch base with his new friends at the restaurant. When the Foundation's business made trips to the Capitol more frequent, Casa Roma and the Hotel Andrew became a regular part of his schedule.

As dinner progressed it occurred to Samantha and Harte that what brought them together was the work they were doing for Mike Prince. Other than snippets of personal history, circumstances prevented them from engaging in deep conversation about their work. Casa Roma and the story behind it, gave them a point of reference during what might have been an awkward evening.

They arrived at the car, parked in one of those lucky spots a visitor sometimes finds on third Street at the base of the Hill. Standing across from the reflecting pool in front of the Capitol Building, Harte gazed up and down the breathtaking expanse of the Mall. His eyes came to rest on the awe-inspiring domed structure that housed the U.S. Congress.

"You know Sam, sometimes you get so wrapped up in the issues and the people in this town, you almost forget what a stunningly beautiful place it is." He looked at her accusingly. "Mike didn't tell you to bring me down here, did he? The little pinhead knows how I feel about this place. Is this some kind of psychological thing to make sure I'm on the team?" he asked in obvious humor.

"Excuse me. The walk on the mall was your idea," Samantha replied in her best official tone.

"Oh yeah, that's right." Harte looked at her innocently. "I was just making sure you knew."

"This is not going to be easy, is it?" Samantha replied with a smile and a shake of her head.

In the car the conversation was more open. "You're not really a flight attendant are you?" Harte mentioned, bringing up a point that had been on his mind most of the evening.

Samantha seemed to turn inward.

"Wrong subject?" He asked gently.

She loosened a bit, groping for words. "No, not really."

"We can change the topic."

She sighed. "I'm an analyst by trade. It's just like being a regular nine to five commuter. Of course, I happen to commute to Langley. But because of certain language skills, my last assignment was in the field. Things went off plan."

Harte recognized the understatement. "We don't have to talk about this. I didn't mean to bring up anything—"

"I don't mind. The assignment was in Latin American. No one knows exactly what went wrong but a bomb went off at what we thought was a safe house. Two agents died. One minute I was standing on the porch. The next thing I knew I was lying in the back yard." Her look grew distant. "The book says 'don't get close to anyone in this business.' I guess this kind of thing can happen at any time. But it's hard not to get attached to the people you work with."

Harte considered the irony as he stopped in front of her townhouse in Rosslyn. "Sam, I'm sorry I brought it up."

"I really don't mind. I don't have any friends in this town to talk to about this. As you noticed this evening, small talk can be somewhat restricted in this line of work. It can really inhibit your social life." She relaxed a little. "The Agency has some 'light duty' assignments for field agents who need to get off the line for a while. The South Air thing was open so I took it. Mike told me to take as long as I needed. He has the right last name as far as I'm concerned." She smiled at her own clever play on Prince's name.

She continued as they walked. "It has been almost four months now. It's time to get back to it." A hint of resolve came to her voice. "There is work to do and I've been sitting on my butt too long."

They faced each other at the front door. "For what it's worth, I'm glad you picked this assignment for your comeback," Harte said.

An uneasy silence fell over them. Samantha did not want the evening to end but she was not sure if she should ask him in. Her social skills were not exactly up to speed lately and she did not want to do something stupid once they got inside.

Harte fidgeted slightly. He did not want to leave her but there was a longer view to take. They would soon be working together and he was afraid of doing something that might adversely affect that situation. If he read her intentions wrong, it could easily turn the whole thing sour. He might destroy his chances with a woman who, from the moment he met her, had knocked him head over heels.

Samantha broke the silence with a halting question. "Do you, uh, want to come in for um, a cup of coffee or something?"

Harte looked into her eyes, knowing that his answer could determine what became of the relationship. "Sam, we have both had a long and tiring day. Tomorrow looks like more of the same. I think you should go into your house and I should go back to my hotel." Not knowing what to expect he leaned forward to kiss her on the cheek.

She surprised them both by turning toward him as their faces met. The kiss was gentle but they held it longer than either expected; long enough to realize that there was more to it than just "Good night."

"I'll pick you up around nine in the morning," Harte said as he reluctantly moved away from her.

"I'll be waiting," she replied dreamily.

He walked to the car and as he opened the door, looked up to see Samantha standing in the doorway not more than thirty feet away. She leaned against the door frame with her arms folded and a contented smile on her face, gazing at him.

The sight of her brought his feelings to words. "There is nothing I would rather do than come in and have a cup of coffee with you. But I wouldn't want to leave and I didn't want to force you to make that decision. I thought you should know that." He smiled warmly and got into the car before she could respond.

Samantha watched him drive away before entering the house. She closed the front door and leaned against it. Looking to the ceiling she brushed the beginning of a tear away. "My God," she said aloud. "There is one left out there after all." She could not remember the last time she felt so good inside.

Harte pulled into the garage next to the Hotel Andrew. The valet greeted him. "That was really close, Mr. Harte. Ten more minutes and I would have been out of here," he said with a friendly grin.

"Sorry I worried you, Juan. I'll try to do better next time," Harte joked back. He always took care to let them know his approximate schedule. They appreciated the consideration as much as his generous tipping policy. He was almost to the elevator when the night desk clerk emerged from the office.

"Mr. Harte, a message came in for you a few minutes ago."

Harte's pulse raced. The evening with Samantha had helped him put aside the problems of the Herbert Loman case. With a sigh of resignation, he opened the message. A schoolboy grin crossed his face as he read the words: "Thank you more than you know. See you in the morning. Samantha."

The desk clerk nodded his approval. "If I may say so, Mr. Harte, from the tone of the lady's voice it appears you did something very right this evening."

"For the record, Howard, I did something very proper this evening. And for once it looks like it was right." The men exchanged a knowing smile. "Would you do me a favor?"

"Of course, Mr Harte."

"Tomorrow, would you send a bouquet of roses to Sue at Casa Roma? And send Martin a top shelf bottle of red wine. Do you have anything resembling a thank -you card sitting around?"

Howard disappeared into the office and returned with a small card and envelope with the hotel's logo. "How about this?"

"Perfect." Harte wrote, "Thanks for making us feel like the Royal Couple of Washington. Samantha and Dan." He put Sue's and Martin's name on the envelope and handed it back to the clerk. "Could you send this along with the flowers and the wine?"

"Most assuredly, Mr. Harte."

"Thanks. Hey, how's your daughter doing at Arlington Tech?"

"She's still getting straight A's. I'll never be able to thank the Wilson Foundation for its help. My wife and I are most grateful."

Harte smiled. "Howard, you people treat me so well there was no way I could pass on the chance to show my appreciation. Tell her to keep the A's coming. She has a great future. I'll see you next trip."

"Good night, Mr. Harte. And thank you again."

Harte leaned back on the bed and stared from the note to the telephone. It was nearly midnight and he was dead tired but he really wanted to make one last phone call. Finally he decided both he and Samantha deserved a good night's rest. There would be time for such things. The decision made he closed his eyes and the day's activities overcame him as he drifted off to sleep.

Chapter VII

"Do you have everything?" Davaron asked

"I wish you would come with me, Barb. Some of those people are really strange."

"Let's not make an issue of it." Davaron stopped the discussion. She knew Harmon understood, but appreciated his concern.

"But what about—"

"End of debate." She worried about someone overhearing them as much as she cared about a painful parting. Their day and night together had been officially productive and socially exhilarating. She knew all the theories about two people thrown together in a stressful situation, but this seemed different. It almost concerned her that they got along so well. The last thing she needed was an emotional involvement with someone she might be working alongside in the near future.

"Okay, but you watch that pretty little butt of yours out there,"

Harmon said in acceptance.

"Do you really think it's little?" Davaron asked in the character SESA enjoyed having around the camp.

"Actually it's perfect, but don't get over confident."

"Not around you. Now give me a kiss that will hold me over for a while and get on that plane." Before Harmon could respond she threw her arms around his neck and kissed him deeply. Her feelings went from facade to genuine attachment and she held the kiss much longer than she planned.

"Can I breathe now?" Harmon asked with a grin, as they ended the kiss but not the embrace.

"You have a flight to catch, Mr. Harmon, and we both have a job to do," she said with mock sternness

"You're right. But this part isn't over by a long shot," Harmon replied holding her gently.

"I know, Bill," Davaron said and gave him one more kiss to show she understood completely.

They reluctantly broke the embrace. "See you soon," Harmon said. Before stepping out to the tarmac, he glanced back to see Barbara standing in the spot he had left her. She looked fondly at him, her right hand moving in a subtle good-bye gesture. He took a breath and walked through the gate.

Davaron sighed as he boarded the plane. She passed through the sliding doors of the main terminal entrance and walked to a sedan at the end of the drop off line.

"That was touching," the driver said dryly.

"Oh, bite me, George. My work day ended around nine o'clock. You got what you needed from both of us and I decided our free time was ours to do with as we pleased. Is that all right with you?"

"Take a break, Barbara! It was a joke, for Chrissake," Gansz replied defensively.

"Sorry. I haven't had much of a life lately and he may be a keeper. You know, he actually offered to sleep on the couch. You don't just toss that kind back without a closer look."

Gansz noticed the blush as Barbara stared down at the seat. He did not want to pry into her personal life. The Bureau had put a heavy load on her and he was not about to add to it.

Her original assignment had come down directly from the White House. She was Morgan Trent's unofficial government protector. With tacit Bureau approval, Gansz changed her assignment to one of monitoring SESA. He worried about her cover being blown. Davaron had to move from carefree air head to careful observer, without changing her character.

So far she seemed to have mastered the transition, but there was always a chance someone in SESA might notice a difference in her approach to her camp duties. Gansz shifted the topic to bail her out of her personal discomfort. "What else do I want to know about Harmon and his friend Harte?"

"I assume you have seen the background file on Harte and his Foundation so we can get straight to the point. Do you know a Herbert Loman?"

"Yeah. He died in a motel fire in Huntsville earlier this month. He is the reason I got this assignment to monitor Harte."

"Harte found a computer disk full of coded entries in Loman's belongings. He and his group broke part of the code and SESA came into the picture. These two are trying to find out what happened to Loman because, apparently, the Huntsville police have been ordered off the case."

"I have confirmation on some of this," Gansz said. "The particulars are not important but there is really high-level involvement in this deal."

Davaron seemed relieved. "It's nice to know I'm not working without a net out there."

Gansz hesitated. "I didn't say that."

Davaron broke the uncomfortable silence that followed. "Talk to me George," she challenged him.

"It's hard to explain. I have no orders to intervene. But it sure seems like a hell of a lot of people are unofficially involved." His explanation did not reassure her.

"Oh shit!" Davaron cried out as she slumped into the seat of the car. Her head came to rest near Gansz's lap.

He looked down in amazement. "Barbara, what the hell are you doing down there?"

"Don't get your hopes up, George," she said, sarcastically. "Do you see the guy in khakis walking toward the parking lot?"

"Got him. Late twenties, about six feet tall."

"Remember that face. It's Al Simmons, second in command at SESA. He's the guy I saw taking pot shots at the Everglades bird population. Can I get up now?"

Gansz could not resist the moment. "I wish you would. I have a reputation to think about."

"Bite me, George," Davaron repeated her favorite snide comment as she returned to her seated position.

"Any ideas where he is coming from?"

"Not a clue. He comes and goes a lot with Trent's blessing. Every time I'm around him I get this kind of military feeling. I felt it even before I saw him shooting. And let me tell you, he was pretty damned good with that gun."

"You watch it around him. I'll check with the airlines and try to track him."

Davaron shifted the conversation. "You never answered my question about working without a net."

Gansz's uneasy feeling returned. The question would not go away. He tried to put things in a good light. "If anyone asks officially, we are out here on our own."

"What is this, *Mission Impossible* or something?" Davaron's voice was decidedly edgy.

"Not exactly." Gansz tried to sound calm, but his partner forced him to consider her position.

"Be a little more specific, will you?" she goaded.

"It's hard to explain but I think that if and when anything goes down we'll have what we need to handle the situation."

"And until that time?" Davaron persisted.

"As I said. We are on our own. Except, of course for your two friends from the Wilson Foundation."

"And what if something happens to one or both of us before we get this figured out?"

"Honest answer?" Gansz looked her in the eye.

"Honest answer," Davaron turned the question on him.

"No one has any idea we even exist."

"How nice," Davaron replied with open disgust. "Just get me back to my car."

"Look, Barbara—"

"Don't bother, George. It's not your fault. I took the job and this is the hand I've been dealt. Let's just get to it."

Gansz started the car and they drove out of the airport pick up area in silence.

LANGLEY, VIRGINIA

"Thank you, Mr. Harte. And remember you only have clearance for Rooms 121 and 123," the security guard said.

Harte nodded as he and Samantha re-entered the working area of CIA headquarters. "Did he seem agitated?" he asked as they stopped at Prince's office.

"They are paid to appear agitated. That way nobody takes security for granted," she replied matter of factly. "I have some reports to file. If we have time I'll meet you for lunch. If not we will get with each other before the day is over."

"Seven-A," Harte called as she walked away.

Samantha turned back in puzzlement. "What are you talking about?"

"My seat number the first time you walked away like that."

She blushed, then eyed him like a correcting parent. "Thank you. But don't even think about a nickname."

Harte looked at the floor, then back at her. "I would never think of such a thing."

"Of course you wouldn't," she replied skeptically. Then her smile broadened. "I'll see you later." She resumed her walk, happy at the compliment but more conscious of her movements.

Harte entered Office 121. "Good morning, Ms. Arnold. I think I am expected."

Janice Arnold looked up with a straight face. "Go right in, Mr. Harte. He's waiting for you."

Harte did a quick double-take. Her reply carried a sternness well beyond her matronly demeanor. He expected at least a casual inquiry about last evening. All he could say was an emphatic, "Yes, Ma'am," as he walked toward Prince's office.

Arnold stopped him. "I'm sorry I snapped at you, Mr. Harte, but things have changed since last night and everyone is a little on edge around here."

"It's okay. You guys are paid to be on edge." Harte repeated Samantha's observation. He entered the office to find Prince staring at a wall mounted TV.

"Take a look at this! We got a heads-up on it two hours ago. Field reports are just starting to come in."

The words "BREAKING NEWS" came up over the CNN logo. A reporter appeared, noted his location in Riyadh, and dropped an information bomb on the world.

"Diplomatic pandemonium has broken out in the Saudi capital in the wake of what must be described as a watershed event in U.S. and Saudi relations. This morning in the Moslem holy city of Mecca, four American soldiers were discovered in an alley along with two dead Saudi women. Early reports indicate the women had been repeatedly raped. Witnesses said the soldiers appeared drunk and defiant.

"Before authorities could arrive on the scene, an angry mob, swollen in numbers because of the Ramadan holy month, dragged the soldiers into the main street and beat them to death. We have raw tape of the aftermath of the incident. I must caution the viewers that this is unedited footage. We are not exactly sure what it will show."

Prince looked despondent. "I hate this raw footage shit."

The reporter's voice spoke over a mob scene on the screen. "As you can see, there appear to be two covered bodies in the alley; probably the victimized Saudi women."

The camera panned over an angry mob shouting in numerous Arab dialects. In front of a shop lay the bloody remains of four white males in civilian clothes.

"These bodies were identified as U.S. soldiers stationed at the

American Embassy in Riyadh. Why they were in Mecca is a mystery. The U.S. embassy has refused comment."

Harte and Prince winced as members of the crowd kicked the bodies repeatedly. It did not take a NSA linguist to translate "Death to the Americans" in every dialect spoken.

"I must remind the viewers that this tape is at least three hours old," the reporter intoned. "Authorities tell us the bodies have been removed. While there is no confirmation as to the disposition, it can be assumed that negotiations are under way for their return to U.S. possession."

The tape mercifully ended and the reporter reappeared on the screen. "The political fallout has reached blizzard proportions, if I may use a winter metaphor in this desert land."

"He's a real Shakespeare." Prince sneered.

Harte stared at the screen. Part of him could not believe what he was seeing. In the back of his mind the wheels of cynicism slowly began to turn.

The reporter continued. "Every Arab embassy in Riyadh has issued a statement of condemnation over the act. Jordan, Qatar, Oman, and of course, Syria are demanding the immediate withdrawal of all American forces from the region. Egypt has indicated it will be forced to follow suit.

"In Teheran, the Iranian government, in what has to be described as an unexpectedly conciliatory statement says, and I quote, 'The Iranian government, while recognizing an unfortunate error in human judgment, wishes only for stability in the Persian Gulf. With great reluctance we agree with our friends and recognize the necessity for America to withdraw its forces until such time as an understanding can be reached, concerning this sad event.'"

"Can you believe such shit? We're screwed over there."

The wheels turned more quickly as Harte searched for something to justify his feelings. "The Saudis have to realize the ramifications of a total military withdrawal on our part."

"Of course they do," Prince said as the frustration grew in his voice. "But it's out of their hands. Religion supersedes politics almost every time in that area. I can't think of anything that would rile those people up more than Americans raping and murdering Arab women in their holiest city at one of the most sacred times of the year. It's like I said. We're completely screwed."

Harte found his opening. He weighed his next comment carefully, and calmly said what was on his mind. "It seems pretty convenient if you ask me."

Prince sat with his head in his hands. Slowly his face came up and his fingertips rested on his chin. His eyes were wide open as he stared at Harte. "Jesus Christ, you're right. But they would never do that would they? I can't believe I didn't think of it, even though it is beyond outrageous."

"I'm sure it would have come to you," Harte said modestly.

"That was sure an unlucky break for us that the crowd killed those guys. I guess we never will know their side of the story." Prince's comment dripped with sarcasm as he reassumed his role of analyst.

"I don't know, Mike, but my first question would be, 'Who has the most to gain from getting the American military out of the region?' From everything I've read, Iraq has more internal turmoil than it can handle. Kuwait and the smaller Emirates won't profit from it."

Prince took up the premise. "None of the G-7 nations want a major supply disruption or price hike. The Russians could possibly be interested since their Caspian oil is nearly ready for distribution. But we would know if they were screwing around down there. I'd say that pretty much narrows it down."

"And they seem so understanding," Harte ventured.

Prince grabbed the phone. "Jan, get me NRO on priority."

Harte looked at him quizzically.

"I'm retasking all non priority satellites to the Persian Gulf," Prince said over the mouth piece. "I want to get as close to twenty-four hour, real-time coverage on Iran as I can get."

Harte's eyes widened. "You can do that?"

"I do terrorism. As of five minutes ago the agency, thanks to you, is treating the events in Mecca as a terrorist act."

Harte watched the television as Prince completed his call to the National Reconnaissance Office. The beleaguered American ambassador was trying to answer questions one at a time although they seemed to come at him in groups of fifty. The intercom startled him back to the moment.

"Sir, the AD is on line two."

"I'll be with him in thirty seconds," Prince replied calmly. He mouthed the words "Assistant Director" to Harte, who sat awestruck as he watched his one-time employee orchestrate the workings of the greatest intelligence agency on the planet.

Prince finished his call to NRO and quickly pushed line two. "Yes, sir. I have a civilian with me, who I was briefing on another situation when this came up...To be honest he gave me an idea on this thing...If you give me twenty minutes I can finish up with him and get back to you...Yes, it's a back-burner situation that we can't handle because of you know who...Right, the Trent deal...Fine with me, sir. By the way, you will be getting a confirmation call from NRO any minute now...Yes, sir. I retasked all available birds to the Gulf region. When I brief you I think you will agree. If not we can call it off. I just wanted to get the jump on things...Very good, sir. I'll see you in an hour with my report."

Prince turned to Harte with a grin. "That wasn't so bad."

"Are you going to the woodshed on this?" Harte asked, still amazed by what he had been permitted to witness.

"Nah. He loves me. I got lucky on a few ops and did some damn good intelligence work on a few others, so he gives me some slack here and there." Prince paused to let everything sink.

"Dan, I told you yesterday that I love this stuff and I'm pretty good at it. Hell, from what just took place here I'd say you have a knack for it too. If you weren't all wrapped up in..."

"Don't even think about it, Mike. I'm not even sure I like what you've gotten me into with Trent. Some of these guys are pretty spooky. And I keep running into people that act like they don't give a damn but then strongly suggest I do this or that."

Prince appeared to drop all thought of the Saudi problem. "Here's the deal. As I said yesterday we don't know what you are doing on this. The FBI has a passive interest even though they haven't officially activated an investigation team."

"I met one of their people in Naples, yesterday," Harte interjected. "She seems up to the task, but it has to be pretty lonely out there."

"They usually don't leave their people hanging out to dry. She is probably part of a loosely organized network. They are still under a hands off order regarding Trent, but I can't imagine them backing off completely."

"Where do I go from here?" Harte asked.

"Follow your instincts. They seemed to be in good order this morning. You can't access government data banks on this. Rita will have to stay off her Cray at JPL from now on. That will piss her off, I'm sure, but that's the way it is."

"We do a lot of communicating over the nets."

Prince brought out an attache case. "These are secure modems. Do you have anyone who can install them?"

"Andy Loman can handle it," Harte said as he examined one of the devices.

"Herb used to tell me all about him." Prince replied and then went silent for a moment. "I really hate not being involved in this."

"I believe you do," Harte said. Suddenly he looked up from the modem. "Hey! this is from National Electronics, in Huntsville."

Prince reacted like a child caught in the cookie jar. "It's a long story but we kind of own them," he said sheepishly.

"I talked to their CEO for nearly an hour the other day and he acted like he didn't know a thing."

"Rich Willis is a good man. That must have been the afternoon of the nineteenth."

"How did you know that?" Harte asked in amazement.

"He called as soon as you left the building." Before Harte could react, Prince took a piece of paper and scribbled a phone number on it. "As far as the public is concerned NEI does a little contract work for the agency and nothing more. Rich is someone you can count on if things get dicey out there."

"When should I call him?" Harte asked.

"With luck you won't have to. Look, I don't expect you to jump in front of a train on this. If Trent is doing something illegal the game is over and the FBI will move in. You are just trying to find out about

Herb Loman for us. So don't be a hero out there. If the fire gets too warm step back and we'll figure something else out. Do you understand me on this?"

Harte breathed a sigh of relief. "Thank's. I wasn't sure you were ever going to tell me that part."

"You're an intelligent man. I didn't think I had to." Prince replied matter-of-factly.

"I better get my butt in gear," Harte said as he put the modem back in the box.

"I'm keeping Samantha here for the rest of the day and evening to brief her on this assignment. I hope you don't mind."

Harte was momentarily disappointed. "I was hoping she could fly to Cincinnati with me."

"I'm sending her out tomorrow. By then you should have your people in order and she won't be compromised by anyone who decides to opt out."

"That's fair," Harte replied. "My initial impression is that everyone will stay on for this one."

"Just remember that this ain't no game, my man. And Sam's first duty is to the Agency. What the we need takes precedence over what you think the two of you need. I know you respect a person's sense of duty and honor, but from what I've seen of the two of you together, it seemed worth mentioning. No offense intended."

"None taken, Michael," Harte said firmly. "I'd like to have lunch before I fly out? Can I borrow her for an hour?"

Prince was already looking through some papers on his desk. "She would kill me if I said no to that," he replied. Without glancing up, he pushed the intercom button. "Ms. Arnold, would you get Samantha on the line for Mr. Harte when he gets to your desk?"

"Yes, sir," came the monotone reply.

Prince stood and offered his hand. "It's your show now, Dan. Janice will give you a chit to get those toys on the plane. You be careful out there." They held the handshake for a few seconds longer, both realizing the mutual respect they always had for each other had moved up a level.

NAPLES, FLORIDA

Simmons walked into the SESA compound to find the members busy breaking down the camp and loading everything for transport. A quick glance around gave him the chance to locate everyone. As expected, members of his team had assumed leadership roles throughout the camp. Kennedy supervised a group preparing the empty water tank for its journey. Rodvick worked on the generator. Amy Hector organized the breakdown and loading of the tents and supplies. Reilly moved through the area coordinating the overall activity.

Even Maria DeLeon pitched in. Simmons wondered if she had volunteered or was ordered by Trent. To everyone's irritation, she had assumed an air of "Queen of the Camp" since taking up part time residence in Trent's quarters. Either way, Simmons knew that he would be able to use her attitude to his advantage if necessary.

One of the last tents still standing was the large one belonging to Trent. He sat at his work table, still studying the diagrams Simmons had delivered earlier in the month. He looked up from his work. "Welcome back, Al. Come on in."

Trent long ago quit asking about Simmons' travels out of the area. The excursions always resulted in something beneficial to SESA. As they neared their moment of destiny in Louisiana the chance that Simmons' business trips involved illegal activity increased dramatically. To acquire the supplies necessary, SESA would, at some point, have to deal with a lower echelon of humanity. Simmons' handling of these matters enabled Trent to insulate himself from any fallout when the deed was done.

Trent rationalized every action with a line of logic that said he was entitled to just revenge for the senseless death of Nina. Her untimely death gave him the right to respond at a time and place of his choosing. The place had been chosen and the time, while not pin pointed, was imminent. The outcome justified whatever means were necessary to achieve the goal.

"Have you heard the weather reports up north?" Simmons asked as he crossed the room.

Trent perked up. "Good news?"

"The field trip may be shorter than we expected."

Trent was all ears. "Tell me."

"Remember the avalanche story we saw three weeks ago?"

"The one in Montana?"

"Exactly. The jet stream has moved north. The area has had sixty degree temperatures for the last few days. All that snow and ice should be melting and flowing down the Missouri river and into the Mississippi as we speak. If the trend holds for even another couple of days we will have the high water we want in two to three weeks," Simmons reported.

"What about the Ohio?" Trent asked excitedly

"It's raining from Louisville to Pittsburgh. If the data you gave me on past flooding is any indication, I'd estimate our best moment will be around the weekend of the thirteenth, maybe sooner."

Trent looked at the construction plans. "If that pattern could last more than a week or so, much of that area will move beyond the chances of an extended freeze."

"That's the way I see it. Even without that first big flow there's a hell of a lot of water coming down from the north. We will have all spring to pick a time."

"What about the supplies?"

"They off-load in New Orleans on the fifth of March. We'll have them in hand by that afternoon."

"Can we be ready by the thirteenth?" Trent pressed him.

Simmons went over some things in his head. This was too big an operation to let personal enthusiasm get in the way of facts. If everything could not be brought on-line at the proper moment, it was better to wait. The river would run high off and on throughout the spring. But this looked like the best possible time. "If everyone does their job we can be ready any time after the tenth." He hesitated for a moment.

"Is there a problem, Al?"

Simmons enjoyed what he called the "pass responsibility" game. "If the water is up and the Corps of Engineers is concerned, there may be more people at the site than we expect. I'm not sure how we will want to handle that situation." He knew exactly how he would handle "that situation." It was important that Trent understood the plan and approved.

"Al, we have had this conversation before. I thought we decided that people might have to be eliminated if they interfere with the mission." Trent spoke the words automatically by now. Killing was a given at this point. He even considered that some of his own people might have to be eliminated if they jeopardized the success of the plan. The demise of the Southeast Endangered Species Association might also be a result of his mission. Its death was acceptable if it helped achieve his goal. Everything and everyone became disposable when that goal was revenge.

"Then there should be no problems, Mr. Trent," Simmons replied subordinately. "I just want to makes sure we cover every potential situation."

"You are a good man, Al. Don't quit thinking like that," Trent said. He stared at the blue prints and put his finger on the one called the Low Sill. "You will be a part of history," he said to the document. "And so will we."

"Yes, sir," Simmons said as he glanced out of the tent. "I better get out there and make sure the move is going smoothly."

"They can have my tent in fifteen minutes. Are you going to fly over with me and Maria?"

Simmons stopped at the entrance to the tent. "I'll ride with the equipment. If there is a flight connection problem, one of us will still be there when the gear arrives."

"Then let's get going," Trent said.

As Simmons moved into the compound a cheerful female voice interrupted his thoughts. Barbara Davaron entered the camp lugging a large picnic cooler.

"Sorry I'm late, Al. It took a little longer to get this together than I thought."

"Barbara, we are on a different schedule here. You have to be here when we tell you." Simmons scolded her gently.

"I'm sorry," she replied sheepishly. "Look. I made a few sand-wiches for the trip."

Simmons looked into the cooler and saw enough food for a platoon of men on a three day patrol. "What are you? The President of the Red Cross or something?" he said, laughing in spite of himself.

Trent emerged from his tent. "What's so funny?"

"Barbara made a small snack for the trip west. She must think we are going to Butte, Montana."

Trent peered into the cooler. "That pretty much eliminates a stop at McDonald's on the way," he said with a grin.

"Why the hell did you make so much?" Simmons asked more out of idle curiosity.

"I figured when we get wherever we are going we might be too tired to set up the grill and cook. This should be enough for lunch on the way and something when we arrive."

Trent and Simmons exchanged an amused yet approving glance. "That's one I didn't think of," Simmons said with a shrug.

"Maybe we can stop on the way and have a picnic. There has to be a preserve or something that we can take a look at." Davaron quickly reverted to her air-head approach.

Trent reached over and hugged her gently. "I doubt there will be time for a picnic. But you certainly have made a fine contribution, Barbara." He gave her a fatherly peck on the cheek. "And I'm glad you are coming with us."

"Good work, Barbara," Simmons called as she walked away. He surprised even himself with his sincerity.

DeLeon looked up from her work in time to see Trent hug and kiss Barbara. "Bastard. Bitch," She nearly spat the words as she watched them.

Chapter VIII

CINCINNATI, OHIO

Harte drove along the deserted country road to his home, twenty miles west of Cincinnati. From the passenger seat Lassick looked wistfully at the passing country side. They had met by accident at Greater Cincinnati International Airport. Their respective flights were part of Delta's 5:00 P.M. complex at the air line's second largest domestic hub.

"Do you realize how far out of New York City I'd have to drive to find an area like this?" Lassick asked.

"It's nice isn't it?" Harte replied. "When I bought the land from the farmers out here, I promised to build only one house that they would not even be able to see. In return they gave me a first option to buy another twenty acres to the north and east in case a developer tries to move in."

"I think the main reason I keep showing up for these meetings is just to hang around the place." Lassick unconsciously brought them back to the subject of their get together.

"Things have taken on quite a different aspect since the last time we spoke," Harte said warming Lassick up to the topic.

"Nice understatement. I don't know what you found in Naples but I got a lot of food for thought in this baby." Lassick tapped the attache case in his lap lightly as he spoke.

"Let's wait till we get inside." Harte turned off the road, drove up a slight incline and passed a long landscaped mound of earth.

"It looks like we already have company," Lassick said as they passed two parked cars and parked at the end of the mound.

A car screeched as it turned into the drive way and raced past. "Rita," Harte and Lassick said with a laugh. They waited patiently as Lowry parked. The passenger door opened and, to their surprise, Harmon emerged with a shaken look on his face.

"I will never ride with her again," he said as he walked past them.

"Oh, give it a rest, Billy. I was in a hurry," Rita replied as she joined Harte and Lassick.

Harmon stopped at the front entry way. "That truck driver is going to kill you if he ever sees you again."

"He'll get over it."

"Do we want to hear this story?" Harte asked.

"She has a peculiar way of exiting an expressway. From now on I'll just get here on my own. Now if you don't mind I'm going to see if I can swallow my heart, lungs and balls, because they have been in my throat for the last ten minutes." Harmon stayed in character through the entire conversation.

"He has absolutely no sense of adventure," Rita said as she walked through the doorway.

Harte stood at the head of the table. "Do any of you remember Mike Prince?" A couple of nods of recognition and a couple of blank stares greeted the question. "I spoke to him yesterday and today at CIA headquarters." A total lack of sound told Harte he had their attention.

"As of yesterday I am unofficially on assignment for them. If any of you want out because of this new development, you have my complete understanding and blessing. You also have the right to hear what I was told before you make your decision." Harte spoke to the group but kept his eyes on Andy.

"Herb Loman was investigating terrorism for the Agency. Mike wants to know how SESA came up on his disk. Technically, we are out on a limb here, and I have no idea how it will end up. Frankly, some of SESA's people are pretty scary." He looked toward Harmon who nodded agreement.

"The Agency is sending out a liaison to work with us. Even though we are off the record with them, Mike thought it would be a good idea to have one of his people on hand. This individual arrives tomorrow and will take up residence here. Mike doesn't want anyone outside of the loop to know this person for obvious reasons. So you can all sleep on it before you make your decisions if you want to."

"Does this have anything to do with why I could not log on to my Cray?" Rita asked pointedly.

"You're kind of the reason we are at this point. When you logged on the first time, Mike was alerted that Mr. Loman's coded file had been breached. They will probably be taking your satellite over to the Persian Gulf for a while too."

"If that's the case I certainly have some time on my hands. Count me in." Rita knew when to joke and when to be serious. If the Agency needed her survey satellite there must be a major emergency.

"We're all in, Dan. We talked while you were in Naples and want to see this thing through to the end, no matter what." With Lydia's "pronouncement" the matter was settled.

The meeting resumed as if never interrupted. As Lassick was preparing to brief them on the information he had compiled, the doorbell rang.

"Who the hell could that be? We're too far away for a pizza delivery." Harte tried to hide his concern with the comment. A touch of paranoia crept over him but as he walked to the foyer. Through the peep hole he saw a vaguely familiar face and opened the door.

"Mr. Harte?" the visitor inquired.

"Yes," Harte replied, trying to place the face.

The visitor held out a business card. "George Gansz, FBI. We sort of met in Naples, Florida, but if you don't remember then I did my job well. May I come in?"

Harte's eyes widened with recognition. "At the lounge and then again in the hallway of the hotel, right?"

"Yes. Look, I can stand out here and say what I have to, but I'm from the South and no real fan of the great outdoors in February."

"I'm sorry." Harte swung the door open. "I was putting a few puzzle pieces together and got lost for a minute. Please. Come on in." He could not resist one question. "Do you happen to drive a Red Escort on occasion?"

Gansz broke into a grin. "Only in Huntsville, Alabama."

"Thank you." With all that was going on, Harte was greatly relieved to have solved the mystery of the "Huntsville tail."

"I noticed from the driveway that you have company. Is there someplace we can talk that won't disturb your guests."

"Are you here to arrest me, or something, Mr. Gansz?" Harte asked, ready to play the Michael Prince trump card.

"Quite the contrary. I'm here to compare notes. And I prefer George, if it's all the same to you."

"Fine with me," Harte led him down the hallway. "You won't be interrupting anything, George. In fact you might want to talk to my guests."

Only the whirring sound of the computer's cooling fan broke the silence in the dining room. "This is George, everybody. He's with the FBI and he's on our side. George, meet the heart and soul of the Wilson Foundation." When the introductions were finished Harte invited Gansz to take the lead.

"I am investigating the death of Herbert Loman. The problem is my orders call for 'passive monitoring' of this case. That means I'm not really at liberty to assist you and I can't take preemptive action regarding SESA. I think it's a bunch of bullshit but, unless they do something felonious, I have to sit on my hands on this."

There was no response from the table. He took a deep breath. "Well, screw all that. I have an agent in the field down there and you people are putting a hell of a lot more on the line than the government has a right to ask. Give me an idea of where you are going on this and

I will get whatever information to you I think is helpful once I get back down South. And if something goes down where any of you are left hanging out, I'll be there to help." Gansz knew his offer was wholly inadequate. He waited for someone to unceremoniously show him to the door.

Harmon walked to the kitchen. When he returned a couple of seconds later the room was still uncomfortably silent. With both hands clasped behind his back, he walked up to Gansz at the head of the table. He brought his hands forward and each held an open bottle of beer. "Come on, George, we have things to talk about. Leave the computer nerds alone for a while and they will come up with some good stuff for you." He grinned at Gansz as he offered one of the beers, and motioned him out of the room toward a wing of the house.

Without warning they were bombarded with wadded up computer paper from the dining room. "Eat shit, Billy," Loman called out.

"That means they agree," said Harmon. They walked toward the great room to discuss their mutual concerns over SESA. Barbara Davaron would be a significant part of the conversation.

LANGLEY, VIRGINIA

Prince stopped briefing Samantha to watch the press conference that had most of the world holding its breath. No one could predict what the speaker was preparing to announce. The anticipation, along with the anxiety level, was extremely high.

The Saudis were playing it close to the vest. A major policy statement was forthcoming in the aftermath of the tragic incident at Mecca and only the Royal government and the Saudi Ambassador knew its content. Even the White House had been kept in the dark on an official level, although the back channel talk pointed to a nightmare scenario.

The CNN reporter finished her brief introduction and the press room went silent as the Saudi Ambassador prepared to make his state-ment. He read from a single sheet of paper in a monotone voice, never once making eye contact with his audience of reporters.

"Saudi Arabia considers the unfortunate incident in the Holy City yesterday a tragic case of misguided judgment on the part of a few individuals. The Royal Family accepts the profound apologies of the President and heads of the U.S. Military in the spirit of peace and conciliation intended."

The Ambassador paused to weigh his statement one last time. Prince gave a hopeful look to Samantha. It melted as the Ambassador read the next paragraph into the bank of microphones.

"However sincere the apologies might be, the fact remains that the Holy City of all Islam has been desecrated. As such, all children of Allah are desecrated. The outcry has been swift and legitimately harsh and the Royal Family has heard the cries for justice. Therefore, the Saudi Royal Government reluctantly announces the following action, effective immediately."

Prince closed his eyes. Samantha looked over and thought she could see him mouthing the words along with the speaker.

"Until a review of procedure can be completed Saudi Arabia requests the immediate redeployment of the United States Armed Forces to an area outside the Persian Gulf Region. The decision as to where to redeploy belongs unilaterally to the government of the United States and there will be no further input from the Saudi government on this matter."

Prince's expression turned studious. Samantha noticed the change. "What are you listening to?" She asked point blank.

He waved a hand for silence. "Let him finish."

The Ambassador continued. "It has been related to the Saudi government by representatives of Qatar, Oman, Bahrain and the United Arab Emirates that they concur and desire that this statement speak for their respective governments. They will not be briefing the press in the foreseeable future. They also express extreme regret over the incident.

"It is further requested that the diplomatic staffs at United States embassies in all five nations be reduced to minimum status until the situation is resolved. The Saudi Government and its Gulf Region allies do not wish to curtail diplomatic ties with the U.S. but feel this staff reduction is commensurate with the gravity of the situation."

Prince drummed his fingers on the desk. "Come on. Just give me one more statement and we're in," he said to the television screen.

"The Saudi government will honor long-term oil contracts with the United States and will continue good faith negotiations on future contracts. We shall not punish the American citizens for the wayward actions of a few misguided men. There will be no further statements and I will take no questions in this matter. Thank you for your attention." The Saudi Ambassador departed the room under a barrage of questions from the press.

"Yes!" Prince pounded his fist once on the desk. He pressed a button on his intercom. "Did you get all of that, Jan?"

"I'll have a rough transcript in about thirty seconds," came the monotone reply.

"Excuse me," Samantha interrupted. "Did we just watch the same announcement? I could have sworn the Saudi Ambassador just kicked Central Command out of the Persian Gulf. Am I missing something here?"

"They think the whole thing is bullshit. The guy just said as much in diplomatic-ese."

"You've lost me," Samantha said as Janice Arnold entered with a sheet of paper and a video cassette. She put the paper in front of Prince and looked at him sternly. "I don't want to hear a word about spelling or typos. It's the best I could do under the circumstances."

"You are the Queen of Langley," Prince said as he looked over her hastily typed transcript. "Put it on the screen and we can go over it. We'll correlate with the video later."

Janice Arnold was an analyst before she took the promotion to Prince's office. She relished a chance to employ the skills that had enabled her to move through ranks to her position as Executive Assistant: Western Hemisphere Special Operations. It was a title and office few people in the building knew about, never mind anyone outside Langley. Arnold did not care. She was part of the inner sanctum of the intelligence community, and had the respect and confidence of her boss. Right now that was all she wanted in her life.

"Okay, ladies. Let's translate the Ambassador's statement for the folks at home," Prince said in a Game Show voice as Arnold ran the paper through a scanner. Her typed transcript of the press statement appeared on the TV screen.

"Not a single harsh word," Arnold said as she read through the transcript.

"Exactly, Jan," Prince followed up. "Look at the statement, Sam. There is no fiery rhetoric. The Saudi's pass that off on the rest of the Arab nations. Not only that, the ambassador never once refers to American soldiers in Mecca. Where is it? Right there. 'The misguided judgement on the part of a few individuals.' I think that's a signal they believe it was someone else's work."

Samantha was into the analysis. "You're right. The whole statement is conciliatory. All 'regrets, reluctantly, properly resolved.' They don't want any part of this decision do they?"

"The guy is scared to death," Arnold interjected. "He did not look up once in the entire statement. And the part about the diplomatic staff reductions—"

"Bingo! And the other countries four countries are all on board for this," Prince continued. "It's going to leave them wide open and they might not be able to protect our people. They are all going to batten down the hatches and ride this thing out the best they can."

"I can guess where they fear that action might come from," Samantha stated the obvious.

"It's a pretty short list. Two real possibilities. Only one, with all of the internal turmoil in Iraq," Prince replied. "A rough translation probably says 'We're sorry you have to get out for a while but please don't go far and we will get you back in here soon.'"

"That explains the oil contracts. There's that phrase again, 'a few misguided men.'" Arnold was in full analyst mode. "He might as well have said 'Somebody is screwing with our relationship and we want to know who.' We could probably run our own 'op' in there on this one and we'd have their blessing."

"I could not agree more," Prince concurred. "Type a report on everything we just discussed. Put your name on it and I'll put a cover signature on it."

"Mr. Prince, I couldn't do that."

"Why not?" Do you agree with the analysis?"

"Of course I do. But I'm not—"

"You are an analyst. And a damn good one. Remind them what they lost when they made you a glorified secretary. It's made my life a hell of a lot easier but it was the Agency's loss."

Arnold could not remember the last time she blushed uncontrollably. "Thanks, Mike. I'll take care of it right away."

"I'm sure the whole building was watching this. Let's scoop them on it." Prince sent Arnold back to her desk.

Samantha watched the secretary depart and thought she detected a little extra bounce to Arnold's step. "That was really decent of you. How did you learn to be such a good boss?"

"I worked for Dan Harte while I was in college," Prince replied without hesitation. "You'll see what I mean starting late this afternoon when you get to your assignment."

"I'm nervous, you know."

"Don't be. You know who you work for and so will everyone out there, at least on the official level. By the way, you should probably take some evening clothes along. Many people make demands on his free time. He has trouble saying no so he winds up at a lot of dinners and boring official functions. He might ask you to go along."

"Why would he do that?" Her question was sincere but it dripped with naivety.

"Duh! Because he likes you. Look Sam, this is an important assignment but you are allowed to be human. Dan understands the line between business and pleasure. I'm sending you out there because I think you do too. So just be yourself. Everything will be fine.

"Dan once told me that even though it cost him some short term satisfaction he always tried to do the proper thing. I wish I could say that about myself. Hell, as we get older I suspect most men wish they could. It would eliminate a lot of skeletons from our closets. As far as I know, Dan Harte's closet is clean. Enough said."

"I feel like saying 'Thanks, Dad'," Samantha said as she prepared to leave.

"One more thing." Prince stopped her. "Keep everything that went on here today in mind while you are with the Wilson Foundation. Dan was the one who put me onto this line of thought with the Saudis."

"Really?"

"Yeah, when the news report got to that sappy statement by the Iranians, he looked at me and said 'Isn?t that convenient?.' As soon as he said it the thunderbolt struck me. But up till then I was an intelligence basket case. I don't have anything but a hunch to go on with this, but the world is real weird today and nothing surprises me anymore. Know what I mean?"

"More than hectic coincidence, or something like that?"

"Something like that." Before Prince could continue a light on the phone bank started blinking. "Oh Christ."

"Do I want or need to know about this one?" Samantha asked, expecting no reply.

Prince stared thoughtfully at line ten. "You know what I just said about no surprises? This call is a direct line from Moscow."

"Son of a bitch!" Samantha blurted out. She quickly covered her mouth, embarrassed at the expletive.

"I agree. Well so much for my short Saturday work day. Do you have everything you need?"

"I'll be airborne in about an hour."

"Keep me posted. We'll be in touch."

Prince waited for the door to close before lifting the receiver. "Hello?" He cursed to himself for sounding tentative.

"Hello, Mikail. How are you today?"

"I'm up to my ass in other people's shit. Who the hell is this?" He could not place the voice though it sounded vaguely familiar.

"I love your colorful metaphor and having watched CNN myself, I can certainly understand your reply. I am General Viktor Gorki. Do you know me?"

Prince dropped the phone on the desk. He cursed himself again while trying to regain his composure. "I know you, sir. But the question is, are you really you?"

"If it would help we can talk about Beijing."

Prince was convinced. The head of the KGB had hand-delivered information to the Agency that helped the United States extricate

Chinese dissidents in the aftermath of the Tianamen Square riots in 1989. Only Gorki could have known about that. "I thought I recognized your voice, sir, but I had to be sure. My apologies."

"None necessary, Mikail."

"Why are you calling me, sir? I'm a little down the totem pole for the director of KGB to be placing personal phone calls on a Saturday afternoon."

"It is already a cold evening here in Moscow, Mikail. And I called you because your area of expertise is just what is necessary in my situation. You see we have a problem here and we may need the help of people in your field."

"You mean my Agency don't you?" Prince was fishing.

Gorki chuckled nervously into the phone. "No, Mikail. I mean Western Hemisphere Special Operations."

God, he's good, Prince thought. "We don't have a department by that name sir," Prince lied again.

"Be that as it may. The fact remains that we have a problem and you are the one I called. Considering what you claim to be up to your backside in, I believe we might be of assistance to each other."

"You have my attention, General Gorki."

"I thought I might. Let me ask you a question. Have you ever heard of General Anatoly Kasarov?"

Prince sat bolt upright at the mention of the commander in chief of the Russian Western Forces. "Yes, sir. Of course."

"That is the problem I wish to discuss with you, Mikail."

Prince fished a fresh file out of his desk drawer and quickly scribbled the word "KASAROV" across the top. Then he settled back into his chair for what promised to be a most peculiar conversation with the head of the KGB.

MOSCOW, RUSSIA

Kasarov glanced at the half-empty vodka bottle on Cherkin's desk. He noted, with satisfaction, the trembling hand as Cherkin raised the glass of clear liquid to his lips. He will need it, Kasarov thought, and turned his concentration back to the draft of the speech.

"It is an excellent speech, Mr. President," the General announced and handed the draft across the desk to Cherkin. "This is the only way to accomplish what must be done for the country. I wish my approach could have been less confrontational, but I had to follow my convictions. I hope you understand."

Cherkin bit his lip. "I concluded some time ago that drastic action would be necessary. To be honest I am glad you had the courage to come forward with so bold and sweeping a plan. For the first time in a long while I feel good about the future of the country."

Kasarov was taken aback. He expected Cherkin might have to be dragged to the podium to announce the cabinet change. A wave of suspicion washed over the general as he again glanced at the vodka bottle. "Those are most kind words, Mr. President. I applaud your ability to see through the fog of politics and grasp the central point of the matter."

Cherkin saw Kasarov eyeing the half empty bottle and seized the opportunity. "General, would you join me in a drink to our future success." He retrieved another glass from his desk and poured a stiff shot of vodka. You patronizing little weasel, the Russian President thought, as he smiled and slid the glass toward Kasarov. He topped his own glass off with another ounce or so of the Russian national beverage.

"The toast is yours, Mr. President," Kasarov said, in deference to the protocol he was preparing to trample under foot over the next few weeks.

"To our success, and to a much brighter future for Mother Russia," Cherkin said as their glasses clinked together over the center of the desk.

Kasarov downed his shot and exhaled contentedly. His suspicion disappeared as the vodka settled in his stomach and a warm feeling moved through his body. He closed his eyes momentarily, to savor the euphoric afterglow.

Cherkin used every muscle he could muster to control the grimace that tried to overcome his outwardly calm expression. Though his drink was diluted by the almost alcohol-free solution in his glass, the addition of full strength vodka was a harsh reminder that his program of self weaning was already showing signs of success. The very concoction that had numbed his senses to the ongoing crises in his country now caused him such a nauseous feeling that he feared he would vomit and destroy the facade he presented to Kasarov.

His luck held when the general closed his eyes for a moment and missed the shudder that overtook Cherkin as he put his empty glass down. The success of his deception was assured when Kasarov rose to make his exit.

"Mr. President," he announced, "tomorrow we begin putting our house in order. Our actions will set Russia on a course to future greatness. I will do my best to earn the confidence you have placed in me."

Cherkin extended a shaky hand and held on as Kasarov shook it vigorously. He smiled meekly, belying his feelings of utter contempt. "Until tomorrow, General."

"Until tomorrow, Mr. President." Kasarov stepped back from the desk, executed a perfect salute, followed by a tidy about face and marched out of the office.

Cherkin waited to insure he would not be disturbed, then leaned to the side of his desk and vomited with gut-wrenching force into the waste basket. His misery ran unabated for nearly a minute as he disgorged the vodka, which for years had been the source of his political and social courage.

When the wave of nausea eased, he groped for the edge of the desk to right himself. As his vision cleared, he noticed a white handkerchief on the desk. He wiped the effects of his bout with the trash can from his face and the figure of Viktor Gorki came into focus.

"The things we do for Mother Russia," Gorki said dryly.

"I'd rather face the parliament on a recall vote," Cherkin replied, righting himself. He tried to return the handkerchief.

"We will make that a present to you," The KGB director said, pulling his hand back like a child who had just touched a hot stove.

"You are a merciless bastard," Cherkin replied with a shaky laugh.

"It is how many perceive me. What is it that young Western tennis player says? 'Image is everything.'"

"I did not know you played tennis, my friend," Cherkin said, happy for a moment of small talk.

"I don't. But I do play 'image.' And I am very good at it," Gorki replied with a wry smile.

"So you are," the president said. He regained his composure and motioned Gorki to a seat. "Speaking of image what did you think of the little vignette we presented for you?"

Gorki had observed the meeting from behind a two way mirror across the room. "Kasarov is the most dangerous man in Russia. He will stop at nothing to return to the old ways."

"I agree. Where do we go from here?"

"The situation is grave. The Western Army is loyal to him, and he is in contact with many former Soviets. The contacts have been more open lately. I think he is developing a political base along with his military standing. There is but one option, Yuri. He must be stopped."

"There are many pieces to this puzzle," Cherkin said.

"That is true, my friend. How do things go on your side of this equation?" Gorki wanted all facts before he made his proposal.

"Agriculture and Interior understand and will cooperate," Cherkin said with conviction. "The key to everything came from their status reports earlier this week."

Gorki leaned forward. He thought he knew what was coming but he wanted presidential conformation. "Tell me more."

"Interior reports the Caspian Sea oil fields are now on line and will soon be able to deliver to the world market. If Kasarov controls the oil distribution he can refund the military to its former level."

"He would need a major market for that oil," Gorki said, hoping that the president would pick up the trail.

Cherkin was a step ahead of the KGB chief. "Only one customer could initiate a purchase contract of the magnitude Kasarov is looking for."

Gorki decided the President was on the right track. "I have been watching the developing situation in Saudi Arabia with more than a passing interest."

"So have I. Tell me what is on your mind."

Gorki collected his thoughts. "The Americans are not stupid

enough to let such a thing happen. I find the timing curious in the context of what we are dealing with."

Cherkin straightened in his chair. "Do you think Kasarov is involved with the Saudi problem?"

"Not directly. But he could be involved with those who are. If this situation disrupts the American oil supply they will need a new source. What a stroke of luck for them to find a willing supplier in Anatoly Kasarov and his underling at the Russian Interior Ministry. Mr. President, we both know these kind of coincidences do not just happen anymore."

"I am listening," Cherkin said.

"I have contacted a man at CIA. He is mid-level, involved in counter terrorist activities. He is approachable."

"What about his superiors?"

"Our information says they have confidence in him. I am working on a plan to take care of Kasarov and control any backlash from those who are loyal to him. If executed properly it can also alleviate the American crisis in the Persian Gulf. They might be extremely grateful for help like that."

"Tell me more," said Cherkin.

"No, Mr. President," Gorki replied, surprising his friend with a suddenly formal address. "This will be a delicate operation. It could fail miserably. Even if it should succeed some governments may be offended if they find out about it.

"I will run the operation myself and you will be insulated. If we fail, you can disavow me as a renegade and your government will survive. Even if we achieve the desired results, we will not be sending out press releases. The Americans will know what took place and they are the only ones who matter. This might give you a bargaining chip or two at a future Summit meeting."

Cherkin was stunned by his friend's display of loyalty. "But Viktor, I would want you to share the credit in this."

Gorki shook his head slowly and smiled. "No. If this works, the Americans may think that I am a clever fox. It makes my job a lot easier if they think I am a stumbling bureaucrat."

"You are certainly no stumbling bureaucrat, Viktor. And I suspect the Americans already know that." Cherkin said solemnly. "What you are is Russia's most loyal friend. And also mine. Now go to work on your plan."

"I will give you reports so there are no surprises. It is an important time for Russia. The new ways must succeed. I will do my duty and you will be proud of me." Gorki stood to go.

"I already am," Cherkin said as he escorted the KGB chief to the door. The two men shared a brotherly embrace and Gorki left the office to begin his effort to save Mother Russia.

CINCINNATI, OHIO

Harte watched Gansz pull out of the driveway. The agent looked fit and ready to go after a good night's sleep and a day of conferring with the Wilson Foundation. "Is there anything else I should know before I go blindly stumbling along?"

Harmon stood his ground. "That's not fair. He and Barbara came to my hotel room. They said not to tell you anything because some one else had plans for you. They threatened to arrest me on a security violation, for Chrissake. What else was I supposed to do?"

"And now?" Harte trusted his young friend implicitly but decided to let him squirm a little.

"He said once he contacted you, everything was on the table. I'll tell you the truth, Dan. I was prepared to go on with this whether you got on board or not."

"Mike contacted you didn't he?"

Harmon did not hesitate. "Yes. He wanted to bring you in and when I said you might not be too keen on the idea he set up the South Air plan to make sure you got there safely. You might as well know. I've worked on a few domestic ops with him."

"They are not allowed to work inside the U.S. borders," Harte protested.

"Get a grip, Dan. We don't have borders anymore. Washington has taken down the walls. All we have is lines on a map and the bad guys don't read maps too well. Sometimes the lines blurred and Mike has to run an 'Op' here and there. That's just the way it is."

Harte relented. "I know how it is, Billy, and I understand. I just love torturing you."

"Asshole," Harmon replied with a laugh. He peered down the road at an approaching car. "Looks like our babysitter is about to arrive."

The car stopped in front of the house and Samantha got out of the passenger side. Lydia got out of the driver's side and exchanged a knowing glance with Harmon. Harte saw the exchange and assumed there had been some 'girl talk' on the way from the airport.

"What did you bring us, Lyd?" Harmon asked as he pulled Samantha's luggage from the trunk.

"I've brought us Ms. Samantha Schmidt, Billy." Lydia looked around secretively. "She's a spy," she whispered loudly.

Harte walked over and greeted Samantha, "Hi. Welcome to the Cincinnati Mental Zoo. Don't mind the inmates. They tend to be a nosy bunch, by nature. They probably know what was on the menu already," he tried to keep the greeting professional.

"Pasta at Casa Roma on L street." Lydia laughed as she and Harmon entered the house.

Samantha shrugged in resignation. "What can I say? She asked and I said we had dinner."

"I am really glad to see you," Harte blurted out. They both blushed. "Sorry, I'll try not to act like a schoolboy."

Samantha looked around and saw no one. "I'm glad to see you too. Now can we get inside? It is still February, you know."

The slight warm spell and the reunion with Samantha made Harte forget, for the moment, that they were still over three weeks away from the end of winter. "We'll get you situated and introduced to everyone," he said as he led her into the house.

Within an hour Samantha was working alongside Lydia and Rita. While she was not an integral part of the team, no one at the table seemed threatened by her association with Langley. Solving Herbert Loman's coded log book commanded their attention. One more mind working on the problem could only be a plus.

"This is a brick wall as far as I'm concerned," Loman said as he studied the time line chart he had created from his father's log. "Now that we have Albert Simmons on file we at least have a link between Dad's log and Trent's group. But from there it gets pretty foggy.

For nearly a year Dad seems to concentrate on Simmons and SESA. But before that, it's this Fernandez guy. Then, at the end, someone named ER. Once in a while he leaves Simmons to check on the other names. If we are reading this right, they each contact this HB character once. That's all I have to show for two weeks work. I'm stuck."

"Let's approach it from another direction," said Lassick from the far end of the table.

"I'll try anything at this point," Loman said hopefully.

Lassick paced the room. Suddenly, he looked up to find six faces staring at him expectantly. "I'll be right with you guys," he said indignantly. "I think better when I'm walking."

"That explains why the articles you sit and type are so unfocused," Rita sniped good naturedly.

"If you can't think while you're sitting, then who sat and wrote your Pulitzer story?" Harmon joined in the taunting.

"You people are like a bunch of sharks searching for an open wound," Lassick complained.

Samantha looked curiously toward Harte. He shrugged. "That's about how it is around here, Sam. They are not a mutual admiration society." He assumed she saw through his lie.

"Okay, think about this." Lassick had the floor again. "We have four names; Estaban and Carrilo from Mexico, Enzio from Peru and Mondros from Haiti. What do they all have in common?"

"They are all many degrees below normal body temperature and apparent victims of foul play," Lydia answered.

"Arturo Fernandez looks like the perpetrator," Harmon added.

"Forget him for a minute. Concentrate on the victims," Lassick continued. "I did more research and came up with an interesting link. What department of government do you suppose that Enzio, Carrilo and Estaban headed?"

Harte felt his neck hair stand up. "The oil ministry."

Lassick's mouth dropped open. "How did you know? I did a two day Nexis search to find that."

"I didn't." Harte replied. "But a bunch of loose ends just fell together and suddenly I think I know where this is heading. Keep talking, Tim,"

"Dan's right. Not only were they all high-ranking officials in their countries' Oil Ministries, but as Lydia said last week, they were all friends of the U.S. Their successors, on the other hand, are unknown quantities in terms of U.S. relations." Lassick took a seat.

Silence came over the room. Rita broke it as only she could. "Since you are sitting down does this mean you are done thinking for the day?"

"He's right, you know," Lassick said pointing toward Harte.

"About what?" Rita asked innocently.

"You really are a brat."

"Yes, but I'm lovable once you get past that," the JPL computer whiz replied, grinning.

During the exchange Harte walked to the corner of the room and turned on the television. One by one the Foundation members shifted their attention to the ongoing news story. CNN supplied quarter-hour updates from Saudi Arabia on the debarkation of the U.S. Central Command from a deployment that, until last week, seemed as permanent as the Pentagon.

"One word keeps jumping to the front of your mind as you watch this?" Harte said rhetorically as he studied the screen.

"Oil." Samantha's response startled them and brought an abrupt end to her "observer" status.

"Go to the head of the class, Sam." Harte said without looking away from the news story.

Lassick picked up on the implications. "That would have to be a hell of an operation."

"I know. And it could go even beyond what we are seeing," Harte said. "Let's look at the facts. We have three random political assassinations that could, to some degree, destabilize the oil markets. Then a major problem arises with the number one supplier in the world and its biggest trading partner. Am I the only one that finds that a bit peculiar?"

"How does Mondros fit in?" Rita abandoned her cutting humor.

"Haiti is our on going Western Hemisphere nightmare." Samantha spoke up and all eyes turned her way. She was officially part of the team. "I'm not saying a situation exists here, but if I wanted to divert U.S. attention in its own back yard, the number one way is to cause turmoil in Haiti. And for the record, the Mondros assassination put the administration in a tizzy they still haven't recovered from. They had the agency assign assets down there that some of us didn't know were still active."

"What did you come up with?" Lydia asked and then recoiled slightly thinking she had crossed a security line.

"Relax, Lydia," Samantha said. "You have the same answer we came up with: Arturo Fernandez; description undetermined, where-abouts unknown. We could have just called you and saved a lot of time." Her frustration was obvious.

Harte took the lead. "Billy, do you remember my walk in the Everglades with Trent? Everything was nice and friendly. You know, his goals, the Foundation's interest and all that. About the last ten minutes or so, he launched into this dire speech about the evil big oil companies. He became incredibly focused. It was a little scary."

"You know how his wife died?" Lassick interjected.

"I know all that," Harte said in a troubled tone. "But this went beyond grief. I mean, he seemed obsessed. It sounded like Captain Ahab talking about that damned whale."

"Jesus Christ!" Harmon nearly shouted the words as a thought hit him like a thunderbolt. "Barbara told me that SESA was moving their camp to Louisiana. If Trent has decided to screw with the oil companies, either his timing is incredibly lucky or he and his operation are a part of everything we are talking about here."

"I don't follow you," Harte said trying to catch up with the line of thought.

"We have to get down to Louisiana so you can talk to Chuck Haisley. He can explain it."

"Who is Chuck Haisley?"

"I told you about him on the flight to Naples. He is one of the engineers in charge of the flood control project on the Lower Mississippi River. It's too much to go over again now but if we pay him a visit you will understand exactly what I mean."

"Oh yeah. I kind of remember. But to tell the truth, Billy, I didn't pay much attention to anything on that flight," Harte said apologetically.

"No shit. You didn't even notice her." Harmon pointed to Samantha as he taunted his best friend.

Harte looked at Samantha. A sheepish expression came over him. "I don't suppose you would believe I did notice and was just being cool." His embarrassed look belied the fact that he really wished that he was telling the truth.

"You're just lucky that she offered you a ride to Washington and gave you a second chance," Harmon continued his needling.

Loman brought them all back to the matter at hand. "If anyone is interested, I have a synopsis of what we just discussed. You may find it a little disturbing."

"Give it to us, Andy," Harte encouraged.

"According to my correlation, and remember this is just a theory, we have a two year conspiracy involving assassinations in Latin America, diplomatic upheaval in the Persian Gulf, and the possible targeting of U.S. oil supplies. And it looks like the work of four guys whose initials are ER, AF, HB and AS. And the only identity we are reasonably certain of is AS, who might be Albert Simmons of SESA. If nothing else it's a staring point."

"I thought from the tone of your voice that it was going to be something significant." Rita Lowry was back in character, but her comment brought only forced chuckles. Everyone focused in on Loman's analysis and Lassick's hypothesis. An acute sense of sobriety covered the room.

"We don't have a lick of hard evidence to prove that any of this is true," Harte said. "But I see too much coincidence to discount it. Unfortunately no law enforcement agency in the country would get involved on this alone. If we pursue this angle we will be totally independent of the authorities. With luck we can find proof and get someone to come on board in time to prevent any major damage."

Samantha was busy studying the printout of Herbert Loman's log. "I have enough evidence." Six pairs of eyes stared a hole through her, making her terribly uneasy. Shaking the feeling off she continued. "There are two Beirut entries. That in itself just screams the word 'terrorist' at me. I'm not sure who HB is but if Mr. Loman was on an assignment for Mike Prince, I'd bet he at least marked the guy as a member of a terrorist organization. He may have just noticed him in passing or he might have actually spotted him with 'ER.'

"Wait a minute." She sat bolt upright. "Last month we had a guy on South Air out of New Orleans named Gene Russell. I marked him because he paid cash for the flight. When we landed at Tampa he made a long distance call from the airport pay phone. I checked the time and he hung up before an operator could break in. That told me he didn't want the other party to know that he was at a pay phone."

"Did you say Gene Russell?" Harte asked.

She beat him to the punch. "Yes I did. And yes it could certainly be Eugene Russell." She smiled proudly and looked around the room.

"Two down and two to go folks. Good work, Sam," Loman said as he entered "Eugene Russell" into the slots on the log marked "ER." "Now all we have to do is find out who the guy is and we will have something to work with."

"Let's take a break. I don't want anyone to overload on this stuff," Harte said. Some of them looked a little ragged.

"In case you hadn't noticed, it's 11:30. I'm taking a break in the bedroom until tomorrow morning." Lydia's announcement caught them all by surprise. No one had glanced at a clock for hours. The reality of time hit them, and their energy seemed to instantly drain. Within ten minutes everyone had made their way to their respective sleeping quarters.

Harte and Samantha were the last ones to leave the room and they walked slowly toward the door of the guest room Samantha shared with Lydia. "You did a great job in there this evening," he said as they stopped at the bedroom door.

"They are a good group. I felt like I fit in," she replied, as she leaned against the door frame. The exhaustion of her long travel day and the session in the dining room was quickly catching up with her.

He kissed her lightly on the cheek. "See you at breakfast. You've earned a good night's sleep."

"See you in the morning," she whispered as he walked down the hallway to his room.

At his bedroom door Harte, on a whim, looked back up the hall. Samantha was still leaning against the door frame smiling just as she had been at her front door in Rosslyn. She gave him a gentle wave of the hand and disappeared through the doorway.

Harte entered his room. He was sure that his dreams would not be dominated by his problems with Morgan Trent.

"He's a good man, Sam."

Samantha was startled by Lydia's voice as she turned into the room. She relaxed on one of the twin beds facing Lydia who sat with a book in her lap.

"That's an understatement. Does he have a white horse tied up out back?" She was tentative. In spite of their conversation during the ride from the airport she wondered if she might be trampling on the history professor's feelings.

"You would think so," Lydia replied. "I know there is no man I respect more than Dan Harte. When I first joined the Foundation I developed something of a crush on him. One night, in my own academic way, I hinted that I was available and interested. He told me he viewed us on a different level and couldn't do a one night stand with me. Of course I was totally disappointed and frustrated at first. Then I started thinking with my brain and realized that it was about the nicest thing a man had ever said to me.

"He is one of my best friends and easily my most valued colleague. I would not trade the relationship we have now for anything. If I wasn't such an academic, there's that word again, I would envy you. Sleep well, Samantha Schmidt. Somebody smiled on you this week."

"Good night, Lydia. And thank You."

"Don't mention it. It was as much for him as it was for you." Lydia turned out the light and the day's events overcame them both in a matter of minutes.

OLD RIVER AREA, LOUISIANA

"You can't do that! It will screw the entire system...Yeah, fine. Get back to me. That will be a big help." Haisley slammed the receiver down in disgust.

Roosevelt and McMahon looked up from the charts they were studying. "Bad news, huh?" McMahon ventured.

"They just opened the gates at Barkley and Kentucky Lakes. The system is full and they have to bleed it off. You might as well forget about the Missouri for now. It isn't going anywhere until the Ohio is done." Haisley studied the wall map of the United States. He focused on Western Kentucky at a point near the confluence of the Ohio and Mississippi rivers.

The huge lakes behind Barkley and Kentucky Dams were full to the brim. Most of the year they provide recreation and drinking water for the citizens of western Kentucky and Tennessee. During flood season on the Ohio River, five miles to the north, the dams create a holding tank for the Cumberland and Tennessee rivers until the Ohio returns to normal levels.

But the situation had become desperate. The thaw and massive runoff in the eastern U.S. overwhelmed the system from both sides. The Tennessee and Cumberland were pouring water into the lakes from the south. The bulging Ohio had filled the two dams' outflow channels. The water level rose steadily against the north face of the structures' flood control gates, forcing the Corps of Engineers to open the gates of both dams and drop the lake levels to an acceptable depth.

By doing so, the Corps saved the area around the lakes and the two river basins from catastrophic flooding as the weight of the water bulled its way into the outflow channels. But as the cliche goes, "for every action there is a reaction." Towns and villages along the last sixty miles of the Ohio River were now at the mercy of Mother Nature.

"How far did they open the gates?" Roosevelt asked.

Haisley shook his head. "They wouldn't say exactly. But they apologized and wished us good luck. What does that tell you?"

"They probably just doubled the discharge of the Ohio. How long do you think we have?" McMahon looked over his silt level readings.

"A week. Possibly ten days." Haisley continued to stare at the map, as if trying to will the situation to change. "I need to get out of here for a while. I'm going to make my rounds. Anybody want to come along?"

Roosevelt grabbed a clipboard from the wall. "I'll go with you. I can use the fresh air."

"I'll check these readings and watch the phones," McMahon said. "The calls should start coming in pretty quick."

"Good thinking, Henry. If it's anything important we will be over on the Auxiliary Structure. Come on, Aaron. Let's get the hell out of here."

When Haisley and Roosevelt had pulled away from the office, McMahon reached for the telephone. He had a quick personal call to make before the lines got tied up with official messages. After two rings an answering machine gave a generic message. "A week to ten days," McMahon said. He hung up and waited for the official calls to start.

Within minutes after the gates holding back Lake Barkley and Kentucky Lake cranked open, a seething wall of water churned through the outflow channels heading rapidly north. The already flooded Ohio River received an extra 600,000 cubic feet per second of flow from the Tennessee and Cumberland Rivers. The river level rose two feet in the first five minutes with the infusion of new water. The force of the outflow pushed the current speed to over fifteen miles per hour as the initial "bubble" careened toward Paducah.

The old weir dams at Paducah and Olmstead disappeared under a torrent that pushed relentlessly toward the confluence of the Ohio and Mississippi Rivers near Cairo, Illinois. At Olmstead, a fifty foot coffer dam protecting the construction site of a new lock system, was completely inundated.

At Cairo, the river gauge on the town's eastern riverfront disappeared under the rising river, its highest reading of forty eight feet lost under swirling waters. The town nearly vanished as the Ohio and Mississippi rivers came together a mile above the normal confluence. A two story observation building at "Confluence Park", at the extreme southern tip of Illinois, disappeared in a matter of minutes under the surging flood.

The additional water, coupled with the already high volume of flow, brought the Ohio's discharge rate to beyond the catastrophic level. By mid morning nearly one million cubic feet per second, more than either of the previous worst floods in 1973 and 1984, poured from the mouth of the Ohio into the already swollen Mississippi and headed south.

Chapter IX

LANGLEY, VIRGINIA

"I can't believe we are doing this." Prince could only shake his head as the news unfolded on the TV screen. The report originated from the U.S. military installation at Dhahran on the Persian Gulf coast of Saudi Arabia. A reporter spoke in grave tones, while the camera showed soldiers and equipment loading onto transports at the dock.

"On the pier behind me a scene is unfolding which must be considered a watershed moment in the dramatic and often volatile history of the Persian Gulf region."

"He tosses that word 'watershed' around a lot," the man across the desk from Prince said unemotionally.

The reporter continued. "As a result of the tragic events in Mecca three days ago, United States military units deployed in the Persian Gulf since Operation Desert Storm have been summarily evicted by the Royal Saudi government. In addition to Saudi Arabia, units in

Bahrain and Qatar are also redeploying as the famed U.S. Central Command complies with similar notices issued by the respective governments of those small Persian Gulf Emirates and the collective Arab world."

The accompanying tape jumped to ports throughout the Persian Gulf as CNN's electronic eyes captured, for the world, the sight of the mass embarkation of the U.S. forces and their equipment.

The camera shot returned to the reporter. "In a surprising snub to the majority of Arab governments, Kuwait has requested that Central Command keep a detachment of tanks and combat planes 'in country.' The Kuwaitis want the force as a deterrent to Iraq, whose compliance with terms of the Gulf War cease-fire, and U.N. resolutions in general, has been less than acceptable. In a rare show of pragmatism the collective Arab governments acceded to the request, but have asked for and received assurances that U.S. activity in the area will be kept to a minimum."

Arthur Henderson looked away from the screen. "I've seen enough. What do you think is going on over there?" At age fifty, Henderson ran the International Special Operations Division of the CIA. He was Prince's direct superior and coordinated Agency counter terrorist activities around the world. He was visiting Prince in response to a "heads up" on the call from Victor Gorki the day before, in addition to the problems in the Gulf.

"This sucks, Arthur," Prince replied succinctly.

"That's a really strategic analysis." Henderson chided his young colleague good naturedly.

"Sorry, but that's my first impression. It looks pretty cut and dried on the surface but the whole thing just stinks to high heaven."

"How so?" Henderson probed.

"There is no way four American soldiers simply wandered into Mecca and raped and killed two women. I don't think the Saudis believe it either. The ambassador practically begged us to stay within earshot."

Henderson nodded in agreement. "I figure they were kidnaped while on a weekend liberty. We should be getting their unit location pretty soon. Maybe that will shed a little light on it. They were probably drugged and whoever did it killed the women and arranged for the crowd to be there when our guys came to. In my opinion the entire thing was orchestrated to get the exact result we are watching."

"I agree completely."

"So where do we go from here?" Henderson asked.

"We could run a counter-op inside Saudi Arabia. It probably wouldn't do any good though, since the Saudis had nothing to do with this." Prince stared at the wall. "We better concentrate on what might happen when we get out of there. We are laying the largest oil reserves on earth bare to the world. Anyone who thinks they can handle the Saudi military can take their shot. We have to figure out who that might be and how we can stop it from happening."

"My short list contained one name the last time I looked."

"Same here, Arthur. I don't care what the politicians say. We can't let them have those oil fields."

"Then it's time to shit or flush." Henderson leaned back.

Prince picked up the phone, pushed line ten and exchanged a silent glance with his boss as the connection worked through. "Hello, General Gorki. This is Michael Prince. I have a visitor here. Arthur Henderson. Will it be alright if he joins us in a conference call?" Prince looked incredulously at Henderson as he returned the receiver to its cradle.

"Hello, Viktor. It has been a long time."

"Hello, Arthur. I have not seen you since Iceland in '86."

"Yes you have. You just didn't realize it," Henderson said with a chuckle. "And I'm sure I've seen you or at least your handiwork, since then."

"We are both sly old foxes are we not?" Gorki replied.

"Yes," Henderson said, "but I think we must be more sly than ever this time. If what Michael says is true, we must fool many people and we must do it together."

"I think so too, Arthur. Mikail, have you briefed your boss completely on our talk yesterday?"

"Yes, sir. We are all up to speed here."

"Good. I have watched your developing problems in the Persian Gulf on the television. Things do not go well for you there, I fear."

"You aren't gloating, are you?" Henderson asked.

"No, no, my friend, far from it. The problem is grave and I think it may be related to my problem here in Russia. I did some snooping and found an interesting thing. Not so long ago General Kasarov flew down to the Southern Provinces on a routine inspection. There was a brief period where he was off his official schedule and incommunicado. I have managed to find someone who confirmed that the he made an unscheduled short trip across the southern border."

"Iran," Prince blurted out.

"You get an A in geography class, my young friend," Gorki said. "He was not there very long but you can accomplish much in a short time if you know where to go and who to see."

"Victor, this is serious stuff," Henderson took over. "If Kasarov had an unsanctioned meeting with Iranian officials we are looking at a conspiracy with world wide repercussions."

"Arthur, it seems that you and I never do things in a small way," Gorki said in confirmation. "Perhaps now you understand how your problem in Saudi Arabia might be related to our problem here."

"Just how bad is it there?" Henderson asked.

"There will be an announcement from Moscow today. Consider that the change is far more sweeping than the words imply. I will give you time to weigh the information, along with what I have told you and then get back to you. If you see things my way we can proceed."

"Can't you at least give us something to go on?" Prince nearly pleaded into the speaker.

"I'm sorry, Mikail. You must draw your own conclusions before I initiate anything. It is important that we all enter this by our own decision making process. Then there can be no turning back as things unfold. Please understand this. I believe you know what I mean, Arthur."

"Yes, Viktor. You can count on my honest assessment."

"That is all I ask. My problem must be dealt with, and I hope to avoid a blood bath. You must deal with your problems. If we can solve these things together then that will be good. If not we will both do our best and, how is it you used to say, 'our asses will be hanging out there.'"

"That's close enough, Viktor. We will be in contact." Henderson indicated that the call was finished.

"Till we speak again, my friends," Gorki finished as Prince cut the call off.

Henderson was up and pacing. "Mike, everything else just went off the table, including the Loman case."

Prince looked troubled. "I have a civilian working on that. And he is a friend of mine."

"Not anymore. As far as we are concerned he is an operative on his own. You can let him know that if you want. I'll give you that much. But as of now," Henderson pointed emphatically toward the CNN story on the television. "this is the only operation we are concerned with."

"It's that big?" Prince asked, knowing the answer.

"I've known Victor Gorki, both as an enemy and once in a while as an associate for twenty years. In all that time I've never known him to be truly scared until just a minute ago. Keep me up to speed on this. I have to get the ball rolling on some things." Henderson left the room.

Prince stared at the television. He did not really see the pictures or hear the words. His mind raced to sort out everything that had just transpired.

NAPLES, FLORIDA

Gansz drove slowly down Route 29, watching for the side road Barbara Davaron had described. All he wanted was a quick look around Trent's compound. After his meeting with the Wilson Foundation he pretty much discarded the Bureau's "passive monitoring" orders. Though Barbara's descriptions had been helpful Gansz needed a firsthand look. He had learned the rule early. No matter how good the source do not rely on second hand information if you can view the problem. The time had come to "view the problem."

His cover was simple. Newly arrived in Naples, he had read Trent's newsletter often while living in Birmingham, Alabama. All he wanted to do was help out in any way he could. A Sunday visit eliminated suspicion concerning taking a day off work. It might also mean the camp would be more sparsely populated than usual but he felt the trade off was worth it. At this point the camp's logistics were far more important to him than the people.

A side road appeared to the left. Gansz checked his mileage and found it matched Davaron's information. He turned and, according to her instructions, immediately looked for a place to park. Before he realized it he came to a clearing and slammed on the breaks.

The camp was gone. A quick scan showed not a tent, piece of equipment or human being in sight. SESA had vanished almost without a trace. Gansz's first impulse was to assume that he had the wrong road. Barbara said the camp would be visible before he reached the clearing.

Once out of the car he saw evidence of human activity that confirmed that he had the right location. Worn spots marked the former locations of tents and equipment. Newly covered holes marked what Gansz assumed to be the final resting place of SESA's the waste products. He considered unearthing it to see if there were clues in the trash. The thought of digging into the wrong hole removed the idea quickly. Besides, he thought, if Morgan Trent was on a mission of foul play, the chances of his leaving a clue behind were slim at best.

Gansz sat on a log and considered his next move. He figured that the SESA crowd was on their way to, or possibly already in Louisiana. The first order of business would be to alert Harte to this new development. After that a return trip to Huntsville, Alabama, was in order.

Until now, he had resisted contacting Sgt. John Dutton of the Huntsville Police to see if he could be of any help. Gansz knew the detective did not appreciate being taken off the Loman case. He hoped Dutton was one of those curious cops who just could not leave things well enough alone. Most of the time those guys became a pain in the ass to the Bureau. But Gansz was looking for just that kind of persistence on this case. He decided, as an afterthought, to pay a visit to Richard Willis at National Electronics.

CHATTAHOOCEE, FLORIDA

Simmons sat against a palm tree eating his sandwich. In front of him the Apalachicola River meandered by. From the looks on the faces of the SESA members sitting around the rest stop, the break had come at the right time. The middle of the night departure from Naples had caused grousing among the troops. Eight more hours of drive time awaited.

At Simmons' urging, Kennedy, Reilly, and Hector resisted the impulse to sit apart from the group. The three proteges moved around the rest area, chatting idly with the others. Simmons was determined that no one would feel left out. One bruised ego could unravel a year of planning.

Even the normally useless Barbara Davaron had been afforded the chance to feel like a contributor. The food break, near a town Simmons had never heard of, by a river whose name he could not hope to spell, had come at her urging. He watched her move from cluster to cluster of people, offering a sandwich here, sharing a lazy laugh there. She was like a nurse mother to the young idealists as they lolled in the morning sun.

The thought again crossed Simmons' mind that this stupid blond had a knack for doing the right thing at the right time. As he added up her contributions he kept coming back to the lounge and the men from the Wilson Foundation. He could not put his finger on the problem, but he knew she was a loose end that needed tying.

"Great day for a picnic, Al." Davaron said as she approached him.

"You picked a good place to stop, Barbara," He replied, surprised again at his sincerity.

"Another sandwich?"

Simmons looked around furtively. "You got any roast beef in there? All we ever eat is chicken and fish and those stupid vegetable sandwich things. Sometimes I go into town just to eat red meat."

Davaron dug to the bottom of her cooler. "Here you go. Roast beef and swiss on rye with mayo. I made two, assuming someone else would want to indulge." She handed over a sandwich and opened the other for herself. "You know we will both be ostracized for this if anyone finds out."

Through his chuckle Simmons noted her expanded vocabulary. She usually had the conversational level of a high school graduate who didn't pay attention in English class. Once again he determined that Davaron was more than the dizzy blond everyone was accustomed to. He kept up the small talk, all the while confirming that his original plan for her disposition was correct.

"You better save some of that food. We probably won't reach our new campsite until the early evening. As you figured, we might not have enough time to set up the equipment and cook dinner. That was good thinking."

Davaron blushed at the compliment. "If you guess often enough, you are bound to be right once or twice."

"You have been right more than once or twice, Barbara. I may not say it very often but I consider you an asset. And I am glad you decided to come along with us."

The alarm bell rang in Davaron's head. Simmons had again gone out of his way to make her feel welcome. She put herself in character. "Well thank you, Al. I just hope I can help."

"Hey, Barbara! You got any more food?" The call from Kennedy broke the awkwardness of the moment.

"Duty calls," Davaron said, grateful for the interruption. She picked up her cooler and crossed the rest area, hoping Simmons did not notice her sigh of relief as she walked away.

Simmons stared at the river. He tossed the last bit of his sandwich into the water. A fish struck it causing him to jump. "It won't be that quick for you, bitch," he mumbled as he stood and prepared for the final leg of the drive to Louisiana.

CINCINNATI, OHIO

Harte, Samantha and Harmon picked at their breakfast amid idle conversation. Across the spacious great room Loman, Lowry, Lassick and Rogers lounged around the television reading various news publications and watching the Sunday pundit shows. All the shows focused on the U.S. withdrawal from the Persian Gulf. Only the "talking heads" varied from network to network.

The venerable commentator on the screen announced the show's theme and guests. When the camera focused on the mild-mannered man with the bow tie, a collective cheer went up from the area around the television. Harte noted the surprised look on Samantha's face. When the dark-haired firebrand reporter came on the screen a cascade of boos replaced the cheers.

"Did you teach them this?" Samantha prodded good-naturedly.

"No. But I think I secretly used reaction to this panel as a litmus test," Harte replied, only half-joking.

Samantha shook her head and smiled.

"Before we get into our discussion, here is some other news since the morning papers," said the senior correspondent on the television screen. "In the eastern United States, the surprising warm spell has led to spot gasoline shortages as people take advantage of the nice weather and get in some early weekend getaway trips.

"An oil industry spokesperson said there is no need for alarm. Refineries are presently switching over to gasoline from heating oil and everything should be back to capacity in a week. Demand such as this weekend's does not usually occur for another two or three weeks. He urged people not to panic. The gasoline supply is not in jeopardy.

"Elsewhere, President Yuri Cherkin in Moscow announced a major cabinet change today by appointing General Anatoly Kasarov the new Defense Minister. Kasarov, a veteran of the Afghanistan campaign, recently supervised the redeployment of the Russian Western Forces from the former Warsaw Pact countries and the newly independent republics of the former Soviet Union.

"While Kasarov is thought by Western analysts to be an eminently qualified military leader, some observers expressed surprise at the promotion. They consider him to be one of the old-liners who argued bitterly against the breakup of the Soviet Union and the ensuing troop pullout. Others see him as a soldier who simply tried to protect his 'turf' as all dedicated military men should. They note that since the redeployment, Kasarov has toed the government line loyally. We will keep you informed.

"And now to our guests and today's topic..."

"That should keep Mike Prince on his toes for a while," Harmon said, as he left the table for a closer look at the talk show.

Samantha brought her coffee cup to her mouth to prevent Harte from noticing her frown. The move failed.

"I hope that is due to an Agency problem and not the coffee or the company," Harte said in an effort to break the silence.

"The company and the coffee are just fine," she replied weakly. "That news report bothered me."

Harte took the lead. He put his finger on the table and drew an imaginary line between them. "This is agency business," he said pointing to Samantha's side of the line. "This is our situation." He indicated the area on his side of the line. "I do not cross this line unless invited. You cross it only when you think it necessary. I have no problem with that and neither should you. If you want to be alone I'll join the peanut gallery over there and harass some reporters on TV."

Samantha looked around quickly and leaned a little toward him. "While Mike was briefing me on this assignment his phone rang and he turned sheet-white. He told me the call was on the direct Moscow line. I left before he took the call."

She was clearly troubled. "They know his specialty. I'm sure they have a dossier on him. I keep thinking that the call was not related to the Gulf, at least directly. They would have called another department or at least, his boss."

"You don't have to continue this, you know," Harte said and redrew the imaginary line on the table.

"Yes I do." She collected her thoughts. "I believe the call was a 'heads up' on the Kasarov promotion."

"Why call Mike?" Harte crossed the line with the question, figuring she would send him back if she wanted to.

"Mike eliminates terrorist problems for people." Silence ruled the table.

Harte rubbed his forehead. "Do I want you to explain that?" he asked without looking up.

"The statement is self-explanatory," Samantha said solemnly.

Harte looked around the room and took a deep breath. "That certainly adds spice to the chili doesn't it."

"Dan, if this changes your feelings on what we are doing here, I can get you out of this. It won't be a—"

Harte interrupted her. "Listen, I could have backed out when I realized Herb Loman's death was more than an accident. I knew then there were risks. And when Dutton and Willis nudged me in certain directions it was my choice to go forward."

He thought about the discussion with Prince and suddenly things came into crystal clear focus. "I worked for NSA in the Marine Corps You probably know that already. No matter what other bullshit things went on, I could always walk away from my work station feeling like what I did made a difference in the world that day. I never forgot that feeling and the pride that came with it. And nothing I have done since has come close to measuring up to it."

Samantha frowned. "Yes, I have seen your dossier. You've done a lot of worthwhile things and made a difference in a lot of lives over the last few years." She pointed to the group around the television. "Doesn't that matter?"

"Of course. It matters a lot. These people motivate me. But this is different. Maybe I'm trying to answer some nagging inner question or something. Look, Sam, I've had a few 'what ifs' in my time and if I walk away from this one it will haunt me for the rest of my life.

"Someone I have confidence in has returned that trust and asked me to do a service to the country. If I stop now, all that I have ever stood for is philosophically invalid. I hope you can understand that."

She reached out and touched his hand. "Understand? They should post that on every office wall at the Agency. We have had our last discussion on the matter as far as I'm concerned. But what about them?" Again she pointed across the room.

"Tell them your concerns. I'll stand by their decision."

"Are you that confident in them?"

"Completely," Harte said without hesitation.

Suddenly a thought struck him. "Sam, do you think Mike let you know about the phone call assuming you would eventually tell me about it?"

"Officially, no. But he has to figure we will talk about things. It's funny. He drew a line just like you did in terms of my duties here. And I got the feeling that he deliberately made it blurry."

Across the room Rita picked up the telephone after one ring. "Hey, Dan. It's George Gansz. He says it's important."

Harte and Samantha exchanged a puzzled look as he crossed the room. "What's up, George?...No shit! When...Good idea...You bet. You do the same."

He looked back to Samantha once more. "Listen up, everyone. SESA is on the move. George Gansz just got back from their camp near Naples and there wasn't a scrap of paper in sight. Let's get ourselves together and figure out where we go from here." He weighed his next statement.

"You should know that we may be getting into some pretty high level stuff here. A lot of strange things are happening around the world right now. I want to work under the assumption that these events might be related."

After a brief silence, Rita leapt from the couch and headed for the dining room. "All right, let's get it in gear."

Harmon and Samantha joined Harte as the others filed out of the room. "Dan, we really do have to go to Louisiana. I've been working on an angle to all of this. You have to talk to my friend at the Corps of Engineers."

Harte recognized the serious tone in Harmon's voice. "We leave tomorrow morning, Billy. Pack enough to stay awhile. I'm not coming back until we find Trent."

"I want to come along but Mike will not allow it," Samantha said. "I can coordinate things here and keep you up to speed."

"That will work. I want to be a step ahead of everything, not running along to catch up. Let's get to it."

SIMMESPORT, LOUISIANA

Reilly turned off the levee road and maneuvered the Land Rover through standing water. Just past the tree line he stopped and let his passengers look back.

"Nice touch," said Trent as the water reformed, covering the Land Rover's tracks and the roadbed.

"We thought so, Mr. Trent," Reilly replied with a grin.

"Let's see the camp." Trent patted Maria's knee gently.

Simmons completed his inspection of the new SESA base camp. The tents were ready for occupation. He wanted to change the configuration, but Trent insisted on the same semicircular array they employed outside of Naples. The only consolation came in the form of some tall trees growing on the high ground he had chosen for the encampment.

The sound of an approaching vehicle brought everything to a standstill. Simmons noted the group's reaction with satisfaction. Even Barbara Davaron appeared on guard, looking down the trail toward the oncoming sound.

Amy Hector, stationed thirty yards up the trail, signaled "all clear" back to the camp. She waved at Trent as the vehicle slowly passed her position. He unconsciously returned the gesture while continuing to survey the surroundings.

Everyone gathered as Trent crossed the compound. He stood under a tree in the middle of the camp and signaled for quiet.

"Ladies and gentlemen, congratulations on a job well done. From this spot we take our place in history. If we all do our parts, SESA's actions will mark the moment when the human race began the task of returning earth to nature. Our objective is to deal a crippling blow to the foundation of man's technological assault on the environment; the evil oil empire. No person or thing will stand in the way of our final goal.

"Always remember that a greater good will come from what we do. Discard any personal qualms that may arise at the moment of action. Dispel any inner questions and do what is necessary for the success of the plan. Earth's survival depends on us doing our duty to our maximum ability. The mission begins now."

Cheers and applause broke out. The cheers coagulated into a one-word chant. "Trent! Trent! Trent!" they shouted in unison accompanied by rhythmic hand clapping. He basked in the adulation. Were it not for his all-consuming desire for revenge, he might even have believed what he had just told his followers. With a wave he turned from the crowd and entered his tent.

Davaron clapped and shouted along with them. She made sure her gestures and expression sent the right message to any eyes that might be watching. Her mind worked desperately to come up with a plan.

Trent's speech, while not specific, confirmed to her that SESA planned to take militant action somewhere in the bayous of Louisiana. Nothing could be gained by sabotaging a few nearby oil wells. The plan had to involve large-scale disruption of the industry itself— in production, refining and delivery.

The group dispersed and returned to work. Davaron tended to her duties around the cooking facilities. The work afforded her time to try to figure out what SESA was up to. She assumed that once the action began, the presidential restraining order went out the window and the authorities would step in. Trent and Simmons had to know that the window of opportunity would slam shut almost immediately.

She had caught glimpses of weapons around the camp, only rifles and handguns. They were not the tools with which someone did major damage to a behemoth like the Louisiana oil and gas industry. Something was missing. Until she could identify that missing element her considerations meant nothing.

As Davaron leaned over a crate of produce a hand came to rest on her shoulder. She jerked slightly and muffled a cry of shock. Getting into character, she turned to confront what she assumed would be the grinning face of Simmons. "You scared me to death...Mark," she said in genuine surprise to Mark Rodvick, one of Simmons' proteges.

Rodvick seemed pleasant but often showed her far more attention than she was comfortable with. She controlled the feeling of uneasiness. "I was so wrapped up in counting oranges I almost forgot about everyone else."

"Sorry, Barbara. I just wanted to say thanks for packing extra food. By the time we got everything unloaded and set up last night, nobody wanted to screw with cooking. Everyone was grateful."

Davaron was taken aback by the gesture. "Thank you, Mark."

"You're welcome." Rodvick hesitated for a moment. "Do you think I could have an orange?" he asked with a schoolboy look.

Davaron retrieved an orange from the crate. "All you had to do was ask. You didn't have to butter me up with all that talk." She chastised him gently.

"I meant what I said, Barbara. The orange was an afterthought." He smiled warmly again. "I'll see you later."

Davaron returned to her work, still on guard but feeling a little more welcome than before.

Simmons stood near the entrance to Trent's tent. He caught Rodvick's signal as the young man crossed the compound peeling the orange. Simmons returned a nod and entered the tent to find Trent studying the blueprints on his work table. "Everything is on schedule, Mr. Trent. The supplies have been topped off and we can go a month, if you want, without going into the community. It wouldn't bother me, but I think some of them will go stir crazy with no outside contact. I'll arrange trips into town just to get them off site for a while."

Simmons put a map of Louisiana over the blue print. "Look here. We are a quarter mile west of the Atchafalaya River. The target is a ten or fifteen minute drive away, but only five miles northeast as the crow flies. You and I should drive over there so you can get the area down. We can take Tom with us. Mark should probably go along so he can take a good look at the crane. I'll go over with Jim and Amy a day or so later."

"Good plan." Trent moved the map and went back to the blueprint. "What about the other supplies?"

"They arrive in New Orleans in two days."

"We can't have any problems on that end."

"Don't worry. It's under control." Simmons weighed his next statement carefully. "When everything goes down there is a real chance of losing this camp and everything in it. I figured you should know, in case you want to relocate." He braced for Trent's reaction.

Trent considered the point. "Al, we are stepping onto a new level with this action. I see no finer way to end the work of SESA than in this manner. The camp stays here."

Simmons silently exhaled. "That's good enough for me, sir. If you will excuse me it's time for my introductory visit to Mrs. Reese, in Baton Rouge. I may be gone most of the day."

"Take the night off. You've earned it. I won't expect you until tomorrow. You did an admirable job getting everything here and set up. I'm truly grateful."

"Thanks, Mr. Trent. It was a pleasure. I think I'll take you up on that. My last visit to Baton Rouge was not quite a tourist trip. See you tomorrow morning."

LANGLEY, VIRGINIA

Prince disconnected the conference call. "I'm glad it was nothing important," he said, trying to lighten the pall covering the room.

"Those people have some real problems over there, Mike," Henderson said brushing aside Prince's comment.

"Is Gorki serious on this?" Arnold asked incredulously.

"I'm certain of it, Jan," Henderson replied. "I knew something was wrong yesterday when Cherkin announced the change of defense ministers. Karchev is his strongest political and military ally. Hell, he saved Cherkin's ass once during a coup attempt. Cherkin would not let him go voluntarily. Kasarov must be making a political move to take control."

"Arthur, are you talking about a coup?" Prince asked warily.

"Exactly. A bloodless, completely legitimate coup," Henderson replied stoically.

"How do you think Kasarov managed it?" Prince asked.

"Hard telling. But we have to assume the Western Forces figured heavily in the mix."

"He wouldn't bring the tanks into Moscow again would he?" Arnold joined the speculation.

"I doubt it," Henderson replied. Suddenly a cat-like grin crossed his face. "But he could threaten to discharge half of them and leave the western front defenseless."

"No way," Prince said, in obvious disbelief.

"Why not?" Henderson asked matter of factly. "It's a paper army at best. It's been almost two months since our satellites saw so much as a trace of a heat pattern from most of the vehicles. That army is parked."

"It could just be a winter stand down," Arnold suggested.

"Not a chance," Henderson countered. "Estimates say they don't have more than two hundred thousand troops still active out there. Cherkin can't gamble on Kasarov exposing the western front. At least I hope he can't. There are some pretty long memories in the capitals of Russia's neighbors.

"Kasarov would have nothing to lose by making the threat. What's left of the army is loyal to him so Cherkin doesn't dare remove him. So he plays his cards and with luck Cherkin has to fold. I'd bet on that scenario."

"Gorki said there was more to the announcement than meets the eye," Prince said. "He indicated a back room cabinet reshuffle. What do you make of that?"

"Figure it out, Mike. What does an immobile army need?"

The light went on in Prince's head. "Food and fuel. Jesus. Kasarov may have control of Interior and Agriculture too?"

"It would give him all the food and oil he needs for the military." Henderson calmly replied.

"That's back to square one of the Soviet system. Take care of the military first. The civilians get what's left over." Arnold squirmed as she spoke.

"Exactly. And when the civilian population rebels at the lack of supplies, Cherkin is history and Kasarov can run for election with a promise to fill the shortages, and the army to insure victory. No shots fired. Government changed. Thank you very much. Now, about those pesky Americans." Henderson leaned back in his chair.

"That amounts to a restart of the cold war." Prince said.

"Precisely."

Prince was troubled by Henderson's matter-of-fact approach to a potential world crisis. "Is there something else I should know here?"

"It isn't going to happen." Henderson said calmly.

"You seem pretty sure of that." Prince replied, unable to hide his uneasiness.

"If Gorki can get it together on his end we will take care of his problem and in turn, he will help us with our situation in the Persian Gulf. You may not want to know more than that."

"The 'Black Squadron.'" Prince had a feeling this was coming but he had to say it anyway.

"The ball is already rolling."

"Arthur, this is not a drug lord or some paid assassin. Kasarov is a high-ranking official of a foreign government. I don't care how he got his position. It will not sit well with a lot of people."

"Michael, this is the real world." Henderson said tersely. "There will be an oil crisis if things go the way we expect them to in Saudi Arabia. Our sources indicate the Russians have a delivery system in place for their Caspian reserves. Three quarters of the world's oil supply could be in the hands of Iran and a hard line Soviet General in less than a month. Sorry, but I don't have time to worry about who is going to be miffed."

Prince and Arnold knew he was right. But the plan still troubled them greatly.

"If you two are uncomfortable with this you can opt out. Jan, you can go back to that desk out there, no questions asked. Mike, you will come to a moment like this sooner or later if you stay around long enough. There's a job to be done. I will do it with or without you."

"That's exactly what Gorki said yesterday," Prince realized that a moment like this came along, hopefully, just once. All he stood for and worked for pointed to an event such as Henderson was describing. Prince knew he was in. He just needed a little shove in the right direction.

"That's right," Henderson said. "It is how things are done in our world. You make a decision and stick with it, regardless of the consequences."

"Tell us what you need." Arnold read Prince's thoughts and spoke for both of them.

"Good," Henderson replied. "I have to get back to my office and make a few calls. Viktor will want to communicate with me through you, Mike. Jan, make sure there is no record of anything. We'll figure out what kind of report to file later. Keep any information we acquire safe. As far as anyone is concerned, this is a non event."

Prince was back in his analyst mode. "What if this goes farther than the Russian and Persian Gulf thing?"

"I don't know how it can get any bigger." Henderson decided to give Prince a little leeway. "If you think there may be one or more tie-ins to this, run with it. The only rule is this operation does not leave your office."

"Fair enough." Prince replied.

Henderson stood to leave. "Remember. We are the good guys on this one. It's why they pay us the big bucks." He rolled his eyes and left the room.

Prince and Arnold stared at each other across the desk. Again Arnold read his thoughts. "I'll call Samantha once we are up and running on this."

"What would I do without you?"

"You'd manage. But I'd like to think it wouldn't be as easy for you," Arnold replied.

The door closed and Prince was left to consider how his place on the world's chess board had just been dramatically enhanced. He worried that one of his best friends might become a pawn on that board.

Chapter X

HUNTSVILLE, ALABAMA

Dutton took one more look at the red Escort in the rear view mirror as he turned into the parking lot at Baker Precinct. He had noticed the vehicle five minutes earlier and felt better now that he was on police property. His concern turned to curiosity when the Escort pulled into the parking space next to his and the driver waved an acknowledgment. Dutton eyed him suspiciously as they met in the middle of the gravel lot.

"Are you tailing me?" Dutton asked, his alert level high.

"Not at all, Sergeant Dutton. You are Sergeant John Dutton, aren't you?" the man asked nonchalantly.

"Yeah. Do you mind if we get on equal footing in the name department?"

The visitor reached into his sports coat and Dutton tensed. "Relax. It's just ID coming out." He produced a business card. "George Gansz, FBI. We can do the badge-in-the-wallet thing if you want."

Dutton found Gansz's manner somewhat disarming but, in a way he felt even more guarded. "What have I done?" He knew it sounded like a speeding motorist playing stupid but the question just came out.

Gansz chuckled. "Please relax, John. May I call you John?"

Dutton nodded cautiously.

"Good. I'd like to talk to you in private about a case we have in common; the death of Herbert Loman."

Dutton recoiled visibly. "I am no longer assigned to that case."

Gansz sensed the edge in Dutton's response. He took a step toward the precinct house and waited for Dutton to assume the lead. "Yes, I know that. I'm the guy they assigned the case to when they took it away from you. But things are starting to get a little dicey out there and I thought you might be able to help me out. Now, do you think can we talk?"

"I don't see how I can help you, Mr. Gansz."

"Let's find an office somewhere. And call me George."

Dutton relented and led him down the precinct hallway. When they reached his office, Gansz wasted no time. "Do you remember Daniel Harte?"

"Hell, yes. He's a good man."

"Well he has had quite an interesting few weeks since you last spoke to him. Here's the deal, short and sweet. Loman's death may have been a terrorist hit. Harte and his Foundation were checking on an environmental group in Florida which may somehow be related.

"The next thing you know the CIA called him in. They asked him to work the case on his own with no official cover and believe it or not, he, and his entire group said 'yes.' I'm not going to let someone with that sense of duty work without a net. So, do you want a piece of the action on this?"

Dutton looked nervously around the room. "I did some off-duty snooping around on the Loman case. In my opinion, the entire thing stinks to high heaven. As far as Harte is concerned, his outfit put my kid through Space Camp a couple of years ago. I owe him a big favor but I can't just blow off all of this." He pointed to the mountain of files on his desk.

Gansz produced a sheet of paper. "Would it help if, as of one hour ago, you are on temporary duty with the Bureau as a special agent for unspecified assignments?"

Dutton's eyebrows rose as he read the order. "That would help a whole lot," he understated, even as a ball of excitement formed in his stomach.

"I believe that is your supervisor's signature. He figured we would come for you some day. They don't want to lose you downtown. I promised I would return you if I could."

"You're kidding." Dutton read over the temporary orders with genuine surprise.

"Come on, John. You know what kind of work you do. And I don't work with hack cops. So get through this moment of false modesty and we can get to work." Gansz could not hide his grin.

Dutton removed a thick file from his desk drawer. "This is what I have on Loman. Most of it was a dead end for me, but you might make something out of it."

Gansz had to use both hands to lift the file. "A little snooping around, eh? I think I've come to the right person."

Dutton shrugged. "I was curious."

Gansz leafed through the paperwork. "Do you know Richard Willis at National Electronics?"

"He's a straight shooter from everything I've seen and heard. Solid in the community, up-front businessman, he does all the right things. He's not involved is he?"

Gansz leafed through the file. "Everything got put in motion after Harte visited him. I also did a little 'snooping around' and discovered some interesting aspects of Mr. Willis and his company. It's time to pay him a visit."

"No calls, Sheri," Richard Willis said to the intercom as he greeted his visitors. "What's on your mind, Agent Gansz?"

Gansz settled into his chair. "Mr. Willis, we'd like to discuss Daniel Harte, and you should know that Sergeant Dutton has been cleared for this level of discussion."

The phrase caught Dutton off guard. Gansz had informed their host that he knew Willis was more than a corporate CEO. The case had just moved a few rungs up the official ladder.

Willis appeared outwardly calm. Ever since he had pointed Harte to the limb and nearly ordered him onto it, the President of NEI had been waiting for some official backup for the guy. This meeting appeared to be just that backup. He was not about to give the store away to these two, but he was more than willing to let them browse the shelves pretty thoroughly. "Exactly what level are we discussing here, gentlemen?"

Gansz cleared his throat and headed into what, in his career, were uncharted waters. "Sir, I have over-stepped my orders and spoken to Mr. Harte. He said that when he talked to you about Herbert Loman's death he felt there was more going on than just a consultant and a defense contractor."

"Interesting." Willis wanted to see what his visitors knew before he started handing out state secrets.

"He said you used the term 'need to know', and the coffee cups had NASA's logo and Langley on them. My math is pretty basic but when I added that up the answer came to three letters." He wrote "CIA" on a scrap of paper and slid it across the desk.

Moments later Willis deposited the paper in small pieces in the trash can. "If I had realized that the Bureau so was actively involved in the case, my choice of phrases and coffee cups might have been different."

Gansz knew the game. "As I said, the active status is unofficial," he replied, looking to Dutton for a reaction. The detective stayed calm and Gansz continued. "Harte went to the Southeast Endangered Species Association. I have an undercover agent with them. She was supposed to be watching out for their interests at the behest of the head of EPA."

Willis shook his head in disgust. "That figures."

"She contacted Harte and reported that a high-ranking official of SESA was using live members of the Everglades bird population for target practice. I got a little antsy and took it upon myself to move her assignment and mine up to the active level. I feel the circumstances warrant it."

Gansz figured the time had come to pass the ball to Willis. "If I am out of line on this, I'm sure you have the means to stop me." He turned to Dutton. "And if you want out after what I just said I have no problem with that."

"I have wanted to move on this for over two weeks. You aren't getting rid of me just because you broke a rule or two," the detective said eagerly.

They exchanged a resolute nod. Gansz turned back to Willis. "That settles it. Unless someone steps in and says otherwise, we are not walking away from this."

An uneasy silence filled the room. Willis' eyes darted back and forth from Gansz to Dutton. He concluded the time had come to step to the plate, take a swing, and screw the consequences. "So, do you guys want a cup of coffee or something?"

Dutton's eyes widened and he could not resist. "Can we drink out of the Langley cups?" he asked with the innocent enthusiasm of a grade schooler.

The double-edged question brought a collective, tension shattering, burst of laughter. "I believe we can arrange it, John." Willis replied, as they settled into the business of planning their next course of action.

NEW ORLEANS, LOUISIANA

The *Queen of Brindisi* lay nearly motionless near the west shore of the Intercoastal Waterway, awaiting her turn in the St. Claude Lock. St. Claude was the busiest of the numerous lock and gate structures that kept the waters of the Gulf of Mexico from inundating New Orleans and its below sea level surroundings.

Most ships entered the port of New Orleans through the twenty mile long Intercoastal waterway, running just below and parallel to Lake Ponchartrain, from the Gulf of Mexico to New Orleans. The canal permitted ships to avoid the ninety mile stretch of the Mississippi River below the "Crescent City." Any delay at St. Claude was far more preferable than attempting to navigate the treacherous shifting sand bars of the lower river delta.

On the bridge, the first officer stood watch at the ship's console. A blinking panel light indicated that a hatch was open on the exterior hull. He glanced around the bridge. The rest of the duty section was engaged in idle activity. He calmly reached over the console and turned off the light.

Near the water line, on the port side amidship, three men stood in the open hatchway and studied the shoreline. "It is two hundred meters, and the lock will be closed for another thirty minutes, so there will be no current," one of them whispered.

"Is our man waiting?" Bantar asked as he adjusted the fit of his wet suit.

"He has followed the ship since we entered the canal." The man pointed toward the shoreline. "Shall I signal him?"

"Let us not draw attention to ourselves." Bantar picked a spot on shore for an aiming point.

"We will make certain the cargo is properly handled. The driver knows where to go."

"And who is the driver? I do not like to work with an unknown quantity."

"It is Rashur."

Bantar nodded his approval. "Of course. I have not seen him since we staged his death four years ago. I must remember to wish him belated condolences." He chuckled and prepared to enter the water. "You have done well, my brothers," he said while stepping onto the rope ladder for the ten foot descent into the canal. "Are the rest of your travel plans in order?"

"We sail for Panama later today, to catch a plane for home and await your return."

"This will be our finest hour."

"God is great!" one of them replied confidently.

Bantar nodded and lowered himself into the muddy water.

PERSIAN GULF

The captain of the cruiser *Arlington* surveyed the plots on the board. Ahead the U.S. Persian Gulf Fleet steadily made its way in single file through the narrow Straits of Hormuz toward the Gulf of Oman. He shook his head as he considered the ramifications of the redeployment.

The Gulf was an international waterway, but he could do little without at least one local port of call. The political events since the incident at Mecca had removed the U.S. Navy from the welcome list at all ports in the Gulf region. Even Qatar, whose size and location made it a natural target for aggressors, had caved and requested the U.S. withdrawal.

The only reason for optimism came from a joint Saudi/U.S. decision, made and executed beyond the eyes and ears of the world's intelligence communities. The commanders had agreed to secretly billet a portion of the American armor and its ordinance in remote bunkers in the Saudi desert. If any problems arose, at least a semblance of response could be put in place with relative speed.

In addition, a sizable cache of supplies and equipment had been deemed unretrievable by Central Command and handed over to the Saudis. The Captain assumed the unretrievables could be recovered quickly if necessary. He did not doubt that necessity for a second. The Saudi military force was, for its size, a formidable contingent. But the fact remained that the largest known oil reserves on earth had been effectively laid open to the world. To anyone willing to take substantial casualties, those oil fields could be secured in a quick strike action.

As the *Arlington* made its way into the Straits, the captain moved to the sonar station. "How's it look, Chief?"

"Everything nominal, Captain."

"Keep on it. We've done the drill dozens of times, but this is the most hateful stretch of water I know."

"Aye, sir."

The captain was not really worried. He figured that someone had arranged for the eviction of the U.S. fleet. They had to realize that just one questionable encounter with a hostile ship would give the U.S. and Saudi Arabia an excuse to reverse the entire redeployment. The sonar and radar screens had been clean since the *Arlington* departed Dhahran. It seemed as if every ship in the region had pulled into port so as not to antagonize the American Fleet.

"Boy, that's going to be a problem."

The hair on the captain's neck stood up but he maintained a calm demeanor. "Report, Sonar."

"Sorry, sir. It's no big deal. I was just pinging the channel and noticed an anomaly on the starboard floor. It looks like there was an underwater land slide or something. It's too big for any subs we might be hunting."

"Give me positive ID, Sonar." The Captain said tersely.

"Got it, sir. It's just a mound of new rock and sand. I didn't mean to fire you up."

"No problem, son. We're all a little tense. Chief, make a note to alert the chart people. They will want to tell SubFleet about it."

"Aye, sir," the sonar chief replied.

The captain rubbed his forehead and stared at the deck. A smile came to his face. Maybe things were not so bad after all, he decided. He stretched and looked around the *Arlington's* Combat Information Center. "Lieutenant, take the con. I'm going on deck for some air."

As he departed the room, the watch chief passed the word. "Captain on the deck. Exec has the con." The executive officer assumed the duty in the CIC as the ship finished its run through the Straits of Hormuz.

NEW ORLEANS, LOUISIANA

At the massive Chalmette Port Facility, the *Queen of Brindisi's* main davit slowly lifted a cargo pallet from the forward hold. The crane operator worked with particular care, landing it on the dock without a nudge.

A priest made his way through the army of longshoremen and

forklifts. He smiled broadly as he gently stroked the rough wooden side of the container. "Come, my sons," He beckoned his helpers to the cargo. The priest's personal driver tried, in vain, to keep the old clergyman out of everyone's way.

As the forklift operator prepared to place the crate in the truck, he stopped in front of the priest and gently lowered the crate almost to the ground. "Father, we're a little ahead of schedule. Would you like to take a look before we load up?" the lift operator asked with a gentleness that belied his outward crusty appearance.

"Oh, may I please, my son?" the priest implored like a child on Christmas morning.

"Of course." The man effortlessly loosened the fastening nails of the crate and, with the help of one of the delivery men, lifted the lid.

All who looked into the crate and were startled by the beauty of its contents. The seven foot statue wore Teutonic robes and the face had the ruddy look of the northern European people. One hand clutched a Bible to the breast and the other held an axe that extended past the knee.

"St. Boniface," the forklift operator noted with approval.

"You of know him?" the priest asked.

"He chopped down the oak tree of Thor and brought the church to Germany." His reverence turned to curiosity. "But how did he wind up in this neck of the woods?"

The priest replied without hesitation. "By the time the parish was founded, all of the major French and Latin church entities were taken. So the parishioners voted for him."

"It makes sense to me," one of the delivery men remarked and a chorus of laughter broke out among the men.

"Okay, Father, let's get St. Boniface into the truck and back to Hammond," The lift operator resealed the container and slid it into the closed rear cab of a delivery truck. Pausing once more near the priest, he asked a final question.

"Are you sure you will be able to handle that thing? It weighs over a ton."

The priest smiled gently. "There are many stout hands at the parish who have waited eagerly for this delivery. I pray they show the same care as you have. God bless you, my son."

The forklift operator bowed his head as the priest bestowed the sign of the cross on him. "Thank you, Father. It was my pleasure."

The delivery men exchanged a look of relief as they finished securing the crate in the truck. They checked their watches. It was 9:59 A.M. The dock worker had caused just enough of a delay. It occurred to them that it might have been planned, though the man's sincerity had been undeniable.

The truck driver leaned out his window and called to the priest's driver. "Remember to give us some space back there. We don't want you under the truck if we have a sudden stop. Once on the highway you can take the lead if you want."

"Don't worry about us. Just do what you have to do," the driver of the sedan said as he waved to the men.

The truck moved down a warehouse-lined street toward the access road of the port facility. As it passed an intersection, a semi-trailer truck entered the road from the right and came between the two vehicles. The semi driver looked down and saw the oncoming sedan. In a panic he squealed the rig to a stop, straddling the intersection.

The priest's driver yelled a warning as he hit the brakes hard and brought the car to a screeching halt two feet from the cab of the huge truck. The priest tumbled to the back seat floor. "Father, are you all right?" the driver said frantically groping to assist as best he could.

"I'll be fine, my son," came the reply from the floor.

The semi driver was at the window of the car as the priest picked himself up and slumped into the back seat. "Hey, man, I'm sorry. I didn't—" He noticed the Catholic collar. "Oh, shit. I mean. Oh, no. Father, I'm sorry. I wasn't looking. It's all my fault. Please forgive me."

"Be calm, my son. We all should pay closer attention in life."

Beyond the semi, out of their view, a duplicate delivery truck with three men in the forward cab emerged from a warehouse. Two of its occupants quickly switched the license plates while the third conferred with the driver of the first truck.

"Did you see it?" Simmons asked the man.

"It's perfect. He'll never know the difference."

Simmons looked past him. "Finish mounting the plate inside, Tom. Get that truck off the street."

Reilly pulled the first delivery truck through the vacated garage door. Kennedy approached Simmons from the second truck and handed him the screwdriver. "Here you go. She's all set. I'm going to the end of the street."

Simmons checked his watch. Forty-five seconds had elapsed since the near miss between the sedan and the semi-trailer. He handed the driver a blank envelope. "Here's a little bonus. Let's get moving." He entered the garage and closed the door.

The delivery driver made his way around to the priest's car. "Is everything okay back here?" he asked as he approached the sedan.

"Everything is fine, my son." The priest turned to the semi driver. "Would you please move your truck and we can all be on our way."

"Yes, Father," the semi driver said as he returned to his rig. The truck moved slowly through the intersection.

"Is the statue all right?" the priest asked nervously.

"Everything is fine," the delivery-man replied. He looked down the side street toward the departing semi. "That guy was a clown," he muttered.

"Yes, but he is God's clown and we must be understanding," the priest said as graciously as his sore leg and shoulder would permit. "Now let us be on our way."

The driver mounted the replacement delivery truck. He looked back once more to the priest's sedan and waved to the driver. The two-vehicle convoy headed out the port's main access road toward the St. Claude Avenue gate.

Kennedy emerged from his lookout post as the duplicate delivery truck emerged from a garage. He signaled Reilly to drive to the end of the road. "We should give them a few minutes in case the Poland Street drawbridge is up," he said. "After all we went through, it would be a waste if we pulled up behind them in line."

"Good idea," Simmons said, concentrating on the plan ahead.

After the short delay, Reilly drove out of Chalmette Port and onto St. Claude Avenue. The road turned into Elysian Fields Boulevard, a wide avenue that passed through one of the rundown areas that surround the French Quarter and the downtown New Orleans business district. A mile later the truck turned west onto I-610.

The warehouse street was deserted. Another garage door opened near the intersection where the exchange had occurred. A four wheel drive vehicle emerged and slowly proceeded to the main access road. At the wheel, Bantar went over his mental notes. He memorized the faces of Kennedy and Reilly. They acted like Simmons' lieutenants.

Bantar had refined many of Simmons' skills and he began to paint a picture of what the strike team would look like. Now that he knew some of the faces it would not be hard to spot the rest of the key players. Once the action started their movements would identify them.

Bantar planned to get in and dispose of his targets quickly, muddying the waters for the relentless investigation the Americans would conduct. They would eventually get to the bottom line. All he needed was a two-week window for Kasarov to move and for the Saudi initiative to activate. After that the wheels would turn on their own and the Americans would be powerless to alter the outcome.

He planned his reconnaissance of the area northwest of Baton Rouge. According to the map it was relatively unpopulated, with numerous back roads and secondary highways. That was a good start. The rest of the plan would fill in as he grew familiar with the area. The drive up Interstate 10 would be heady.

SIMMESPORT, LOUISIANA

Harmon pulled into the poorly-paved parking lot of the Simmesport Market. Simmesport seemed more like an oversized village, nestled against the levee on the western approach to the Route 1 bridge over the upper Atchafalaya River. The Market was little more than a convenience store at the town's main intersection.

Harte spread a map of Louisiana on the hood of the car. A systematic series of slashes covered the map. The pattern ran north and south from the lower Atchafalaya basin area near Morgan City, to Simmesport. It extended west, nearly to Lafayette.

Harmon returned from the market and handed Harte a soft drink. "We've spent the last four days at every bullshit campground on every back road in the central part of this state. All we have to show for it is a sore back and a ton of mileage fees for the rental car company."

"I wish that woman from the Environmental Office would get back with us." Harte replied. "You'd think that between Wednesday and Friday she would find time to at least leave a message acknowledging my call."

"In the store I checked with Alexandria. The innkeeper said no calls came in." Harmon replied with growing frustration.

"Billy, we could spend the next two weeks criss-crossing this state and still not cover every place on this map."

Harmon tossed out a gambit. "I don't think we would find them if we hit every spot on the map."

"What are you getting at?"

"I am convinced that Trent does not give one rat's ass about endangered species in Louisiana. And I don't believe he wants his camp located."

"I'm listening."

"Trent's Naples operation reeked of military organization. It was almost oppressive, in a way. Those people were not just innocently counting birds. I haven't been so relieved to get away from a place since I left Statistics class at Purdue. I'm telling you, they are here to screw things up."

Harte's own discomfort surfaced. "For what it's worth, I haven't had a good feeling about this since Huntsville. But I have no idea where to go with it."

"What about Mike Prince?"

"You know the deal. Unless we come up with air tight proof of a national security threat, his people are out of the mix. Besides, he probably has a pretty full plate right now with the Saudi problem."

Harmon nodded thoughtfully then abruptly changed the subject. "We're not accomplishing anything here. Let's take a little break. Do you want to see something really amazing?"

The sudden change of pace caught Harte off guard. "Are you saying there is more to this place than the Simmesport Market?"

"You asshole," Harmon said with a chuckle that had been rare in the past few days. "Really. Let's go see my buddy Chuck Haisley. Remember, at the Old River Project?"

"You keep coming back to that."

Harmon pointed toward what he figured was the Northeast. "It's only about fifteen minutes from here. Chuck should be on site, if he kept to his schedule. I'm telling you, you really have to see this place to believe it."

Harte knew that the search for Trent was wearing on him. "Okay, we'll go see your friend. And when we're done I'm going back to Cincinnati for the weekend. I need to get away from here for a few days and put some things in order."

"I think you will find something back there to get your mind off all of this stuff," Harmon said with a sly grin.

Harte read his friend's mind. "Go to hell, Billy. She's just someone I'm working with at Mike Prince's direction." Harte shook his head in exasperation. Then he promptly admitted to himself that for the last four days, when he was not actively thinking about the Trent case, his thoughts immediately drifted to Samantha Schmidt.

There really was a lot to like about her. There were also some natural obstacles. They had spoken on the phone often during the week but it was almost exclusively about business. A couple of times he imagined the artificial barrier between work and their personal life starting to melt. But he always steered the conversation back to the official level. It seemed the proper thing to do.

With any luck there would be time, when this was over, to remove the barriers and find out if the relationship went beyond professional. They seemed, at least, to be exchanging signals that indicated something more personal. Harte tried to dismiss the thoughts from his already cluttered mind. "Let's get over and see your friend."

"Yes sir, Mista Harte. Whatever you say, sir," Harmon replied in his best "Rochester" voice.

"You are a shit," Harte playfully smacked him on top of the head.

A delivery truck, followed closely by a Land Rover, rolled off the Route 1 bridge and stopped at the intersection. The driver looked both ways and then straight ahead into the Simmesport Market parking lot. His eyes widened as they came to rest on the sedan. He quickly turned right and drove about fifty yards down the levee road before stopping.

"Why the hell did you stop?" Simmons yelled as he met Reilly between vehicles.

"Did you happen to look into the parking lot of the convenience store back there?" He did not wait for a reply. "Remember Harte and Harmon, at the Naples camp a couple weeks ago? They just got into a car back at the intersection."

"That fucking bitch," Simmons muttered. "Did you see which way they went?"

"No. I just got through the intersection so they wouldn't see us."

Simmons looked down the road. "What kind of car was it and what color?"

"Late model white sedan. Probably a rental."

"All right, good work. Head on to the camp. I'll stay here for a few minutes in case they come back this way. If I'm not along in fifteen minutes put everyone on alert. We can't have these two stumbling into the compound."

Simmons returned to the Land Rover convinced that Harte and Harmon were not just stumbling around in central Louisiana. He waited a few minutes and moved on, content they had left the area. He recalled the evening in the lounge back in Naples and contemplated the demise of Barbara Davaron. Her last few hours on earth would be enjoyable for him and one or more of his close companions. She, on the other hand, would wish for death long before the actual moment arrived.

Harmon turned off Route 1 at the village of Lettsworth and headed north on State road 15. After a few gentle bends, the road straightened and ran northeast roughly along the levee that protects central Louisiana from the whims of the mighty Mississippi River.

"What's that?" Harte asked, pointing ahead.

"Part one of the Old River Flood Control Project," Harmon announced as they approached a concrete and steel structure spanning the road.

On a stone pillar off to the right of the bridge entrance Harte read the words "Old River Lock." Once on the bridge he saw that it crossed the east end of a lock and dam structure.

"The Mississippi River is about a quarter of a mile that way," Harmon said, pointing to the right. "The Red River is five miles to the west." He pointed to the left

Minutes later they emerged from the trees in a sweeping left turn along a broad flatland. Directly ahead, a towered structure slowly filled the windshield. As they approached, Harte swallowed as the true size of the gated dam became obvious.

"Billy, it's huge." He leaned forward to look up at the piers as they crossed the dam.

"Pretty neat, isn't it?" Harmon said with a grin. "This one is the Auxiliary Structure, believe it or not. Now you know why I said you have to see this thing."

They crossed the dam, passed a towering crane on railroad tracks and moved off into another gentle left turn. Directly ahead was a second structure. It had no towers but was flanked by two massive overhead cranes, also on tracks. As they crossed Harte looked to the left and saw water churning over a hundred yards beyond the dam.

"They call this one the Low Sill. It's the original structure. The big one wasn't built until the eighties. I suppose that's why it's the Auxiliary Structure but it still seems odd to me." Harmon stopped halfway across and turned off the engine. The rush of water was unmistakably loud. "Can you feel that?"

Harte became aware of a rhythmic vibration that gently rocked the car. "Is the water doing that?" he asked in amazement.

"Yep. The river is way up. What you feel is water coming through the gates. Amazing, isn't it."

"I see your point. Do you mind if we get off this thing?" Harte said nervously.

Harmon laughed and started the car. "Relax. It's been a lot worse than this, according to Chuck, and the thing is still standing."

He finished crossing the dam and pulled into the parking area on the north side of the Low Sill. "Chuck should be in the office. He'll give you all the details. You are going to love this."

Harte looked back toward the Low Sill as he followed Harmon to the Corps of Engineers office building. He was quickly developing a healthy respect for the River, the flood control project, and the men and women, whoever they were, who made the whole thing work.

Harmon knocked on the office door and opened it before anyone answered. "Hey Chuck. Are you home?"

"If I was home I'd be back in Vicksburg," came the response from across the office. Haisley turned from a table full of charts. "How you doin', Billy?" he said with a grin as he met them in the middle of the room.

"Terrific, Chuck. This is Dan Harte. We were just in the neighborhood and decided to stop by for a look around."

Haisley shook hands with Harte. "Good to meet you. But give me a break. Nobody is ever 'just in the neighborhood' out in these boondocks. What are you guys doing here?"

"We were doing R&R in Alexandria, and Billy said we had to see this place before we go home. The next thing I knew we were driving across that thing back there." Harte pointed in the general direction of the Auxiliary Structure. He dismissed Harmon's puzzled look it with a glance.

"You picked a fine time for a look around. The river is up and still rising," Haisley said. "It could get pretty hairy out here in the next week or so. Aaron says we may get a flood like '84 or maybe even '73. Those were the two worst on record. Isn't that right, Aaron?"

Two men emerged from an adjoining room. "It could be a good one," said a tall, late thirtyish man in a blue T-shirt.

"Dan Harte, meet Aaron Roosevelt," Haisley announced. Harte's hand collapsed in the grip of the chief engineer.

"Sorry," Roosevelt said as Harte flexed his fingers. Traces of gray that offset the engineer's dark hair suddenly seemed out of place as a boyish grin crossed his equally dark face.

"No problem," Harte replied as the tingling sensation in his hand slowly eased.

As Roosevelt reacquainted himself with Harmon, the second man came forward. "Hi. Henry McMahon."

"Henry is the night supervisor of the project. I wanted all of the supervisors in for a briefing, so Henry came in early." Haisley always walked a fine line between complimenting and patronizing McMahon. There was no reason to expose visitors to the fact that his promotion in the Corps of Engineers had come at McMahon's expense. He appreciated McMahon's ability to put the situation aside when duty called.

Harmon came over to greet McMahon. "Good to see you again, Henry. Jesus, you look like shit. Don't you ever sleep?" he said with a laugh.

McMahon really did look run down. Though no one at work ever called him on it, he always had a ready made excuse on hand just in case. "Normally I'd be sleeping right now. I'm just dedicated," he replied with a weak grin.

The front door opened while McMahon was replying to Harmon's question. "He's run down from all that time on the gambling boats," said Mardi as he entered the office.

"Kiss my ass, Randall," McMahon replied.

Before Haisley could begin proper introductions the guard sniffed the air and bolted for the stove in the corner of the room. "Dammit, Aaron, I told you not to leave them on too long." He removed a large skillet from the burner and examined its contents. "You nearly burned my mud bugs."

"I'm sorry, Randall," Roosevelt said humbly. "I didn't think you'd mind if I worked on the river problem. It's up two more feet. I'll remember my place from now on."

Haisley watched the exchange with amusement. "Nobody knows exactly when Randall became the boss. It started out with little stuff here and there and the next thing we knew it was his operation. We try to measure up to his expectations."

The guard approached them with skillet in hand. "Come on, Mr. Haisley. I just asked him to keep an eye on my mud bugs while I made a quick round."

"Dan, this is Randall Mardi. He is the main security officer here at the Old River Control Project."

"Hi, Dan. Do you want a mud bug?" Mardi held the skillet under Harte's nose.

Harte backed away a bit. "Hello, Randall." He looked tentatively into the skillet. "What are they?" he asked.

"Crayfish," Mardi replied. "Thanks to Aaron they nearly burned. But I got them in time. Want one?"

Harte declined and Mardi went back to the stove to finish his cooking. "Is he the security guard or the eccentric chef?"

Haisley smiled and lowered his voice. "He shot the head off a snake at 50 feet from a draw with that," he said, pointing to the .357 Magnum on Mardi's hip. "Frankly, we're glad his cooking talent is all we have to deal with."

The comment set off a small alarm but Harte put it aside. Around the office everyone slowly returned to their duties.

"Telephone, Henry," Roosevelt called out as he walked toward the door. "I'm going out to check the silt levels, Chuck."

Haisley and Harte followed Roosevelt out of the office. "So do you want the ten cent tour of the place?" Haisley asked as Harmon joined them on the lawn.

"Sure," Harte replied. "They seem like a good team," he noted as they walked toward the Low Sill.

McMahon watched them through the window and considered what his life had come to. In the late seventies the Corps of Engineers did a major review of the Old River Project. The Low Sill had come dangerously close to failing in the 1973 flood.

MacMahon presented a study which called for letting the Mississippi River migrate into the Atchafalaya since the big river had been trying to do so for years. His plan was ecologically sound and cost efficient.

Haisley, recently out of college, advocated augmenting the Low Sill with a second structure and keeping the river in its present bed. His study pointed to the economic disaster that would come with the loss of the river through Baton Rouge, and "Refinery Alley" on down to New Orleans. It was an aspect McMahon had not even considered and it swayed the Corps to adopt Haisley's plan.

On hearing of the decision McMahon confronted the board of directors and informed them of their mistake in what turned into a personal exchange. The shouting match cost him any chance for career advancement. The final blow came when The Auxiliary Structure was christened and Haisley was named project director, in spite of McMahon's seniority.

McMahon's life spiraled downward, through alcohol, compulsive gambling on the river boats, a divorce and financial ruin. Within that lifestyle came a series of accidental contacts that led him to the phone call that awaited his attention.

He took the call in the adjoining office, checking once more to make sure Mardi was fully engrossed at the stove. "McMahon here...Visitors? Yeah. A couple friends of Haisley's. He took them out for the tour. Other than that nobody...How the hell did you know that?...Christ. We don't need this kind of problem...You're the one who knows them. What are YOU going to do about it?...Okay let's think this through...I agree. Can you do it?...That's good. I'll suggest it if Haisley doesn't. I'll let you know about the timing...Don't worry about it...Good bye."

Haisley pointed to a small confluence a half mile to the west. "The outflow channels of both structures meet there. Everything flows to the Red River, about seven miles out, then south into the Atchafalaya and finally, the Gulf of Mexico."

"How much water do you send through?" Harte asked.

"We allow seventy percent of the river go on to Baton Rouge and New Orleans. The other thirty percent is bled off to the west. We use the gates of the Auxiliary Structure and the Low Sill to regulate the volume. It all depends on the flow level in the Mississippi."

They crossed the roadway to the Mississippi side of the Low Sill. Harte leaned over the railing and watched the water course through the gate assembly. The sight was both mesmerizing and intimidating.

"The key to the equation is silt," Haisley continued. "As the Mississippi increases its volume the silt content increases. We take water samples and match the silt content to charts in the office and that tells us how much water to send through."

"Why the seventy/thirty number?"

"It's a flow velocity equation. If more than thirty percent of the Mississippi goes through our complex the river doesn't have enough strength to carry the silt downstream. A deposit builds in the main channel. Eventually it would be blocked off and the entire river would simply turn west and abandon its channel. That's the layman's explanation but it covers it."

"What happens then?" Harmon asked.

"We do not even consider that possibility." Haisley's tone turned decidedly ominous.

"It's that serious?" Harte was startled by Haisley's change of expression.

"It would be, in a word, devastating. That's why Aaron is out at the end of the channel right now." He pointed to the figure of Roosevelt, a quarter mile away where the Mississippi entered the Low Sill's inflow channel. "We normally take silt samples every six hours. In flood season we take them on the hour. That's how quickly the situation can change."

"He's a good man isn't he?" Harte said, testing his first impression of Haisley's assistant engineer.

"Aaron's the best. He knows the river better than most towboat pilots. He's been with the Corps since he was eighteen. For my money he should be a supervisor by now, but sometimes things don't happen down here the way they should." He did not use the word discrimination but the inference was obvious to Harte.

"I talked to him once about coming up to Vicksburg with me. I was sure I could get him into management. You won't believe his answer," Haisley said as they walked beneath the overhead crane and back toward the office.

"He said thanks but this is where he can do the most good. It's the lynch pin for the whole Lower Mississippi River and he considers it an honor to work on it. What could I say? How often do you find someone who believes so much in the concept of duty? He is a blessing. That's for sure."

MORGANZA, LOUISIANA

Harte lounged in the passenger seat as Harmon drove south on State Route 1. Baton Rouge was about an hour away. Then it would be home for the weekend.

The road ran near the top of a levee and periodically the rising Mississippi burst into view on the left. Two hundred or more yards from the road, the tree line marking the river-bank stood in water up to the lower branches. The river lapped at the base of the levee. The only thing between the flat forested land of central Louisiana and disaster was the man-made mound on which they drove. And it seemed to grow even more narrow and far less protective with every new sighting of the swirling backwaters of the river.

The road inclined to the top of the levee and they came onto the Morganza Spillway. For more than half a mile they drove across the gated structure with the water, by now a huge lake extending out to the river channel, hitting the dam's gates well above the normal level.

As Haisley had explained, the spillway is the sixth element of the Old River Flood Control Project, and the last line of defense. If the Mississippi River should overwhelm the Old River Complex, the spillway can be opened. The river will, in theory, drain into the bayou that runs along the eastern side of the Atchafalaya River down to the Gulf of Mexico. According Haisley, no one knows precisely what effect opening the Spillway would have on the course of the big river. Mostly they just hope it never comes to that.

Harte broke the uneasy silence as they came off the Spillway into the town of Morganza. "I don't like this a bit."

"No kidding. It's like driving on a strip of land over nothing but water," Harmon replied.

"I don't mean that," Harte said abruptly.

"I should have read your mind," Harmon replied, stung by the mild rebuke. "I was thinking about something else."

"Sorry, Billy. I keep thinking about Trent and after the tour from Chuck it bothers me even more."

Harmon was back on track. "I'd sure feel better if we knew where he was."

"Or what he is up to," Harte added. "I cannot come up with one good reason, outside of political hay, for him to just pack up and move his entire operation to Louisiana. Then somewhere out on the Auxiliary Structure I got this vision of Trent just screwing up the works."

"Like how?"

"That's the problem. I have no idea. I don't suppose you can just blow the thing up or anything like that. At least not with conventional explosives."

"I doubt if Trent has access to a nuke," Harmon said jokingly. "And from what I saw of the Auxiliary Structure that is about what it would take."

"You don't need to destroy something to sabotage it. What if they altered the out flow equation somehow."

"They'd need inside help for something that sophisticated. None of the people we met today reminded me of the Rosenbergs."

Harte nodded. "I must be getting paranoid. Get me to the Baton Rouge Airport. I need to get back home and see Sam." A pained expression came over his face and he turned and looked out the window. "Ah, shit. Can I take that one back?"

"No way, Jose." Harmon got out the needle. "Do you mean Sam who you only deal with professionally on the orders of Mike Prince?"

"You really are a terrible man."

"Is that the Sam you show extra attention to when you think no one is looking?"

"Do we have to do this now?" Harte was defeated.

"Come on. Help me out on this. Is that Sam who had you pacing the floor and watching the clock while waiting for her to arrive last weekend?"

"I hate you so much right now that I can't even begin to tell you how—"

Two simultaneous explosions shattered the light-hearted taunting session as the car jerked wildly to the left. A furious vibration rocked the vehicle as it swerved back and forth. Harte held on for dear life as Harmon fought for control. The car careened across the two lane road. Finally it came to a screeching stop in a gravel parking lot.

"What the hell was that?" Harte asked, out of breath.

Harmon was already out of the car and inspecting the damage. "Both the front tires blew, for Chrissake!" he said as Harte joined him.

Harte looked back up the road. "We didn't run over anything. I can't believe both tires just failed."

Two hundred yards down the road, Simmons moved quickly through the trees to his Land Rover. He returned the telescopic sight to its case, placed the modified M-16 under the seat and drove back onto Route 1.

McMahon's call came with just enough time to spare. Simmons knew Route 1 and was able to get to Morganza and into position. The scope allowed him to fire an amazingly accurate burst into the oncoming vehicle. A shot while the car was on the Spillway would have been better. The river would have finished the job. Unfortunately there was no decent cover near the structure.

The driver had managed to control the car and the ultimate objective was missed. With luck the event would scare Harte off long enough for SESA to accomplish its mission. If not, he could be dealt with. Trent could not stand the guy and made no bones about his desire to get eliminate him when he found out Harte was in the area. Simmons was sure that even if Harte did stay around, the camp was secure and by the time anybody figured out what was going on, the mission would be successfully completed.

The mechanic lifted the shredded tire off the mount and an object dropped from the inner lining. He stooped to retrieve it. "Ya'll got any enemies around here?"

Harte and Harmon stared silently at the deformed chunk of metal, then at each other.

"Ya'll know this is a bullet, don't ya?" the mechanic said in a slow drawl. He removed the second tire and another slug dropped out of the lining. "M-16, I'd say. I picked up enough of these in my time to recognize the old 5.56 millimeter. The good news is ya'll are alive. The bad news is somebody out there maybe wishes you wasn't," he chuckled at his own remark.

"This is getting serious," Harmon said, unable to control the edge in his voice.

"Trent," Harte said not hearing his friend.

"Well, no shit, pal. Who the hell else would it be?"

"Take a break, Billy. Think about this for a minute."

"I am thinking about it and I don't like it."

"I know." Harte kept his wits. "But like I said. Just think. What does this tell you?" He took Harmon out of earshot of the mechanic. "If Trent ordered this, then obviously he doesn't want us in the area. Why should it matter to him if we are down here? Everything he does is supposed to be sanctioned, at least passively, by the government." He did not wait for a reply. "This confirms a lot of what we've been thinking."

Harmon relaxed a little. "Suppose we are right. Where do we go from here?"

"We stay on plan. Get us to the airport. I'll talk to Sam about going higher up with what we have."

Harmon shook his head. "Dan, we have nothing."

"We were shot at." Harte was now the incredulous one.

"I realize that. But without a suspect in hand all we have is a hunch. You know what George Gansz said. It's hands off when it comes to Trent."

Harte considered the logic. "You're probably right on that count. But I still want to get this information higher up the ladder. Who knows? Maybe there are other pieces being looked at and this might fit in somewhere."

"Okay." Harmon hesitated.

"What's on your mind, Billy?" Harte prodded.

"I want to stay down here."

"I understand." Harte knew exactly what was on his friend's mind. Field agent or not, they knew that Barbara Davaron was most likely in a dangerous position. "Look, you keep a low profile on this. Stay in touch. And contact George. The last I knew he was in Huntsville. Let me know what he says."

"When are you coming back?"

"As soon as I can. If I can't get answers in Cincinnati, I'll go to Washington and try to talk to Mike. He may not even see me but I'll deal with that if it comes up. For now let's get to Baton Rouge. I want the quickest flight out. Come on. Let's do our duty."

Somewhere along the road it occurred to Harte that "let's do our duty" seemed like the most natural thing to say. He thought about the people he had met over the last month. From Mike Prince and Samantha, to Aaron Roosevelt and Randall Mardi. He considered all the heroes had lost as he grew up and wondered if, perhaps, he was rediscovering them in this collection of individuals and others like them. Even amid his darkest thoughts of Morgan Trent, he managed a slight smile. Maybe there is hope for all of us, he thought to himself.

Chapter XI

MOSCOW, RUSSIA

Cherkin held the glass to his mouth long enough for the grimace to pass. Sergei had put the usual dosage of alcohol into the liter of water to help maintain the President's public persona, especially during visits by the new Defense Minister. It was important that Kasarov think that he held all the cards, and his impression of Cherkin as a drunk was a necessary part of the charade.

"My next initiative, Mr. President, involves removing the Army from harvest duties in the fall. It is demeaning to take a man from the front lines of national defense for two weeks a year and have him pick potatoes. The Agriculture Minister is working on an alternative plan which he will submit for your approval within the next month."

Kasarov glanced up from his notes as Cherkin put the nearly empty glass on the desk. The General shook his head. Any feelings of sympathy for the President were offset by the fact that Cherkin's alcoholism produced indecisiveness which made the newly appointed

Defense Minister's job much easier.

He prepared to announce his next initiative when the intercom interrupted. He was tempted to answer the buzzer himself but resisted turning the political knife which he had firmly wedged in the President's back.

Cherkin fumbled for the button on the intercom. "What is it, Sergei?" he asked with disinterest.

"The director requests an emergency meeting, sir."

Cherkin and Kasarov came to attention in their seats and exchanged a puzzled glance. "We better see what's bothering Viktor," Cherkin said good naturedly.

"By all means, Mr. President."

Gorki came through the door quickly. "Mr. President," he announced before he reached the desk, "I have some— Oh. I apologize. Your aide neglected to tell me you had the Defense Minister in. I will return later."

Kasarov's curiosity was killing him, but he did not assert himself. If Gorki wanted a private meeting, it would be easy enough to get the information from Cherkin later. "I can leave if you would like. These matters can be discussed another time." He deftly walked the line between gracious and patronizing.

"Actually, General it might be better if you stayed. I will probably have to brief you eventually."

Kasarov was hooked. "Thank you, Mr. Director. I appreciate the invitation." He settled in for Gorki's briefing.

Gorki paced the room. "Mr. President, there more bad news in the south."

Cherkin leaned a little forward. "Not Georgia, again."

"It is worse than that. I have reports from agents on the situation in Chechnya. The independence movement continues but there may a more sinister aspect to it. These reports are preliminary and I must stress there is no evidence of overt activity at this time. But I am disturbed nonetheless."

"Why don't those people understand reality? Chechnya is nearly a ward of the state. What can they gain by attempting independence?" Cherkin said in frustration.

Kasarov wanted to leap from his seat. How could information like this have eluded him? He forced himself to sit quietly and let the discussion to take its course.

"Mr. President," Gorki continued, "It is not that simple anymore. There is another element to consider."

"And what is that?" Cherkin asked.

"Chechnya is the focal point of our recently developed oil delivery system. We need them in the fold or everything falls apart. Without the ability to get the Caspian oil to market our economic survival is, at best remote. We need those oil sales or the country may disintegrate before our eyes."

Kasarov's mind raced. He resisted the urge to take over the discussion. It was important that everything emanate from the President, especially with the KGB director in the room. His entire ascension to power depended on the Caspian oil. If all went as planned the world's greatest oil consumer would soon become Russia's best customer and at premium prices.

"Mr. President," Gorki continued, "This is a National Security matter and I would like to get the Defense Minister's input on it, with your permission."

"As you wish," Cherkin replied.

Gorki turned to Kasarov. "General, as you probably know, there really is not a sophisticated political apparatus at work down there. Nor do they have anything approaching a well armed military." He resisted mentioning the success of the Chechen guerilla units against the Russian Army. "It is possible that another force is at work here."

Kasarov took the cue. "It might be organized crime."

"I am considering exactly that, General," Gorki replied deferentially. "It is perfect cover for them; another satellite seeking freedom. Most of the Western World's press would be on their side. If they play their cards correctly, the criminals could wind up with their own oil company."

"I agree completely with that analysis. That is how we must approach it," Kasarov said calmly. He tried to make the comment sound like an opinion instead of a command decision.

"The question is how do we deal with it?" Gorki measured his next statement carefully. Everything depended on Kasarov's response. "The local police are not equipped to handle this. I could go there myself but if my visit became public knowledge it might trigger the entire movement, not to mention the political fallout around the world from the KGB putting down what is viewed as a political uprising. I am at somewhat of a loss as to how to deal with this."

Kasarov decided to take control. "There is a way."

Cherkin leaned forward. "Speak your mind, General. This is too important to stand on ceremony."

Emboldened by the endorsement, Kasarov stood up. "I can make a surprise inspection of the region's armed forces. It will be easy to find them inadequate and order divisional maneuvers for the Southern Sector. I will insert forces into the area, root out the criminals and put an end to this independence nonsense. As for Western reaction, all military training is subject to error. If a situation of force does arise, we can simply attribute it to a mistake during training and express the nation's sorrow for the innocent lives tragically lost."

Gorki warmed up to the topic. "There is nothing quite like major divisional maneuvers to remind the people where the power lies." He turned to Cherkin. "Mr. President, the Defense Minister's plan is viable and I am ready to endorse it. General Kasarov must operate by presidential decree and at his own discretion. I also believe this conversation should not leave this room."

Kasarov's heart nearly burst through his uniform jacket. KGB had just recommended that he be given free rein in the most strategically significant area of Russia. "I am honored by your show of confidence, Mr. Director."

"It is well earned, my friend," Gorki replied graciously.

Kasarov paced the room. "Mr. President, with your permission I would like to start on this as soon as possible."

"Of course, General," Cherkin replied. "Do you know when you might travel to the region?" he asked nonchalantly.

Kasarov paused at the door. "This weekend and early next week I have official events to attend. But next weekend is good. I can give you the exact plan and the date by Wednesday, if that is acceptable."

"Excellent. Thank you for your contribution in this effort."

Cherkin hoped the show of sincerity hid his disdain for the man he considered an autocratic charlatan.

"It is my honor to serve the country, Mr. President," Kasarov departed with a short wave of the hand.

Gorki picked up the vodka bottle. "He has not the faintest idea, does he."

"Ambition blinds him, Viktor. It is our secret weapon. He thinks only he and I know of his plans and that my ego prevents me from talking to anyone."

"He is a patronizing little weasel if you ask my opinion."

"He is the devil and must be returned to hell," Cherkin said with resolve.

Gorki lifted the vodka bottle and took a deep drink. "Yuri, this is nearly water. I should arrest Sergei for treason," he said with a laugh.

"He is a good boy and he looks after me."

Gorki turned serious. "You are doing well, my friend?"

Cherkin gave a tired smile. "I am doing better. Soon I hope to be doing well. I think that if I have survived these past three weeks, there is some hope for me."

"And maybe for Russia too, Yuri."

"I suspect much of that hope depends on you and our American friends," Cherkin said as he looked away.

"We can depend on them. I have no doubt of it."

"It is not right for you to stand alone out on this limb, Viktor."

Gorki moved toward the door. "I have been on that limb before, Mr. President. I am comfortable out there. It is where my duty lies. And here is where your duty lies." He gestured around the room and bid his friend and leader good evening.

SIMMESPORT, LOUISIANA

Simmons nodded with satisfaction as he watched the young SESA members perform their assignments. Kennedy's team readied a Land Rover to receive its door panel logo. They applied spray paint over the stencil Henry McMahon had provided. After a few minutes they removed the stencil to reveal the castle insignia with the words "U.S. Army Corps of Engineers" encircling it.

On a table in front of the supply tent, Reilly inspected another rolled length of gray claylike material. He measured the roll, removed it from the table and disappeared into the tent. Workers quickly moved to a large pile of the compound that lay amid the broken pieces of what had once been a seven foot tall statue of St. Boniface. They cut another ten pound wad of the material and repeated the rolling process.

A few yards away Hector's group meticulously pruned the ends off lengths of electrical wire. They arranged the lengths in pairs and capped the ends. A team member then folded the wire and carried it into the supply tent.

Davaron moved among them delivering soft drinks and food. As soon as Simmons broke the statue open, she recognized the contents as plastic explosive. From the color she knew it was not standard C-4. Reports inside the Bureau indicated a former Eastern Bloc country had developed a more powerful form of the explosive. She seemed to recall the name CS-5 but that was not important. Her immediate problem was that she had no way of getting the information to an outside source.

She spotted Trent in front of his command tent and made her way over to him. "Coffee or juice, Mr. Trent?" she offered with the inviting smile that seemed to charm most male members of the group.

"Juice would be fine," Trent replied pleasantly.

"Everyone is working so hard around here, I feel like I'm not helping much," Davaron said in her air head character.

"We have important work ahead, Barbara. Every contribution matters greatly."

"From the looks of things everything will work out fine."

The tent opened and Maria emerged with rage in her eyes. She swept past Trent and confronted Davaron. "You bitch. Stay away from him." Without warning she pushed Davaron to the ground and jumped on top of her, flailing wildly with both hands at her fallen victim.

Davaron suppressed her instinct to dispatch the woman. The last thing she needed was for someone to recognize standard self-defense tactics. She shielded herself from DeLeon's attack, trying to appear as helpless as possible. All the while she pleaded for assistance.

Simmons looked up from one of the work stations. He silently cursed both women as he walked over and pulled DeLeon off just as Trent stepped in to break up the fray.

DeLeon's assault turned verbal as Simmons restrained her and Trent helped Davaron to her feet. "You've been after him for over a month. Leave him alone or I'll rip your tits off and shove 'em down your throat."

Davaron decided to respond to a month of actual and implied accusations. She summoned up her best Southern accent and looked DeLeon straight in the eye. "I'm not after anybody around here. But if I was and it was between you and me, you wouldn't stand a chance. All you do is bitch and moan. You're the biggest pain in the ass I've ever met, and besides that you smell funny."

A collective cheer went up from everyone who had stopped to watch the confrontation. Maria had become almost unbearable since becoming Trent's regular bed companion. Most of them had waited months for someone to stand up to her. In deference to Trent they had held their feelings inside.

Trent and Simmons looked at each other like parents who were totally amused but still had to scold their children. Trent helped Davaron to her feet and straightened her clothing. Simmons unceremoniously ushered DeLeon back into the tent. "Now stay in there and cool off," he said sternly as he backed away from the entrance.

"Okay, everyone let's get back to work," Trent announced. The camp slowly returned to its routine. "Go clean up and take a little break, Barbara. I promise this will not happen again," he said gently.

Davaron realized a possible solution to her situation. "I'm tired of everyone around here treating me like I'm stupid. I want to go home. This isn't fun anymore." She thought she detected a hint of panic on Trent's face.

"Don't be silly, my dear," he said with a slight quiver in his voice. "Do me a favor. Relax and think about it. All will be fine in a little while. Give it a few days and we can talk again if you want." He patted her shoulder and smiled.

Davaron's crestfallen expression was more sincere than she planned. It was obvious Trent did not want her off the camp-site. She shrugged in resignation and walked away.

Simmons caught up with her and gently put his hand on her back. "Don't let her get to you, Barbara. We all know she's a pain. Mr. Trent thinks the world of you. And from everyone's reaction to your little speech, you can tell that they all like you," he gestured around the work area. "If it matters, I think you do good work and contribute far more than you suspect. I'd consider it a personal favor if you stayed on."

Davaron hoped Simmons did not feel her cringe at his touch. Even when he spoke with sincerity he seemed evil. She hedged a bit. "Thank you, Al. I have to admit that almost everyone treats me okay around here. I'll give it till the end of the week. But if I feel like I do now, I'll leave then. Okay?"

"That's all I ask. By the end of the week this will be no more than a remote memory. You have my word on that. Now go get cleaned up and take a break like Mr. Trent said." Simmons congratulated himself on his diabolical ambiguity. By the end of the week her entire life would be no more than a remote memory. He caught up with Trent and they walked to a clearing away from the main area of the camp.

"I'm getting Maria out of here," Trent said.

"I don't know if that's such a good idea, sir," Simmons said nervously.

"Don't worry. I'll let her stew for a day, then send her off to Naples to take care of some things at the office. We'll make it seem like she is necessary and the trip is important."

Simmons was not enthusiastic. "What if she starts talking around and gives us away?"

"She will buy it long enough for us to do what we have to here. For the first day or two she'll bury herself in the work. You know how obsessive she is. By the time she gets to feeling abandoned all of this will be over."

"How can you be so sure?"

Trent grinned broadly. "I suggest you tune into CNN and find out what's going on upriver. Then you can tell me if Maria will be a problem. You can also give me a revised timetable for the operation if the spirit moves you."

Simmons knew smugness when he saw it. The weather patterns in the north must have worked their magic to perfection. "I'll get right on it, Mr. Trent. We can move any time."

"That's what I wanted to hear. Get back to me as soon as you have a revised schedule." Trent walked away. He preferred solitude when pondering his destiny.

BATON ROUGE, LOUISIANA

"Bring it on in. A little more. Got her." With a gentle tug the fireman dislodged the body from the bridge pier and brought it into the rescue boat. The pilot backed away from the pier while the two fire fighters in the bow section began their initial report.

"Central Station, this is River 1. We have a female caucasian on board. We'll do a preliminary and get back to you."

"Copy that, River 1. State your location."

"Copy, Central. North side of the east pier of the I-10 bridge. Repeat, north side of east pier of the I-10 bridge."

"Copy, River 1. Will stand by for preliminary."

The body showed little sign of the disfigurement that comes with protracted time in the river. The rescue team conducted their examination with routine precision.

"Any obvious marks?" the team leader asked.

"There is a small lump on the back of the head. That could have happened when she hit the bridge," the young woman said as she worked her hand around the base of the neck and up the right side of the victim's head.

"Too bad she didn't hold onto her purse," the fireman said rhetorically as he wrote down the results of his inspection and his partner's examination of the body. "If you can't find any other marks this could be a jumper."

"She hasn't been in the water more than forty eight hours, seventy two tops," his partner said. "Did any of the gambling boats report an 'overboard' this weekend?"

"Not according to our records. We got the sighting from a passing towboat."

"I'd say she is in her early fifties. Seems like she was in good shape. It didn't take much water to start stretching the skin." The woman rolled her eyes as she recalled one of her first recoveries. The body had been in the river for over a month and water had inflated the corpse to grotesque proportions. She thought, at the time that the dead man resembled a five hundred pound water balloon.

"Wait a minute. Here is something." She reached into a small pocket of the dead woman's skirt and removed a plastic coated badge with a clip attached to it. "What a break! Her employee I.D. badge. It looks like we have a civil servant type here." She passed the badge to her partner.

He attached it to his clip board and squinted as he tried to read the name on the waterlogged identification card. On his report sheet, in the spaces marked "name" and "address" he wrote "Reese, Virginia" and "Louisiana Environmental Office."

"How about that. She probably spent her career worrying about this damn river and this is how it showed its gratitude. Oh, well. I'll call it in. I'm sure they will have to notify somebody in the morning that they have been promoted." He shook his head and reached for the radio.

CINCINNATI, OHIO

Harte stared at the clock on the nightstand. The digit changed to 6:01. It was the tenth time he had seen the number move forward. A voice inside said it was time to get up. His body said another hour in bed would be extremely helpful.

Saturday and Sunday had been all-day attempts at analysis of the nearly deciphered disk of Herbert Loman's personal log. The cities, dates and all but one of the two-letter groups were in order but the information seemed to lead nowhere.

Some time late Sunday afternoon Lydia excused herself just to get out of the house. Shortly thereafter, Rita announced that she was taking Andy into the city for some R&R. Harte felt that the entire situation reeked of a "friendly conspiracy."

He and Samantha found themselves alone together for the first time since Washington. They ate a quiet early dinner and spent some time on the patio. Nature cooperated with a lull in what had been more than a week of cold rain. As evening approached, they built a fire and settled in to watch TV.

The dream date ended unceremoniously around 10:00 when the week's activities caught up with Harte and he nodded off to sleep on the couch with Samantha sitting next to him. He awoke around midnight, to find himself alone on the sofa with a small cushion pillow on his chest and a light blanket for cover. A touch of the pillow yielded the still warm imprint of Samantha's head where she had curled up next to him and slept.

On his way to the bedroom he stopped in the dining room and found a piece of paper on which he wrote the word "Sorry." He slipped the note under her door and retired to bed where he slept in fits and starts until the clock watch began.

Once again he tried to fit the pieces of Loman's log into a picture. With the exception of one set of overlapping entries, the Latin American and Southeastern U.S. entries implied two distinct time frames. The only deviations from the pattern were the Beirut entries, one near the end of the Latin American chronology, and one in the middle of the U.S. listings. And HB was still a complete mystery.

The telephone prevented Harte from rehashing the sequence again. It dawned on him that a very limited number of people would be calling on his private line at this hour. Irritation quickly gave way to anticipation.

"Hello." Harte snapped the greeting.

"Dan, it's Tim. If you are in bed get up. If you are up make coffee. I'll be there in ten minutes."

"Where are you, for God's sake? It's 6:15 in the morning."

"I'm at your exit on I-275. It's a long story. Just get ready. You are going to love this one."

Harte replaced the receiver as his feet hit the floor. Within minutes he was in the kitchen. The phone must have acted as an alarm clock. One by one the house guests filed into the area in various stages of alertness.

Samantha entered the kitchen as Harte finished filling two coffee cups. She held the note up and looked at him with still dreamy eyes. "Don't worry. You were comfortable."

When Rita arrived, Harte and Samantha exchanged a quick smile and left it at that. "Good morning, kiddies," Rita announced in a remarkable state of good cheer. "I hope we all had an enjoyable evening." She resisted a more probing comment.

The comment and attitude cemented Samantha's suspicion of the Saturday night social conspiracy. "Mine was wonderful," She said on her way out to the dining room.

Harte looked at Rita with a shrug and a dumb grin. "Me too," he said, leaving her alone in the kitchen.

She stood by the coffee maker as Lydia walked in. "Well?" the history professor asked her young colleague.

Rita clenched her fist. "Yes!"

"Well thank the Lord," Lydia said as they joined the group at the conference table.

Moments later Loman ushered Lassick in. Tim wore the look of an all-night traveler but his enthusiasm belied the exhausted facial expression.

"This better be good," Lydia warned good naturedly.

"This is better than good," Lassick replied, unable to hide his excitement. "I found this late last night while researching a story on the Persian Gulf crisis. It was too hot for a phone call." Lassick produced a folder from his briefcase and pointed to the name on the cover. "Ladies and gentlemen, meet Hamur Bantar, or HB as we've come to know him."

Five pairs of hands grabbed for the folder. Loman got control and quickly rifled through the papers inside. A white letter-size envelope fell onto the table.

"Those are the pictures you got from the FBI agent down at the SESA camp. I didn't get anything from them," Lassick said to Harte, before turning his attention to the contents of the folder. "The paperwork is a short outline of an Iranian named Hamur Bantar. Most reports consider him a small time terrorist, if there is such a thing. His name keeps popping up through indirect links and references to some notorious activities around the world. But there is not a scrap of hard evidence on him."

He waited for comments but none came. "Some of these actions go back ten years. That's a long time for a bit player to remain active in that line of work. Small-timers usually wind up as sacrificial lambs so the authorities can act like they've made a major arrest. Or they wind up dead when the organization has no more use for them.

"So I tried a different take. What if his name came up by accident on those reports? Say some cop is questioning a prisoner and Bantar's name comes up in passing? Maybe the cop enters the name on the report as an afterthought and suddenly there is this recurring character and no information.

"Even with central filing it would be easy to consider him a low level nobody. If you're not looking for something it probably is not going to be there."

Loman studied one of the papers in the folder. "This looks like some kind of official dispatch."

"That's the good stuff," Lassick said triumphantly. "Don't even ask how I got this, but it's a copy of a diplomatic message from Teheran to their embassy in Tripoli after we bombed Lybia in '86. It instructs the embassy on the official response to the fact that one our 500 pound bombs 'accidentally' landed in the front yard of their embassy.

"Look at the signature line in the lower left. After the signer's name and title there is a slash followed by initials. What are they?"

"HB," Loman said curiously.

"Exactly. My source on this says that when you see initials after the signature line like that, it indicates who dictated the message. It signals that the message is authorized from much higher up the chain than the signer."

If silence is golden, the dining room of Harte's home was the vault at Ft. Knox. When Lassick felt that everyone was on the same page, he made his assessment. "I'm convinced that 'HB' is Hamur Bantar. He is a high-ranking Iranian official who is, in all probability, one of their chief terrorists. Someone from our list has contacted him. And all of a sudden I get the feeling we are dealing with more than an environmental nut case named Morgan Trent."

Harte's gaze fell on Samantha who studied one of Barbara Davaron's pictures. The look on her face was one of anxious puzzlement. "Something wrong, Sam?"

She held up the picture of Simmons and dropped a bomb of her own on the table. "When did Gene Russell join SESA?"

"What are you talking about?" Harte asked half seriously.

"This is the guy I marked on the South Air flight to Tampa. His name is Eugene Russell."

"Are you sure?" Lassick asked skeptically

"It's my job to be sure," she snapped back indignantly.

"All right, All right," Harte announced raising his hands over the table. "Let's all take a breath and put this into perspective."

"Sorry, Tim," Samantha volunteered.

"Don't worry about it. I feel just as strongly about my information. At this time of day I would have snapped at anyone who questioned it." He looked around the table. "We have a big bag of shit on our hands folks and I do not have the foggiest idea what to do with it."

"How about this?" Rita said looking up from the computer screen. "From the beginning we've had Andy's father tracking three guys. That always bothered me. Shouldn't that be a one-on-one proposition? Am I in the ballpark on this, Sam?"

"Certainly. You put ironclad coverage on a primary target." Samantha replied.

"Okay. We've agreed that AS and ER are the same individual.

That tells us Mr. Loman was tracking one person. If he was on, what did you call it, Sam, 'ironclad coverage,' the why can't AF be that same guy? I've checked through the chronology. The only sets of initials that never appear in the same multiple entry are AS, ER, and AF. I think they are aliases for the same person. And if all of our theories hold up, he does assassinations for a living."

Lydia spoke up. "Mr. Loman's log has our man meeting with Bantar in Beirut twice in the last eighteen months."

Throughout the discussion, Harte watched Loman. What had occurred to him a few minutes earlier was slowly dawning on the young computer analyst. Loman's expression slowly moved from enthusiasm to brooding. The brooding turned to pain as he discovered the identity of his father's murderer.

Harte got Rita's attention. She casually moved to the open chair next to Andy and put her arm around him lovingly.

Loman nodded gratefully. "Thanks, Rita. It's okay. I've had my grief. But I appreciate it. I surely do."

"Anytime, partner," Rita replied and hugged him gently.

The implications sunk in with each of them. Samantha realized what her discovery had triggered. "Andy, I'm so sorry. I had no idea it would come to this."

Loman looked at her sadly. "It's okay, Sam. It's part of what we have been trying to accomplish here. I think, deep down, I knew that it could come to something like this." He reached across the table and gently touched her hand. Then he looked resolutely around the room. "Now, somebody tell me what we are going to do about it."

Harte reached for the telephone. "I know what we are going to do. We are going to get some help and find Morgan Trent and Albert Simmons quickly. And I know just the man to help us out." He dialed a number in Langley, Virginia.

"Prince here," said the weary voice.

"Mike, it's Dan."

"What can I do for you?" The voice seemed decidedly matter-of-fact compared to Harte's urgent tone.

"I'm getting ready to come to D.C. and I need a favor when I get there; the sooner the better."

Prince's voice registered a little more interest. "Is this related to our project?" he asked, knowing the answer.

"No. I need an oil change and I want you to set up an appointment for me. What the hell do you think?" Harte looked incredulously at Samantha, who put her hand to her mouth to hide her smile.

"That was a good one," Prince replied with a chuckle. "Since you kept it clean I assume Sam is listening in."

"I have us on the conference line. Look Mike, this is really kind of urgent."

"What do you need?" Prince's tone said that he was up to speed on the conversation.

"I need aerial photographs of a ten square mile area around the town of Simmesport, Louisiana. I can be at your office by 10:30 to pick them up."

"No problem. I'll have Photo Mat whip something up."

"I'm serious," Harte said impatiently.

"That's the problem," Prince replied, his voice stern but official. "I can't do it."

"You don't realize what's going on here."

Prince cut him off. "I know what's going on. First, I'm holding a memo that strongly restates the administration's position regarding the Southeast Endangered Species Association. A report came into EPA concerning what Morgan Trent considered harassing tactics by a couple of government agents."

He did not wait for a response. "Second, even if I wanted to get your pictures there's no way. Everything is up over the Persian Gulf right now. I don't have any assets to spare."

Harte tried to think quickly. "Can't you, uh..."

He looked toward Samantha who mouthed a phrase. Harte nodded. "Can't you retask one of the satellites for a couple of passes over Louisiana?"

"Nice one, Sam," came the reply through the speaker.

Samantha looked around the table and smiled smugly.

"No way." Prince said. "We need every detail we can get over there as close to real time as possible. I can't order a bird out of there for a domestic shoot. They would never allow it, especially in light of this memo. If word got out that we retasked a satellite to snoop on Trent, they'd drag us naked down Pennsylvania Avenue."

"Does that memo mention areas to avoid?" Harte asked.

The conference speaker was silent for a moment. "No. What's you're point?"

"If I wanted to ensure compliance I would state, in no uncertain terms, what area to avoid. That would lay down the law in black and white."

"That's one for you, I suppose."

"Okay, then try this. Since there is no specific 'off limits' area, and you can't tell the cops to avoid an entire state, whoever authorized that memo probably has no idea where Trent is." Harte held his breath.

Prince was evasive. "It could be a general cover memo. That would explain the lack of specifics."

"Listen to me, Mike. Billy and I have been on everything that resembles a road down there. I cannot locate a compound with eighteen people, thirteen tents, a generator, a water tank and five vehicles. Call me overly suspicious but I think that is just a little odd."

"I like your thought process, Dan, but I am in no position to help. It's not my decision to make."

Harte made a last attempt. "Try to understand this. Trent is a complete loon. I believe he is planning a militant action somewhere in Louisiana. One of his followers may have murdered people, including Herb Loman. And if it wasn't for Billy's driving skills the tally might be higher. I am going to try to stop this guy, but I need some help. What are you going to do about this?"

A sigh came over the speaker. "Here is the official word. I cannot authorize a photo reconnaissance of your area on what the higher-ups will call speculation and hearsay. If you want out because of this, I understand and that's the end of it. I wish it could be different but there is nothing I can do."

Harte set his jaw. "Michael, I'll be on a plane for D.C. in a little over two hours. If they do not let me through the gate at Langley, my next stop will be Capitol Hill to discuss the matter with a couple of acquaintances. Where it goes from there is anyone's guess."

"Do what you have to. Because that's exactly what I am doing. I'm sorry. I hope this is not the last time we talk to each other but that will be up to you."

A soft drone told them the connection had been broken. Harte drummed his fingers and looked to the ceiling. "Andy, confirm me on the next flight to Washington. Dulles or National, I don't care. I can get to the airport in about an hour and a half." Without another word he left the room.

Samantha looked at the others who sat quietly at the table. Each silently considered the ramifications of the call. All that they had worked so long and hard for had come to a crashing halt, and just when they seemed so close to a solution. An emotional balloon had exploded leaving them exhausted in their chairs. "This is just bullshit," she said, to everyone's surprise, and reached for the phone.

"Dan, I told you I'm sorry about this..."

"This is Samantha."

Prince became edgy. "Sam, don't do it. You know I am right on this one."

"Mike, you have to do this. Dan would not ask if he didn't think it was important."

"How can you say that?" Prince asked impatiently.

"Because these people have done everything on their own so far without a lick of help from us or any other agency, and they have a solid case."

The truth hit home. "Don't you think I know that? I had no idea it would go this far. But I cannot get the photos. I don't even have a U-2 available. Everything in the inventory is on priority coverage over the Gulf."

Samantha looked around and winked. "You can get them if you have to, and you know exactly what I'm talking about."

"We better not be on conference right now."

"We are. And if you hang up I will tell everyone here what we are talking about."

"Sam, you can't do that. It's against the law. You just don't understand what is—"

"No, you don't understand. This is beyond 'need to know' and all that stuff." She assumed a sisterly tone. "Michael, do something for me. You know that Rolodex by your phone?"

"Yes," came the slightly irritated reply.

"Thumb through it and count the number of names that you can truly call friends. I'll wait. It should not take long."

"That isn't fair," Prince said, his voice faltering.

"You are absolutely right for a change," she said, regaining the upper hand. "Dan Harte is one of your few good friends and you have used him and everyone in this room on a garbage detail you did not have time for. They put their lives on hold and made personal sacrifices for what they each decided is more important than individual achievement. Now that they have something to show for it you've cut them off at the knees.

"You have no right to use them like you did and then discard them because of a momentary inconvenience or a lack of will. If that's how we are going to do business then I will get on that plane with Dan and drop in just long enough to type up my resignation. The Agency will get along fine without me. But I don't know how well I could get along without the people at this table and others like them.

"And the real truth is, if you keep walking away from the Dan Hartes and Bill Harmons of the world, you will eventually be nothing more than a fat ass bureaucrat, whining about how the system abuses you and worrying about your lousy pension. Don't do this for me or Dan. Do it for the country. Do it for yourself. Duty doesn't always go by the book, Mike. It is time for you to do yours."

"Was there anything else?" Prince asked meekly.

"Does there have to be?" Samantha asked bluntly.

"What time is his flight?"

Samantha breathed a sigh of relief as she looked at the monitor. "Flight 292. It arrives at Dulles at 10:05 at Gate 12. That's enough time for at least one pass and maybe two."

"I know. Relax. You made your point."

"Don't be angry with me, Mike. It had to be said."

"I'm not, Sam. I'm angry at me for losing sight of things. You are right. It had to be said, and it was far better to hear it from you than from someone I don't care so much about."

"Thanks, Mike."

"I have to roust the boys over at NRO. Keep in touch, okay."

Samantha smiled, "Of course. Say hello to Janice for me. And while you are at, it take her to lunch. You might be surprised at how things go."

"I'm a step ahead of you on that one. I don't have to be hit over the head with a board on everything. Talk to you soon."

Four sets of eyes stared a questioning hole through her. "Don't ask. I don't even think I'm supposed to know about this one. Mike will tell Dan, if he thinks it is necessary." She shuffled some papers as Harte re-entered the room.

"You got my flight, Andy?" he said as he adjusted his tie. He noticed the increased activity at the table.

Loman handed the flight information to Samantha. She picked up a briefcase. "I'll walk you out to the door," she said as she came to Harte's side.

He glanced around curiously. "Is something going on that I should know about?"

Samantha took his arm and led him to the front door. "No, I think we are just all finally awake," she said, dismissing his concerns. At the doorway she stopped him long enough to re-adjust his tie. "There. Perfect. You might need this." As she handed him the briefcase it occurred to her that she almost added "honey."

Harte was quick on the uptake. "This looks disturbingly domestic to me," he said wryly.

"We can discuss that another time. Have a good day, dear." She kissed him lightly.

OLD RIVER AREA, LOUISIANA

Haisley shook his head as he read the incoming messages. Along the Missouri, Mississippi and Ohio Rivers, reporting stations kept him abreast of conditions. The overall message was crystal clear. A late-winter flood in America's midsection had reached catastrophic proportions.

From the Rocky Mountains to the Appalachians, over a hundred thousand streams and rivers were cycling their water through the system and into the Lower Mississippi River. The only bright spot came when Cincinnati and Pittsburgh reported that the rain seemed to be easing. Though the Ohio River was not dropping, it might level off. If the trend held, at least the long-term outlook was optimistic. Still, a massive volume of water was working its way down the Lower Mississippi river toward Baton Rouge and New Orleans.

"Aaron, take a look at this," Haisley called into the adjoining office.

Roosevelt entered the room studying a chart. He handed it to Haisley and looked over the flood reports. "This matches up with the silt readings through the afternoon collection."

Haisley studied the readings. "I think we'll find out this time if we know what we are doing down here, or if we've just been pissing in the wind all these years. Sometimes I wish they would have shot old Captain Shreve before he could dig his damn outflow."

The two engineers smiled weakly at the reference. Captain Henry Miller Shreve had constructed the first connecting channel between the rivers in 1831. Located ten miles downstream from Haisley's main complex, the canal enabled the famed river boatman to economically get timber from the Red River to markets along the Mississippi. Little did the Captain know at the time how much money and manpower would be expended to maintain his six mile long canal.

"We better start easing the pressure on the Low Sill right away," Haisley said. "Get on over to the Auxiliary Structure and take Gates Three and Four up a couple feet."

"Two at a time may just keep things under control for the whole run," Roosevelt said hopefully.

"From the looks of this incoming information we won't even see the main bubble for another two days or so," Haisley replied, rubbing the stubble of two days' growth of beard. It's going to get pretty hairy out here."

"We'll handle it," Roosevelt said on his way out the door.

Haisley leaned on the window sill. "If you say so Aaron," he said to the empty office as he looked across the water covered flood plain toward the raging Mississippi River.

DULLES INTERNATIONAL AIRPORT

Flight 292 touched down on the main north/south runway. Harte knew the flight to Washington was a waste of time and energy. But his gut instinct told him to make the trip. He tried to formulate a secondary plan if, as he suspected, the guard at Langley refused him entrance.

He had no hard evidence to back up his assertions, a fact which continued to gnaw at his confidence. He was sure something terrible would happen soon in Louisiana, but he simply could not prove it. In that regard he stood out on a limb, alone but for the loyalty of a few good men and women. A nagging inner voice kept hammering at the idea that the problem with Trent fit into some much larger picture.

The threat to go to Capitol rang hollow. If a friend with the insider knowledge of the CIA refused to act, there was no way an elected official could muster any interest; at least not in the time frame Harte needed. His only real option was to follow through on his original plan and see where the chips fell. He stopped at a bank of seats inside the terminal to get his identification and paperwork for the rental car in order.

"Mr. Harte?"

He jumped at the sound of his name and turned abruptly to find a young man in the uniform blazer of Delta Airlines. "Yes. What do you want?" he responded tentatively, then silently chastised himself for his suspicion. There were few places on earth safer than the area around a boarding gate at Dulles.

"I didn't mean to startle you, sir. I was told to give you this when you arrived." He held out a sealed envelope.

Harte took the envelope. "Sorry I snapped."

"No problem, sir. If you need anything else the assistance desk is at the end of the concourse," the young man replied pleasantly before taking his leave.

The only thing written on the envelope was his name. He opened it, half expecting a message from Samantha or somebody else back in Cincinnati. The note inside was a seven-word, hand-written sentence with no signature: "Meet me at the cornfield at 11:00."

A trace of a smile crossed Harte's face as he let out a barely audible sigh. He had a little less than one hour to get out of the airport and cover twenty seven miles on mostly back roads. The time frame was perfect. For some reason he was not at all surprised.

ANTIETAM NATIONAL BATTLEFIELD

Harte stared out over the field he had visited so often in the past. In early March "The Cornfield," freshly plowed, showed a mere hint of life. Whatever time of year he stood on the spot he could always envision that dreadful September morning in 1862. The corn stood well over six feet high and the dawning sun bathed the crop in its life giving light.

History became the present as Harte imagined himself riding with General Joseph Hooker as the Union Commander's Corps approached the battlefield from the northeast woods. Their conversation was interrupted by the General's sudden attention to the front. A glint of sunlight on steel in the cornfield ahead alerted Hooker to an ominous presence. Stonewall Jackson's men were waiting.

Immediately Hooker ordered his infantry into firing lines and at 6:30 A.M., the Union Army unleashed a withering artillery and rifle assault on the Rebels hidden among the cornstalks. Jackson's men broke and ran leaving over a thousand dead or wounded in the field. Hooker's Corps gave chase and thus began the bloodiest and, according to some, most pivotal day in American history. By six o'clock that evening, the first Confederate invasion of the North had been stopped and over twenty three thousand men lay dead or wounded on ten square miles of gently rolling hills on the outskirts of Sharpsburg, Maryland.

Harte became immersed in history as he leaned on a map stand that describes the events of that morning to visitors touring the battlefield. An envelope landing on the glass enclosed chart shattered his concentration and brought him back to reality.

"A good friend once told me the Nation was saved here that day," a voice said from his left.

Harte stared ahead. "Some of us think so. I had no idea you could be so dramatic."

"It's as much practicality as anything," Prince said as he came around and stood between Harte and the field. "You've had me hopping around the area all morning and I wanted a place out of the way but familiar. This seemed like the right place at the right time."

Harte looked through a stack of pictures. Even his untrained eye recognized the enhanced satellite photos.

"That one will probably interest you the most," Prince pointed out as Harte came to the fifth photograph.

The picture showed a river bank and the land along it. Harte's eyes came to rest on a slightly fuzzy grouping near the upper right hand corner.

"Try this," Prince said offering a small magnifying glass.

Although Harte could not make out precise definition, an unmistakable design came into focus under the glass. A semicircular line of light colored objects and a straight line of three larger objects directly across from the arc caused him to exhale deeply. "How did you know?" he asked without looking up.

"A few years ago we did a fly-over of Trent's camp in Naples and took a couple of pictures. You just never know when something like that will come in handy."

"You said all the satellites are assigned to the Persian Gulf."

"They are. And so are all of our low altitude assets."

"How could you retask one of them so quickly?"

"We didn't," Prince said in a slightly smug tone.

"Gimme a break, Mike. You know this is killing me."

Prince looked away toward the battlefield. "Every ninety minutes or so, a Russian bird flies over the area. We lifted the shots off its downlink."

"You're kidding," Harte said almost bursting out laughing. "How the hell can you do that? It's all computer-run."

Prince shrugged. "Where do you think they got all their hardware and software? Nothing goes out that we can't override. Everyone in the industry knows that. For the last ten years or more we've made sure the Russians acquired certain components so they would build the system we wanted them to."

"No shit. I've always had my suspicions about that." Harte was nearly giddy.

"Yeah, I know," Prince replied without emotion. "When I was briefed on all of this I told the Agency you had once talked about something like that. They asked where you got the information. I told them that, as far as I knew, from logical assumption. I was correct, wasn't I?"

"Yes. Yes, of course," Harte replied honestly. "This is too good to be true. I can't wait to tell—"

"No one," Prince interrupted him emphatically.

"What?" Harte said. His smile faded as reality set in.

"That information is part of a classified Agency briefing, given while you are temporarily cleared to certain security levels. If you reveal anything you learned through your cleared status, it is a felony punishable by up to ten years in prison and a fifty thousand dollar fine. Welcome to spook world, Dan." Prince grinned maliciously.

Harte was crestfallen. He looked at the picture of Trent's camp. "I guess there are no freebies in this game, huh."

"Especially this game." Prince instinctively looked around to confirm that they were alone. "I can't begin to explain all that is going on right now. It has nothing to do with clearance. We just don't have time to get into all of it. I got the problem in the Persian Gulf, which you know about from the news. I got a big problem with the Russians and I'm beginning to think the two may be related. Hell, for all I know, Morgan Trent might be involved in it too."

Prince did not want to alarm his friend but he needed to bounce his ideas off someone from the outside to see if anything made sense.

"Everything I look at has two words plastered all over it; oil and Iran. I have a report that the new Russian Defense Minister was actually across the Iranian border in Tabriz not long ago. I think the Iranians are making some kind of move and General Kasarov may be in on it."

Harte decided to add his two cents worth. "Tim Lassick thinks one of the names in Herb Loman's log is Hamur Bantar," he said as calmly as possible.

"Jesus Christ! Is that all?"

"No." Harte cleared his voice. "It's only speculation on our part, but if we are right, one of Trent's people met with Bantar on one or two occasions."

"I want you out of this right now," Prince said as he made a swipe at the stack of photographs.

Harte pulled the pictures out of reach. "No way, Mike."

"I can't let you go any further on this."

Harte stood his ground. "I have to stay on this. Billy is in Louisiana right now. There is an undercover FBI agent stuck in Trent's camp. Along with a few other people I've come to know, they are counting on me. If I don't see this through who will? You already said your hands are tied on the matter."

"We'll figure something out."

"That's not good enough. Think about it for a minute. If, as you say, all these things are interrelated, exposing Trent could throw a monkey wrench into the whole plan. I assume you have an overall plan."

"Yes," Prince replied with irritation.

"Fine. So if you come down on Trent the whole thing could unravel. Not to mention that if he's just out counting birds, you guys will be in so much hot water, from the White House and some of their friends in Congress, that it could screw things up for a long time. On the other hand, If I'm wrong about this it's no big deal. The worst that can happen is that I'll be trashed by the media. I can live with that. If I'm right, you can bring in the cavalry."

"That's not the worst thing that can happen to you," Prince said ominously.

"Yes it is. Unless I'm stupid. Look Mike, I'm not without assets of my own on this. All you have to do is give an unofficial nod in a few places and I'll put something together. You know what I mean."

Prince understood, but a question nagged at him. "Why are you doing this?"

"Because sometimes you just have to stand up and be counted. It's all a matter of duty and honor. I've met a lot of people in the last few weeks who quietly live their lives by that code. It hit me when Billy and I were driving back from the Old River Complex. I kept thinking they are like the heroes I thought I lost when I grew up."

Harte gathered his thoughts. "It's like this place. The cemetery here is full of names on headstones. Some don't even have names. Just a bunch of ordinary guys. But what men they must have been, on both sides, to stand and fight like that."

He gestured around the battlefield. "You know the first time I ever came here, it was a warm June morning and I got a chill up my spine, almost like I was here on that day. I need to act with that sense of ultimate duty and loyalty, at least once more in my lifetime. And I think this is that moment." He looked out over the cornfield one more time. "I don't know, Mike, maybe this is my Antietam. Maybe not. But I'm absolutely certain it is something I have to do."

It was useless for Prince to attempt to dissuade him but he tried one more approach. "If something happens to you out there, Samantha will kill me."

"She understands. She can handle it."

"Come with me," Prince said. They walked through the trees and into another clearing. He made a circle over his head with his index finger. On cue the pilot fired the engine of the waiting helicopter. By the time they reached the doorway the noise forced them to shout.

"He will take you back to Dulles. There's a South Air flight waiting to take you back to Louisiana. You will get the details on the way to the airport."

"What about the car?"

"I'll drive it back," Prince shouted. "I want to spend a little time here. It's been a while since I visited the place. After all that's gone on this morning, I need to take a look around and get a few things in order."

"Good for you, Mike." Harte offered his hand.

Prince ignored the gesture and embraced his old friend. "Watch your ass down there. I want to sit around and laugh about all of this when it's finished. Do you understand?"

"No problem, boss," Harte said. He boarded the helicopter and watched Prince head back through the tree line.

"Next stop Dulles, Mr. Harte," the pilot announced.

"Let's go," Harte said as the chopper lifted off and banked hard toward the south.

Chapter XII

ZELENOGRAD, RUSSIA

Kasarov looked over his deployment plans. Chechnya would be at most, an inconvenience. He agreed completely with Viktor Gorki that the ongoing independence movement was a cover for a major move on the oil industry by the burgeoning organized crime element in the new Russian Republic.

The Defense Minister planned to nip the situation in the bud with little fanfare. Already three companies of special forces were on hand securing the inspection route. The visit would appear as a routine activity but along the roads of the renegade province, the true meaning of the "inspection" would be unmistakable. Chechens would understand the folly of supporting a move toward freedom.

If the criminals still did not see the light, Kasarov had an armored division and a reinforced infantry division, ready to deploy on a "training mission." The deployment could become permanent with the stroke of a pen. After a few pesky questions at a press conference or two, and heart-felt apologies to the United Nations, the Caspian Sea oil would be secure and the plan would be back on schedule.

He marveled at how simple things could be when politics did not cloud the issue. All one needed was the will to use force and anything could be resolved. Chechnya might damage Yuri Cherkin politically, a situation Kasarov welcomed, but the Defense Minister would be immune to any political fallout. Kasarov's control of the Defense, Interior and Agriculture ministries precluded any possibility of his removal from office.

In reality, Cherkin's government could fail and dissolve with Kasarov's blessing. A new administration would be forced to build itself around the General's power base. He might even get to pick the next President if all the cards fell properly. At the very least he would have major input on new cabinet selections which would further cement his status as the behind the scenes ruler of Russia. Kasarov stretched in his chair and considered how smoothly his plan was proceeding. In a way he owed the Chechen criminals a debt of gratitude. Their stupidity had paved the way for the final entrenchment of his power. A weekend on the Caspian shores seemed more inviting with each passing minute.

LANGLEY, VIRGINIA

Arthur Henderson allowed himself a moment of compassion. "I understand how you feel, but we are talking about fundamental changes in the political and economic flow of the world."

"I know that. But he is my friend," Prince said weakly.

"We have had this conversation before." Henderson replied more sternly. "You offered him the door and he stayed in the room. He may not know the entire scope of what we are doing, but he must feel his end is significant. I assume you hinted that there is more to this than dogging Morgan Trent."

"To tell you the truth, He mentioned it himself. I didn't give any details, but I confirmed that there might be a bigger picture."

"Then you baited him. What's your problem?" Henderson had invested too much time and effort in Prince's rise through the Agency to allow his young protégé to buckle under the weight of personal feelings.

"That's exactly what bothers me. I feel like I led him into this. I could get him killed."

"He could have stepped away at any time. Have you considered that he might want in, and allowed you to lead him along?"

Prince recalled the conversation at The Cornfield. He had seen a side of Dan Harte he never expected. Harte had a lot to lose and yet demanded a chance to put it all on the line. Prince had heard the words when they were both much younger, talk of duty and honor, but he had never seen Harte in a situation where the words had to translate into action.

So many people in Prince's life talked the talk perfectly but managed to disappear when it came time to act. He found, in the renewal of his friendship with Harte, someone who was at least attempting to stand by the words he spoke. And the bitter irony was, that after waiting so long to find a kindred spirit, Prince had to send his friend into harm's way.

"Are you still with me on this?" Henderson asked in an effort to get Prince back to business.

"Yeah, Arthur," Prince replied. "I just had to get a thought or two in order. Dan will be all right, I think."

"You did have the good sense to give him access to some assets."

Prince nodded his head. "I can't assign a strike team but if he continues to use his head, he can put something on the table that will give him a decided edge."

"Tell you what," Henderson said holding up an Executive memo. "If things goes down right we may get a little payback on this piece of shit. You can be the 'angel of death' if you want, and take your friend Harte along if he's interested."

Prince read as far as the EPA logo. A smile crossed his face. "I think Dan might like to be in on that. Of course I might have trouble getting him away from Samantha long enough to make the visit."

"I can see where that might be a problem, but for him, a pleasant one I'm sure," Henderson said with a chuckle.

"Okay, I'm back. What have we got here?"

Henderson rubbed his hands and studied his game board, as he like to call his tactical plan. In his early years at CIA he had often gone through feelings like Prince was experiencing. Eventually he trained himself to treat everything as a game; a deadly serious game with historical consequences in many cases. But unless the humanity of the situation became moot, no agent could truly do his or her duty.

"Here we go, Mikey." He picked up the telephone. "This is Big Boy. Activate Hunter 1 and 2. Big Boy out."

"Big Boy?" Prince said with a grin.

"It was their idea not mine. I would never be so pompous," Henderson said with mock sincerity. He dialed again. "This is Big Boy. Activate Black 1. Big Boy out."

Prince studied the map of the Middle East and Southern Russia. "It's really hard to believe that such a small area can be the root of so much shit."

"You are probably only the billionth or so person to ever make that statement. Good to see you back on the cutting edge of analysis again, Mike." Henderson's uproarious laugh drowned out Prince's muttered expletive.

PERSIAN GULF

Two hundred and twenty feet below the western entrance to the Strait of Hormuz, the sand swirled gently as Hunter 1 and 2 powered up their engines. The twin Sea wolves lifted off the sea bed and glided into the Persian Gulf. The new rock and sand formation, logged by the *Arlington's* sonar operator on its last passage, ceased to exist. It was transformed into identical killing machines; the fastest, stealthiest, most powerful attack submarines ever built.

"Report, Sonar," said the Commanding Officer of Hunter 1.

"Sonar reports all clear, sir," came the reply.

"All hands, this is the Captain. I'll make this short and sweet.

You pretty much know the situation topside. The good news is we are not alone out here. Hunter 2 is patrolling on the Saudi side. Our mission is to identify and track specific targets in the Persian Gulf. You know that means the Iranian Submarine force. Fortunately, they make it pretty easy for us.

"We will receive additional target data as the mission proceeds. The circumstances can change in an instant and we have offensive authorization on CO's discretion. So keep your heads in the game.

"Gentlemen, let me emphasize that this is not a turkey shoot. Leave your cowboy hats back in your foot lockers. We will almost certainly end up putting a few fish in the water, and before this is finished we are going to give some people a real bad day. So keep it quiet and do your jobs. Let's find them first. Things always work out better that way. Captain out."

He turned to the Executive Officer. "Keep her near the bottom ten miles off the coast. Let's find those rattletraps real quick."

"Aye sir," the Exec replied. "Steer 305, Chief. Adjust at helm's discretion to maintain distance."

"Steer 305. Helm's discretion," The watch chief repeated methodically.

"Sonar contact bearing 262!" a young voice called out.

"Course and speed," the captain replied.

"Course 292. Speed twelve knots, submerged."

The captain glanced at his chart. "Identify."

"It's either an Iranian Sub or a wedding car dragging tin cans along the floor."

A chuckle wafted across the room as the crew responded to the sonar report. The Captain concealed his own amusement. He often made similar remarks regarding the noisy signature of the diesel submarines Iran had purchased from Russia. Some veteran sonar operators claimed they could track the subs by simply putting an ear to the bulkhead.

"I get the picture, Sonar. Let's keep it by the book," the captain replied without emotion. It was more a reminder to the crew than a rebuke of the sonar operator.

"Sorry, sir. He's coming around to course 295. Maintaining

twelve knots. Range 10000."

"Captain, he's heading toward the tip of Qatar. My guess is that he will proceed on up the Saudi side," came the unsolicited report from the Navigation station.

"That sounds good to me. Hunter 2 should be picking him up pretty soon."

"They should be on him already, sir," the navigator replied.

"Captain, Sonar. The way those guys throw off noise, I can go 'passive.' There's no reason to blast away with an active search."

The captain now became the diplomat. "Good idea, Sonar. Make it so. Okay, everyone, that was a good exercise. If we do them all like that, you guys will make me look like the genius the Navy thinks I am." The announcement officially closed the book on the sonar operator's verbal miscue.

"Take over for a while. I'm going to my quarters." The Captain moved toward the hatchway.

"Captain in quarters. Exec has the con," the watch chief announced as the Captain headed down the main passageway.

Once inside his small but amenable cabin, Captain Robert Farragut removed his operating orders from the safe. He considered the phrase, "at captain's discretion." The Navy had put the ultimate power of life or death in his hands. If the mission played out anywhere near the scope of the briefing paper, his discretion could lead to peace or war.

His family name said he had sailor's bloodlines. The Navy banked on the fact that some of the legendary Civil War Admiral's blood had made its way into the young Submarine Captain's veins. Farragut knew this mission would answer that question.

SIMMESPORT, LOUISIANA

Frustration gnawed at Harte. "The photos show it plain as day."

"The good news is there is only one road left," Harmon replied as they looked over the map.

"Let's see what we can find before sunset."

Harmon turned onto a road running northeast along the Atchafalaya River Levee. The bed was a loose surface of uneven asphalt that quickly turned to gravel then, just as quickly, to dirt. "It looks like trucks have been along here. I can't tell when or how big they were," Harmon pointed to marks left by a six-wheeled vehicle.

A mile down the road they encountered a large pool of standing water. It covered the right of way for well over fifty feet and extended past the tree line to the left, into the swampy woods. "What do you think?"

"How deep can it be?" Harte replied.

"You're the boss." The water rose around the wheel wells as Harmon gently urged the car on. Halfway through the tires were submerged to the axle. Slowly the water level dropped and they came back onto the dry road bed again.

"That was exhilarating. I'd like to recross that in daylight if you don't mind." Harmon said pointedly.

"Give it another mile or so," Harte replied tersely.

"Hey. I'm as anxious to find these goons as you are. Maybe more so," Harmon said as he thought of Barbara Davaron.

"Sorry, Billy. This is just frustrating. It's like Trent is right in our laps, and we can't get our hands on him."

Harmon stopped the car as the road turned to a grass-covered path. "It's getting darker. Let's head back and try tomorrow. I don't want to be back here when the lights go out."

"Your right. Turn around."

"You mind if I turn the radio on?" Harmon asked as he retraced his path.

"Keep it low. I'm going to listen out the window if the bugs don't eat me alive."

Harmon found a Baton Rouge station and kept time with the music on the steering wheel. Harte's concern over the insect population became reality and as they approached the standing water he rolled up the window. The top of the hour struck and the radio station began its local news summary.

"The body pulled from the river Saturday has been identified as

Virginia Reese, an employee of the Louisiana Environmental Office. A preliminary report lists the death as an accidental drowning. Ms. Reese had been—"

"That's the woman we've been trying to get in touch with. Jesus Christ, Dan. Don't you think the bodies are starting to pile up just a bit around here?"

"Stay cool." Harte stared into the woods.

"I'm trying. But these guys are killing people. Can't we call someone to take care of this?"

Harte read through the words to Harmon's true concern.. "Billy, she understands the deal. This is a lot bigger than you, me and Barbara. I'll explain it all later. For now just keep your head on straight. I don't need you in pieces. Hey! what was that?"

"Where?" Harmon jumped as he hit the breaks.

"Keep the car moving." Harte nearly shouted. He silently thanked the Louisiana mosquito population for forcing him to roll up the window.

Harmon brought the car smoothly back up to speed and out of the water. "What the hell is going on?" He begged as he drove toward Route 1.

"I thought I saw a light in the thicket back there. Maybe I was just hoping, but it sure looked like a light."

"So what do we do?"

Harte's frustration with the search and his disdain for Trent boiled over. He had originally viewed the environmentalist as a demagogue who had thrown life at the Wilson Foundation life out of sync. Now Trent appeared responsible for at least two deaths. In addition, he had probably ordered someone to try to kill Harte and Harmon and was threatening a lot of innocent lives. All for cheap revenge.

"You probably won't like this but you have to trust me. Get us back to Alexandria."

"What the hell for?" Harmon demanded.

"Because we can't do a thing the way we are. We need sleep and time to see we can get together for this."

Harmon's agitation turned to curiosity. "What do you mean?"

Harte watched the road ahead. "We are going to call on some

people and see what they are ready to ante up for this deal."

"What if they don't come through?"

"One way or another, they will. And once we have everything in place, I'm going to shove Morgan Trent's head so far up his ass the only thing he's going to recognize is shit."

Harmon's eyes widened. "You're really pissed aren't you?"

"You're damn right I am. Now get me back to Alexandria."

"Yes, sir, Mr. Harte," Harmon said with a salute.

"Don't be an asshole, Billy."

"I'm not," Harmon replied. "I'm trusting you with my life and Barbara's, and this is the first time since we started this deal that you've shown me that you are more than just an interested observer. I need you to stay that way." He stopped at the intersection of the levee road and Route 1. "And if you do, I'm prepared to do anything you say. So what's it going to be?"

Harte looked over with a firmly set jaw and a fire in his eyes that Harmon had not seen in years. "Okay, partner. You've got it," he said as they shook on the deal. "Now let's go."

Harmon clapped his hands once. "Now you're talking, boss."

Simmons made his way from the observation post back to the camp and went straight to Trent's living quarters. "We need to talk, Mr. Trent."

"Come on in, Al," Trent's voice beckoned.

Simmons noted no evidence of Maria DeLeon's presence. In some ways it was a relief, but he still considered her absence a potential trip wire. She had not been happy about returning to Naples, even though Trent assured her it would only be for a few days. Simmons did not like her being out on her own, but he bit his lip and went along with the plan. At least there was less tension with her out of the way. "We may have a problem," he announced unceremoniously when the tent flap closed.

"Tell me about it."

"A car just went down the road and I swear that Harte was in the passenger seat."

"Son of a bitch!" Trent threw his pencil. "I'm going to get rid of that nosy bastard if it's the last thing I do."

"The only reason he would be on that road is if he thought he might find us. At least that's how I see it."

Trent fumed at the prospect of Harte interfering with his moment of destiny. "He might not be doing this on his own."

"Exactly. We should move our time table up. I don't want a confrontation with the authorities."

Trent was steps ahead. "The river is up fifteen feet. Forecasters expect it to rise ten more feet by morning. We can move tomorrow. Get everything ready and make sure everyone is well rested. We will be up late tomorrow night."

"Yes, sir." Simmons left the tent in a state of elation. One more night and he would be set for the rest of his life.

The camp was a beehive of activity for the next three hours. Davaron pitched in and tried to hide her anxiety. She still did not know exactly what Trent and Simmons had in mind. Obviously the event would be significant and for now she was powerless to prevent it. She was on her own with a little over twenty-four hours to think of something.

IZMIR, TURKEY

The pilot tried to imagined what his formation must look like to the NATO radar operator. A single C-5A could turn heads when it entered a radar screen. Five of the massive cargo jets in a tight "V" formed a large white blob on whatever screen tracked them from the air base at Izmir. The sight might easily unnerve a rookie tracker or a trainee.

Normally the planes traveled in an extended single line formation, but recent events in the Persian Gulf had altered both the NATO and United States' military routine. The commanders decided to eliminate the twenty five mile no-fly zone which the engine wake of a standard formation would have dictated, so the tight "V" was ordered.

Most of the supplies on board would have gone by ship to Izmir, the Headquarters of Allied Land Forces Southeastern Europe. The developing Saudi crisis made rapid delivery imperative and the C-5As were called in.

The flight leader activated his radio as they approached one hundred and fifty miles from the base. "Blue Five, Giant One."

"Copy, Giant One," came a tense reply. "Have you on screen."

"Roger, Blue Five. Is there a problem?"

"Negative," the voice replied a little more calmly. "You guys sure paint quite a picture."

The Flight Commander grinned at his copilot. "Copy, Blue Five. Sorry we didn't warn you. Let's try not to make this a general information broadcast."

"Copy that. Sorry."

"No harm. Assuming approach formation in three minutes. Standard procedure from that point. Giant One, out."

"Will contact at standard time. Blue Five, out."

The pilot switched frequencies. "Did you get that?"

"Roger. Thanks for the lift."

"Your luggage is on schedule. We break in two minutes. Thanks for flying 'Air-Med,'" the commander replied in his best civilian pilot impression.

"Hope to fly with you again soon."

Seconds before the giant transports broke for their approach, five F117-A's dipped from beneath the huge transports. They dove quickly to the deck and assumed formation five hundred feet above the Mediterranean sea. Turning east northeast, they skimmed above the waves toward the Turkish coast.

"Blue Five, Giant One. Assuming approach formation now." The pilot kept on course as the four accompanying cargo carriers fell into single file for approach to the NATO base.

"Giant One, Blue Five. Did you have accompanying aircraft?"

"Negative. Just the escort service." The flight leader referred to the F-14's far off his starboard wing.

"I have them. Anyone else along for the ride?"

"Negative, Blue Five. Is there a problem?"

"I thought I saw something just as you changed formation. It could have been residual turbulence from your wake but I sure thought I got a glimpse of something. Oh well, it's gone now. You are cleared for approach. Handing you off to tower. Blue Five, out."

"Giant One, out." The flight commander turned off the radio. "He was good. Most operators can't see them even when they know they are coming."

"You didn't expect them to have some 'boot' standing the watch, did you," the copilot replied.

"Good point. We better call Langley when we get in. They may want to debrief him. He won't know whether to pat himself on the back or shit his pants. Let's do the checklist." The Flight Commander chuckled again as he began his approach to Izmir.

Mark Sanders watched the coast of Turkey approach. He swayed slightly in the cockpit as his Stealth Fighter's on board computer adjusted its flight through air currents and temperature changes. The jet moved into a gentle climb and shot over the rugged coastline.

He took manual control and alerted the rest of the flight. "ETA five. Break now."

No call signs and no wasted words. The formation moved from "V" to single file. A slow left turn put them on a northerly course. Minutes later, Sanders peered into the darkness over the Turkish landscape. Two thin lines of yellow light appeared on the ground ahead. With no ground to air communication he focused on a single blue light between the lines and brought his craft to a smooth touchdown on the secluded runway.

He taxied, at full ground speed, toward a looming hill at the end of the runway. A series of red lights dimly illuminated a large hangar bay built into the hillside. Sanders maneuvered into the hangar, swung his plane around facing outboard and shut down the engines. When the remaining four units of "Black 1" followed suit, a curtain of close- weave camouflage netting dropped across the front of the bay. Lights came up and ground crews appeared from the back of the hangar to service the planes.

Sanders walked quickly to the rear of the bay. A civilian met him at an open doorway. "Good to see you, Mark."

"I think I'm glad to be here. What's the agenda?"

"This is going to be a hairy one. Arthur Henderson said he was sending the best he had, if that's any consolation." The two men disappeared down a darkened passageway into the catacombs of the Turkish hillside.

NAPLES, FLORIDA

Gansz could not believe his good fortune. He wondered how many Bureau investigations over the years had succeeded due to this kind of blind luck. Probably quite a few.

He had returned to Naples hoping to find the one piece of evidence that would permit him to move against Trent. Another trip to Trent's former camp, including the odious task of digging into the refuse pits, had revealed nothing helpful. His only consolation was that he managed to stay relatively clean during the work.

On the way back to his hotel he drove by the organization's office and everything changed. A car with rental plates sat in the parking lot. Gansz parked across the street, in the shopping center lot, and waited.

His patience was rewarded when a woman emerged from the office and walked unsteadily to the parked car. Through the zoom lens of his camera Gansz recognized her, from Barbara Davaron's description, as Maria DeLeon. He could hardly control himself. He had the boss's girlfriend alone and half drunk. And from her expression, she did not look happy. If he handled this right it could be the mother lode.

He tracked her from a safe distance, praying that the Naples Police would not show up and pull her over. Finally, she turned into, of all places, the parking lot of the hotel he was staying at. To his utter amazement she went straight to the lounge.

Calming himself, Gansz walked to the hotel desk and showed his ID to the clerk. "Would you call the lounge? I'd like to speak to the bartender. Please explain who I am. I don't want to have any unnecessary conversation with him."

"Yes, sir, Mr. Gansz," the young clerk replied.

When she had completed her task, Gansz took the phone. "I'm George Gansz. Relax and keep the conversation to a minimum, okay?" He tried to sound friendly but was sure the bartender would feel otherwise.

"Yes, sir. What can I do for you?" came a confident reply.

"Good answer. A woman just entered the lounge. Can you see her? Yes or no will do."

"I can help you with that."

Gansz relaxed. The kid was playing the game perfectly. "Is she anywhere nearby?"

"We have everything you need right here at the bar. I'm sure you will like the arrangements."

"You're doing fine. I'm coming in to sit with her. I can't tell you how important it is that I get some information out of her." Gansz chose his words carefully. "As you can see she is on her way to 'ga-ga land.' I need her to answer some questions. Then I need her out of action for the rest of the night. You can't imagine what is riding on this. Will you help me?"

"We can put that together anytime for you, sir."

"Good man. I'll be right in," Gansz replied as sincerely as he'd ever said anything.

"I'll have room service bring it right up," the bartender added his own final covering comment.

"Is he always on the ball like that?" Gansz asked the clerk as he handed back the house phone.

"He's my boyfriend," she said proudly. "That woman is a drunk. She has been causing problems in there since she arrived last night. Will you get rid of her for us?"

"You did your part. I'll try to do mine just as well." Gansz made his way to the lounge.

DeLeon sat at the bar, mumbling into her nearly empty Margarita. Gansz nodded to the bartender and pointed casually to the phone on the bar. The young man acknowledged him and the game began.

"The gentleman would like to buy you a drink, Ms. DeLeon. His name is George and he's okay."

When DeLeon turned and squinted at him, Gansz smiled warmly and said the only thing he could think of. "You looked like you could use someone to talk to."

The bartender rolled his eyes good-naturedly at the stale pick-up line. To his utter amazement it worked and DeLeon warmed to the new arrival instantly. Gansz noticed a distinct lack of alcohol in his scotch and soda and subtly signaled his appreciation to the bartender. Maria became more talkative with every sip.

"So when is your husband supposed to get here?" Gansz asked hoping his timing was right.

"He's not my husband. He was my lover. At least until we went to Louisiana and he started eyeing that blond slut." She nearly spat the words.

"Louisiana, huh? Great place for a vacation." Gansz led slowly and deliberately.

"They're not on any vacation. They're supposed to be out there counting birds and snakes and shit. But they don't give a damn about any of that."

Gansz gave silent "thank you" and skipped the next five questions on his mental checklist. "I'm sure they are doing good work, whatever they are engaged in."

"No they aren't," she blurted out. "They are going to do something evil." In her drunken state DeLeon saw a chance to get revenge on Trent, Simmons, Davaron and all who had made a fool of her. "Think what you want, but I've been there. They have guns and all kind of stuff. They are going to do something to a bridge or a dam something. I've seen the plans. And I hope they burn in hell." She stared defiantly, daring Gansz to disagree.

Gansz had all the information he needed and probably all he was going to get. "I could use one last drink," he said, counting on the bartender to catch his drift.

"This should do the trick." The bartender said put a scotch and another Margarita on the bar. "If there is anything else just say the word," he said with a grin.

"You've done fine." Gansz replied before returning his attention to his drunken companion. "What do you say we down these cocktails and grab a bite to eat, Maria. I missed lunch and I'd love some company for dinner."

DeLeon squinted at him. "I'll down the drink but I don't want no dinner." She took the Margarita, drained it in one gulp and wiped her mouth on her wrist. "That's to Morgan Trent and all his assholes, wherever they are." The drink hit her like a sledge hammer. She rocked back and forth on the bar stool. A day of anger and alcohol caught up with her in one fell swoop.

Gansz looked across the bar with curious amusement. The bartender grinned and pointed to the bottle of grain alcohol he kept for the flaming drinks the tourists loved.

Gansz returned the grin. "Check please. Why don't I get you to your room and you can take a nap. Maybe in a couple of hours you'll want to eat something."

DeLeon was a mess. "I don't feel too good. Can you get me to my room so I can take a nap? Maybe in a couple of hours I'll feel like eating something."

"Great idea. I'm glad you thought of it." Gansz paid both checks and put a fifty dollar bill on the bar.

"That's not necessary, George," the bartender said graciously.

"It's not enough, believe me. There is a desk clerk out there who deserves a nice dinner one night next week. It's on me." He winked and began the task of removing DeLeon. From the lounge.

The elevator passed the second floor about the same time DeLeon passed out. Gansz abandoned any sense of propriety and threw her limp body over his shoulder, managing to get her inside the room before anything truly embarrassing happened. He flopped her unceremoniously on the bed and searched the room for something to help him locate Trent. Some one had been smart enough to relieve her of anything related to Louisiana.

He was about to leave when DeLeon moaned and rolled toward the side of the bed. In a final act of gratitude to the hotel, and for her own protection, Gansz adjusted her position so that she lay on her stomach with her head slightly over the bed side. He put a trash can directly beneath her face. At least the room would stand a fighting chance when her body rejected the day's intake, he thought hopefully.

CINCINNATI, OHIO

"Wilson Foundation," Lydia Rogers said into the phone.

"I need to talk to Dan Harte," came the agitated reply.

Lydia's eyes lit up in recognition. "George, is that you?"

"Yes. Who is this?"

"Lydia Rogers. I was here last weekend. How's it going?"

"Oh, yes. You're the historian from Columbus."

"That's me. Dan's not here. Can we help with something?"

"I just got big-time information on Trent."

Lydia's approach instantly turned serious. "I'm going to let you talk to Samantha Schmidt. She is coordinating things here. Just a second." She looked toward the kitchen. "Sam, get in here. We have a phone call you need to be in on."

Samantha entered the room mouthing the words, "Is it Dan?"

"It's our FBI guy," Lydia whispered as she activated the speaker. "George, I have you on conference."

"I'm Samantha Schmidt, Mr. Gansz." Samantha said.

"Are you a law enforcement or government agent?"

Samantha appreciated his caution. "I'm a government liaison. Sorry, but anything else is on a 'need to know' basis."

"We may have a mutual friend in Huntsville, Alabama. Do you know Richard Willis?" Gansz asked searching for confirmation of Samantha's credentials.

"We've met." Samantha smiled. Maybe the Agency was more involved than she originally thought.

Gansz was relieved. Samantha's response confirmed that more government agencies were getting involved in the case. "I just questioned Morgan Trent's girlfriend. She thinks they are going to blow up a dam or a bridge or something in Louisiana. I need to get this information to Dan as soon as possible." To his further relief, neither of the women asked Gansz about the information extraction process.

Samantha weighed her options. "Dan is already down in Louisiana with Bill Harmon. It's better if we contact him from here. We have secure phones."

"He's searching for Trent's camp, isn't he?"

"Yes, and without much luck. He may need more assets than he has on hand." Samantha tried to sound unemotional.

"Does he have access?" Gansz asked.

"No one will give an official okay on anything. But I think there are people he can call on if he really gets stuck."

Gansz understood completely. He recognized, in Samantha's voice, more than a passing official interest. "We're on the same page here, Ms. Schmidt. I'm going back to Huntsville. Whatever call Dan makes on this will probably go through there. If he needs me he has my number."

"That's a good plan."

"It sounds like we are in business then." Gansz took a chance. "Samantha, he is going to be all right."

Samantha let out an audible sigh. "Thank you, George. I appreciate that. We will be in touch soon." She switched off the intercom. "Was it that obvious?"

"It is to me. I guess it's his job to read people," Lydia said. "Hey, don't worry about it. It's surely not a crime to be attracted to Dan Harte. There aren't many like him around anymore."

Samantha blushed and looked down at the table as Lydia continued. "You may expect more of yourself but he doesn't. So if you won't give yourself a break give me one. I've seen the look in his eyes when you are around. He won't let you just walk away when this is over. I'd bet my tenure on it."

"How did he ever find a group of friends like you guys?"

"We found him and he's stuck with us. Now you have another call to make." Lydia stood to leave.

"Don't go." Samantha put her hand on Lydia's arm. "He may have questions you can answer. Or I may."

"You show a lot of promise."

"I'm working on it." Samantha said with a wink.

"Hello," a sleepy voice said over the speaker.

"Dan, it's Samantha. I just spoke with George Gansz in Naples. Lydia and I are on the conference line and Andy should be along any minute."

"What about the others?"

"Rita's catching up on some sleep, and Tim is in New York." Samantha noticed Loman and motioned him to a chair.

"What's George doing back in Naples?" Harte asked.

"He was checking around and ran into Maria DeLeon. She apparently told him that SESA is going to blow up a dam or maybe a bridge. Does that make any sense to you?"

"Good work, everyone. That confirms what Billy and I have been thinking. We still haven't found his camp. That could change though since Mike Prince came through this morning. Sounds like there's a guardian angel hanging around somewhere."

"Whatever you say," Lydia spoke for the group.

"We've covered the area by car and came up empty. We need to be in the air for this. Maybe a call to Huntsville tomorrow will get us what we need."

"That is the impression I got," Samantha added hopefully.

"I want to be there for this one," Loman said. It was a statement everyone had been expecting.

The speaker was silent for a few seconds. Finally Harte's voice came across, calm but resolute. "I can't let you do that, Andy. I can go through all of the reasons and you will have an argument for each one so I'm just going to leave it at that."

"But Dan, I deserve—"

"The matter is not open for discussion." Harte hated having to be so blunt but it was the only way to handle the situation.

Loman threw down his pencil and left the table.

"I'll take care of it," Lydia whispered and followed him.

"Sounds like we lost a few listeners on that song," Harte said to whoever was still in the room.

"Andy's pretty upset. Lydia went to talk to him." The long day's work began to come through in her voice.

"Are you okay, Sam?" Harte asked with concern.

"I'm fine. I haven't slept very well since I got here."

"There's a lot going on. It's understandable."

"That isn't really the problem."

"What's wrong?" A note of apprehension came into his voice.

"It's just that I..." Her voice trailed off.

"Sam, you can tell me. What's the problem?" Harte asked with more obvious concern.

"Well," Samantha said tentatively, "don't be offended but the bed you put me up in sucks."

"What!?" Harte asked through a laugh.

"Well, it does," she said defensively. "It's like a piece of plywood. I can't get comfortable on it."

"Problem solved, Agent Schmidt," Harte replied officially. Then his voice softened. "Sleep in my bed. It's a lot softer. I'm sure Lydia wouldn't mind having a room to herself again."

"I couldn't do that." Samantha sounded like a school girl.

"Why not?" Harte asked sincerely. "It's not like I'm there, though I wish I were."

She blushed in spite of the empty room. "I wish you were too, Dan. I truly do."

"When this is over we'll work on that, if you want to."

"I keep expecting to look out and see a white horse grazing by the lake." Samantha recalled her conversation with Lydia.

"No. Just a blue sedan in the garage," came the matter-of-fact reply. "But if you want a white horse in the back yard I'll see what I can do."

"You've done more than enough. But just the same, thanks. I needed that." As Samantha finished, Lydia returned.

Harte's voice softened even more. "Now go ahead and sleep in my bed. It will appreciate the company. I know I would."

"I better get off the line now. You never know who will come in on this conversation," Samantha said sheepishly.

"Good night, Lydia." Harte's voice was slightly raised as if he knew he was talking across the room.

"Good night, Dan. I only caught the tail end," Lydia called back, thoroughly enjoying Samantha's embarrassment.

"I'll talk to you soon, Sam," he said in a low voice. "Get yourself a good night's sleep."

"I'm here if you need anything," Samantha said, ignoring the double entendre. "Stay safe down there." She clicked off the speaker and looked up at Lydia.

"Andy's not happy but he's calm. We need something to get his mind off Louisiana."

"I have an idea," Sam said, still a little dreamy from the phone call. "The Agency will want a report on Herb Loman's log. No one is more qualified than Andy to do the job. It's not busy work. He'll have to make a presentation at Langley."

"What if he decides to pack up and head south?"

"Technically, Dan's orders constitute an Agency directive. I'll threaten to have him picked up and thrown in jail if he violates the directive. With any luck the analysis assignment will be enough to get his mind right, and I won't have to resort to the threat."

"Smart girl. Now you only have one other thing to take care of tonight."

"What's that?"

"Figure out a way to leave your mark in his bedroom," the history professor replied calmly.

"What are you talking about?"

"The next time Dan Harte goes into his bedroom something should tell his subconscious that you are a part of the room and part of his life."

Samantha blushed profusely. "I don't know anything about that sort of stuff, Lydia. I wouldn't have the first idea," she said with utter sincerity.

"That's probably the attraction. You don't know the game and its peculiar rules. When you meet someone like that life changes. It works for both men and women. It just doesn't seem to work very often." Lydia's analytical comment concealed a tone of frustration. She shrugged and flicked off the dining room light. "Don't worry about it, Sam. Let's get some sleep." They walked down the hallway together. "Hell, you've already left your mark on his heart. At least that's the way I see it."

ZELENOGRAD, RUSSIA

Technicians scrambled on and around the Backfire Bomber. Formerly part of the Soviet nuclear Triad, the plane had been refurbished to serve as the official aircraft of the Commander of the Russian Western Forces. The interior, spartan by western standards, represented the lap of Russian airborne luxury. A stateroom for the general and sleeping facilities for a staff of ten was complemented by a state-of-the-art galley and dinning area. Near the flight deck a Combat Information Center and Communication station gave the newly appointed Defense Minister up to the minute status reports on every active and reserve unit of the Russian armed forces.

Kasarov preferred the Backfire to the civilian Aeroflot Jet his predecessor used. He considered it far more reliable and easier to maintain. The psychological factor also played a part in the decision. The Backfire was a more impressive display of authority as it touched down on a runway and taxied across the tarmac. To all who witnessed its arrival, there could be no doubt as to the stature and power of the plane's occupant.

A technician walked gingerly across the starboard wing to the running light fixture at the wing tip. He removed the plexiglass cover as he had on the port wing. The maintenance schedule called for replacement of the lights well ahead of the bulb's life expectancy to prevent a malfunction that might cause delay or even embarrassment during a mission.

Kasarov was a stickler for details and went ballistic at the least hint of inefficiency or lack of readiness on the part of his forces. The extra costs of the increased maintenance schedule were returned handsomely in the pride and attention to detail that quickly became the hallmark of the "New Russian Military," as he referred to his restructured armed forces. The replaced parts were recycled to the reserve forces, saving procurement costs in that area.

The technician removed the bulb and gently placed it in a pouch on his hip. After installing the replacement, he attached a small gray box to the rear of the light compartment. The color matched the interior of the light compartment perfectly, just as the box on the port wing had.

He replaced the glass cover and crossed the wing to the open hatchway on the fuselage. Inside the plane he reported to the maintenance chief, then left to turn the used bulbs in at the supply desk. He put the old bulbs on the counter and exchanged a nod with the officer on duty.

The quartermaster dismissed the technician and reached for the telephone. Recognizing the voice on the other end of the line, the officer said, "I have the running lights you requested. You may pick them up at your convenience." Without waiting for a reply he hung up and returned to his paperwork.

MOSCOW, RUSSIA

Kasarov walked the long Kremlin hallway, mentally putting the final touches on his master plan. One agency head stood between him and control of Russia. He liked Gorki personally, and considered him a truly competent official. But there was no escaping the fact that the KGB head believed in the president's reform movement. He would have to be replaced.

In the Chechnya visit, Kasarov saw a solution. If Gorki perished at the hands of the revolutionaries the General could literally kill three birds with one stone. He would be rid of the KGB head and have a major say in his replacement. More importantly, he would have a ready-made excuse to station troops in the region. The deployment would be a presidential order due to the assassination of a high government official. Kasarov could get what he wanted and Cherkin would continue to bear all of the political heat.

"General Kasarov to see you, sir."

"Send him in," replied Victor Gorki pleasantly.

Kasarov entered the Director's office and inhaled the aroma of a recent paint job. "I love the smell of fresh paint. Most people find it offensive but I feel it means progress. It is much brighter in here. I like it."

"Thank you, General. Just because my department operates in the shadows doesn't mean I must spend my day working in one. A fresh coat of paint can do wonders for one's outlook. Please join me in a cup of tea, or would you prefer coffee?" Gorki knew how to be pleasant without being patronizing.

"Tea is fine, Viktor. May I be informal?"

"Of course, Anatoly. How can I help you?"

Kasarov sipped the tea and measured his words. "It is the Chechen problem. I am flying down Friday and will land a little after midnight. I have been considering the handling of this situation. It really is well within your sphere of authority. Perhaps we should undertake this mission together."

Gorki held the tea cup to his mouth breathing in the aroma. While Kasarov's offer was stunningly conciliatory, one did not get to the top of the Russian spy industry without covering all contingencies. "It is good that you suggest this, Anatoly. By coincidence I was prepared to offer my assistance in the matter. Perhaps we think more alike than either of us imagined."

Kasarov let a smile cross his normally stern countenance. "Perhaps we do." In spite of the seeming comraderie, he waited for Gorki to make the next move.

Gorki did not hesitate. "I see only one problem. Much effort has gone into separating the Military from the KGB in the eyes of the people. They will always think of us as skunks but they no longer look at the Army as a tool of KGB. That can, in some ways, work to our advantage."

"A good point, Viktor, but how does it relate to this?"

Gorki chuckled inwardly. The little worm had no concept of subtlety. "If the Defense Minister and the head of KGB are seen traveling together it could get to the press. The people will think we are back to business as usual."

The statement caught Kasarov completely off guard. "I never considered that side of it."

Gorki made his move. "There is an alternative. I have a summer dacha near Sevatstopol. I will fly down to the Crimea on Thursday. I am overdue for a vacation. From there it would be easy to get to Grozny unnoticed. I can meet you on Saturday with the latest intelligence reports."

"Can you do that without being noticed?"

"I once took the White House tour in Washington. When it was over I called their CIA director and discussed the beauty of the art work along the hallways. He was not happy."

Kasarov could not hide his amazement. This man might truly be a valuable ally, or a terrible thorn in his side. He briefly considered revising his plans to eliminate Gorki, but determined that he could eventually become a problem. KGB had to be the Defense Minister's personal arm of enforcement. "How will we meet up in Chechnya?" he asked, groping to regain control of the meeting.

Gorki noted Kasarov's reaction to his story. He chastised himself for being so vain. The last thing he needed was a moment of suspicion on his adversary's part. He retreated to a more patronizing tone. "I have people on the ground in Grozny. One of them will contact you at the air base when you touch down. He can see you in person or convey the message through one of your people. Whatever you are comfortable with."

"A personal contact would be best, Viktor. My personal aide will arrange it. The fewer people that are aware of this the better, don't you think?" Might as well take out one of his henchmen while we are at it, Kasarov thought.

"It looks like I am in for a long overdue rest at the sea shore," Gorki said as he stretched in his chair.

The meeting ended cordially. When Gorki felt sure of Kasarov's departure from the building, he opened a desk drawer and dialed a red telephone. He gently drummed his fingers as the connection went through. A familiar voice came over the receiver. Gorki took a deep breath. "Friday night at midnight the party begins. Frequency 10582.

I hope you can attend." He closed the drawer and reached for his desk phone. Another familiar voice came through the receiver. "It has begun," was all Gorki said before hanging up.

An ocean and a continent away, Arthur Henderson stared at the wall of his Langley, Virginia, office and sighed. Finally he reached for his desk phone and punched the far right button on the console.

"This is Big Boy. Alert Black 1. Rendezvous 03132000 Zulu. Frequency 10582. No drill. Repeat, no drill."

He hung up and activated the intercom. "Find Mike Prince and get him up here. As soon as he is on the way, get me the President."

Chapter XIII

ALEXANDRIA, LOUISIANA

"Don't you think you should give him time to let his ass warm up the chair?" Harmon asked dryly as he lounged in the hotel room's easy chair. "Take a look at this for a minute."

Harte replaced the receiver and paced the room, keeping one eye on the television. CNN's chief meteorologist stood in front of a large map of the United States. Lines on the map indicated a change in the weather pattern that had dominated the country for the previous two weeks.

"The good news," said the forecaster, "is that the jet stream has migrated northward. This has permitted the Bermuda high pressure system dominating the Lower Midwest to push north, removing the threat of added rain in the Ohio valley."

The map behind her changed to news footage. "The bad news is that the rivers of the central U.S. drainage basin are full to the brim. This is Cape Girardeau, Missouri, and the water is beginning to wash over the top of the levee. Local authorities say there is no danger of the levee failing but that can't be very encouraging news for residents as they see the water lapping into the streets near the river."

The tape changed to an overhead shot of what appeared to be a huge lake. "Other places aren't so lucky. Somewhere beneath all this water is the confluence of the Mississippi and Ohio Rivers. The roof-tops you see amid the swirling waters is what's left of the riverside business district of Cairo, Illinois, a mile above the confluence. These are three-story buildings.

"The river depth meter on the banks of Cairo tops out at forty-two feet! And there is a fifteen-foot flood wall on top of the bank. So you can see that the residents will have major clean-up problems when the flood gate north of the city finally reopens and they can return to their homes. Fortunately, the evacuation effort went smoothly and, as of this morning, there have been no deaths reported from this truly historic flood."

The background changed to a map of the Lower Mississippi River from below Memphis, Tennessee, to New Orleans. "Now for the really bad news. Even though the rain has finally stopped, when all is said and done this water will end up flowing down the Mississippi, past Baton Rouge and New Orleans and into the Gulf of Mexico. The Father of Waters may well become the Monster of All Rivers.

"I spoke to Charles Haisley earlier this morning. He is the Army Corps of Engineers Assistant Director of Operations on the Lower Mississippi. We caught up with him at the Old River Flood Control Project above Baton Rouge. He told me that if the rains abate along the Ohio and its tributaries, the channel will hold all the water presently in the system."

A new background shot produced a diagram of the outflow area around the Old River, with its two arms extending the seven-mile distance between the Mississippi and the Red River. "Mr. Haisley explained that the gated dams at the Old River Complex siphon water west into the Red River and eventually on down the Atchafalaya through central Louisiana. It is a delicate operation based on pretty complex flow equation. If more than thirty percent of the water flows west, the Mississippi could actually change course and move into the

Atchafalaya. He declined to discuss the ramifications of this.

"Well, there you have it. The rains have stopped for now and so far the dams and levees are holding. But it looks like the next five to ten days will be pretty hairy along the Mississippi River as the this truly abnormal late winter runoff works its way down the streams and rivers of the central U. S. 'CNN Morning Edition' will return after a local cable break."

"They always smile at the end of their segments," Harte remarked with irritation as he reached for the phone.

"They can afford to. They're three stories above dry land in Atlanta," Harmon replied to the non question.

Three rings later a male voice answered. "Richard Willis."

Harte jumped in his chair. He expected a secretary. "Mr. Willis, this is Daniel Harte. We spoke a few weeks ago concerning Herbert Loman."

"Oh, sure. The Wilson Foundation, right?"

"You may also remember suggesting I talk to Morgan Trent down in Naples, Florida."

"I remember. What can I do for you, Dan?"

Harte detected no change in Willis' tone at the mention of Trent. He decided to take the direct approach. "Since you asked, I'm out in the Middle of Louisiana and I could really use a helicopter."

A mild chuckle came over the phone line. "No problem. I'll just run to the bathroom and shit one for you."

"I am deadly serious about this," Harte said icily.

"I'm listening," came the even reply.

"Mike Prince told me I had assets if I needed them."

Willis' reply had an edge. "Where are you calling from?"

Harte smacked the table top lightly. "I'm in Alexandria, about a hundred miles northwest of Baton Rouge." He decided to make sure the discussion was going in the direction he wanted. "Don't worry. Mike gave me a device to secure the phone with. You wouldn't happen to know what company makes devices like that?"

"We make them. So do a lot of other companies."

Harte hoped the "insider small talk" would make Willis more receptive than he sounded. "But I doubt seriously if they sell them to the CIA. It doesn't seem like something the Agency would take open bids on."

"What is you point here, Mr. Harte?" Willis' tone seemed more irritated than interested.

Harte's frustration boiled over. "Here's the damn point. I believe Morgan Trent is going to attempt to sabotage the Old River Flood Control Project near here and if he succeeds it will be a catastrophe like you cannot imagine. You people have been sending me after this guy for three weeks with hints and suggestions. You have nearly led me around by the nose at times and maybe it's my fault for not putting a stop to it.

"But I owed it to a friend and I began to feel that maybe I owed it to the country. Now I finally have something to show for all the work and it's like pulling teeth to get anyone in authority to come on board for this.

"Everything about you screams CIA. Mike Prince told me I have assets so I added one and one and the answer came up 'you.' Now what are we going to do about it? If you won't help me, please say so right now, so I can try to find someone who will get his head out of his bureaucratic ass long enough to understand what the hell is happening down here."

Harmon stared up from the paper with raised eyebrows. Harte shrugged as if to say, "What have I got to lose?"

Willis broke the uneasy silence. "How many people do you think Trent has with him?"

"I guess between fifteen and twenty." Another period of silence caused Harte to shift uncomfortably in his chair. "Look, are you going to help me or not? That's all I want to know." The sharp edge was off his voice.

"You will have what you need at the Alexandria Airport by 9:30 this evening."

"What was that?" Harte felt a lump in his throat.

"It takes a little time to get things like that together. I can't just go shit you a helicopter, okay?"

"Sorry. I didn't expect you to say yes." Harte felt his pulse racing.

"I had to know how sure you were of your situation. This is really touchy and we can't go off half-cocked on it. Mike already filled me in. He said to expect your call. It's at my discretion whether to go forward. My discretion says it's time to move."

"Do you mind if I ask what convinced you?"

"I've learned that when a civilian says the government has its head up its bureaucratic ass, the civilian is usually right. Be at the airport at 9:15. Arrange for refueling. You will have night search capability onboard and the pilot will want to top off the tank."

"I appreciate this more than you know," Harte said.

"So do we. Good luck and watch your ass out there." The line went dead before Harte could reply.

"Come on, Billy. We have until 9:15. Let's take one more look around the Old River Complex just to get a feel for the land. After that we ought to try and get a little sleep. It looks like we'll be doing a night search and who knows how long we will be out there."

"Dan, if they hurt her, I'm going to wind up committing serious crimes out there."

Harte put his hand on his friend's shoulder. "We will do what we have to and that's a promise."

"I know we will."

OLD RIVER AREA, LOUISIANA

"Right. Eleven thirty. I'll be ready...I agree. It's too close to take a chance...Right. See you then." McMahon looked around the empty room as he hung up the phone. It made life easier if he did not have to explain his personal calls. On leaving the office, he instantly regretted Simmons' decision to cease contact until the SESA people arrived on site. In the parking lot stood Harte and Harmon.

"What's happening, fellas?" He said with a friendly wave.

"Hi, Henry," Harte replied courteously. "Where's Chuck?"

"Out on the crane with Aaron. I'm heading over to the Auxiliary Structure. Can I help you with anything before I go?" he silently added, "you nosy little prick."

"No thanks. I just want to ask Chuck a few more questions. Mind if we go out and see him?"

McMahon pointed to the huge crane moving slowly across the Low Sill. "Be my guest, but it's kind of loud out there. You might need a gun to get his attention." McMahon chuckled at his own dark humor.

Harte was not amused. "I'll figure something out."

Halfway across the nearly six hundred foot span, a twenty-by-forty foot steel gate dangled from a cable beneath the enclosed control room of the towering crane. The entire assembly moved slowly in their direction.

"The vibration out here is worse than before."

"That's just your imagination," Harmon scoffed. "I think."

Haisley waved from the control room and pointed toward the end of the Low Sill from which they had come.

"Good idea, Chuck." Harte said to nobody. "We'll just wait over there for you."

Roosevelt gently slid the steel gate into a slotted bay outside the flow channel and waved to them from the window of the crane, forty feet above. Haisley descended the access ladder and greeted them with a huge grin. "Man, she is really flowing. We're down to two gates in the two deep channel bays. They normally hold four each." He shouted over the roar of the water.

"Will you be able to hold it back?"

"No problem. Henry's going to take the Auxiliary Structure gates up another two feet. That should stabilize everything. I can still go up three more feet over there, and pull a gate or two out of this old girl. The Mississippi isn't going anywhere we don't want her to. Let's ride over and see how Henry is doing." Haisley signaled his intentions to Roosevelt who waved an acknowledgment and continued his attention to the crane.

They crossed the short road separating the two flood control dams. Harte guessed the distance at three quarters of a mile. From the Auxiliary structure, he surveyed the surroundings. Water covered much of the area around the complex. A spit of land between the two structures extending out to the Mississippi River was the only dry ground in view. A levee topped by an access road protected it from the rising water.

"Will that stay dry?"

"Probably, but most everything else will disappear. By nightfall this area will look like an island. Only the road here and some of our infrastructure will be dry, along with this baby and the Low Sill. We may have to open gates on the Overbank Structure, on the other side of the Low Sill."

Harte tried to envision the area at night from Haisley's description. The volume of water hurling through the open ports of the project was beyond his comprehension. "How much water is going through here?"

"Let's see," Haisley replied nonchalantly. "If we get maximum flow, and it looks like we will, it should be around seven hundred thousand cubic feet per second, give or take ten thousand. That's about five and a half million gallons."

"Per second?" Harte was incredulous.

"Per second," Haisley repeated. Any concern he had was masked by the nonchalant reply.

"I have nothing to equate that to," Harte answered blankly.

"Let's find a comparison. Ah, here we go. Do you know Lake Okeechobee in Florida?"

"Yeah."

"Good. That lake is twenty-five by thirty miles or seven hundred and fifty square miles, with an average depth of twelve feet. Let me see. That's around two hundred and fifty billion cubic feet." He noted their bland stares. "Hey, I'm an engineer. Math is what I do.

"So. If Lake Okeechobee was flowing through here at our maximum volume we could drain the entire lake dry in a little over three and a half days. Does that help put it into focus for you?" Haisley grinned at him.

"You're kidding."

"Not a bit. We are draining two thirds of the United States through here. And it's been raining for nearly two weeks."

"You talk about it like yesterday's baseball game," Harte said in disbelief.

"That's the only way to deal with it, Dan." Haisley calmly replied. "Hell, if the people working this project stopped to consider the magnitude of what happens here, some of them would just toss their hard hats into the river and walk away.

"It's like a lot of jobs. Take coal miners. How many of those people do you think would ride into those shafts every day if they thought about the roof falling in? The only thing to do is block it out and get the job done. Most people never understand that."

"I see what you mean," Harte agreed lamely.

"Don't think for a minute that anybody out here is kidding themselves. They can't completely block out the obvious. This won't be just another day at the office. It's going to be a real test and some people on this project are going to find out what they are made of before this run is all over. You mark my words." The young engineer walked away toward the towering complex.

BANDAR-E BUSHEHR, IRAN

The water level in dry dock number two of the massive Al-Sabat shipyard slowly climbed above the pylons under *Revolution One*. The million-barrel oil tanker would soon be afloat, ending a three month stay in the facility on Iran's Persian gulf coast just southeast of the Kharg Island Terminal. Its sister ship, *Revolution Two*, was already partially afloat in the adjoining dock. Soon the ships would be back on the world's sea lanes, and Iran's oil delivery capability would be back to full capacity.

The decision to overhaul the ships simultaneously had caught the industry, and most western governments, by surprise. But when OPEC members took up the production slack, economic fears quickly eased. Economists around the world agreed that Iran's claim of huge savings in labor costs was financially viable. Greenpeace put the final seal of approval on the action by praising Iran's rapid reaction to the environmentalist's demands to refit and repaint the world's super tanker fleet.

One hundred and seventy five miles above, *Intelsat Five* moved into position above the massive shipyard. Until recently the former reconnaissance satellite had been engaged by NASA's Jet Propulsion Laboratory, in Pasadena, California, updating the geodetic survey map of the planet.

Unlike most intelligence satellites tasked over the Persian Gulf since the U.S. ouster from Saudi Arabia, *Intelsat Five* flew a pole to pole orbit. More importantly it flew outside the known schedule of the other birds. It would be able to fly its track for seventy-two hours or more before being accounted for by the various organizations which tracked the world's orbiting vehicles. If Iran was working in concert with known fly over patterns of the U.S. reconnaissance fleet, *Intelsat Five* might just catch them off guard.

At the National Reconnaissance Office in Virginia, a photo analyst studied the initial transmissions from *Intelsat Five's* "real time" surveillance. Infrared images turned the Persian Gulf night into a semi- animated afternoon. The blue tint of water flowing into the dry dock surrounded yellow to red shades of the ship's outline. The stern of the tanker glowed bright red as the engine room powered up in anticipation of its launch. Everything on the screen confirmed the routine nature of the event.

Suddenly the analyst's eye was drawn to an odd color pattern amidship. From the outer port hull of *Revolution One*, a thin green line ran across the blue of the rising water, to the dock. On the line, a row of red dots blinked every fifteen seconds or so along the side of the ship.

A glance at the clock told the analyst he had three minutes of real time photography left before his bird moved out of range. He quickly signaled the satellite and the camera zoomed in on the dots. They were definite heat sources but something prevented him from detailing the point of origin. They seemed to be under some sort of protective cover.

Just before *Intelsat Five* moved out of range the analyst sent one more signal and the satellite marked the dots. Seconds later the dry dock disappeared amid a snowy image that took over the screen. He crossed his fingers and activated the computer imager at his console. The signature photograph came into focus. With a sigh of relief, he highlighted a red dot and ordered the image scanner to find a match among the thousands of heat signatures which NRO had acquired over the years. Having no idea where to focus he entered "general search," and went for a soft drink while the computer searched its files for a match.

"That was fast," the analyst mumbled, as he returned to see the words "Source Match" blinking on the screen. He retrieved the file and nearly spilled his drink when an animated image of a Soviet T-72 tank appeared on the screen. "Holy shit," the analyst said to no one. He entered "Match all" and in seconds the computer confirmed that the heat dots on the satellite photograph were a column of Russian T-72's. Stranger still, all evidence indicated they were moving, in single file, into the side of the ship.

The analyst's trembling hand betrayed the calm expression on his face. He carefully entered a coded command and sent the photographs and analysis to the office of Arthur Henderson at the Central Intelligence Agency. After taking a moment to compose himself he called out to the rest of the watch section, "Come here, everybody. You ain't gonna' believe this one."

SIMMESPORT, LOUISIANA

Simmons guided the runabout along the Atchafalaya River. The span of the Simmesport Bridge dominated the night sky above. To the right, the tree line was awash and water lapped a few feet up the thirty foot levee running along the bank beyond. He found an opening in the trees a few hundred yards down stream from the bridge and steered the boat in. Reilly heaved the concrete anchor a few feet up the levee.

Fifteen feet from the crest of the earthen structure, Simmons began digging with a military entrenching tool. "Henry was right. This stuff is like goose shit," he said with a quiet laugh. He quickly finished the first hole and moved a couple of yards up the slope.

Reilly lowered a wad of explosives into the hole and strung one of the attached wires off to the left. After a tug to make sure the firing pin was secure, he moved up the slope to where Simmons had already finished digging another hole.

"This one's three feet," Simmons whispered and moved a few more paces up the levee as Reilly repeated his work.

Simmons quickly dug another hole. "I'm going to the other side of the road," he whispered from the top of the flood wall.

"Make it three feet deep near the top."

"You got it." Simmons disappeared over the levee's crest.

When Reilly finished setting his third charge, he removed a coiled mass of the claylike explosive and carefully untangled it. In a few moments, a fifteen foot line of CS-5 lay stretched on the grass. He secured wire to each end and moved to the top of the levee.

"What's this?" Simmons asked as he rejoined Reilly.

"I call it a 'leveler,'" Reilly said calmly. "It will put a three foot wide gash in the top of the levee. This is going to be one nice hole when it goes up."

Simmons checked his watch. "Finish up here. I'll fill the holes in."

Reilly placed the final charge on the landward side of the levee and attached the wire to his leveler. He rejoined Simmons at the first hole. "Where do you want this?" he asked as he examined the box attached to the end of the blasting wire.

"How does it work, again?"

"When water gets into the chamber it shorts out the safety switch. The charge heads down the line and whammo. Fourth of July comes to Simmesport."

Simmons started loading equipment back into the boat. "Put it six feet from the top. We may get to see it blow before we hit the road."

Reilly positioned the box. "It might be fun to watch. I've never taken out anything like this before."

Simmons guided the boat back up the river. The lights of the bridge helped him avoid the debris that cluttered the waterway. They anchored a mile north of the bridge, and rejoined the group assembled in Simmons' tent.

ALEXANDRIA, LOUISIANA

Harte paced on the tarmac, alternating glances between his watch and the eastern night sky.

"Will you please stand still for a minute? It'll be here. If we weren't a half hour early you wouldn't be going through this." Harmon's outburst was as much a ribbing as a request.

"I want to get moving on this," Harte replied excitedly.

A soft whirring noise from above interrupted the conversation. They turned and were startled to find the dark outline of a helicopter approaching from the south, and nearly on top of them. In the night sky the craft's lines seemed bulkier than the standard commercial choppers flown by corporations and private owners.

"That's a 'Huey!'" Harmon shouted. The UH1 had been a staple of the U.S. armed forces well through the 1980's. "We should have heard that thing coming from miles away. Wow!"

As the helicopter touched down the pilot turned control over to his co-pilot and jumped out, ducking under the prop wash. Once clear, Richard Willis straightened up and removed his flight helmet. He extended a hand in greeting.

Harte's jaw dropped. "What are you doing here?"

"I haven't flown in a while so I came along to log some hours." He pointed to the cockpit. "Jack usually does all the flying but once in a while I pull rank on him just to keep from getting rusty."

Harte watched through the cockpit window as Willis' co-pilot shut down the controls. "Bullshit. I don't know a whole lot about these things but I do know a perfect landing when I see one. Not to mention you snuck up on us in the middle of a completely open area."

Willis grinned sheepishly. "Okay, I'm busted. I flew these things in Southeast Asia. We had an air cargo outfit called 'Air America,'" he dead panned the reference to the CIA's covert air operation during the Viet Nam war. But if you really want to see some flying you should catch Jack's act. I hear his CO nearly cried when he mustered out of the service after 'Desert Storm.' Anyway, Mike said it could get a little hot out here. So I figured you could use an old chopper jockey and a few of his friends."

The side door slid open and two more helmeted figures emerged. Before Harte could react, the helmets came off revealing the grinning faces of George Gansz and John Dutton. They rushed forward to greet him.

"Can I get in on this?" Harmon asked impatiently, after greeting Gansz warmly.

"Sorry, Billy," Harte replied. "This is Sgt. John Dutton of the Huntsville P.D. and Rich Willis, from National Electronics, also in Huntsville. Apparently we have been working together on this from the beginning, much to my surprise."

After exchanging greetings, they walked toward an out of the way terminal. Willis explained how Gansz and Dutton had made contact with him. He confirmed that Prince had been indirectly keeping the investigation on course.

Harte figured Samantha for the guardian angel in all of this and he whispered "Thank you, Sam," to himself as they entered the terminal. One item still nagged at him. "You almost landed on our heads before we spotted you. How did you do that?"

Willis smiled. "That's what took so long. I won't get technical on you. Let's just say we put a muffler on her. I also had a couple of other modifications put on. Some we will need. Some I hope we won't. Now show me what we are looking for."

Harte spread the satellite photos and a map of the area on a nearby table and waited while Willis studied them.

"Okay what's the plan?" Willis asked.

"Aren't you going to take charge?"

"You're the one who knows the area and the situation, Dan. I just got here. If I have anything to add I'll jump in. But as far as we are concerned, it's your show. We'll be gassed up and ready to shove off in about an hour. After that just point us where you want to go and we're on our way."

Harte stared at him nervously.

"Don't worry. I'll let you know if something is not doable.

Follow your instincts. You've done pretty well so far. If I have to do anything impromptu out there, just go with it and I'll get you back on plan as quickly as I can."

Dutton stood quietly by as the group conversed. He moved his wind breaker aside and removed a nine millimeter service gun from its holster. As he checked it he became aware of four sets of eyes riveted on him. He focused on Harte and Harmon. "There is at least one and maybe more murderers out there. They will have no problem killing again. This ain't no fucking picnic, guys."

His terse comment and weapon check gave stark confirmation to the gravity of the mission. They exchanged a determined nod and dispersed in silence as each man wrestled with his thoughts.

SIMMESPORT, LOUISIANA

Davaron moved quietly through the camp. A dull glow and the sound of activity emanating from Simmons quarters drew her toward that tent. Something big was about to happen. If she could just find out what it was and escape, it was only a mile to the main road. Once there she would have to figure things out as she went since, whether by accident or design, she had not been out of the camp since SESA's arrival a week ago.

As she crept along side the tent, she recognized Reilly's voice. He seemed to be discussing his and Simmons' recent trip out of the compound but she could not determine much from the conversation. Her eyebrows arched as she became aware of another noise, the sound of two people engaged in something far more intimate than small talk. She leaned forward to hear better. Suddenly a searing bolt of pain shot through her scalp and her head snapped back. She looked up to find Simmons face staring menacingly down at her. His eyes glowed with hatred.

"Hello, Barbara. We were hoping you might join us this evening."

Davaron felt another burst of pain as Simmons dragged her by the hair to the front of the tent. She was about to scream when she caught sight of Trent standing idly at the entrance to his tent across the compound. Her pain turned to horror as he shrugged and disappeared into his quarters.

"Look what I found," Simmons announced triumphantly as he yanked Davaron to her feet inside the tent.

A look around told her that she was in for a nightmare she would never forget, assuming she survived. She began shutting down her mental and psychological functions, hoping to physically weather whatever they had planned for her.

Simmons maneuvered her across the tent to a table. He displayed the undercover agent like a trophy. "We all have a lot of adrenalin built up tonight. Maybe Barbara can help us get rid of some of the tension. Amy, grab an arm."

Simmons and Hector draped Davaron across the table face down. Already in a slight daze, she looked up momentarily to find Simmons staring into her eyes as he held her out-stretched arm. She had never seen such evil on a human face.

"Who's first?" Simmons announced the beginning of her ordeal without looking away.

From behind she recognized the voice of Rodvick. "After watching Amy and Jim, I'm already halfway there. I'll take a shot."

"Give her a good one, Mark," Hector cackled as she held Davaron's arm tightly.

Simmons never quit staring into her eyes. "I've been waiting for this since the night I saw you in the bar with that bastard Harte and his pussy-ass little buddy. You might as well relax and enjoy it because, lady, it's the two minute warning and the game is over for you."

Davaron felt panic as hands tore at her clothing. She looked away from Simmons and stared down at the table as Rodvick positioned himself behind her. He spread her legs roughly and prepared to do his business. "Let's try something just a little different," he said with an ominous chuckle.

Trying to remove herself from the situation, she focused on some papers on the table. She was able to make out a crude sketch and two words before she discovered, to her utter horror, that Rodvick's violation of her would be as far from conventional as she could imagine. The shock and the pain of his initial entry sent her over the edge. She forced all of her attention to the sketch beneath her face and when sheer disgust at Rodvick's actions combined with everything else, she passed out on the table.

"What should I do with her?" Rodvick asked when everyone had finished with Davaron. Throughout the ordeal they continuously awakened her, but to their dismay, she passed out with each new onslaught against her womanhood.

"Toss her out in the swamp. If the animals don't get her the flood will. She will be just one more victim of a terrible disaster." Simmons was pleased with his ingenuity.

Rodvick flopped Davaron's body over his shoulder and left the tent. A hundred feet from the camp he unceremoniously dumped his burden at the base of a tree near some standing water. "You should have stayed awake, honey. It was really a good time." He whistled a tune as he walked back to the compound.

The camp was alive with activity. Everyone gathered up their equipment and loaded the vehicles. Trent caught up with Simmons near the supply tent. "Are we ready?"

"It's time. Do you want to say anything before we move out?"

"Everyone knows what this is about, Al. Let's get on with it." They boarded the vehicles, and the Southeast Endangered Species Association moved out of its compound for the last time.

OLD RIVER AREA, LOUISIANA

Haisley waved to the passengers as the Land Rover crossed the Low Sill. The four occupants seemed a little young at first glance. It troubled him enough to check with Roosevelt, up in the Low Sill's overhead crane.

"Hey, Aaron," Haisley shouted into the walkie talkie, "Did you hear anything about a new vehicle issue in this area?" He could barely hear the reply over the sound of rushing water.

"It's news to me, Chuck. Anything wrong?"

"I don't know. Where's Randall?"

"Making his rounds, I think." Roosevelt looked down from the control room as Haisley approached.

"I guess it's no big deal. I just wish they'd let us know about these things." Haisley looked across the spit of land separating the Low Sill from the Auxiliary Structure. Headlights swept the dark grassy area as three vehicles rounded the bend in the road to the south of the complex and moved toward the Auxiliary Structure. Haisley thought he saw a fourth vehicle stop at the bend but it was too far away to be sure.

"Randall, where are you?" he said into the walkie talkie.

"I'm coming south on Route 15 just above the power plant."

Haisley nodded. The security guard was less than a mile away and on the move. "I want you on the alert. A Land Rover just went by with our markings on it, and I didn't recognize the passengers. Check on it if you see it and get your butt back here as soon as you can. Something seems goofy around here."

"Roger. It's parked at the end of the Overbank Structure. I'll check on it. Security One, out."

"Henry, are you there?" He cupped the communicating device over his ear.

"Yeah, Chuck. I'm on the Auxiliary Structure. What's up?"

"Take a close look at those vehicles coming toward you. Let me know if you notice anything odd."

"You got it. I'll get right back to you."

Haisley put the communicator in his pocket and looked back to the south. The first vehicle was across the connecting road. It entered the Low Sill's roadway and stopped next to him. He noted the Corps of Engineers logo and gave the six passengers a quick once-over, searching for a familiar face. A middle-aged man in the front passenger seat stared back at him with a look somewhere between hate and scorn.

Instinctively Haisley reached for his walkie talkie. Before he could remove it the intruder aimed a forty-five caliber handgun at him. Haisley recognized the silencer on the end of the weapon and closed his eyes in surrender. The last sound he heard was the voice of the weapon's holder.

"My name is Morgan Trent and I'm taking over this site." The bullet entered Haisley's chest, passed through his spinal column and exited his body before he ever heard the thud of the gun firing. He reeled backward from the impact and fell over the railing into the seething caldron below. His lifeless body emerged seconds later in the foamy torrent that churned through the open bay and down the outflow channel toward the Red River, seven miles to the west.

Roosevelt deposited the twenty-five ton gate gently into a slot at the south end of the Low Sill. He extracted the crane's giant hooks and moved out toward Bay Number Six, the middle of three "deep water" bays in the center of the Low Sill. Once he removed another gate from Number Six, there would be only one barrier left in each of the eleven outflow bays.

Roosevelt could not remove those gates for fear of weakening the structural integrity of the dam. If the river rose any more, the Auxiliary Structure would have to control it. They might have to open gates on the Overbank Structure, which normally sat on dry land, but even now had river water lapping at its base.

He peered out over the front of the crane and saw a parked vehicle and people scurrying around on the Low Sill. Another vehicle stopped and its passengers got out. One ran toward the crane on the north end of the road. Roosevelt's heart rate increased with every second he could not locate Haisley. A noise distracted him and he turned to see a figure on the catwalk outside the control room. "What the hell's going on here? Get off my crane."

"Shut up and do your job and you might see your wife and kids again." The intruder aimed a gun at Roosevelt's head. "Keep taking the gates out."

"I can only take out one more before it becomes structurally unsound," Roosevelt said, trying to sound official.

"Do it or I'll blow your brains out and do it myself."

Fear gave way to anger as Roosevelt returned to the controls. He continued to search for his boss on the ground below but a gut instinct told him the search would be in vain.

Mardi cautiously approached the north end of the Overbank Structure. At the edge of his headlights, a vehicle straddled the road on the far end of the gated structure. He quickly crossed the three quarter mile straightaway. The sight of someone trying to flag him down put him on guard.

When the signalman saw Mardi's uniform he took aim with an automatic rifle. Mardi ducked to the seat, swerved to the right and floored the accelerator. Bullets tore into his car. He regained the road as he came back up to a seated position.

The car shook with the effects of two flat tires as it slid to a stop. In the rear view mirror Mardi saw an orange glow as sparks ignited gasoline from the ruptured fuel tank. He jumped from the car and rolled away. The tank exploded, sending a smoky yellow plume of fire into the night sky.

Keeping low to the ground, he scurried toward a row of hedges near the security office on the north side of the Low Sill. He leaned against a fence post and tried to survey the area. There was a lot of activity on the Low Sill but he could not determine what was going on. He took a few deep breaths and slowly worked his way toward the dam. What he really hoped for was some help to arrive.

ALEXANDRIA, LOUISIANA

"Don't you guys have some sort of uniforms or something for this kind of stuff?" Harmon shouted as the Huey lifted off the tarmac.

"We're just a bunch of good old boys out for a joy ride," Willis shouted back over the sound of the motor. "We aren't even out here, for all anyone knows."

"I was afraid you would say that," Harte joined in.

"Don't worry. We won't be out there hanging by our asses." Willis pointed to the instrument panel. "I evened up the odds a bit before we left Huntsville."

"That's fine by me." Harte replied and brought out his map of the Simmesport area. "I figure the camp is along this road and not too far into the trees. It can't be more than a mile or so from the main intersection. If we fly a north south/pattern we can cover the area in a lot fewer passes."

Willis turned to his copilot. "Jack, use Route 1 down there for your directional line. Stay a couple miles to the south of it. We'll turn at the river and start right in on the search pattern."

The copilot took the Huey out of its hover position at full throttle. "We'll be at the river in twenty minutes, Mr. Willis."

Willis returned his attention to Harte in the passenger compartment. "We'll swing out over the levee and go quiet above the river. That way we won't panic the locals. Take a look at this." He activated a view screen between the ship's control seats. The display showed an ever-changing animated pattern of colored lights and figures on a dark field.

"Is that the ground directly below us?" Harte asked.

"You got it. It's an infrared imaging scan of the area. It will outline a human body, in case you want to count heads."

"What about something like a tent?" Harte asked.

"If it's occupied it will glow like a light bulb. Even if it's empty, the residual heat will give us a pretty decent image. Either way you will be able to determine the configuration on your satellite shot."

Harte looked around and found Harmon seated between Dutton and Gansz. In the dim light of the cabin, they studied a hand-drawn map of the Old River area. "Did you mention that most of the surrounding area will be under water?"

"I'm getting to it," Harmon snapped.

Harte understood his friend's concerns. While the potential danger to the Flood Control Project nagged at them, Harmon had a further concern over Barbara Davaron. Were it not for his instant attraction to Samantha, Harte would have wondered how Billy could be so caught up with the young agent in such a short time. He remembered how Gansz and Harmon had gone off together back in Cincinnati. It could be assumed that Davaron was a main part of the conversation and things made more sense.

"Hey, Billy," he called over the engine.

"What do you want?" Harmon snapped again as he looked up from the map.

"Everything will to be all right out there. Okay?" He saw the doubt in Harmon's eyes. "I mean everything."

Harmon relaxed slightly. He nodded and waved his hand. It was the best he could do under the circumstances.

A gentle prod to the ribs brought Harte's attention back to Willis. "There's the Simmesport bridge at about eleven o'clock."

Harte looked slightly left of straight ahead. The bridge lights arched over the blackness of the Atchafalaya River. "The levee road has no lights so you will have to eyeball it."

"No problem. Watch this. Jack, I'll take it from here." Willis steered the Huey over the levee and the viewing screen between the seats turned a deep blue.

Harte recoiled at the sudden change of color. "Water shows up blue on this thing," he said trying to assimilate the ongoing cram course in infrared telemetry.

"Close enough. The colder the temperature the deeper the blue. The warmer the temperature the brighter the red. If you have an idea what's beneath you it all makes sense," Willis shouted back just before he cut in the silent drive on the helicopter's engine.

"That's impressive," Harte shouted before he realized that the roar of the engine had died to no more than a loud hum.

"I think he heard you," Harmon shouted just as loudly. His seat mates vented a lot of built-up tension at Harte's expense as they fell over themselves laughing.

"Gentlemen, get your eyeballs to the windows. We are going in for our first run." Willis brought the ship to a northerly course. "I'll take us in at three hundred feet. Keep the river on the right edge of your screen. If it disappears let me know and I'll adjust." He reached for the goggles on his helmet.

"What are those?" Harte asked.

"Night vision. I want my own eyes for this. Your screen is a lot more detailed but these will give me the lay of the land. We'll be flying over at about seventy knots so stay on the ball. Here we go."

The Huey flew silently over the now familiar Simmesport Market. Almost immediately the lights of the town passed from view and the darkness of the Louisiana bayou dominated the ground below. Harte studied the view screen, noting patches or streaks of blue that denoted standing water on the animated landscape.

Suddenly, in the upper right portion of the screen a much larger patch of blue appeared. If Harte had passed his quickie course, this would be the standing water which he and Harmon had driven through. His fascination with the "puddle" nearly caused him to miss the pattern of reddish orange in the left center of the screen. "I got something!" he called out, not knowing what else to say.

"Where?" Willis asked excitedly.

"We just passed it. Did you see the water to the right?"

"Yeah, I saw it."

Harte's pulse rate increased. "I saw red to the left center of the screen as we went by. It was the first heat reading since we left the town."

"I'll double back. The water will be to your left this time. Keep you eye on the right part of the screen. Don't get distracted."

"Can we go a little slower? I want to be sure."

"Trust your instincts. You know what you are looking for and you have a spot to focus on. If it's the camp, you'll see the pattern even at this speed." Willis steered the helicopter over the trees for a second run. He brought the ship down a little to make sure the read on the view screen took. "Is the river in the same position on the left as it was on the right?"

"Yes." Harte concentrated on the growing patch of red to the right of center. As they passed over the heat source, he felt the Huey slow a little and silently thanked Willis. Like an animated smiling face the outline of a semicircle of squares appeared, with another set of three larger squares forming the nose and eyes just above it on the screen.

"That's it!" Harte shouted. He sat back from the screen and a troubled feeling came over him. Even in the excitement of discovery something didn't seem right.

Gansz was the first to notice Harte's subdued demeanor. "What's wrong? You look like you lost your wallet."

"Something is missing."

"We're getting back toward town. What do you want to do?" Willis asked, looking straight ahead.

"Circle over the river." Harte ordered. "Let me see the satellite shots," he said to no one in particular.

The pictures appeared from the back of the passenger compartment. He scanned the photos, looking for something out of place. The muffled sound of the motor was his only distraction. The overhead shot seemed more cluttered than the image he had just seen.

Willis broke the silence. "This isn't a pickup truck that you can just sit in the parking lot with the engine idling."

"Pickup truck," Harte mumbled as he pored over the photos. "That's it! All I saw was tents and some stationary equipment. I didn't see anything resembling a truck or car." He raised his hands over his head as if signaling a touchdown. "Yes!" Just as suddenly his hands dropped to his head and he slumped in his seat. "Shit. The place is deserted. They're all gone."

Harmon, Gansz and Dutton sat waiting, nearly at attention. Harte looked back to the photo, nodded resolutely, and officially took command. "Get back over the camp site and hover. If anyone is home we'll find out quickly enough. If not we can get down there and check it out"

"What if there's no one home and nothing to go on?" Willis tried to keep Harte thinking one step ahead.

"We head northeast. Some good people are going to need help tonight. We're not going to let them down."

"Now you're talking." Willis took the Huey back up the search route at full throttle.

Seconds later they hovered over the abandoned SESA compound. Nothing on the ground moved except debris scattered by the prop wash of the helicopter. There was not a soul in sight.

Harte studied the screen at his feet. "What's this?" he asked, pointing to a reddish dot at the left edge of the viewer.

"Take the stick, Jack." Willis twisted in his seat and studied the dot. "Bring her left a few yards." The dot moved to the center of the screen. He took a breath. "It could be a body."

Harte saw the fear in Harmon's eyes. "We have to check it out, Rich. Can you get us down there?"

"Let's make absolutely sure first." Willis turned on the searchlight and the ground below was instantly bathed in the glare of half a million candle power. In the center of the light field lay a body next to a stand of trees.

"Where can you land this thing?" Harte asked urgently.

Willis looked around. "It'll be tight but I think I can get down near the tree line."

"Then do it."

Willis brought the Huey down in a clearing at the edge of the camp. Before it came to rest Harmon slid the side door open and stood on the ground looking around. Harte joined him. "George, you and John look around and see what you can find. Let's go, Billy. You keep your head on straight, you got it?"

Willis adjusted the searchlight as they moved through the trees. Thirty yards from the camp they spotted the object of the search. Harmon sprinted the last distance and fell to his knees. Harte arrived as Harmon turned the body over to discover the face of Barbara Davaron, eyes closed and covered with muck.

"Son of a bitch," Harmon said as he clutched her to his chest. He rocked back and forth as the tears streamed down his face. Davaron did not respond. Harmon went through the entire emotional gamut from sorrow, to frustration to rage.

Harte did not interrupt. His task would be to channel that emotional flow into determination. He reached for Davaron's arm and felt for her pulse. A sigh of relief escaped his lips and he put his arm around Harmon. "She's alive." As he inspected the unconscious woman more closely he saw the tattered condition of the remainder of her clothes and bruises on her upper thigh area.

Harte dropped to his knees and shook his head. "They aren't even human if they can do this." The disdain he had expressed for Trent combined with his disgust over what had been done to Barbara and a subconscious switch went off. His stomached churned as a totally foreign feeling invaded his senses. He found himself pondering a word which he would never have entertained until the last week.

Harte stared beyond the glow of the searchlight into the damp cool darkness of the Louisiana bayou. He silently vowed to get *revenge* on Trent, Simmons and their followers. For all the pain and suffering they had inflicted on Barbara and, by association, William Harmon, and for all the innocent lives they now threatened, SESA would pay dearly.

"Let's get her back to the chopper. You can't sit out here all night." Whatever he said was going to be inadequate but they had to get moving.

When Harmon finally looked up, his eyes, so often twinkling with mischief, stared straight through Harte. "There will be payback for this." He cradled Barbara in his arms and walked away with his precious burden.

"I know there will, Billy," Harte replied to the retreating figure of his best friend.

At the helicopter one look told the rest of search party what had transpired. Willis took control. "My son's flight suit is in the back compartment. It should fit her. There is a first aid kit too, if it will help. You know this changes everything. They've assaulted a federal agent. We can bring the troops in now, if you want."

Harmon gently wiped the muck from the unconscious woman's face and hands and dressed her in the flight suit. Her eyes blinked slightly and her head moved to one side. "I think she's coming around a little," Dutton said tentatively.

Slowly Davaron's eyes slowly opened. She squinted to focus and instinctively lashed out as she realized she was surrounded by men. She landed a blow to Harmon's face.

"Barbara, wait!" Harmon ducked another wildly thrown fist. He moved in and surrounded her with his arms as she pounded on his chest. "Barbara! Barbara! It's me, Bill Harmon."

Her eyes glazed briefly and she slowly ceased her attack. She stared in confusion around the passenger compartment.

"Look," Harmon almost begged. "Here's George. You know him. And Dan Harte, my buddy from Naples. You're safe now." He eased his hold on her. "They are gone and we are here for you."

Davaron's rage subsided as she recognized Gansz and Harte. Tears welled up in her eyes. As suddenly as she had lashed out, she collapsed in Harmon's arms. "Oh, Bill, it was terrible. They held me down. I couldn't stop them. I wanted to die." Her voice cracked and the words would no longer come out. She tried to purge the nightmare from her mind as she leaned against Harmon's chest and sobbed uncontrollably

Harte watched Billy bring the young woman back from the brink of shock with steady understanding and a gentle touch. He had never seen this side of Harmon but knew, from that moment, that their relationship would change. The jokes and needles would still abound but the substance beneath would be far superior to what they had known before. Harte liked the thought.

But now there was business and the business was grim. He sat down next to them. "Barbara, I need you to be a field agent for just one more minute. Do you know where they went?" He asked gently.

Davaron disengaged slowly from Harmon. "I'm not sure. They have a lot of what looked like explosives." She tried to compose herself. "It looked like C-4 but more green in color."

"You're doing fine. Take your time on this."

Davaron struggled with the words. "Just before I passed out..." Tears formed again. "I saw a sketch on the table. I don't know what it was but I saw the words 'Low Sill.' Then it started and I—." The discussion ended in another flood of tears.

Harte leaned over and kissed her gently on the top of her head. "We'll take it from here." He stepped out of the helicopter to give Harmon and Davaron some privacy. The rest of the men gathered around him.

"Should I call in the Cavalry?" Willis asked.

"Do you just fly helicopters or do you work for his other boss?" Harte asked the copilot, point blank.

"Sorry, sir. You do not need to know that," Jack replied with a hint of a grin.

"Good. We don't have time to get anyone else in here. As far as I'm concerned we are the Cavalry and it's time to get up to the Old

River Project. Will you give me a lift?"

"Jack, we got a mission and it looks like we got us a team leader," Willis said. "Crank her up." He turned to Harte. "With your permission, of course."

Harte looked to Gansz and Dutton. They removed their firearms and chambered a round. With a curt nod to Harte and Willis, they boarded the helicopter.

"That settles it," Harte said. "Head east till you pick up the Mississippi River. About fifteen miles to the north those goggles should show you an inlet on the left and a tree line just above it. When you clear the trees there's a spit of dry land between the two sites. Run this thing with the muffler on and we should be able to get pretty close to the road between the Low Sill and The Auxiliary Structure. The water going through the gates should cover any noise the copter makes."

"When did you figure all that out?" Willis asked in genuine amazement.

"I got the lay of the land this afternoon."

"How did you know?"

Harte shrugged. "It seemed like the best possibility. I tried to cover all the bases."

Willis and Harte ducked under the Huey's spinning rotor. "If all your hunches are this good, I like our chances. The flight up should take about ten minutes or so. Can you figure something out and brief everyone?"

"I've been working on the plan since you told me I could have this thing," Harte said patting the side of the Helicopter.

"I knew you were going to say that."

"The bad news is if it wasn't the Old River Project, I didn't have a clue."

"You just keep guessing right." Willis climbed into the cock pit.

Harte jumped into the passenger compartment. The first order of business was Davaron. "Barbara, how are you doing?"

As her senses continued to re-awaken and the immediacy of the mission became clear, Davaron made a valiant attempt to put aside her pain and feeling of humiliation. "Pretty rotten, but I'll survive, if that's what you mean."

"That's what I mean. Billy, I know Barbara needs medical attention, but we have to get up to the Old River. Sorry, but that's the way it has to be," he said firmly.

"We can't get there quick enough for me."

Harte chose his words carefully. "I want your head on straight for this. If we screw it up we are all going to be in deep shit. Are we clear on that?"

"Dan, we've been on this road for more than a month. Let's get to it." Harmon's normally animated face showed no trace of emotion.

Before Harte could continue, another dose of reality thrust its way into his life. A hand reached back from the flight deck holding two nine millimeter sidearms in web belts and holsters. "You may need these," Willis said as the Huey lifted off and headed east over the Atchafalaya River.

Chapter XIV

OLD RIVER AREA, LOUISIANA

McMahon stood near the railing by Gate Three of the Auxiliary Structure watching the SESA members do their work. Suspended by a rope hooked over the top of the gate, Kennedy carefully molded the grayish-green compound around each two-inch steel cable until all thirteen draw lines were completely encased in a thick wad of the claylike substance.

He swung back to the walkway and handed the rope to Reilly who maneuvered himself into position while Kennedy moved to the right side of the gate and repeated his task. Reilly secured pre-cut wires and firing pins to each wad of CS-5. Swinging back to the railing he secured the trailing end of the wire and ran to the next station. He arrived just as Kennedy was swinging back to the walkway.

They leap frogged along all six of the Auxiliary Structure's gates.

When all of the charges were set and wired, they went back to the first gate and began the process of attaching the trailing wires to a central electronic detonator.

"I told them they had an hour, Henry. It looks like they are ahead of schedule," Simmons noted his stopwatch with satisfaction. "Let's go to the office and do our business."

"Good idea. I want to hit the road as soon as I can," McMahon replied with a broad grin.

"Amy, get the truck to the other site. They should be ready now," Simmons called. Hector waved and drove off the Auxiliary Structure, down the connecting road toward the Low Sill.

"Where are you heading?" Simmons asked idly as they walked toward the log cabin style office.

McMahon had always found irony in such a frontier looking headquarters for such a technologically advanced complex. After tonight it would not matter. "I'll get over to Mexico first. Then pick a place far away."

"With a casino, I'm sure."

"Probably. And lame extradition laws." McMahon's laugh was interrupted by the sound of an explosion to the north.

"What the hell was that?" Simmons snapped as he looked in the direction of the noise. "Those idiots are jumping the gun."

"Relax, Al. From the looks of the plume, whatever it was happened on the other side of the Low Sill. Chances are someone tried to run the northern road block. They're probably toast right now." McMahon said as they reached the door to the office.

He sat at his desk and removed some papers from the drawer. "Airline tickets and a passport. I have an early hop out of Shreveport to Houston. From there it's 'hello Mexico City.'"

McMahon became engrossed in his travel plans. As a shadow passed between him and the overhead light, he looked up to find Simmons standing slightly behind him. The engineer briefly caught a sniff of a pungent odor as a handkerchief covered his nose and mouth. He struggled to free himself, inhaling deeply from the ether-soaked cloth. Moments later he slumped unconscious at the desk.

Simmons examined the ticket and passport. "This is good work," he said of the passport. "I can use these myself." He booby-trapped McMahon and the desk then ran a wire to the door, where he planted another wad of CS-5. Carefully setting the trip wire, he closed the door and walked back to the Auxiliary Structure.

Reilly tightened the last screw on the electronic detonator. He and Kennedy walked off the Auxiliary Structure as Simmons approached from the office. "All done, Al."

"Excellent," replied Simmons. "Let's do one final check before we move out." He beckoned them back out onto the dam. At the third gate he looked closely at the explosive charge. "Did that one come loose?"

"No way. I wrapped it with duct tape," Reilly protested.

"It looks loose to me. Check it out. You too, Jim."

The young men shrugged and stared across the railing to inspect their work. Simmons stepped back, removed the silencer-equipped gun from his jacket and calmly put a bullet into the back of Reilly's head from ten feet.

At the sound of the thud Kennedy looked over to see Reilly's face explode forward and splatter onto the smooth surface of the flood gate. He turned to Simmons with a question on his lips. The question was never asked as a bullet entered his head just above the left eye. The force of the shot spun his body around leaving it draped over the railing next to Reilly.

Simmons replaced the weapon and stepped toward the dead men. "Sorry, guys. It's nothing personal. I have to tie up all the loose ends. You understand." He calmly grabbed the bodies by their feet and flipped them over the railing into the churning water below.

Willis gasped as he turned the UH-1 north along the channel of the Mississippi River. "Dan, look at this."

Harte peered over the control panel and caught his breath. The mighty river, awesome in a normal flow pattern, spanned the entire scope of their view from the cockpit, as they raced a scant fifty feet above its surface. In the dull glow of the new moon, they saw the tops of trees that should have been standing tall on the dry flood plain.

The river was a monster whose ends crept inexorably up the slopes of the surrounding levees. The incredible volume of water created a river-bed three miles wide, a giant churning lake as far as the eye could see. Entire trees floated past as the central United States disgorged its runoff toward Baton Rouge, New Orleans and the Mississippi Delta.

"Are you sure we will have a place to land?" Willis asked with mounting concern.

"Don't worry. The levees will keep the landing area dry."

Willis shook his head. "You might not say that if you could see through these." He tapped his night-vision goggles.

"You'll want to get rid of them before we cross the tree line. The site is pretty well lit. If memory serves me it could blind you for a few minutes."

Willis nodded. "Jack, as soon as we clear the trees take the stick. Put us as close to the road as you can."

"Yes sir."

A dim glow painted the shape of the tree line across the wind shield. Harte turned to the passenger compartment. "Everyone has his assignment. Be careful out there. Barbara, I know you are hurting but stay alert. If someone makes a try for the copter you will have to deal with them. Can you handle it?"

Davaron was weak but her reply was feisty enough to give Harte hope that she would recover from her trauma. "Just give me a gun. Nobody will board this craft."

Gansz reached down to his ankle and drew a snub-nosed service revolver. "Use this."

She inspected the weapon then looked down toward Gansz's foot. "George, you've got to be kidding me."

"What's the problem?" Gansz asked in amazement. "It's a gun, isn't it?"

"I know, but an ankle holster? I'm sorry, but that is just too tacky." The team shared a last nervous laugh, courtesy of Barbara Davaron, and at George Gansz's expense.

"We're coming up on the tree line," Willis announced from the cockpit.

Rodvick backed the huge crane toward the north end of the Low Sill. Below, the last of the dam's twenty-five ton steel gates swayed at the end of a cable. The controls were easier to operate than the manual had implied. In a series of start and stop movements he managed to get the gate swinging back and forth on its steel tether. Over the dry bay on the bank of the outflow channel he stopped the crane and released the tether controls in one quick motion.

The gate dropped into the slotted bay with a resounding, clanging crash. Steel collided with concrete, ripping chunks from the casing and cracking the gate bay to the base of the eastern wall which faced the rising Mississippi. The gate came to rest in a skewed position, knocking other gates from their slotted housings and rendering the bay unusable.

Rodvick stared into the mess as he backed the crane off the Low Sill to its original parking spot. He jumped with a shout as a spray of water came through the crack in the concrete wall of the gate storage bay. The first blow to the Low Sill's armor had been landed.

He scampered excitedly down the access ladder to join the rest of the SESA team, jumping the last three rungs to the ground. Straightening up, he turned flush into the barrel of Randall Mardi's .357 Magnum.

"Move and you die." Mardi steadied the barrel two feet from Rodvick's face. "Tell me what the hell is going on here or I'll blow your ass into the river."

Rodvick weighed his options and chose bravado. "You're too late, pal. We've taken over the site and by the time we are finished it will be a memory in your little mind. That is, assuming Mr. Trent even lets you live."

"Who's taken over this site?"

Rodvick saw his chance. "See for yourself," he shouted over the roar of the water.

Mardi turned his head slightly to view the events on the Low Sill. Rodvick rushed forward and they fell to the ground in a tangle. They tumbled out from under the crane into a grassy area on the north bank. Mardi managed to push Rodvick off and roll away. He came to one knee and, as Rodvick prepared to pounce again, fired point blank into his attacker's chest.

Rodvick tumbled down the short incline. He landed face-down in the water which covered the flatland north of the Low Sill and now lapped within six feet of the raised road bed of State Route 15. The dark of the night hid the pool of blood which slowly formed around his body.

Once Mardi was sure of the kill, he surveyed the situation on the Low Sill. At least eight people were running on the structure stringing wire at various points. None were looking his way. Apparently the rushing water had covered the sound of his pistol's discharge. In the window of the south crane he saw Roosevelt and an unidentified person. The crane retreated with a steel gate suspended beneath.

Mardi was vastly out numbered and assumed that Roosevelt and Haisley were now hostages. In addition to the people on the Low Sill, there were at least four more intruders to the north at the entrance to the Overbank Structure. His only option was to begin reducing the odds.

He crawled along the water line to avoid being outlined in the light of his still-smoldering automobile. Two intruders worked around the wheel assembly of the crane while the other two stood by the Land Rover. Mardi closed the distance, all the while knowing that he needed the saboteurs closer together.

"What the hell. It might work," He scooped a handful of gravel from the roadside. Coming out of his crouch, he heaved it at the crane. The stones rattled against the steel support legs.

Instinctively the two road guards joined their companions at the base of the crane to search for the origin of the noise. Mardi raced the last few yards. "Freeze! Drop your weapons!"

Four sets of hands went up and two of the intruders lost control of their bladders, as they stared down the barrel of Mardi's Magnum. "Move away from the crane and face the vehicle with your hands on the roof. Do it now!"

The four SESA members moved to the Land Rover and assumed the position. Mardi went to the base of the crane. "What's this?" He looked over the wad of grayish-green clay. "I said what is this?" he shouted when there was no response.

"Plastic explosives," replied a whimpering voice.

"No shit. Do you have any idea what you are doing?" He shook his head in disgust. "Of course you do, you little pricks. We'll just take care of this and then get back to your buddies over there."

"Don't screw with it, man," the whimpering voice pleaded.

"Shut up." Mardi carefully pried the compound from the wheel housing. A large chunk came away in his hand. He immediately saw a small black box taped to the steel structure. A toggle switch, held in place by the CS-5, flipped to the left and a red light came on. He had only enough time to bow his head before the booby trap activated and the explosives erupted in a flash of flame and raw power.

Mardi died instantly as the blast blew him into pieces. Two SESA members also died in the explosion. The remaining two lay on the ground gasping for breath. Before they could recover, the massive crane teetered on its shattered legs and slowly toppled toward them. Unable to move, they watched in horror as seconds stretched into eternity. The steel and concrete structure hesitated above them and finally crashed to the road, reducing the Land Rover to a metal pancake and crushing the SESA team members under its weight.

Simmons walked off the north end of the Auxiliary Structure in time to see the Overbank crane hit the ground in a ball of flame and dust. "Jesus Christ, what ever happened to timing?" he said, unaware of the reason for the crane's premature destruction. "What the hell. Let's get on with it."

He removed a black box from his jacket and raised an antenna on the remote control device. "It's show time," he muttered and pushed the button.

Twelve individual explosions melded into a continuous loud blast as the CS-5 erupted along the face of the massive gates of the flood control structure. Groups of thirteen steel cables groaned and buckled, finally snapping and flailing in every direction as they lost the battle against sabotage.

Deprived of the cables' support, the sixty foot long, fifty-five ton gates succumbed to gravity and dropped in quick succession into their housings. The foundation of the Auxiliary Structure shook as the rolling thunderous crash of the six gates traveled across the entire site, signaling the closure of the first line of defense against the Mississippi River. The Old River Complex suddenly stood on the verge of losing its historic battle to contain the mighty water-way.

Simmons admired his handiwork for a moment before moving out toward the Low Sill. A dark object flying silently over the land between the structures caught his eye. He abandoned his Land Rover and ran along the road to a defile opposite the field. He assumed a sniper's position and waited to see what the helicopter had in mind.

At the southern approach to the flood control site, a Land Rover sat unattended in the road. A few yards away, three bodies lay on the pavement. Bantar finished his last victim with a round to the head.

The explosion at the Auxiliary Structure had distracted the young road guards. As they stood in a line across the road, Bantar, crouched in the bushes on the levee, made his move. Coming silently up from behind, he fired at nearly point-blank range into the backs of the first two SESA guards. The third victim had time to turn half way before the bullet entered his side, necessitating the head shot.

The Iranian moved along the levee near the tree line. He found his boat already floating a few feet farther from the bank than when he tied it up an hour ago. Thanks to his earlier reconnaissance, he easily navigated among the trees and rushes to the main channel.

He guided the boat to the mouth of the Auxiliary Structure's inflow channel. The closing of the gates eliminated most of the current so he quickly darted across and continued up the river to his next observation point. He anchored the boat on the south bank of the flooded entrance to the Low Sill's inflow channel and resumed his surveillance.

The black UH-1 raced across the tree line in near silence. As the passengers began their observation of the site, a loud rumbling explosion to the left distracted all but the pilot.

"Holy shit. They got the Auxiliary Structure!" Harmon shouted as he saw smoke waft above the towers of the southernmost structure of the complex.

"It looks like it's still standing. You guys be careful over there," Harte replied.

"We better call in some help." Willis' concern was obvious. "Even if we stop this, there will be plenty of work to do."

Harte agreed. "Anyone we can get a hold of quickly?"

"Jack will put a few calls in once we touch down. We'll get some people out here one way or another."

The Huey quickly covered the distance to the road. Harte steadied a pair of binoculars as the craft swooped in to land. "There's a lot of activity on the Low Sill, but I can't see anyone looking this way. I think we snuck up on them." The Huey bounced to a landing. "Let's go." The doors slid open and two teams moved out in separate directions.

Roosevelt looked south toward the sound of the explosion. He had watched, in anguish, the destruction of the crane at the Overbank Structure. Now the Auxiliary Structure was under attack. When he pulled the final gate out of the Low Sill he knew the precarious situation he was putting that structure in. It was now nothing more than a row of concrete pylons at the mercy of the erosive effects of the raging flood waters.

The gun at his head reminded him of his helplessness. Whoever had planned this operation knew exactly what was needed to put the entire complex on the way to failure.

"Move away from the console," the gunman ordered.

As Roosevelt stepped aside, the intruder landed the butt of his gun across the base of the engineer's skull. He reeled from the pain but maintained consciousness. He felt himself being maneuvered across the control room and before he could resist, the gunman muscled him out the door and onto the catwalk. Roosevelt struggled to no avail as his assailant dragged him to the side of the crane and pushed him off the towering assembly into the river below.

He landed between the bank and a sixty foot wall built to direct water through the Low Sill's bays. The river level saved him from the jagged rocks that lurked beneath the surface during normal flow times. His body was racked with pain but he was out of the current that sent the waters of the Mississippi coursing through the Low Sill at what was now an alarming rate. Roosevelt whispered a prayer of thanks and made his way to the gravel bank where he collapsed.

Trent watched with satisfaction as his followers planted the predesigned CS-5 charges around the Low Sill. He missed the expertise of Reilly, but recognized the need for his services at the other site. "Let's keep it moving, everyone. We will be drawing attention soon and I want this project to go to completion."

The pace picked up noticeably. The age and wear of the Low Sill was evident from the many gaps around the joints of the structure's concrete slabs. SESA members put wads of explosive into every crack and crevice they could find. Before long the entire roadway was criss-crossed with blasting wire.

Hector approached Trent, "I was going to let you know that everything went smoothly at the other site, sir. They must have decided to let you know in their own special way," she reported.

"I wish they had waited till we completed our installation." A hint of disappointment tempered Trent's enthusiasm.

Hector looked at the maze of wire strung about the roadway. "Do you really think we can blow this up, Mr. Trent? It sure looks pretty solid to me."

"We don't have to destroy it. All we have to do is weaken it at a few critical points. Nature will handle the rest as the water pours through."

In Trent's best-case scenario, the erosive force of the water would completely remove the Low Sill as the Mississippi River began its westward migration. The least he expected was a major degradation of the project to insure any repairs would be delayed long enough to accomplish his goal. According to his research SESA's actions would show immediate results.

The oil and gas fields of Louisiana would be under water as soon as the Atchafalaya Levee failed at Simmesport. River levels at Baton Rouge and New Orleans would begin dropping almost immediately. Refineries along the Mississippi, between the two cities, would eventually be out of commission. Nina would be avenged, and the country would have to consider life with a severely curtailed energy supply. His disappointment vanished.

"Load it up," he shouted to a group setting charges at the base of the Low Sill's cranes. "I want them rendered completely useless."

Harte and Willis crept toward the Low Sill. "There must be at least ten people out there," Willis said. "Those aren't the best odds."

"I doubt if all of them are armed, and we can probably count on a few of them to just pack it in if we force the issue. I don't think many of them have ever come under fire, if you know what I mean."

"You've guessed right so far. I suppose we can go to the well one more time," Willis said with a shrug.

They moved to the base of the south crane. Two of Trent's people were putting the finishing touches on charges around the wheel base. "We can knock the odds down a bit," Harte whispered.

"It might alert the rest. I have an idea."

They let the saboteurs finish and move away. Quickly they crept to the base of the crane and examined the charges. "Don't rush into this. They could be booby-trapped," Willis cautioned.

An examination revealed a straight charge with no hidden surprises. Willis took out a pocket knife and cut the connecting wire. Then he cut the wire leading out to the Low Sill and wrapped the end around a bolt to maintain the appearance of a connection. "We'll be fine as long as they don't reinspect."

They made their way along the Low Sill managing what cover they could from the parked vehicles. "This will have to do," Harte said as they crouched behind Trent's Land Rover. "If we can get them into a group we might be able to take them."

"I hope they cooperate," Willis said without enthusiasm.

Suddenly, the SESA members began to congregate across the Low Sill roadway. They attached the ends of their blasting wires to a central connection on the railing. The connector was wired to a small black box with a short needle antenna.

Harte looked at Willis and shrugged. "Well, that worked," he said nervously. The roar of water permitted them to converse in near-normal voice levels.

"We're getting awfully lucky here, pal. I'm waiting for the roof to cave in on us."

"You could have put that differently." Harte tried to ease his own tension with the lame attempt at humor. It did not work.

Willis studied the assembly carefully. "There has to be a remote triggering device somewhere. My guess is they'll blow it from the south entrance and head back the way they came."

"Then we have to move before they load up. Trent probably has the detonator. If he shows it I'll go for him and you cover his people. I'm sure you are a lot handier with that thing than I am." He tapped Willis' drawn handgun.

"What if he doesn't show it?" Willis asked pointedly.

Harte took a deep breath. "We have to stop them."

"Are you ready for that?"

"They have made this personal. I'll do whatever is necessary." Harte's hand moved to the gun at his side.

"That's what I wanted to hear," Willis said calmly as he gave Harte a gentle pat on the shoulder.

Trent's people gathered around him in the middle of the roadway. He reached into his jacket as he began his speech. "That was good work everyone. Let's get all the vehicles off the bridge and—"

"Now!" Harte shouted when he saw the electronic device in Trent's hand. He jumped forward and threw a textbook roll block at Trent, who flailed backward as his legs went out from under him. The detonator slid across the pavement stopping near his Land Rover.

"Don't move!" Willis drew a two-handed bead on Trent's followers. Two of them instinctively moved toward Harte and Trent as they lay in a tangle on the pavement. Willis calmly put a bullet into one. "I said don't move!" Seven pairs of arms went skyward as brashness disappeared in a wave of fear.

Harte finally got control of Trent and pulled him to his feet. "You stupid son-of-a-bitch. Who the hell do you think you are?" he shouted as the adrenalin coursed through him. He put his gun squarely on Trent's chest.

"You are attempting to stop God's work here," Trent replied with utter defiance.

"Right. Get over to that railing and you can check with God and see what went wrong." Harte's voice dripped sarcasm as he man handled Trent past the line of parked vehicles.

Willis signaled the rest of the SESA members and they quickly moved across the roadway to join Trent. He picked up the detonator and examined it. "We're all clear, Dan."

Gansz and Harmon approached the office at the north end of the Auxiliary Structure while Dutton proceeded onto the dam to inspect the damage. They moved cautiously, with weapons drawn, to the office. "Push the door open and cover me," Gansz whispered.

The office seemed deserted but the night had already yielded far too many surprises. "Just don't shoot any good guys." Gansz put his hand tentatively on the door. He turned the knob slowly as Harmon positioned himself. "Now."

Harmon kicked the door open. Gansz saw the trip wire and re-acted instinctively. "Look out!" He pushed Harmon away from the entrance.

The simultaneous explosions shattered every window as flames ripped through the interior of the one story building. Gansz took the full force of the door charge as the blast threw him across the front lawn. He was dead before he hit the ground, the front of his body reduced to red jelly.

Dutton came running from the Auxiliary structure to find Gansz's body stretched out in the grass. "Oh, no." He ran to his fallen comrade and realized instantly that the young field agent was gone. He spotted Harmon near the front of the office.

"Bill! Bill!" Dutton called nervously as he turned Harmon onto his back. A low moan told him Harmon had survived the blast. In the glow of the fire Dutton saw a stream of blood running down the side of Harmon's face. He found the main cut and fashioned a wrap with his handkerchief.

Harmon's eyes slowly came open. "What happened?"

"They booby trapped the entrance."

"Where's George?"

Dutton shook his head. "Over there. He didn't make it."

"He pushed me out of the way. He saved my life," Harmon said, as tears formed in his eyes.

Dutton tried to be understanding, but there was work to do. "Can you move at all?" he asked, helping Harmon to his feet.

"I think so." Harmon took a few unassisted steps before collapsing against the policeman's chest.

Dutton picked him up and carried him down the road. "I'll get you back to the helicopter and then I have to get to the other site. They may need a hand."

He quickly covered the distance to the Huey. "Barbara, take care of him." Dutton swung Harmon's body into the passenger compartment. When there was no reply he took the time to look inside. "Where the hell is she?"

Willis' assistant looked back from the cockpit. "Oh shit." He reached for a walkie talkie. "Mr. Willis, are you there?"

Bantar crouched on top of the levee near the mouth of the outflow channel. The rising river enabled him to tie his boat up less than three hundred yards from the Low Sill. Binoculars nearly put him on the structure as he watched the proceedings.

The explosion to his left told him that Simmons had probably covered his tracks at the southern facility. The body count on the Low Sill was already encouraging. At this rate there would be no one left to tell the tale of what had transpired on this momentous evening. The American investigators would find ample evidence of massive sabotage. But with no one in custody, at least no one with any knowledge, the event would go unsolved. A nice clean operation.

Bantar quickly unsheathed a high powered rifle and attached the telescopic sight. He cradled the weapon in a "Y" shaped stick and watched the scene on the flood control structure unfold. His target would eventually appear.

The explosion to the south startled everyone on the Low Sill. The SESA group started to milling about. "Get back over against that railing and shut up. I'm in no mood for any of this." Willis glanced back and forth from his prisoners to the Auxiliary Structure.

The sound of a pager caught his attention as he herded the SESA members back to their assigned place. "What is it, Jack?" he said impatiently into his communication device. He shrugged at Harte. "I like to keep in touch."

"I'm sorry about this, sir, but we've lost Agent Davaron. Sergeant Dutton brought Harmon in. He got hurt in that last explosion but it looks like he'll be okay. Anyway, when I looked back into the passenger section she was gone."

"It's okay. We'll be on the lookout for her. Everyone here is in custody and things are quiet here. Keep the channel open in case I have to get back to you quick."

"Copy that, sir."

A belch of smoke and flame and an ear-splitting blast shattered the uneasy calm on the Low Sill as the charges exploded along the roadway and under the crane at the north end of the road. Two of Trent's people were instantly thrown from the structure into the raging water. Willis found himself half over the railing groping to regain his senses. Harte and Trent, shielded by the five-ton truck, were knocked to the ground amid the hail of debris and the cloud of smoke and concrete dust.

Harte looked down the roadway to see Simmons calmly striding toward them. He seemed an almost apocalyptic figure moving in and out of view as he passed through the smoke and dust of the explosion's aftermath. He brought an assault rifle from his side to the ready position, as he approached.

The sight of Simmons distracted Harte from a far more significant sensation. He shook the cobwebs out of his head and realized that, in spite of the explosion, the Low Sill was still standing against the force of the rushing water. As he groped around for his weapon he saw huge fissures where the charges had been planted. The road was covered with rubble but the dam was still up and holding its own.

Harte's gun lay near the wheel well of an overturned Land Rover. He crawled to it and, as his hand got to within inches of the weapon a shoe came down on his wrist and a bolt of pain shot up his arm. Pinned to the ground, he managed to roll halfway over, only to stare up at the barrel of an automatic rifle. Just beyond the barrel he focused on a face more consumed with pure hate than he had ever encountered.

"Do you think I am stupid or something? Didn't it occur to you that I would have a back-up plan?" Simmons sneered as he flashed the remote device before Harte's face. "No speeches, Mr. Harte. Just good-bye."

Harte closed his eyes and grimaced at the sound of the weapon's discharge. A moment later he felt no pain and his arm was free. He looked up to see Simmons leaning against the Land Rover clutching a spot between his left shoulder and lung. The rifle lay a few feet away. Over his shoulder, Harte saw a figure in a flight suit approach them with a drawn police revolver.

"No more!" Barbara Davaron screamed as she stopped and aimed the gun squarely at Simmons' heart.

Simmons stood his ground but his eyes betrayed the fear. He was at the mercy of one of his victims. It was a situation he had never encountered.

Davaron steadied the revolver with both hands. "You are an animal." She nearly spat the words.

Everyone stopped to watched the confrontation. Even Trent, still on the ground and in pain, watched the impending demise of his trusted assistant.

"Don't do it, Barbara," Harte said tentatively. "There is a lot of information we need to get from him."

"You'll get nothing," Simmons said. His fear for his life tempered the defiance in his voice.

Davaron remained rigid but the gun slowly dropped from its bead on Simmons' chest. He started to relax. Suddenly the gun ceased its descent and came to bear directly on his groin. Fear degenerated into outright panic.

"You are still a field agent, Barbara," Harte pressed. "Now more than anytime in your life you must remember that."

"I know what I am. And I know what he is. He's a pig. They castrate them don't they? Why shouldn't he get the same treatment as any other pig?"

The entire left side of Simmons' stomach and chest suddenly exploded in a rain of blood and organ tissue. Some of the bloody mass splattered on Davaron as she stood poised to fire. Simmons collapsed in a heap. Everyone dove for cover as she stood rigidly over his body.

"Barbara, why?" Harte said as he reached her side.

"I didn't do it," she said, her voice trembling.

"What?"

"I didn't shoot him. This gun couldn't possibly do that." She began to tremble.

The realization hit Harte like a thunderbolt. He grabbed Davaron and pulled her to the ground.

"I saw a flash out near the river," Willis shouted. He reached for his communicator. "Jack, we have shots fired from the end of the channel. Wait a minute. Okay, there's a boat in the water. It's heading downstream. Get airborne. Take him out if you have to. It's on my authorization." He looked toward Harte. "I told you we had some modifications done on the Huey. I wasn't coming out here bare-ass naked."

Harte got to his feet. Dutton arrived to help corral the prisoners. He herded Trent and his people to the back of the truck and checked it for weapons. As Hector passed Davaron the fire returned to the agent's eyes. Before she could act on her feelings, a troubled look came over her. "Where's Bill?"

Harte joined them near the truck. He was about to ask the same question when an eerie sound of metal scraping on concrete washed across the structure and the roadway moved beneath them. The pavement buckled and the Low Sill swayed slightly as they tried to steady themselves.

"She's going to fall! Let's get out of here," Harte shouted. A crashing sound below signaled the loss of a concrete support beam under the road bed.

People scrambled in all directions. Harte tried to direct everyone to the south end of the structure but there was no controlling the panic. Hector muscled past Harte and Davaron and ran for the north end of the road. Suddenly the pavement buckled beneath her and a section of the structure gave way taking Hector along with Simmons' body and the Land Rover into the channel.

Harte and Willis urged everyone toward the south exit. Concrete and steel crashed into the channel behind them as the Low Sill disintegrated like a row of dominoes. As Harte reached the span over Gate Ten the road bed beneath him gave way in a slow collapse into the river. He pushed Davaron to safety and managed to grasp an exposed piece of rebar steel as the footing dropped completely out from under him.

A tremendous weight pulled at his shoulder sockets and he felt arms clenched around his waist. He looked down to see Trent holding on for dear life. While his hands fought for a better grip on the rebar, his mind wrestled with the disposition of Trent. Every ounce of feeling screamed at him to dislodge his passenger and let the river do as it pleased with the egomaniac. It would be the just revenge he had allowed himself to contemplate at the SESA camp.

From somewhere deep within his brain an inner voice, undeterred by the adrenal rush and the emotional flow of the night's events, spoke out. It reminded Harte that all that differentiated him from the Morgan Trents and Albert Simmons' of the world was plain and simple civility. Without that he was no better than the men he had confronted on this night.

Harte gained some footing on a concrete outcropping and slowly pulled himself even with the remaining roadbed. As his head cleared the top of the wall he saw the survivors gathered on the south end of the Low Sill. Once again he fought off the temptation to dislodge Trent and, when he had a solid hold, reached to help his prisoner up the concrete facing.

When Trent was at eye level, Harte looked into the defeated man's face and saw smug defiance. It suddenly dawned on him that Trent now held a position advantage over him and was attempting to pry his arm loose from the rebar.

Harte panicked. His grip on the steel rod loosened and he stared down into the swollen, boiling water. Just as his hand began to slip from the rebar, the pressure on his arm eased and the weight of Trent's body disappeared. Harte grabbed the steel with both hands and held on tightly. He looked up and saw Roosevelt dragging Trent up by the collar. Trent was helpless in the engineer's grip.

"Let go of me, you stupid black bastard." Trent nearly spat the words as he struggled to free himself. He never took his hate-filled eyes off Harte.

"What did you say?" Roosevelt asked in disbelief.

"You heard me. You are screwing with God's work here. Now take your filthy hands off me." Trent struggled desperately against Roosevelt's attempt to subdue him.

The events of the night and Trent's verbal assault put Roosevelt over the edge. The fire in his eyes flared into an emotional conflagration. In one motion he lifted Trent off the ground and hurled him into the raging torrent below.

As Harte watched Trent disappear under the surging water, two hands grasped his shoulders and lift him to safety. He and Roosevelt stood on the remaining section of the roadway and looked across the opening that used to be the Low Sill. Harte shook his head sadly. "I'm sorry, Aaron. I did the best I could."

"I believe you did." Roosevelt shuddered as he contemplated what he had just done.

Harte looked toward the south bank. Willis stared back at them and nodded before returning his attention to the prisoners. "Trent was not going to let it be any other way. I can live with that if you can," Harte said to the engineer. They made their way toward the south bank, leaning on each other for support.

Bantar put the runabout's engine to full throttle as he skimmed along the swollen river. Even at this speed he would have enough fuel to reach Baton Rouge. He looked over his shoulder and thought he detected something flying near the water line. Hearing no sound but the boat's motor he dismissed it as a shadow and turned his attention to the river ahead.

"We're kind of close to the water aren't we?" Harmon leaned against the bulkhead and watched the river surface race past beneath him. The Huey's "muffler" permitted a reasonable conversation level.

"It's just like flying over the desert only we can't land." Willis' copilot grinned as he stared ahead through his night-vision goggles.

"Good idea. Don't land," Harmon mumbled. He tried to find a comfortable position. Pain was still his overriding feeling.

"I have him spotted. Hold on. We are going up." In quick succession Jack pulled back on the throttle, flipped up his goggles, and activated the Huey's powerful search light.

Straight ahead and fifty feet below, the runabout was bathed in light. Jack immediately fired four rockets from the pods he and Willis installed in Huntsville. The missiles hit just ahead of the speeding boat and showered it with water as they exploded.

Bantar was momentarily blinded by the intense light. The explosions ahead shocked him back to reality. He did not have time to figure out where the helicopter had come from. It was obvious he would need all his skill and luck to escape.

He veered left then right to no avail. The silent pursuer and its dreaded light stayed with him. He pulled a quick one hundred eighty degree turn which nearly flipped the boat. The helicopter seemed to pivot in mid-air, never letting him out of the light field.

In desperation Bantar reached for the rifle. Before he could get into firing position a burst of large caliber machine gun fire ripped through the boat nearly cutting it in half just behind the steering compartment. The strain of the motor and the river current finished the job and the boat broke neatly in two leaving Bantar weaponless and in the water.

Jack brought the Huey to a hovering position. He activated the rescue apparatus and lowered the harness to the helpless Iranian. To his amazement, the swimmer ignored it and continued his futile attempt at escape. "Take the damn thing, dummy. You're going to drown if you don't," he called through the ship's external speaker.

Bantar knew that escape was impossible but he could not stomach the idea of being captured by the Americans. Suddenly, a solution came to him. If he could overpower his captors he would have the fire power to complete the job at Old River and a means of escape. He waved to the pilot in surrender and reached for the rescue harness.

"It's about time," Jack said aloud as the swimmer positioned himself securely in the harness. He pulled into a gradual climb and began to reel in the rescue apparatus. "Can you keep this guy covered once we get him on board?"

Harmon sat in the passenger compartment assessing his condition. "To be honest I don't know. I've been in a hell of a lot better shape than this."

Jack nodded and looked down at the slowly rising figure of Bantar. "Not a chance, buddy," he said with finality. He pulled the ship into a much steeper climb and switched off the lift motor on the rescue tether. Leveling off at three hundred feet he spotted the outline of the tree line at the Old River Complex and headed for it. His water-logged prisoner dangled helplessly some thirty feet beneath the passenger compartment.

Bantar cursed as he felt the rescue line stop. He looked down and quickly realized that he was too high in the air to jump. He concluded that his situation was hopeless and looked up with hate-filled eyes to find a smugly smiling face staring down from the cockpit.

Jack made one final announcement over the Huey's outboard speaker. "Please remember to keep your seatbelt fastened and note that the captain has turned on the ' No Smoking' sign." He could not resist adding, "Dickhead."

Dutton and Willis corralled the remaining four SESA members into a manageable group. "I'm no expert, but the water looks like it's rising pretty quickly," Willis said as Harte and Roosevelt approached. "Where is the highest ground around here?"

"Over near the Auxiliary Structure." Roosevelt, still weak from his ordeal, tried to support Harte's sagging body.

An orange glow appeared in the sky beyond the south tree line. Seconds later the unmistakable sound of explosions rumbled across the flatland. "Now what?" Harte said anxiously.

Willis checked him for weapons. "Unless I miss my guess, Jack and your buddy just caught up with the shooter. Let's get over to the high ground and wait for the Cavalry." He turned to the prisoners. "You two. Get your young asses over here."

Two of Trent's followers came quickly to his side. Willis motioned them over to Harte. "Make yourselves useful and help this man. And don't pull any shit. If he so much as groans I'll put a bullet in both of you. You got that?"

"Yes sir," one of them mumbled. They relieved Roosevelt of his burden and assisted Harte.

Willis assumed command. "Let's move out. John, take the point. Barbara, those two are yours. If they breathe wrong shoot them in the head. Let's go, people. The creek's rising."

SIMMESPORT, LOUISIANA

Seven miles west of the Old River Control Project, the Outflow Channel and the Red River merge. The meeting of the two currents forms a continuous whirlpool which directs the water south into the Atchafalaya Basin. Within minutes of the closing of the Auxiliary Structure's six huge gates, the surge of water through the Low Sill overwhelmed the whirlpool and obliterated the three-river confluence. Waves of water scoured the levee on the western bank of the already bulging Red River, as the Mississippi attempted to disgorge its flood water through the only exit available.

Many Simmesport residents gathered on street corners while others stood on their porches. The discussion centered on the series of explosions to the northeast which still echoed in their ears. A short siren blast from the Simmesport bridge brought all conversation to a halt. It indicated a rise in the Atchafalaya River level to the first warning marker six feet up the levee. The river had reached this marker many times before, but coupled with the explosions, the siren injected a note of anxiety into the people milling around the town.

Thirty minutes later, a double blast of the siren signaled that the Atchafalaya had hit the second warning marker six feet farther up the levee. No one could recall the river rising so far so quickly. The evacuation plan went into effect.

In another thirty minutes, well over half the two thousand three hundred residents of Simmesport were on Route 1 heading toward

Alexandria. Even the three-blast warning from the siren went without incident as the evacuees calmly but quickly boarded waiting cars and trucks. They would be well out of town before the river topped the fourth marker. All they needed was the levee to hold together for another twenty minutes or so.

Ten minutes later the unthinkable happened. A series of rumbling explosions turned everyone's attention toward the levee. Reality swept over the remaining evacuation workers. They scrambled to complete their task but saw confusion and defeat in each others' eyes.

Just below town the levee quaked as a series of explosive charges ripped at its guts. A deep gash appeared near the top of the dirt and grass structure, growing wider by the second as the swollen Atchafalaya poured through with vengeful force. After decades of being bottled up, the river sought freedom from its earthen prison.

The combination of silt and sand in the levee, the Corps of Engineers infamous 'goose shit', stood no chance against the river's assault. Huge chunks ripped away. The scouring effect of the water and the erosion in the core of the mortally wounded earthen barrier increased geometrically, until the mound gave way completely and the Atchafalaya roared out onto the Louisiana flood plain.

The levee disintegrated northward like a sand castle at high tide. Within minutes, a gash ran nearly five hundred yards from the site of the explosions. Only the concrete abutment of the Simmesport bridge stopped the collapse. A wall of water swamped the last group of evacuation vehicles, sending the remaining two hundred townspeople to a quick watery doom. Simmesport quickly disappeared under the weight of the rampaging river and its seemingly endless supply of water from the overloaded Mississippi.

The outer reaches of the flood spread in all directions as three hundred thousand cubic feet of water per second poured through the gap in the Atchafalaya Levee. The volume and force of the initial surge put a square mile of land under a foot of water every minute.

In two hours all of Avoyelles Parish succumbed to the flood. By four A.M., the underpasses of I-49 channeled water into Evangeline Parish, twenty-five miles from Simmesport. The flood moved steadily west into Rapides Parish activating evacuation alarms in Alexandria.

While not as lethal as the initial surge, the relentless water gobbled up a host of small towns as it spread across the open unprotected landscape. Most people got out safely, warned by the citizens of Simmesport as they passed through. With only the clothes on their backs and a few meager belongings the people of Central Louisiana became modern day Bedouins, trying to stay a step ahead of the expanding flood waters; wondering how far they would have to travel to escape the spreading catastrophe.

OLD RIVER AREA, LOUISIANA

Harte's eyes slowly blinked open. His first impression was of a dull pink glow in the distant sky. After the previous night he almost feared what the dawn would reveal. The next sight cut through the sleepy fog and residual pain and awakened his sense of pleasure. A familiar voice came through the drowsiness.

"Welcome back. Some of us have missed you," Samantha said as she lightly brushed his disheveled hair with her hand.

Harte gazed into her smiling face. "It's good to be back," he replied, grasping the reality of her presence.

"How about some coffee?" Samantha offered a styrofoam cup as she knelt at his side.

Harte stared into the cup, savoring the aroma of the morning brew. He put it aside and looked back longingly at her. "I'd rather have a hug, if it's all the same to you."

"I would love one of those." She reached toward him and they held each other tightly. No words were necessary. The warmth of the embrace transcended the events that had brought them to this moment. For a fleeting instant the world went away as they silently took the first step toward that higher bond that men and women are sometimes lucky enough to achieve.

"How did you get here?"

"When Rich Willis called in a strike team, Mike alerted us. He stopped in Cincinnati and picked us up."

Harte came to his feet and helped her up. "How's Billy?"

"Okay. Barbara's with him. I think they will survive."

"She had a rough go of it last night."

"I know. She told me a little about it. It's amazing the way she is dealing with it. If it were me I—"

Harte cut her off. "Let's not think about that." He had often thought through the night how he would have reacted had they found Samantha lying in the swamp near Trent's camp, instead of Barbara Davaron.

"George Gansz is dead." Samantha tried to anticipate his questions. "He pushed Billy out of the way when this office blew up. He took the blast full force." Her voice wavered a little.

"We owe him a lot." Harte collected his thoughts. "Let's see where things stand."

"You can take a break, you know."

"I know, Sam. It's better if I get right back into it." The lawn teemed with activity. Harmon and Davaron stood off from everyone near the Auxiliary Structure. Harte exchanged a short wave with them as he walked. They needed to be away from everything. There would be ample time for him and Harmon to talk about all that had transpired.

The distinctive sound of helicopters grew and faded overhead as the authorities continued air operations in the area. To the left, the extent of the great flood became dauntingly apparent in the growing light of morning. The Low Sill and Overbank Structures were completely submerged. The only evidence of their existence was the superstructures of the massive cranes sticking out of the swirling water. Two lay in tangled heaps on the ground. One, at the south end of the Low Sill, stood erect.

The river slopped over the levee that protected the field between the Auxiliary Structure and the Low Sill, the same field Harte and his team had flown over when they arrived at the Flood Control Complex. Water covered a portion of the access road, and inundated most of the land to the west beyond the structures where their outflow channels used to merge.

The mainland to the south was dry but water in the channel on the

Mississippi side of the Auxiliary Structure slowly rose toward it. The access road across that structure and the presence of the helicopters were the only things that prevented a feeling of being stranded on a shrinking island as the Mississippi River slowly engulfed the surrounding area.

A row of covered bodies lay in the middle of the grassy yard. The immediacy of the overall situation made their removal a low priority. Beyond the grisly display a group of men stood around a work table studying maps and schematic drawings. The discussion appeared quite intense. The first face Harte recognized was that of Aaron Roosevelt. He moved behind the engineer and tapped him on the shoulder.

"Thanks," Harte said as Roosevelt turned to acknowledge him. A hand-shake became a warm embrace. The conversation at the table ceased as the two men reaffirmed their new found-bond.

Harte looked around the table. "Where are Chuck and Randall?"

Roosevelt pointed to the row of bodies. "They found Chuck's body near the end of the outflow channel, along with Simmons and Trent. He'd been shot. It looks like Randall managed to take four or five of them with him."

"Dammit. They were good men."

"The best."

"Aaron, we need you here," Willis said gently. "We still have a river to tame."

Roosevelt rejoined the discussion. Harte looked to Samantha and then toward the table. When he turned back to her she put a hand gently on his chest. "I have to help Andy and Rita." She pointed to a park bench near the office. "They are working new information into the Loman file. We've discovered some pretty interesting things during your nap. I'll let them know you're back in the game." Ignoring the men at the table, she kissed him and walked away.

Even in the gravity of the moment an irresistible urge came over Harte. "Seven-A," he said softly.

Samantha turned and feigned a look that could kill. "You'll pay for that, buster." She failed to control her smile.

"I probably will," Harte managed a tired grin.

"What was that all about, or should I ask?" Prince said as he reached Harte's side.

"Mike! I didn't even notice you. What are you doing here?" Harte faked ignorance.

"Waiting to see if you are going to shake my hand or punch my lights out," Prince said sheepishly.

"Do I have the choice?"

"You will later. There's a lot to explain. But for now get in this discussion. We have some big decisions to make and any input will be appreciated." Prince burst Harte's momentary bubble of levity with his stern reply.

At the work table Willis had the floor. "The flooding has reached Alexandria, sixty miles west of the Atchafalaya. The Red River is acting as a northern buffer, so everything is going south to southwest. Evangeline Parish is pretty well under water and it is bumping up against U.S. 190 on the north boundary of Acadia Parish. St. Landry Parish is nearly gone and Lafayette Parish reports minor flooding in its northeastern section.

"Once the water enters Acadia and Lafayette Parishes we are into high-density population areas. In addition, every square mile of land that goes under water puts another oil or gas field out of business. It's still winter time in the north, and I believe you are aware of the Persian Gulf problem. We have to alleviate the flooding right now."

"No problem. We'll open the Morganza Spillway," said a Corps of Engineers supervisor, recently arrived from Vicksburg.

Roosevelt broke the uneasy silence. "We can't do that. Without the Low Sill and Auxiliary Structure to regulate flow, you'll create a lake from Baton Rouge to the Atchafalaya. When it's full, things will back up to here and the river will return to the outflow channel. Opening the Spillway will just make the flooding worse."

"Then why the hell did we ever build the damn thing?"

"It looked good on paper," Roosevelt said offhandedly. "Maybe you should have asked us down here."

The supervisor grumbled and focused on the charts. "Then what are we supposed to do?"

"I have an idea," Roosevelt said tentatively.

The supervisor started to object, but Prince cut him off. "What's on your mind, Aaron?"

Roosevelt shuffled the charts on the table until he found the map of Louisiana. Running his finger along the line of the Mississippi River he stopped at a point fifty miles north of the Old River area. "There are four small towns in this three hundred square mile area," he said drawing an imaginary circle.

"I've fished up there a few times and there can't be more than four to five hundred people living in the area. If we put everything in motion now they could be evacuated in a few hours, especially if you got some of the isolated farmers out with one of the helicopters."

"What's your point?" Prince asked.

Roosevelt took a deep breath. "We can blow the levee here." He pointed to a town called Waterproof and caught himself before he chuckled at the irony. "It would create a catch basin. The base of that levee is reinforced with concrete matting so you will only lose the top ten or twelve feet. That should distribute the flow enough to prevent a catastrophic event but still ease the flow through the channel over here."

He pointed to the Low Sill area. "If we can get just one or two of the Auxiliary Structure's gates working, we will be able to divert water from the Low Sill Channel. From there we take back whatever the river will give us."

"What about the levee at Simmesport?" Willis asked.

"When the Atchafalaya starts dropping, we'll get bulldozers in there to shore it up. We don't have to rebuild it all the way. All we have to do is get it up to the current river level." Roosevelt stepped back from the table.

The supervisor broke the silence. "That's ridiculous. I can't authorize sabotage of one of the levees."

"I can," Prince announced with little hesitation. "This is a national security matter. Will it work?"

"I don't know. We've never tried it before," Roosevelt replied with innocent sincerity.

Harte stifled a chuckle at Roosevelt's response. "Someone ought to try something." He stared directly at the supervisor.

"I will not be involved in this decision." The supervisor backed away from the table. "Roosevelt, your ass is on the line if you do this. I'll see to it."

"To hell with him, Aaron. If the Corps of Engineers screws you over on this I'll hire you as a consultant down here and pay you a lot better than they can." Harte turned to Prince. "Dammit, Mike, do something here. Take a stand."

"Aaron, do you have any explosive charges?" Prince asked as the authority returned to his tone.

"We recovered a hundred pounds of the stuff from one of Trent's vehicles," Willis chimed in. "From the looks of things around here it should do the job. I can have you there in about an hour, Aaron."

Roosevelt found a junior engineer. He pointed toward the Auxiliary structure. "When the repair crew gets here put them to work repairing Gates Three and Four. It doesn't have to be perfect; just functional. Then call Baton Rouge back and tell them to get levee crews with bulldozers up to the Simmesport bridge via Route 1."

A helicopter set down on the road. Its backwash nearly drowned out their conversation. "What about authorization?" the young engineer shouted over the din.

"Tell them it's on my authority, and Chuck Haisley's, and neither one of us can come to the phone." Roosevelt looked to the row of bodies and then to Harte. They exchanged a knowing glance.

"If they give you any shit, I'll deal with them," Prince called out as the junior engineer headed off to place the call.

Moments later Willis and Roosevelt were airborne and Harte stood with Prince in the yard. "Can we talk?" Prince proceeded before Harte replied. "I don't know how you feel about me right now, but there was a lot at stake here last night. Do you see that prisoner over by Trent's people? Rich Willis' copilot plucked him out of the river last night.

"He isn't talking but we're sure he's Iranian. We figure they must have been in on this and he shot Simmons to cover his tracks. That links Iran to this and changes our whole approach in the Persian Gulf. Once we cross check him with Interpol, I'm certain we will find that he is Hamur Bantar."

"No shit!" Harte said, unable to hide his interest.

"As your people figured out, Bantar is far more than a name on Herb Loman's floppy disk. He is one of the top people in the Iranian terrorist apparatus. I've been after him for six years. We think Simmons was his primary contract killer in the western hemisphere.

"We suspected the same guy was responsible for the political killings you decoded in the file. Those two Beirut entries correspond to confirmed sightings of Bantar. He and Simmons had lunch, for Chrissake, on a patio overlooking the Mediterranean Sea. Simmons probably marked Herb at some point and killed him in Huntsville, at least we think so."

"When did you know what I was getting into?" Harte asked.

"Just before we met at Antietam. That's why I offered to get you out. And that's why I told Rich Willis to look after you like you were his brother."

"You could have told me, Mike."

"We know that now. But did either of us know two days ago?"

Harte considered the logic. "You know it just irritates the hell out of me when you're right about something." He extended his hand.

"Thanks. I appreciate that. Hey, I have to call my boss. He's in New Orleans and wants all the details of what we are doing out here. Then I have to have a chat with our Iranian exchange student. And you have business of your own to attended to. I'm sure we will both be occupied until Aaron and Rich get back." He turned to John Dutton who had stood patiently nearby. "Want to give me a hand with our buddy over there?"

"Gladly," Dutton said. He stopped in front of Harte. "Do you still have my card?"

"It's safe at home, John."

"Good. You call me whenever you need me. I'd be proud to work with you any time. You did a hell of a job here."

Dutton turned and caught up with Prince. Harte walked the short distance to Samantha, Rita, and Loman. He smiled as he noticed that Harmon and Davaron had already joined them.

Chapter XV

ZELENOGRAD, RUSSIA

Kasarov listened intently to the recording as he studied the satellite shots. The pictures bore out the words of the news report monitored out of a radio station in New Orleans. Bantar had succeeded beyond the General's wildest dreams.

The broadcast described rampant flooding in the oil and gas fields of Louisiana. Due to the U.S. Army Corps of Engineers' inability to repair a damaged levee, the water threatened to contaminate the American Strategic Petroleum Reserve near the southern coast of the shoe-shaped state. Even a break in one of the upriver levees had failed to stem the flow of water from the Mississippi River into the flatland of West Central Louisiana.

The refineries' and petrochemical plants along the lower Mississippi River were already experiencing major disruptions as incoming supplies faltered and salt water from the Gulf of Mexico threatened to foul their refining water. The U.S. oil industry was in the beginning throes of a catastrophic event on both the supply and production end.

The pieces of Kasarov's master plan were falling nicely into place. All that remained on his end was the disposition of the Chechnya problem and the little matter of Viktor Gorki's demise. Shortly thereafter, the "sand rats" of Teheran would have control of the Saudi oil fields, and Kasarov would begin negotiating with the Americans. The only topic on the table would be the replacement of their precious oil supply.

The irony of forcing the United States to refund a military machine they had anted out of existence through the 1980s was exquisite. The Defense Minster permitted himself a rare laugh as he imagined U.S. Military and Intelligence officials squirming in their chairs as they received news of the oil contracts.

Kasarov reverently ran a finger over the rows of ribbons above the left breast pocket of his uniform jacket. He would have to create a new medal and award it to himself. Better yet, he would have Cherkin present it on national television— assuming, of course, the drunkard could stand long enough to get through the ceremony.

The world was about to change again, and Kasarov would be the agent of that change. In a moment of well earned self-indulgence, he considered whether or not to wear his military uniform during his inauguration as President.

OLD RIVER AREA, LOUISIANA

"Crank it up," Roosevelt shouted through the bull horn as the last technicians scrambled off gate four of the Auxiliary Structure. In the towers above gates three and four, engineers crossed their fingers and started the lifting motors. The two giant gates slowly rose until they blocked the view of the outflow channel behind the dam. A cheer went up as the roar of over a hundred thousand cubic feet of water per second poured through the open bays and the water level on the Mississippi side of the structure began to drop.

A dredging machine, recently arrived from Baton Rouge, scooped huge shovelfuls of silt from the inflow canal into a line of waiting barges. As flow to the Auxiliary Structure slowly increased, Roosevelt pointed to the entry channel where the Low Sill once stood.

"The river is already dropping over there. We should start to get a silt buildup across the entrance. That will help out a lot. The water level should be below the top of the pylons in a couple of hours."

Harte clapped him on the shoulder. "What a job, Aaron. Congratulations. Now what happens?"

Roosevelt pointed to a convoy of dump trucks lined up on the Auxiliary Structure's roadway. "Once we get the water back into the channel, we can start dumping the rocks in from the south side. Between that and the silt bar at the entrance to the channel, I think we can cramp the flow enough to alleviate the flooding west of the Atchafalaya. Then there's the repair of the levee above Natchez and the levee at Simmesport." He rubbed the top of his head. "We got a hell of a job ahead of us but it's a good crew. We can handle it."

"Damn good work, Aaron," Prince shouted as he approached with the reluctant supervisor from the morning planning session.

"I just got off the phone with Vicksburg," the supervisor said meekly. "I told them what you did here and at the levee up north. I said I disagreed but you went over my head."

Roosevelt eyed him with resignation. "You did what you had to do, man. And so did I. When do they want to see me?"

Harte started to protest but the supervisor stopped him. "They don't. That wasn't all I said. I told them that I've never seen a better display of crisis management and recommended you be placed in charge of repairs and promoted to supervisor of the Old River Project on completion."

Roosevelt was stunned.

"It's your project Aaron. For the record, Chuck Haisley lobbied like hell for you, and he would be truly proud of what you've done here. I just wish he could see this moment, but since he can't I want to say that I'm damned glad you were on the job. Congratulations."

Tears came to Roosevelt's eyes as he accepted the hand of the supervisor. The loss of his friend tempered his happiness, but it did not diminish the realization of his dream. He accepted congratulations from Harte and Prince and gazed across his new domain. "I will get you back together," he said to the Old River Complex.

"We have to get going," Prince said. They walked toward the waiting helicopter. "Now remember. Every ninety minutes close the gates and scatter the equipment."

"That's the second time you told me to do that. What's the deal?"

Prince signaled to Willis to start up the Huey's engine. "Should I tell him?"

"He's entitled," Harte replied. "If he knows the situation he'll probably handle it better, the way he works."

"Good point. Aaron, every ninety minutes a bird flies over and takes photographs of this area. We don't want that bird to see much progress. Can you handle that?"

It occurred to Roosevelt that he did not know the first thing about Prince. "What are you, a spy or something?"

Prince gave him a wry grin. "We like to keep an eye on things. Take care of yourself." He shook the new supervisor's hand once more and turned to a group milling near the bombed out office. "Sam, Billy, let's get loaded up. We're outta here."

As the Wilson Foundation's members boarded the helicopter, Harte stood with Roosevelt outside the wash of the rotor. "Thanks again. I owe you my life."

"You gave me back mine," Roosevelt replied with a gesture toward the flood control complex. Again their handshake became an embrace. They sensed that their lives would somehow be forever intertwined.

As Harte prepared to board the helicopter, Samantha suddenly bolted past him. She ran to Roosevelt and gave him a hug and a kiss before returning to the aircraft.

"What was that all about?"

"Some of us are also grateful for what he did." She nestled into his outstretched arm.

Harte surveyed the cabin. Prince and Dutton talked shop. Rita and Loman spoke quietly to Harmon and Barbara. All seemed in order except for the empty seat George Gansz would have occupied. Harte added a visit to Huntsville to his agenda.

"Are we on the road?" Willis called out from the cockpit.

Harte nodded. "Whenever you're ready, Rich."

"Next stop Baton Rouge and points north and east, folks. Thank you for flying the Huntsville Express." Willis eased back the throttle.

Harte leaned back against the bulkhead and looked out over the Old River Project as the copter lifted into the air. The feel of Samantha against his body was soft and comforting. He gave one more casual wave to Roosevelt who stood with some of his crew watching the departure. He smiled when the engineer responded with a smart military salute.

Harmon reached to pull the door closed, but Harte stopped him. "Leave it open, Billy. Let's see what we fought for." He ignored the wind and stared out the open door as the Huey made its way down the Mississippi River.

PERSIAN GULF

"Bridge, Communications."

Farragut clenched his fist. "Captain here."

"Sir, I have traffic on an unscheduled frequency, with an unlisted priority code." The radioman sounded befuddled. "Sir, it's plain text."

"Read the text."

"All it says is 'Big Boy now.' Nothing further, sir."

"Bring her up off the bottom, Chief. You know the course and speed. Get the Exec up here to verify."

"Aye, sir."

A slight vibration followed by a gentle nudge signaled the Seawolf's departure from the floor of the Persian Gulf. With silent precision the crewmen of *Hunter One* readied themselves for action. The Executive Officer came into the Combat Information Center, stopping by the communication station on his way to the plotting table.

"Message 'Big Boy now' verified. Priority code verified."

Farragut picked up the intra ship microphone. "Gentlemen, this is the Captain. We are at full battle stations and we priority targets assigned. This is no drill. Repeat, no drill. We have been cruising the floor of this bathtub for the better part of a week. It is now time to flex our muscles.

"*Hunter Two* is in the northern sector. They have targets and orders as we do. Our targets are in the channel between Kharg Island and Bandar-e-Bushehr. Load forward tubes and stand by with back-ups. We are about to find out why they pay us the big bucks. Do your duty. Captain out."

"Contact changing course, sir. Bearing 023. Range 10000."

The captain of *Hunter Two* stiffened in his command chair. They had picked up the target near the tip of Qatar. Finally, after a week of silently tracking its every move, sometimes from as close as one thousand yards astern, the orders were in and the time had come for action. "Confirm ID and course change, Sonar."

"ID target Alpha. Speed twelve knots. Course 045. Sir, he is really loud. You can probably hear him from where you sit."

"Steady, Sonar," the captain admonished gently.

"Sorry, sir. He's moving along the shelf slightly beneath the gradient."

"Bring her around to course 039, Chief, and goose her a bit. Weapons station, report," the Captain said calmly.

"Solution plotted, sir. Firing range in 55 seconds."

"On my command, Weapons. Steady as you go, Helm."

"Aye sir." The collective response signaled the crew's readiness for battle. *Hunter Two* cut the angle between itself and the diesel-powered Iranian submarine.

The ships cruised in tandem, one hundred miles from the mouth of the Shat-al-Arab waterway, the entry point of the Euphrates and Tigris rivers into the Persian Gulf. The Iranian navigated in close to the shelf created by countless centuries of outflow from the historic rivers. *Hunter Two* cruised farther out in deeper but still tenuous waters of the Gulf proper.

"Range 5,000 and closing, sir," Sonar reported.

"Weapons, report," the Captain called.

"Firing solution ready. Range in twenty seconds."

"Steady as you go, Helm." Sonar was right in his assessment of the noise level of the Iranian Navy's latest addition. The Captain realized that the exercise had all the excitement of a standard drill. He also knew that the events topside, in the countries surrounding the Persian Gulf, put the stamp of importance on the encounter.

"Firing range now, sir."

"Fire one," the captain announced.

An almost imperceptible rocking motion signaled the release of the Mark 48 torpedo. "Torpedo away. Target lock achieved," the weapons officer reported. The sleek killer reached its nominal cruising speed in seconds as it raced toward the unsuspecting Iranian submarine.

"Captain, Sonar. He's powering up to seventeen knots, sir. It looks like he's on to us."

A collective chuckle drifted across the Combat Information Center as the sonar operator's taunt registered.

"Sorry, sir."

"No harm, Sonar." The Captain could not hide his smile.

The diesel submarine strained to achieve the maximum underwater speed of seventeen knots. But as the Mark 48 sliced through the water at twenty-five knots, the math became fatally academic. The contours along the shelf caused a wide variance in the temperature gradient eliminated any chance of escape.

The Iranian sub captain never considered the possibility of company on his patrol. He would pay for that lack of consideration with his ship and his life.

"Target lock, sir. Cutting wires now," Weapons reported. Fifteen seconds later a dull thud came across *Hunter Two*'s speaker as the torpedo found its mark and eliminated one half of the Iranian submarine fleet.

"Idiot," *Hunter Two*'s Captain mumbled. "Bring her around to course 120. Speed twelve knots. Keep her on the bottom. Chief, I'll be in my quarters. Call me when we approach our rendezvous point with *Hunter One*."

"Aye, sir," replied the watch chief.

The Captain paused near the hatchway and looked around the bridge. "Good work, you guys. You did that one by the book." He looked across to the "comedian" at the sonar station and winked at him. The young seaman could not conceal his sigh of relief or his ear to ear grin as he returned his attention to his tracking console.

"Targets on screen. Range 4000. Bearing 020, stationary. Sir, they're huge."

Farragut checked his watch. "Helm, periscope depth."

"Periscope depth, aye, sir."

Hunter One moved to a depth of seventy feet. "Scope up," Farragut ordered as the ship leveled off. He assumed a position at the periscope column. When the viewer reached eye level he turned his baseball hat backward. Before leaning in he looked at a young seaman third class nearby. "What if all generation Xers were just potential Sub jockeys waiting for their own boats?"

The crewman broke up laughing to the consternation of the watch chief. When the young sailor repeated Farragut's comment, the chief just looked at him blankly and shook his head.

"You're right, Sonar. They are monsters," Farragut said as he sighted on the twin super-tankers laying to, just off the dry dock area. In darkness, with no point of reference, the periscope's infrared lens further enhanced the size of the seagoing giants. "Take a look."

The young crewman's eyes widened as he leaned into the periscope. "Aye aye, sir." This would surely be one to tell the guys in the galley. "Sir, they are almost as big as the Nimitz," the crewman said as he back away in awe.

"Correction, son. They were. I don't know if there is enough water in that channel to submerge them. Weapons station, report."

"Weapons aye, sir. Tubes one through six loaded. Range 3000. Firing solution at your command."

"I want an accurate spread. All six have to hit. Stand by for reload of tubes one and three. Helm, stand by to come hard about to starboard."

"Helm, aye."

Farragut moved away from the viewer. "We'll put a couple of

torpedoes into the dry dock. That should put them behind on the repair schedule," he said with a grin.

"Fire tubes one through six now." The submarine bucked with the force of six Mark 48 torpedoes simultaneously departing their housings. "Hard about, Helm! Come to course 115!" Farragut leaned back into the periscope and maneuvered around the CIC to keep the viewer trained on the dry dock while the Seawolf pivoted to its new heading.

"Captain, Helm. Course 115, mark."

"Weapons, set range at 4000. Bearing 115. Prepare to fire tubes one and three."

"Weapons aye, sir. One and three set to firing solution."

"Fire one and three and hold your wires as long as you can," Farragut called out.

"Tubes one and three fired."

As Farragut gave the order to fire on the dry dock, a sudden flash of light in the left of the viewer caused him to pull back. Three torpedoes had simultaneously struck one of the super tankers. He brought the periscope to bear on the light source and flipped over to "standard viewing" as a series of secondary explosions rocked the target.

A blast of light to the right brought the viewer back to the second tanker as the Mark 48s found made contact along the thousand foot long hull. A mammoth explosion indicated a direct hit on the ship's fully laden fuel tanks, dooming the ocean going behemoth to a swift watery grave.

Farragut set the periscope to wide angle and stared open-mouthed at the panorama of destruction. "Look at this," he said to the young seaman third class.

The crewman stared awestruck at the death throes of the super-tankers. As he backed away from the viewer to make room for the Executive Officer, a huge grin came over his face and he instinctively offered the Captain a high five. Farragut returned the gesture enthusiastically.

"Helm, bring her hard about to course 285. Ahead flank. Maintain periscope depth."

"Aye, sir. Coming about." The engines roared to life and the Seawolf nearly pivoted in a one hundred eighty degree turn.

"Chief, check on the dry dock."

"Aye, Captain." The watch chief turned the viewer past the dying tankers to the dry dock area. "Sir, it looks like we have at least one hit. I can see fire and secondary explosions, but I can't tell if the second fish hit."

"Maybe the damned thing is still going," the Executive Officer remarked in mock horror.

"Weapons, report seven and eight," Farragut called out.

"There were explosions on both fish, sir. We put them in there on top of each other." The weapons officer sounded almost indignant.

"Just like we planned it," the Captain replied with a shrug. "Good shooting, you guys. Reload. We have one more stop to make."

"Sir, you may want to see this." The chief backed away from the periscope. "It's pretty awesome."

Farragut returned to the viewer. As the stern of the second tanker disappear under the water, the bow attempted to come up out of the sea. The weight and size of the protruding bow caused the tanker to buckle amidship. A screech of tearing metal coursed through the submarine as *Revolution Two* broke in half amidship. The stern disappeared in a cauldron of steamy foaming water. The five hundred foot long bow section floated aimlessly, slowly sinking as the open end filled with water.

Farragut turned his attention to target number one. "Oh, my God," he gasped. The remaining tanker listed thirty degrees to port. It teetered for a moment, before beginning a slow roll. In less than thirty seconds the roll was complete and Farragut turned on the infrared lens to see the massive outline of the capsized ship.

The view confused him. He should have been able to see much more of the overturned tanker. He pulled back from the periscope as he realized that a wall of water, created by the rollover, was speeding toward the submarine. "Holy shit! Take her down, Chief. Brace for tidal wave!" he called into the ship's intercom as he reached his command chair.

Farragut held on to his armrests. The submarine began a slow lean to port as the water displaced by the capsized tanker caught the conning tower flush. Anything not nailed down fell to the deck as the list reached fifteen degrees. Crewmen shouted out expletives as equipment fell on heads or bodies tumbled to the deck.

Slowly the list subsided and *Hunter One* came back to even keel. Farragut looked around and saw no sign of damage. "Well, that certainly was stimulating. Are you guys alright?"

Collective "Aye, sirs," came back from all departments.

"Contact, sir," the sonar man called out.

"Talk to me, Sonar."

"Bearing 296. Depth 075 feet. Range 8000. Course 285 parallel. He just powered up to fifteen knots."

"He's heading for Kharg Island," the Executive officer said.

"What a coincidence. So are we," Farragut replied without emotion. "Helm, close to 3000 yards and follow him in." He turned back to the Executive Officer. "Are we going to be this lucky?"

Hunter 1 fell in behind the Iranian submarine as it noisily chugged along. Around the CIC the crew took advantage of the time to put their work areas back together. Thirty minutes later sonar reported a change in the sea bed, signaling their approach to Iran's massive Kharg Island oil facility. "He's heading for the terminal, sir," the sonar man reported.

"Periscope depth, Helm." *Hunter One* glided back up to the seventy foot mark. Farragut resumed his place at the periscope.

"Sonar reports all clear."

"Radar reports all clear."

"Up scope." Farragut returned the viewer to eye level. The baseball hat went backward again as he searched for his target. "You won't believe this one." He shook his head as he made room for the Executive Officer.

The second in command took a look, then backed away with a disgusted sigh. "Did these guys go through the 'Gumby School of Naval Combat' or something?"

Farragut bent into the viewer. The Iranian was coming alongside a support ship moored near a massive oil platform. "That is one of their ships, isn't it?"

The Executive Officer already had the ID book out. "Got it, sir. She's Iranian all right. According to this she does double duty, both civilian and military."

"If that's they way they want it. Weapons, set solution on tubes two and four."

"Tubes two and four ready, sir. Solution set. Bearing 285 Range 3000. Target stationary."

Farragut spoke into the periscope column. "Did you think we would play by some sort of rules or something, you stupid bastards? Fire tubes two and four, Goddamit." He backed away from the viewer in disgust.

Around the CIC faces turned as Farragut's epithet sunk in. He noticed the surprised expressions and his became more stern. "They try to run us out of the Persian Gulf and then lollygag around like we are supposed to call for reservations before we do anything. Nobody fucks with the United States Navy." He pointed around the Combat Information Center. "Don't any of you men ever forget that."

He turned back into the viewer unaware of the smiles, nods and straightening of postures that followed his speech. The watch chief glanced quickly around the spaces and, as he walked past the periscope, patted the Captain on the back.

Farragut looked through the viewer in time to see the Mark 48s strike home in an eruption of flame as the Iranian submarine exploded into the night sky. A secondary explosion in the hold of the support ship ripped into the oil platform, mortally wounding it.

The massive steel and pipe tower swayed back and forth trying in vain to survive the breach in its flotation apparatus. Fire engulfed the base of the platform as pipelines ruptured. A series of three explosions hurled pieces of the superstructure in all directions as the three story support platform disintegrated into the sea.

"Periscope down," Farragut said with finality. "Helm come to course 210 and take us to the bottom. We'll rendezvous with *Hunter Two* and get back to the Strait of Hormuz. Somebody has to be there to welcome the surface fleet back in."

WASHINGTON, D.C.

"This is ridiculous," the Director of the Environmental Protection Agency said as she finished studying the report.

"No. This is what's ridiculous." Prince held up a copy of the public statement the Director planned to deliver on the Morgan Trent incident. He held the woman's career, and quite possibly the administration's political fortunes, in his hands. Her defiance made it difficult control the disdain he felt.

"Morgan Trent attempted to sabotage the nation's oil and gas industry. And he did so behind the cover of environmental activism." Prince pointed to his report. "We have a dead body which has been identified as a contract political assassin. We also have in custody a man who will soon be confirmed as a high ranking Iranian terrorist. There is more than enough evidence to link these men to Trent's actions in Louisiana. In conjunction with the recent events in the Persian Gulf, it borders on an act of war by Iran."

The EPA Director squirmed slightly. "That is a bit of a reach. How can you make that connection?"

"That is what I do for a living." The Director of Western Hemsphere Special Operations turned testy. "I lost a good man tracking Albert Simmons and another trying to stop him at the Old River Project. And I might have lost two good friends due to your bullshit 'hands off' memo."

The Director looked around the room in disinterest. As her gaze wondered back to the desk she made eye contact with Harte, who sat quietly next to Prince. She squirmed slightly as she realized Harte was staring a hole through her. Obviously he had been a part of Prince's operation. He was probably one of the "good friends" being referred to by the CIA official.

Prince continued his assessment. "I really don't give a rat's ass about you and your damn birds and snails. But the U.S. economy and its national sovereignty nearly suffered a major blow due to your interference with both the FBI and CIA. I plan to put a stop to that kind of intrusion and I do not care who or what gets hurt in the process. Is that clear enough for you?"

"This is blackmail, Mr. Prince," the Director replied, still defiant but starting to cave.

"Call it what you want. But if you issue this statement, I will call a press conference and release my official report on the matter. How do you think the nation will react to that report, considering your personal affiliation with Trent. I suspect that it might put a bit of a cloud over your political and possibly your personal future.

"If that isn't enough for you, consider this. The administration's concurrence with your memo tacitly permitted actions that would, at least, cause an upward spike in energy bills, and at worst, put us on the brink of war. Call me an alarmist, but I have to think the average American will be pretty pissed off about that." Prince might have felt a some sympathy for the woman, had it not been for the condescending tone of her original memorandum regarding Trent.

The EPA Director's life and career flashed before her eyes, from her days as an activist in the southeastern United States, through her attachment and loyalty to Trent, to her friendship with the First Lady. The political and social influence of the environmental movement had propelled her to the powerful position she now held. At EPA she exercised nearly unchallenged authority over America's citizens and its industry. No one dared cross swords with her as she attempted to reshape the social and economic fabric of the nation.

Now she was confronted by a second-level intelligence agent, and one of his cronies, who threatened to undo all that she, her friends and benefactors had achieved. She eyed Prince with contempt as he casually examined the Bald Eagle paper weight on the desk.

"Mr. Prince, if you attempt this I will see that your career comes to an abrupt end," she boldly announced.

Prince fondled the paper weight. Suddenly he slammed it on the Director's desk with a force and sound that shattered her facade of defiance. "Lady, you issue this statement I'll run you so far out of this town that Rand and McNally will give up trying to find you." He tossed the director's statement on the desk and snatched up his report.

"You mentioned blackmail. I'll give you blackmail. When I go before the press, the directors of the FBI and CIA, and the majority leaders of Congress will be on the podium with me, along with the families of the agents who died trying to stop Morgan Trent."

Harte had told Prince he would come along but just to sit in. The EPA Director's incredible arrogance made a liar out of him. He could not resist asking, "Who's going to be with you, a spotted owl and a snail darter?"

Prince did not miss a beat. "How about a white plumed egret. The way Trent's personal henchman used them for target practice, they might be nearly extinct by now."

The EPA Director's surrender was unconditional. "What do you want me to say?" she asked as tears formed in her eyes.

"I suggest an endorsement of the Corps of Engineers and something positive about how, along with the energy industry, they work in concert with the environment. As for your personal situation I know you will think of something appropriate. In return," he held up the CIA report, "I have a deep drawer into which I will file this."

She stared at her desk, chin in hand and waved her assent to the conditions without looking up.

The gesture further irritated Prince. "I'm sorry, but I didn't quite catch what you just said."

"I said I agree. Now get the hell out of my office."

Prince pointed at her. "Put a lid on it, lady. Some good people are dead because of you. So don't even try that high handed shit with me. I do not like you or the way you do your business. Just how deep into my desk drawer this report goes depends on my personal impression of your revised statement. Do you understand me?"

The Director melted in fear. "Yes sir," she replied reflexively.

"Enjoy your day," Harte said, as they stood to leave.

The look on his face told the Director not to respond

Prince stopped at the office door. "By the way, take a few days to think about your statement before you issue it."

"Why?" she asked through a trickle of tears.

"You don't need to know. Just do it." Prince waved his report in the air and waited until she signaled compliance. He and Harte left the office as the dam burst in the EPA director's tear ducts.

"She's really going to be pissed off at you over this," Harte said, as they walked down the hallway.

"She's dead meat," Prince replied with finality. Suddenly, a grin came over his face. "Spotted owl and snail darter?"

"What can I say? It just came out."

Prince held the door of the EPA Building open as Harte walked through. "Dan, I'm telling you. You have a knack for this kind—"

"Forget it. One pinch hit appearance is enough for me," Harte replied as they walked out into the morning sunlight.

AEGEAN SEA

"Nozzle 1, this is Eyeball," said the radar operator from his station aboard the E-3B AWACS high above the sea.

"Copy you, Eyeball," replied the pilot of the KC-135, refueling plane circling twenty thousand feet below.

"I have your last customer gassed up and rejoining formation. Confirm." The AWACS had monitored the refueling mission over the northeast sector of the Aegean Sea. Stepped-up air patrols, there and in the Indian Ocean, were all the United States and its allies could do, for the moment, to remind the world they were still an active player in the Persian Gulf region.

"Confirm final customer, Eyeball. I'll make a last sweep then head for the barn."

"Copy, Nozzle 1. Do you have other traffic in your area?"

"Negative. Do you see something?"

"I thought I had a reading off your port wing but it's gone now. It was probably emissions from your last customer."

"Probably so, Eyeball. We have some pretty heavy convection down here."

"Copy, Nozzle 1. Will monitor on standby. Eyeball out."

The pilot felt a slight nudge as the last of his "extra" customers disengaged from the refueling nozzle that dangled from the rear of his aircraft. The commander of *Black One* acknowledged completion of his refueling with the prearranged signal. "Done."

The tanker pilot tipped his wings slightly to acknowledge the signal. He turned for home as the Stealth fighter headed for the deck.

Mark Sanders guided his F117-A into position at the head of the five plane "V" formation. "Engage," he announced calmly and five black "flying shadows" turned east, toward the coast of Turkey, at wave top level

At the entrance to the Dardanelles the formation shifted to single file as *Black One* made its way through the famous passage. They passed the ruins of ancient Troy on the right. Three minutes later the monument at Gallipoli flashed by on the left.

The Commander of *Black One* considered both events; two great human tragedies separated by thirty miles and three thousand years; two vivid examples of humankind's ability to inflict appalling carnage on itself. And the killing continued almost unabated, between the two historic moments and since. The human toll just since Gallipoli in 1915 was staggering.

Sanders no longer questioned the need for, or the morality of, the missions he undertook for Arthur Henderson. From low-tech, dirty jobs in Latin America and Africa, to sophisticated operations in Europe and Asia, he understood his place on the chess board.

He often prayed that one day humanity would learn to live in relative harmony, and permit him and his team to retire. Unfortunately, potential social and political tyrants continued to prey on the world's population at a rate that left no seeming end in sight. And because these autocrats seemed unable to learn a lesson, Sanders now led his squadron through the historic passage; five civilians on a military mission to try and stop another moment of senseless human slaughter.

Black One exited the Bosporus like rapid-fire cannon shots. Into the pitch dark night the planes flew, heading east by northeast across the Black Sea. One hundred miles south of the Crimea, Sanders uttered another one word command. "Drop."

He felt a slight jolt as the composite wing tanks fell from his craft. One by one, at fifteen second intervals, the members of *Black One* deposited their contoured fuel cells into the six thousand foot depths, as they flew toward the rocky coastline of southern Russia.

Sanders' in-flight computer buzzed a warning. The Caucasus Mountains loomed before him, invisible to the naked eye yet noted by the all-seeing electronic navigator. He felt the nose of the plane rise as the guidance system steered him to the predetermined air route through the rugged mountain range. The computer screen came alive with images as the Nighthawks crossed the shoreline and raced over the Chechen countryside.

"Go," Sanders moved the mission to active phase with the one-word command. He checked his watch, 11:38 P.M. local time, and turned on the TDRS tracking beam.

Kasarov tried to relax in his stateroom. Sleep was out of the question. The anticipation of events in Chechnya kept his senses operating at peak level. When the weekend came to a close he would be the most powerful man in Russia. A knock on the door startled him. "Enter," he said tersely.

A young officer entered tentatively. "Sorry to disturb you, sir. Communications is monitoring an odd transmission."

"What do you mean, odd?" the general asked impatiently.

"The pulse and transmission rates do not fit any established military programs."

"Have they tracked the source?"

"It seems to be originating on board, sir."

"On board what, Lieutenant."

"On board this aircraft, General," the officer replied.

Kasarov bolted past the officer and made his way forward to the communication station. "Report the situation," he demanded.

The senior Comm officer had taken over the controls from an enlisted man. "I cannot explain it, General. In the last five minutes we have been monitoring an abnormal transmission. We cannot pinpoint the source but it appears to originate from in or around this plane. I have never seen anything like it, sir."

Kasarov fumed. "Call Grozny Center and see what they have."

The Comm officer made the call. "Grozny Base. Grozny Base. This is Command 1."

"Grozny Base here. Over."

"We are monitoring a transmission anomaly. Lock onto our frequencies and track it. The general wants an explanation."

The Grozny operator replied calmly, "We are on your assigned frequencies, Command 1. We can detect no anomalies. Perhaps you should re-calibrate."

Kasarov grabbed the headset. "Perhaps you should pull your head from your ass and find out what is going on up here, soldier. What does the radar say?" Kasarov silently cursed the antiquated Russian radar system which gave long range control to the ground stations while the planes had a seventy mile range.

The Grozny voice hesitated but maintained its composure. "General, sir, radar shows only your plane and two escorts at 15,000 feet on course 134, and 20 minutes out. There is no other traffic in the 250 kilometer circle."

"Simpleton." Kasarov threw the headset at the Comm officer.

Sanders recorded the Grozny transmission. "Just like Arthur said it would be." He adjusted his heading to the north and began a gradual climb. Behind him, two F117s peeled off the formation and streaked east. The remaining wing-men formed up loosely behind Sanders and the formation followed the TDRS signal inland.

They made a wide turn to the east, settling in at fifteen thousand feet on course 134. The Nighthawks quickly closed the gap between themselves and three radar blips on their screens. At one hundred miles the underside hatches of the fighters opened and Phoenix missiles dropped into position from the weapons bay. At seventy-five miles Sanders slowed to match the target's air speed. He waited patiently for Units Four and Five to activate their phase of the plan.

Units 4 and 5 approached the Russian bomber and its escorts head on. Seventy miles from Kasarov's command plane they illuminated themselves with a three second radar signal and quickly dove to thirteen thousand feet.

"Radar contact!" the Comm officer shouted through the ship's radio. "Two craft. Bearing 134. Low and closing!"

Kasarov pounded his fist on the bulkhead. "What is it?"

"They are gone, sir," the Comm officer replied. "There was a momentary image of two aircraft. But they have vanished."

"Alert the escorts, quickly," Kasarov ordered.

"Yes, General." The Comm officer switched frequencies.

Sanders depressed the button and two "Phoenix" missiles dropped from the ordinance carriage. On his screen he watched the image of the lumbering converted bomber as it vainly tried to escape the most precise air combat killers on earth. He waited for visual confirmation of the kill.

"I have missile lock. Two missiles. Fifty miles aft. Closing." The Comm officer stared wide-eyed at Kasarov. "General, sir, they are the 'Phoenix.' They do not miss."

A look of resignation crossed Kasarov's face. Seconds later he felt two impact thuds and an engine on each wing exploded in a hail of fire and metal. The flames raced through the lines igniting the remaining gasoline in the Backfire's fuel tanks. A momentary shudder gave Kasarov one last second to consider what might have been.

The explosion ripped through the cabin killing everyone instantly and scattering plane and body parts into the night. The gasoline burned itself out and darkness regained control of the sky.

The Grozny radar and communications operators looked up from their positions with dazed eyes. They had watched and heard the final moments in the life of the Minister of Defense.

Beyond the console Gorki stood with arms folded and a stern look on his face. Behind him stood three armed civilians. He stepped forward and the soldiers came to their feet.

"Well done, my young friends. There are two options for you. If you saw a tragic mid-air explosion which claimed the life of the Defense Minister, you need never worry about repercussions. If you choose to tell what you think you saw and heard here tonight, then I should mention that I have not quite closed down all of the gulags. I have confidence that you will make the proper choice. Good evening."

Gorki and his guards left the room. The two enlisted men stood at their consoles, staring dumfoundedly at each other.

Sanders watched his radar screen as two Mig-30s swept the skies over Chechnya. He kept his squadron outside the Russians' radar range as he waited for Units Four and Five to join up. Two quick beeps in his headset signaled their arrival. As soon as the screen indicated the Migs were heading away, he spoke a one word command. "Home."

Black One made a sweeping left turn and headed back over the Caucasus Mountains. Just as Arthur Henderson had said, the Russian defenses were of no consequence as the Nighthawks dipped back down to the wave tops and headed west. There would be no landing near Izmir tonight. They would refuel over the Mediterranean and make the Atlantic crossing to Langley.

CINCINNATI, OHIO

"Get in here, you guys," Rita called out from the great room. "The briefing is coming on."

Harte watched the car carrying Lassick and Lydia Rogers turn out of the driveway before following Samantha into the house. They caught up with Harmon and Barbara Davaron and walked down the long hallway to the great room. Rita and Loman were already settled in front of the television as the Secretary of Defense briefed the media on the tumultuous events of the weekend. The Secretary was already into his description of the events in the Persian Gulf.

"...In addition to the sinking of the two super tankers, Iran also reports a major explosion at the Kharg Island Oil Facility which destroyed one oil platform and sunk a support ship and one of the Iranian Navy's two submarines. The vessels were apparently moored near the oil platform. Additionally, and I believe coincidentally, Iran has reported her second submarine missing off the entrance to the Shat-al Arab waterway in the northern Persian Gulf.

"As a result of these events, Saudi Arabia, after conferring with allies in the region, has requested that the United States re-establish our military liaison office in Riyadh. The *Arlington* Battle Group should pass through the Strait of Hormuz shortly and resume patrol status in the Persian Gulf. We believe Iran's lack of comment on the matter constitutes tacit agreement to the redeployment."

"Is any of this related to the 'Kasarov incident?'" a reporter prodded.

The Secretary reacted calmly. "The question refers to the explosion of Russian Defense Minister Anatoly Kasarov's command jet over Chechnya early Saturday morning. Some members of the international press have filed reports indicating the explosion may have been a 'shoot down' by planes from the south. We have no details on any reports like that. You people can consult a map of the area and draw your own conclusions as to the origin of a possible air intrusion."

The reporter pressed him. "The Russians are blaming Iran and moving troops into the Chechnya region. Any comment, Sir?"

"As I just said, read a map. We aware of troop movements by the Russian Western Force into Chechnya. Pavel Karchev, who was removed recently from his post as Defense Minister, has been reinstated following the death of General Kasarov. He has personally assured me that the troop movements are routine and represent no offensive threat to the Caspian or Black Sea region. In light of everything, I take him at his word."

Harte looked around. "This guy is good."

Another reporter jumped in. "We've seen reports of dead bodies in uniform and military debris in the water around the two sunken tankers. Does this evidence, coupled with the reports on the Kasarov incident, suggest that Iran planned a major military action in the region in our absence?"

"Good question," Harmon shouted at the television. "Let's see how he dances around this one."

"We have no confirmation of floating debris and no confirmation of any linkage in the explosions in the Gulf and the death of General Kasarov. It is possible the Saudis think so and want the U.S. Navy on hand just in case. Other than that I have no comment."

"There are rumors that U.S. submarines are responsible for the destruction of the tankers and the Kharg Island facility," a reporter called out from the back of the room.

The Secretary cut him off. "We don't discuss submarines."

Another reporter pressed the issue. "But weren't there supposed to be two 'Seawolves' in the Gulf region recently?"

"We do not discuss submarines. Next question," the Secretary announced firmly.

"Mr. Secretary, the main interest in the Persian Gulf is oil. The Caspian Sea, near Chechnya is also home to Russia's main commercial oil field. This may be a reach, but one of our primary sources of domestic oil is the State of Louisiana. I was wondering, Mr. Secretary, in light of rumors of explosions along the Mississippi levee system and the resulting flood in Louisiana, could the three incidents be linked in some way?"

"This guy will get a job offer from the Agency within a month," Samantha whispered.

"The flooding in Louisiana, and the resulting loss of life, is tragic. At this moment the EPA Director is making her official statement on the matter. I suggest you refer to her for information concerning the Louisiana flood. Thank you very much." The Secretary of Defense left the room without taking the usual side questions that the up close reporters tossed in.

"That was a classic non denial, denial," Harte said as the briefing ended and the reporter prepared to analyze secretary's comments. "There's nothing like a boring press conference to start off a Monday morning."

As they filed out of the great room, Harte rehashed the events of the last few days. After parting company with Prince in Washington, he wrapped things up in Louisiana, Huntsville, and Cincinnati. Everyone then spent a weekend of well deserved R&R at Harte's home.

As the Wilson Foundation members, and their newest "honorary members," shuffled toward the main foyer, a slightly empty feeling came over them. In the last five weeks they had, individually and collectively, run the gamut from trauma to exhilaration. Normal life might be a letdown. Harte wondered how they would deal with it.

Harmon and Barbara looked much better after a weekend stay at a Cincinnati area hospital. They would have some well deserved time together while Barbara re-established her own sense of normalcy

Rita had her lab work. That would be a tonic. Lydia and Lassick had shown they were prepared to rejoin society with an early yet emotional departure. Mostly, Harte worried about Loman. Had the affair helped him through the grief of his father's death? Or did it just put things off.

"Andy, are you going to be okay?" he asked as they walked the hallway.

"I'll be fine. We closed a lot of circles in the last five weeks," Loman replied, gesturing into the area which had reverted to its original use as a dining room. Except for some telephone outlets, there was almost no evidence of the time and energy exerted around the table.

Harte put a hand on Loman's shoulder. "Let me know if you need anything." The phone on the dining room table rang. "I'll make it quick. Don't leave until I'm finished."

"Hi, Dan. Mike Prince. Did you see the morning news briefing?"

"That was quite a show. The Secretary of Defense handled everything smoothly. It's nice to know there is at least one competent guy in that administration."

"Oh, yeah. That was good stuff," Prince replied. "But I meant the EPA Director's announcement. Did you see it?"

"Hold on a minute." Harte covered the mouth piece. "Hey, everyone. Mike Prince is on the line."

"I'm not doing this crap anymore. And I want my satellite back." Rita said as she led everyone back into the dining room.

Harte grinned. "Mike, I'm putting you on conference and Rita says she's not interested in another assignment."

"No problem," Prince said through the speaker. "Once again, you people all did a hell of a job and we owe you. I was telling Dan about EPA's comment on everything. I think you will want to hear it."

"You have our attention, Mike," Samantha said.

"Hi, Sam. The EPA director expressed sorrow for the loss of life in the Louisiana flood. Preliminary estimates say five or six hundred people died as a result of the Simmesport Levee break. Off the record, I believe it would have been much worse down there if Aaron Roosevelt had not been on the job.

"Are you ready for this? She said and I quote, 'Contrary to reports of sabotage, the levee's failure was the result of a break in a natural gas line that crosses the Atchafalaya River near the town. That was the explosion heard by eyewitnesses,' unquote. I suppose that's as good an explanation as any.

"She reported the tragic death of Morgan Trent and most of the members of the Southeast Endangered Species Association when their camp, near Simmesport, was inundated by the flood waters. Again off the record, the FBI has the survivors on ice. They picked up Maria DeLeon in Naples. She was drunk and didn't even know what had gone on. Barbara, are you there?"

"Yes, Mike," Davaron replied as she leaned against Harmon.

"We are going to need you to testify."

"Tell me when you need me."

"Thanks. Anyway, the Director said she expects no long-term problems for the local ecology. She praised the Corps of Engineers for its handling of the delicate balance in the region and reasserted support for projects like the Old River Flood Control Complex.

"There was one more point of interest to her statement. On a personal note she is requesting a leave of absence to attend to personal matters. That's a lot like TASS reporting that a Russian leader has a cold. She's probably greasing the skids for her resignation. It's a bonus I'll gladly take."

"Sounds like a good day for the home team," Harte said.

"Not bad for only 10:30 in the morning. Is Tim there?"

"He and Lydia just left for the airport."

"Arthur Henderson wants to give him an exclusive on events in the Gulf and in Russia. Arthur has never done anything like that. That ought to tell you how he feels about the job you guys did.

"Rita, your satellite will be back on line in thirty-six hours. When you're done with your survey call me and name your project. Keep it in the realm of reality and we'll fund it for you."

"Whoohoo!" Rita screamed as she hugged Loman and then Harte. "I'll be getting back to you within the month, Michael."

"I thought you might. Andy, I'll be expecting the report on your dad's file. Take your time. After your presentation, there are some agency matters I would like to discuss if you are interested. Will you check in with me?"

Loman looked at Harte and Samantha. They shrugged, as if to say, "What have you got to lose?"

"I'll think about it, Mike, and let you know."

"That's all I ask. Billy, let's keep in touch, okay? No business, just fun. I've been holed up in Langley too long."

"I'll be traveling for a little while," Harmon said as he gave Barbara a slight squeeze. "There is a project I have to work on but I will stay in touch."

"Fine. Dan, check your mail. There will be a nice donation from South Air for the Wilson Foundation. It can never repay you but it is well meant. And Rich Willis wanted to know if you will administer a scholarship in George Gansz's name funded by NEI."

"Of course, Mike. That's about the best thing you've said so far."

"I agree. By the way, I have a few items on my agenda that I'd like you to take a look at for me—"

"I already told you, don't call us. We'll call you," Harte shouted as Prince broke up with laughter over the speaker.

"Just kidding. Sam, I will see you soon won't I?" Prince asked with noticeable tentativeness.

"Relax, Mike. It's only for a little while," Samantha replied cryptically.

"I'm counting on you. Hey, thanks again, all of you. We got a lot accomplished here. Take a break. You've all earned it."

"See you, Mike." Harte turned off the conference speaker. "That pretty much puts the stamp of approval on everything. Let's get this show on the road."

The good-byes were less emotional than they expected. Between the Wilson Foundation's periodic reunions and a natural desire to strengthen the bonds they had developed, there was a sense that they would all be together again quite soon.

As the last car with Harmon and Davaron turned out of the driveway, Samantha walked through the foyer and stepped out into the backyard. The sun cooperated by removing the chill from the morning air.

"What did you mean by 'it's only for a little while?'"

"I told Mike I would need at least a week or more to wrap up my work here."

Harte played dumb. "Sam, it's going to take about an hour to finish up the Agency's business here."

"Well silly me. I miscalculated. I guess I will have more time on my hands than I realized."

"The good news is now that Lydia's gone you can have your old room back for the week," Harte dead panned.

"You know, you are a pinhead," she said as she elbowed him playfully in the ribs.

"Oh I get it. So maybe we can find something to do for a week... or maybe a little longer."

"I want to take a walk. Show me your home, Mr. Harte."

"It would be a pleasure, Ms. Schmidt." Harte led her down a stone pathway from the house. The backyard consisted of nearly five acres, neatly landscaped out to about fifty yards from the house. The rest was a small lake and surrounding woods.

"It really is beautiful," Samantha said as they walked by the lake. "But something is missing. We should have seen the stables by now."

"That is the second time you've mentioned something like that. Do you ride horses?"

"Not really. I just assumed you do."

"What would make you think that?" Harte asked with a shrug.

"It's just something Lydia and I talked about one night."

"I'm confused," Harte said with a slightly troubled look.

"I'm not," Samantha replied and kissed him lightly. She took his hand and let him lead her back to the house.